Deceived

STEPHANIE ROSE VIGANO

For my very first readers, who encouraged and inspired me,
and for DV, who holds the key to my heart.

Book design by Stephanie Rose Vigano

Cover photo © Tiko Aramyan/Shutterstock

Previously Published as "Deceived" by Stephanie Rose (2016)

ISBN: 978-0-9984336-2-2

10 9 8 7 6 5 4 3 2 1

"Most of the trouble in the world
is caused by people wanting to be important."

– *T.S. Eliot*

TABLE OF CONTENTS

Deceived

CHAPTER ONE
Falling in Love

BRUCE DIDN'T THINK IT WOULD end like this. Ten years of marriage, up in smoke. Ten years of memories, lost in a moment. For ten blissful years, he'd had everything a man could want.

Incredible, how fast that could change.

The course of his life had taken a dramatic turn, but his outlook hadn't always been so grim. A decade before everything had gone to hell for him, he had just moved into his newly-constructed dream home in the growing suburb of Maple Springs, a happening little Northeastern town nestled cozily on the outskirts of beautiful Stirling City. Bruce had personally picked out the large plot of land for his gorgeous estate as soon as he'd managed to amass himself a small fortune, and its construction marked not only the beginning of an exciting new chapter in his life, but also the realization of a childhood dream.

Ever since he was a young boy, he'd had a vision in his head of what his ideal home would look like and just how perfectly it would sit nestled in the picturesque wooded hills of the suburbs. On the day he finally saw that vision come to life, he thought it almost uncanny how well the traditional brown brick mansion in front of him matched the hasty doodles he'd come up with as a child. Beautiful and private with its set-back lot, meticulous landscaping, wrought-iron details, and large in-ground swimming pool, the mansion was a nice retreat from the hustle and bustle of the city and its constant barrage of lights, sounds, and people, while being conveniently close to the metro his business called home. In no time, he happily settled into his new domicile and filled it with countless treasures and luxuries.

Construction of his high-class bachelor pad might have cost a pretty penny, but as far as Bruce was concerned, it was worth every cent - though if truth be told, he could have had his dream home much sooner if he hadn't been so stubborn about paying for it all by himself. The younger of two brothers, Bruce was the son of a wealthy German banker and a well-to-do socialite mother who was a dedicated arts-enthusiast and loved to frequent the Stirling City ballet. The von Essens lived a privileged life and money had never been hard to come by, but despite his parents' wealth, Bruce had been prideful and refused to let them give him a handout. Building the house was something that he'd wanted to do on his own, and it wasn't the first big endeavor he'd undertaken solo. Before he'd even been able to *think* of laying down the first brick, he'd first had to set the foundation.

He'd started up the aptly-named brokerage firm Vonessen Inc. straight out of college, and as its founder and CEO, the determined Harvard graduate quickly proved himself to be a strong-willed, motivated leader who was inherently money-smart and boasted an unwavering work ethic to boot. Within its first few years of existence, Vonessen Inc. became an incredible success and his obsessive ambition paid off. His fortunate upbringings aside, the money Bruce made from running his business alone could've gotten him anything and everything that he wanted.

...Well, *almost* anything and everything. See, even though Bruce had the dream home and all the money and notoriety that a man could want, he couldn't help but feel lonely lounging around in his huge mansion with no one else to share it with. Having a home filled with rooms kind of lost its novelty when he was the only one in them, and aside from the occasional get-together, that was exactly how it was: Bruce was always the lone person in a big, beautiful, *empty* house. When he'd been a younger man and a bit more naïve, he'd assumed that simply being successful and having nice things would bring him all the happiness and fulfillment that he needed. But when his mind wasn't distracted by business matters, he felt an awful, hollow, nagging feeling in the back of his head that there was something missing in his life; something very important that money couldn't buy.

He discovered what that something was when he met the woman who would change everything for him. That fateful afternoon, he'd decided to do something out of the ordinary and go for a quiet walk during office hours, just to get out and enjoy a change of scenery for once. It wasn't often that someone as work-obsessed as Bruce ventured outside of it in the middle of the day, but spring in the city meant that the area by the river had been reinvigorated with color: the vibrant green of fresh buds on the trees, the blue of a sky rid of winter's dulls, and the rainbow of hues that colored the flowers nestled in rustic wooden planters outside the boutique shops. Stirling was a city well-known for its flourishing business economy, but an even more distinguishing characteristic of the vibrant upstate-New York locale was its rich undercurrent of arts and culture, and the area by the river was perhaps one of the most indicative of this. Visitors to the city loved this part of it. They often said that it, the nearby cultural district, and the communities surrounding it made the city feel almost reminiscent of a "North American Paris." Clean, cream-colored buildings, beautifully kept parks full of trees, a somewhat-hip, Bohemian energy radiating from the streets, and all of the homey cafés and charming coffee shops made it especially beautiful and romantic. *That* was the heart of Stirling, and the draw of life here wasn't only contained to the riverfront and the theaters and galleries nearby. Stirling boasted some of the best restaurants in the country, and a little more than a two-hour drive would put you right at the coast, where residents liked to vacation and sail their boats on the harbor. The ride in-between was dotted with vast stretches of dense forest and quaint, cozy farmland - both a nice retreat for those wishing to escape for a little while.

There wasn't much option for such an escape during the weekdays though, so for now this would have to suffice. Downtown, the sidewalks were constantly crowded with fast-walking people wielding cell phones and briefcases and the streets hummed with a steady flow of traffic. Commuters packed the subway and regional rail and passers-by hailed yellow taxis. But by the water, it was quiet and calm. The path he walked was a refreshing change of pace from the monochromatic buildings of the city's downtown business district, and Bruce let himself enjoy the peaceful simplicity of it as he took in the sights around him.

He could see wide cobblestone sidewalks lined with metal lampposts. Lovers walking hand-in-hand over a long bridge. Friends engaging in idle chitchat at a café. Women leaving high-end stores with bags of home goods and designer clothes on their arms. He could hear the chimes and dings of doors opening, the peaceful lull of flowing water, and birds chirping in the trees. He smelled the warm, soothing smells of coffee and croissants. Nearby, an elderly woman sat on a wooden bench feeding bread to the pigeons, and a pensive young man stood silently at his easel, sketching the entire scene against the backdrop of the river.

It was then that Bruce saw *her.* The prettiest sight of them all. He had always considered himself a gentleman and tried not to ogle her as she walked in his direction, but despite his best efforts, he couldn't help but stare. Her dark chestnut hair hung loosely over her shoulders and the simple gray knee-length dress she was wearing was far from bland despite its lack of color. She seemed.to have an aura surrounding her that simply emanated warmth and grace; an aura that Bruce was inexplicably drawn to.

From a distance she was lovely, but when she got closer and he managed to catch her eye, she practically took his breath away. Her lips were full and slightly parted, shaded by an alluring color that could have only come from the stolen caress of a rose petal. And her eyes were the most startling Caribbean blue that he had ever seen, radiant and sparkling behind a fan of thick lashes against the smooth olive undertones of her skin. Everything else about her was beautiful, too. But those *eyes* could stop traffic.

They'd certainly stopped him.

"Good morning," she said, acknowledging their eye contact with a small, amicable smile. She tucked her hair behind her ear, and Bruce, always so steady and unfaltering, could feel the strange sensation of a childlike flutter in his stomach as he gave her a courteous nod and returned the sentiment.

"Good morning."

Their exchange over, the pretty stranger continued to walk past him, the sound of her clacking heels against the cobblestone becoming less pronounced with each step. Bruce thought of letting her go and simply accepting the past few moments for what they were - merely meeting the eye of an attractive woman and an inconsequential "hello" between strangers - but each stride that she took from him made him ·feel a panicky tug at his heartstrings. He couldn't leave it at that. He *had* to speak to her. He didn't want to seem overzealous, but he hadn't felt so dumbstruck in the presence of a woman since he was a much younger version of himself. There was just something about her... something intoxicating. Maybe it was those beautiful blue eyes.

He glanced over his shoulder to see where she was heading and noticed that she'd stopped in front of a quaint little coffee shop and bakery, Café Amadeus. She was looking at the sign over the door in an indecisive way, as if she were considering whether she should just give in to temptation and go in for something sweet or not, and Bruce took it as an opportunity to suck up his uncharacteristic nerve and do something of the same.

"You know, I hear the scones at this place are delicious," he suggested helpfully as he approached her from behind, watching her tap her chin with her fingertips. He saw her jump slightly at the unexpected sound of his voice, but when she swiveled around to see that it was him who had greeted her, that demure smile broke across her lips again. It was such a charming, welcoming smile. One that lit up her whole face, even close-lipped and unassuming, and concurrently left Bruce stunned.

"I was thinking more of an éclair, to be honest," she confessed with a slight flush blossoming in her cheeks. "An éclair and a cappuccino, actually. I'm having a serious sugar craving right now." She paused for a moment and eyeballed his nice suit. "I take it you're on a work break, too?" she deduced.

"I suppose I am," Bruce almost laughed at himself. It was funny to think that the words 'work' and 'break' said in that particular order would ever apply to him, but here he was. He didn't say it out loud, but the woman seemed to catch the vibe.

"I'm guessing you don't do work breaks very often," she assumed, crossing her arms and cocking an inquisitive eyebrow. The gestures looked so endearing on her that the quiet chuckle Bruce had managed to suppress before promptly escaped his lips.

"No," he admitted. "But I wouldn't mind spending this one chatting with you over some coffee if you wouldn't mind the company. A cappuccino sounds like a good idea right now."

He shot her a cordial smile and the woman grinned back at him, that pretty flush coloring her cheeks again. She seemed to consider it for a moment – but a moment, apparently, was all that she needed. "That would be nice," she agreed as she extended her hand towards him. "I'm Cecilia, then. And you are?"

Bruce shook her outstretched palm and could feel moisture beading in his. How strange, that this random woman could affect him like this! He was a confident CEO, the king of handshakes. He could write a book on how to do one properly and was the first to wag a finger at an improper one. And here he was with sweaty digits. "I'm Bruce," he replied. "It's a pleasure to meet you."

Pleasure turned out to be quite the understatement. You never know what might happen when you reach out to a stranger, but that day Bruce discovered over a table of cappuccino and shared pastries a kind of contentment just chatting with another person that he hadn't felt before. Cecilia was undeniably a beautiful woman, but over the course of just thirty minutes, he'd quickly come to believe that the most attractive thing about her - even more than those captivating eyes - was the person that she was inside. Call it cliché or naïve or hopelessly romantic, but he was utterly enamored with her, right from the start. Cecilia was genuine and considerate, polite and personable, optimistic and intelligent. A classic beauty who not only had soft, timeless features, but a soft heart to match. A woman with a smart head on her shoulders, a thirst for discovery, and a penchant for culture, politics, and philosophy. She was startlingly down-to-earth and easy to talk to once he'd gotten past that initial "hello," and luckily for Bruce, their first conversation over coffee didn't end up being their last. By the end of their impromptu outing they'd agreed to meet again at this same place tomorrow, then again the next day, and *again* the next. Soon, getting out of the office to meet at Café Amadeus had become commonplace and sharing a mid-morning drink with Cecilia by the river was Bruce's favorite part of the day. They would always sit outside if the weather was nice, and enjoy a few warm pastries, hot drinks, and good conversations, sometimes completely losing track of time in the process.

Bruce learned more about the object of his unspoken affections with every outing; things that only made those affections grow fonder. He learned that Cecilia was six years his junior, recently out of college and now working as a secretary at one of the law offices not far from Vonessen Inc.'s headquarters on Broad Street. He learned that she was an only child and that she'd moved to Stirling when she was eighteen years old ahead of attending Greenbriar University downtown. And he learned that just like him, she loved the arts, even if her middle-class roots hadn't been as affluent as his. Growing up with a ballet-enthusiast as a mother, Bruce had garnered quite a bit of respect for music, art, and performance by default, and he was thrilled that they had that passion in common. He found it absolutely endearing the way that Cecilia's beautiful blue eyes would brighten as she talked to him so ardently about her love of going to stage shows, visiting museums, and listening to music from around the world. The piano and violin were her favorite instruments, and she regretted that she'd never learned how to play when she'd had the chance.

She'd go on and on about her mother's paintings, and how as a little girl, she would watch her smooth her brushes over canvas from start to finish, creating masterpieces from a few simple strokes of color. Her mother had always played classical music on the record player while she painted portraits, still-life, and landscapes of the French countryside for her modest gallery - melodies from the likes of Bach, Beethoven, Mozart, and Handel. While her mother lived the life of a starving artist and dreamed of one day being recognized for her talents, Cecilia's father worked as a commercial real-estate appraiser in Philadelphia. He was a hard-working Italian man who'd always seemed to put more hours into his trade than his bank account showed, but he always smiled and never showed his family how tired he was. He tried to teach Cecilia about the importance of family, good food, and smart investments, and she'd always taken his life advice to heart.

"A tavola non si invecchia" had been his favorite Italian proverb. *At the table with good friends and family, you do not become old.* Cecilia had always found it silly when she'd heard him say it as a child, but the older she grew, the more she understood what it meant. When he had passed away from lung cancer during her junior year of high school she'd been heartbroken, but she'd never forgotten the lessons she'd learned from him nor the love that he'd given his family. Since then, she'd tried to remember and honor

him in whatever small ways she'd been able to. Her mother had closed her gallery doors in Philly and sold the family home to move to a quiet place in Maine, and Cecilia had set down her own roots in Stirling, eager to complete her schooling. She visited her mother any time she managed to get time off from work, and during every visit she made sure to cook one of her father's favorite recipes. She was a good cook, she claimed, and Italian dishes were her favorite to make. Bruce figured he'd remember that if he ever got so lucky as to invite himself over for dinner.

He admired so many aspects of her personality - her appreciation for creativity, her loyalty to family, and her persevering spirit, just to start - but for all of her positive traits, perhaps the one that he found the most surprising – and maybe even *comforting* - was that Cecilia didn't seem very interested in his wealth and treated him like a normal human being in spite of it. Bruce had grown up with a lot of nice things, but finding nice women had always been a bit of a challenge for him. Money was a big part of his life; a big part of his upbringing. Talk often revolved around it in any other setting, and he knew deep down that most people - *particularly* women - only cared about him because of what he had and what he could give them.

But Cecilia wasn't like most people. Her pretty blue eyes didn't light up at the mention of his big fat paychecks. Her eyes lit up when he told her a good story about life, or they discovered another shared interest, or they laughed together until their sides were sore after one of his particularly horrible cheesy jokes. And the encouraging thing about this was that she wasn't just putting on an act. There was a pure honesty about her. She was the type of person who truly *cared* about other people, and that drew Bruce towards her just as much as those pierce-right-through-him eyes.

She was so relatable and genuine and sincere that Bruce started to open up to her because of it, confiding in her not just as an acquaintance, but as a friend. He found it surprisingly easy to get carried away talking about everything with her: their pasts, their presents... even their futures. Bruce told Cecilia that what he really wanted for Vonessen Inc. was to see it grow as a business and become something bigger. To have offices dotting the Northeast, to make his family proud, to garner his own success independent of their privilege, and to provide good jobs and a good service to the people around him. When he asked her what *she* wanted out of city life, that bashful smile would return to her lips again and a dreamy look would soften her eyes.

She told him that she liked her job at the law office and all of the people she worked with, but what she was really in Stirling for was the lifestyle *outside* of work. She loved how cultural it was, how artistic the area was, and how everywhere you turned there were countless opportunities for a person to learn and experience new things and broaden their horizons. When she'd first arrived in the city, one of her favorite places to visit had been the library. She loved the tall Roman columns out front and the classical architecture throughout and the big, big shelves accentuated by tall wooden ladders inside. For her, it had been easy to get lost in there for hours, and coincidentally, that seemed to be how she approached life as a whole. She got lost in it, always finding wonderment in the most overlooked of things. Always appreciating them, knowing that time was finite. To Cecilia, life was a constant work in progress, a constant journey. There was always more to see, more to do, more to experience. She loved to learn and create, and at heart she was a free spirit... but sometimes, even free spirits can be afraid to let themselves shine.

Before he knew her better, Bruce couldn't have imagined that someone as real as Cecilia could ever be shy or uncertain about anything, but as she told him one afternoon of her hopes to have a big, beautiful garden one day just like the ones in home magazines - the ones with the carefully crafted landscaping, charming stone fountains, and innate feeling of truly being a labor of love - he discovered that even *she* kept secrets from the world.

Maybe one day she would have that garden, she said optimistically, but for now she would just have to make do without because her apartment was located in a good spot close to work that allowed her to walk to the office and anywhere else that she could possibly need to go. But if she *did* have that garden? She would spend all day in it. Reading, thinking... especially painting.

Bruce was surprised to hear this about her. In all the times that they'd talked about their shared admiration of the arts, Cecilia had never mentioned being involved in them as anything more than an appreciative spectator."You paint?" he asked her. "I thought you said that your mother was the artist?"

He was sitting beside her on a wooden bench near the river, his typical dark roast warming his hand. Cecilia was holding a coffee too, though admittedly she'd been a bit too caught up in conversation to drink very much of it. She was wearing nude heels and a breezy pale yellow dress that buttoned in the front. A pretty color that the small flush she could feel creeping up into her cheeks again like it did so often around him undoubtedly clashed with. Painting was a bit of a hidden talent of hers, something she didn't share with many people. But Bruce was into this sort of thing. Maybe it wouldn't hurt to share it with him.

"Well, I managed to pick up a few techniques watching her work at her easel all day," she admitted with a downplaying shrug. "Honestly, I would love to have a gallery like she did someday... but I don't think my paintings are good enough for that. If I had more time for it or started learning a little earlier, I'd probably be better. But that's the way of the world isn't it?"

"I'm sure your paintings aren't anything to shirk at," Bruce disagreed.

Cecilia smiled back at him in appreciation. She was sure that he was only being nice, but it was still encouraging to hear.

"Would you like to see some of them? And give me your opinion?" she offered. "My apartment's not far."

Bruce agreed and followed her down the cobblestone walkway onto regular sidewalk, past the townhomes and apartment buildings that fetched the highest rents closest to the river to an area that was still nice but slightly lighter on the wallet. This was a good neighborhood; a very nice, classy, artsy place with a lot of young professionals in their mid-to-late twenties and early thirties. Bruce wasn't surprised to see that Cecilia lived here.

Her apartment was housed inside a white brick building with a wrought-iron gate out front and black Cape Cod shutters on the windows. She lived on the top floor. Bruce noticed that she seemed a little nervous as she turned the key and opened the door to her own little corner of the world to him, but while shyness was a characteristic he hadn't seen her display much before, it was one that he found just as endearing as her quiet confidence.

The door opened to a charming one-bed, one-bath open floor plan colored in warm, neutral shades of light brown and clean cream. The floors were all hardwood and the vintage decor was sophisticated and traditional with a touch of the artistic and bohemian. Cecilia's furniture was something Bruce could best describe as something of the modern Victorian persuasion, the same style that he'd tried to incorporate into his mansion. The quaint kitchen and dining area were attached to the living room where a small stone fireplace was nestled against the wall, giving the modest space a touch of comfort and understated luxury. A set of narrow skylights let natural light into the kitchen - enough that Cecilia didn't bother turning on more than the dimmers.

"Do you want something to drink?" she asked. "I can make tea." Perhaps it was nerves to suggest such a thing considering they'd just had coffee, but Cecilia had never been the type to invite someone into her home without offering some sort of food or drink. She walked into the kitchen and pulled out a canister of fresh leaves that smelled like lavender and honeysuckle. As she let the leaves steep and busied herself by getting a kettle of water going on the stove, Bruce perused the room, trying to get a better understanding of who this woman was. He could see a bookshelf full of books along the wall, books that all seemed to have spines bent back from use. And in the window near the dining table he could see a wooden planter box just like the ones at the river, full of small red flowers. He stepped closer to get a better look.

"What are these?" he asked interestedly, noticing the way the petals flared up like a miniature tufted skirt. Cecilia peeked over her shoulder and smiled.

"Oh... those are Tuscan poppies. My father's favorite."

"You have quite a green thumb."

She tucked her hair back and concentrated on the tea. "I'd plant more if I had a real garden. One day, maybe."

Bruce moved on to the bookshelf next. From the way it appeared, Cecilia liked to read classics and memoirs and literary essays - mostly nonfiction. Scattered amongst all of the really heady stuff were books on home decorating, gardening, art, travel, and ballet. She certainly had a healthy array of interests.

He looked towards the fireplace after perusing her books and stepped forward when something small and rectangular on the mantle caught his eye; something with intricate carvings in chestnut wood and a gold clasp on the front. It sat next to a petite antique picture frame holding a photograph of a gentle-looking man with olive skin standing beside a woman with eyes as blue as Cecilia's. It was a music box. He opened the lid and a soft melody tinkled out. Cecilia turned to him, pulling two porcelain teacups from the overhead cabinet and placing them on the kitchen island.

"My mother's," she explained as Bruce listened to the beautiful, bittersweet melody. It was a song he didn't recognize. "Before her, my grandmother's. She wanted me to take it with me when I came here for school. It's from France... probably one of the only really nice family mementos I have, come to think of it." Cecilia sighed as Bruce closed the lid. "I know the apartment's not much. But it's close to the river and I can walk to work."

"Not much? It's wonderful. It's very you, Cecilia."

She gave him a flattered grin and cleared her throat. "So... would you like me to show you some paintings while the tea finishes up? They're just in the other room."

He nodded and she led him to her bedroom, a room just as quaint and feminine as the rest of the apartment. Centered against the back wall was a four-poster bed, and alongside it a mahogany dresser. And there, in the corner, was a wooden easel, a stack of canvases leaning against the wall next to it. Some looked to be painted, some were not, but from what he saw - the art supplies on the small table beside it, a set of oil paints left out in a rush - he could tell that this was something that she really got engrossed in.

He peered at the painting on her easel, intrigued. Its subject was so simple in concept - just a plump pair of bluebirds sitting on a branch decorated with pretty white cherry blossoms - but so striking at the same time. As Cecilia showed him more, he noticed that flowers and birds were a common theme. He could see it so clearly, captured here on canvas: she was a dreamer, a person who could appreciate the beauty in little things. A person who reveled at the freedom and simplicity of something as pure as having wings. She loved creating things that were beautiful. It was what made her feel alive. And she was sharing it with him, letting him in on something personal and meaningful to her.

In a way, it was like opening the window to her soul.

"Beautiful," Bruce said softly.

Cecilia's eyes flickered to his face and she realized that he wasn't looking at the paintings anymore. It was hard to tell if his compliment had been meant for them or for her. She stumbled on her words, the sudden intensity of their eye contact taking her aback. "Give me a garden to paint these in and I'd be completely content," she said, tucking her hair behind her ear like she always did and looking away shyly. She regained eye contact with him again when she felt his hand clasp her wrist, gentle but firm.

"You'll have a garden one day," he said with certainty. "I'll make sure of it."

Cecilia felt her breath hitch in her throat. She could see something in his eyes. An admiration... and a desire. They'd met for coffee plenty of times by now, but neither of them had ever spoken of any sort of harbored attraction. Yet it was startlingly clear that they both had to feel it, because as they stood close enough that either of them could have easily pulled away if it weren't true, neither dared to move. Bruce could feel Cecilia's indecision in the way she said nothing at all, yet her blue eyes seemed to speak all that he needed to know... and then, without thinking, his thumb was grazing her chin, he was tilting her face towards his, and when his lips found hers, she didn't edge away.

He kissed her slowly at first, then building, appreciating her just as ardently as her art. Her lips were as soft as they looked, they tasted just as sweet. She shut her eyes and let out a yielding sigh, leaning in to him as her hand glided along the side of his neck and into his dark hair. Bruce had never felt anything more right. The tea kettle was squealing on the stove, but neither of them seemed to notice. The only sound Bruce could hear was that of his own heartbeat as his blood rushed wildly in his ears.

Bruce lied awake in Cecilia's bed, a cup of hot tea on the nightstand beside him. He could feel the warmth of her body as she snuggled up against him, her arm draped across his torso, her leg tangled over his, and her face nuzzled contentedly into his chest. His black suit coat had long been discarded over the corner of her mahogany dresser, a few buttons of his white dress shirt were still left undone, and his tie hung loose around his neck. As Cecilia's fingers traced delicate circles in the exposed skin of his chest, Bruce's hand found its way into her hair, playing with silken brown strands of it as the room filled with a peaceful silence. The squealing of the tea kettle long-contained and his thudding heartbeat slowly calming in his chest, the room was quiet now save for the muted sounds of the city outside and the repetitive rhythm of her breath, easing gently in and out.

They stayed like that for a long time, relaxing in the silence, until Bruce saw something even more curious to him than the poppies in Cecilia's window and the music box on her mantle. It was a long scar on her knee, dotted by tiny staple marks along its length. Her yellow dress had bunched around her thigh, and now Bruce could see why most of her dresses seemed to be a little longer and hit right below it. She was hiding this scar. He wondered how she'd gotten it. Cecilia could feel her skin grow hot as his fingertips traced the outline of it, careful and featherlike.

"What's this from?" he asked her softly.

She hesitated for a moment. Like her art, the scar on her knee wasn't something she talked about often; it was a remnant of something that she'd left behind before. But she trusted Bruce now. After what had just happened and the way that he'd kissed her, she really did. So she mustered up a little courage and told him her story, letting him in on the entire thing.

"It's from the accident."

The accident. Every time she said it, it gave her an involuntary shudder. The accident had happened only a few years ago, just a few years after her father had died. Another blow to a healing heart. She told Bruce that growing up she'd been a dancer... and apparently a pretty serious one, at that. Her parents had gotten her into ballet when she was a little girl to help her break out of her shyness and meet new friends, and she'd quickly come to love it. She'd kept up with dance throughout high school, even after her dad had died, regularly performing in her town's productions of *The Nutcracker* every Christmas. By the end of her senior year she'd chosen to attend college in Stirling because along with getting in to one of the best academic schools in town, she'd also been accepted as a student at one of the best dance studios where she could train between classes. Her father had always loved watching her dance, and at one point she had dreamed of being a part of the Stirling City Ballet... but it was right at the end of her first year as an undergrad that the accident had taken her dream away. She'd slipped on ice and broken her knee, badly enough that she'd needed surgery and extensive physical therapy for it to heal. Yet even after all of that therapy, she could still feel the long-term effects: periodic pain, permanent muscle weakness in the quadriceps of that leg, and a loss of motion in her knee that affected how well she could straighten and flex it. Her doctor had advised her to avoid any exercises that involved squatting or repetitive deep-knee bending to protect herself and prevent future issues, and at the time, a nineteen-year-old Cecilia - just accepted into college and a great dance school - knew what that meant.

She had been devastated. When she'd first gotten hurt, she'd been determined that once her knee was healed enough she'd find a way back into dance and train herself back to where she'd been before... but she knew that it was impossible now. In the beginning, she'd had a hard time coping with it. After all, she *loved* ballet and there was nothing that made her happier and comforted her more than getting lost in the emotion of the music and becoming someone else on that stage. But in time, she'd learned to deal with her situation and make the best of what she had. She took up what little gardening she was able to do in her apartment because it helped her heal to nurture something else, even if that something else was only a handful of Tuscan poppies. And she took up painting because it helped her express herself artistically when she could no longer do it by dancing.

Bruce was touched by her story. He was certain that it had to be difficult for someone who'd lost so much to keep their optimism intact and be as put together as Cecilia was... but Cecilia claimed that she was still the same Cecilia as she'd always been, just a Cecilia who used a different medium now. Crazy how if her dreams to become a ballerina for the Stirling City Ballet hadn't been dashed, she could have been one of the dancers his own mother had always watched so enthusiastically.

"Why don't you become a dance instructor?" he encouraged her. "You can still be involved with the ballet."

"No..." she shook her head against his chest. "That would just be going backwards at this point. I'm ready to move forward."

"Then why don't you open the art gallery that you want so much? That would be moving forward, wouldn't it?"

Cecilia brushed the idea off. She wasn't *that* good. She wasn't *that* brave. It was probably silly to go for it when there was no guarantee that anyone other than him would actually like what she put on canvas anyway.

"I think you might be becoming biased," she teased him.

"Maybe I am," he admitted with an agreeing chuckle. "But you shouldn't brush your dreams aside, Cece."

"Cece?" she cocked an eyebrow at the new nickname.

He shrugged and his hand found its way into her hair again. "I can call you by your full name if you want."

"No..." she sighed. "I like it." She shut her eyes and inhaled deeply, nuzzling her cheek further into his shoulder.

"Just because it didn't work out with ballet doesn't mean you can't still do what you love for a living," Bruce reminded her gently. "I made Vonessen Inc. work. You can make an art gallery work, too. You have a real talent, something that shouldn't go to waste. You're doing the world a disservice by hiding it."

Cecilia couldn't help a skeptical laugh. She appreciated the notion, but opening an art gallery took money. Furnishing her apartment had taken a good chunk of her savings, and the money she made at the law office was just enough for rent and groceries every month. Whatever was left over was comfortable enough to live off of, but not sizable enough to occupy a commercial space.

"Everything is so easy for you isn't it?" she mused.

"No. But I believe you can do whatever you put your mind to if you want it enough. You just have to believe in yourself."

"Maybe one day," she caved just a little.

"If you need help getting started, I'll help you," he offered.

Cecilia felt a quieting pang in her chest. She'd just spent the last half-hour lost in this man's kiss, but she didn't know him much outside of their friendly chats at Café Amadeus. This was such a genuine, selfless offer. One that was much less about impressing her than about helping her realize her dreams.

"Bruce... why would you do that for me? You know you don't have to do anything like that," she frowned.

"But I want to," he confessed. "You're special to me, Cecilia. Before I met you, I never left my office. But you remind me that there's more to life than a bottom line. I enjoy talking to you... spending time with you... kissing you." His thumb brushed across her lips, sending a warm, tingling sensation rippling through her body. "You make me happy. And I want you to be happy, too."

Cecilia's pretty blue eyes met his and the look she gave him said more than just her words alone. "I *am* happy," she whispered. And when she leaned forward to kiss him again and show him just how much she meant it, Bruce didn't have any reason to doubt her. Cecilia was modest and never asked for much. Maybe she really *was* happy and at peace with her life now. But Bruce knew that she could be even happier, and he was determined to do everything in his power to see that happen.

CHAPTER TWO

Reasons to Live

CECILIA COULDN'T DANCE ANYMORE. She didn't have her dream garden straight out of the pages of *Better Homes and Gardens* to paint in. And she didn't have an art gallery like her mother's. But Bruce was certain that one day he could give her at least two of those things, and after his first visit to her apartment and that first taste of her lips, their lunchtime coffee runs inevitably evolved from what had started as friendly outings into serious dating.

With their true feelings out in the open, the pair officially became a couple and found themselves visiting art museums and wine festivals, attending the symphony and the opera, trying out what seemed to be every restaurant in Stirling, and going to plays and charity events in the city together as often as they could. Every outing was a new adventure for them, and spending time with Cecilia brought out the best in Bruce. Any time he felt like anything less, he'd remember her accident and remind himself of the strength that she carried herself with, letting that strength inspire him in return. And as their relationship progressed, he only felt more impassioned and alive. He embraced the day with a smile on his face and went to work with a renewed sense of purpose. His attraction and admiration had blossomed into love, and anyone who knew them could see that Cecilia felt the same.

There would always be those out there who were quick to judge and assume, but for Cecilia, being with the wealthy businessman had never been about the money. Sure, the money was nice because it allowed them to go out and experience new things together that they couldn't experience otherwise. But there was so much more to Bruce von Essen in Cecilia's eyes than a fat wallet and a good family name. In no time at all, he had become her best friend. He knew things about her that other people didn't, and she loved the comfort she felt in knowing that she could open up so candidly around him. She found so many things about him endearing, from his dashing half-smile to the way his brow ruffled sternly when he was concentrating hard on something, to the way his natural curiosity led him to peruse her apartment while she made them hot tea. She fell for the strong, determined, smart man that she knew he was and admired him for his success, but as far as she was concerned, she wouldn't have cared the day she'd met him at the river if he had been the founder and CEO of Vonessen Inc. or just some average Joe working in an office like her. In her heart, she knew that she would have pursued him regardless.

And damn, was Bruce thankful for it. Before meeting Cecilia, he'd always been so tied up with work, been such a big picture guy, that he'd often failed to appreciate the little things and take any time out for himself. Cecilia showed him that while work was always going to be a part of who he was, there was still more to life than being in the office. He was glad that he hadn't let her walk away with just a "good morning" on that fateful first day, because their meeting reminded him that it was always good to take a step back once in a while to take a breather and really *live*.

After all, if he hadn't tried it, he might've never met her.

While Cecilia showed him that life was worth living outside of steel beams, Bruce in turn tried to show her more than just a good time with his expensive dates and access to the best that Stirling City had to offer. Even more importantly, he showed her that it wasn't foolish to go for her dreams. After they'd been dating for a reasonable bit of time, he finally convinced her to open an art gallery, and soon she was carrying on her mother's legacy, creating art on canvas in lieu of the stage and impressing new buyers with her work. As an artist, she actually became moderately successful and well-respected in the area, known for her simple, uplifting paintings of birds and flowers; pieces that brought smiles to peoples' faces, happiness to their hearts, and a touch of soothing purity to their homes and businesses.

"This is all *your* fault," Cecilia would tease every time she managed to forge a new connection to add to her book. But Bruce would insist that the fault was all hers. *She* was the one who put brushes to canvas. All he'd done was buy the gallery space.

But it wasn't the space nor the money that was important. It was the intention behind it. The desire to make another happy, not expecting anything in return but the satisfaction of knowing that the smile on their face came from you and your doing. And that was exactly why, when it all came down to it, Bruce and Cecilia were perfect for eachother. They helped eachother grow, always encouraging and never stifling. Two pieces of a puzzle had never fit so well together. Neither of them had to say it out loud, but they both knew that they had found their soul mate.

The other half that made them whole.

In knowing this, a fire lit in Bruce. He wanted to give Cecilia the world. So they started to travel that world together, jetting off on romantic spur-of-the-moment getaways to places like the Swiss Alps and the Grecian Isles just to savor the new experiences that being in a foreign land could bring. They hiked mountain paths, tasted regional delicacies, and visited every notable landmark they could find. Cecilia's thirst for exploration was unrelenting. She wanted to see and do *everything*; all the things that her books had told her about, but she'd never been able to savor before outside of the comfort of their pages. Her pretty blue eyes would light up as she took in all the new food, new scenery, and new adventures, and seeing her so happy and vibrant made Bruce happy, too. It was during a warm summer night in Costa Rica, drinking cocktails and eating fresh mango by candlelight while the salty ocean breeze blew in through their open bungalow window that he decided once and for all that this was the woman he wanted to be with for the rest of his life.

When they returned to the city, he asked her to join him for a walk by the river, to the same place where they had first laid eyes on eachother. It was there that he proposed to her, offering her a sparkling diamond in exchange for the promise of having her heart forever. Cecilia said yes without a moment's hesitation and jumped into his arms, wrapping him in the biggest hug he'd ever been enveloped in. As her happy tears wet his shoulder, Bruce's heart hammered with joy. He knew that with Cecilia by his side his life would finally be complete. He would not only have his business, his wealth, his notoriety, and his dream home... most importantly, he would no longer spend long, lonely days in his mansion with no one to love or to love him in return.

He had finally found what had been missing.

The couple wasted no time in getting married. News of their wedding graced the pages of the *Stirling City Gazette* with a lengthy depiction of the ceremony written in flawless detail, describing everything from the elegant decor in the church, to the pretty white-rose centerpieces at the reception, to the romantic long-sleeved lace-and-tulle sheath dress worn by the bride, to a tender play-by-play of the couple's first dance as husband and wife. This was big news, after all. Bruce von Essen was one of Stirling's resident "celebrities" being as rich and successful as he was, and now that he was no longer the area's most eligible bachelor, this would undoubtedly *crush* the dreams of all of the petty gold-diggers out there hoping to get their grubby hands into his fortune. Coincidentally, Bruce couldn't have cared less.

No woman had ever affected him like Cecilia did. He wasn't interested in meaningless flings or cheap thrills. Never had been, to be frank. Cecilia was the purest part of his life, a person who even surrounded by this busy city, this rat race, this superficial world, always remained innocent and genuine. He was incredibly happy with her, and to think that his life could've turned out any other way was simply so disturbing that he chose *not* to think about it. Bruce couldn't imagine Cecilia not being in his life and couldn't remember what it was like living without her. Despite all of the money, riches, and material things that he had, she held the most value to him. Cecilia had filled the empty space in his heart, and he looked forward to his future with her and to spending the rest of his years with her by his side.

The couple honeymooned in Paris, then spent the months that followed cavorting around the mansion in Bruce's off-work hours, enjoying the passion of their newly-wedded bliss. Bruce had never thought it was possible to make love to someone every night, but Cecilia seemed intent on proving him wrong. She couldn't get enough of him, nor him enough of her. It was pure heaven being with her, pure ecstasy to hear his name on her lips.

As soon as he could, he made good on his promise to one day give her the garden that she'd always dreamed of, and when Cecilia needed time for herself, she took to transforming the area behind the house into a vibrant, colorful sanctuary. It was her personal sanctum, a quiet place where she could reflect and paint and think, surrounded by flowers with the gorgeous stone fountain in the center providing the perfect relaxing ambiance. It was truly beautiful; exactly what she had always wanted.

Bruce would often go outside to relax in the warm sun and watch his beloved Cecilia tend to her flowers and trim the tall hedges surrounding them, and he adored the way that she glowed when she did what she loved. As he watched her toil over colorful patches of pretty pink begonias, deep purple pansies, red Tuscan poppies, and vibrant yellow tulips, he couldn't help but think that she was the most beautiful woman on the planet. Classy and sophisticated, yet not at all afraid to get her hands dirty. Sometimes it was hard for him to believe that she was real. He wasn't one to believe much in luck or fate; in his experience, hard work reaped the most reward and most anything else was coincidental. But he sure felt damn lucky to have her as his wife.

"Stop gawking at me!" Cecilia would scold him with a playful smile when she finally noticed Bruce's eyes focused on her cute little rear as she bent over her garden, hard at work.

He would chuckle, caught red-handed, and pull some stupid, sappy line to make her blush. "But how can I not gawk at you?" he'd counter. "You're the prettiest flower in this garden."

Cecilia always laughed at his cheesiness, no matter how blatant and tacky it was. "Bruce, you're so ridiculous! Don't let the geraniums hear you. They might get jealous."

"Let them be jealous, then," Bruce would suggest, pulling her away from her gardening and down onto his bench for a different kind of toil. Cecilia never seemed to mind the distraction; getting side-tracked from her work was never a problem so long as it involved spending some quality time with her husband.

And quality time they certainly spent in that garden. That was where they would talk the very most. Cecilia would sit in his lap with her arms laced around his neck and they'd talk about everything from the arts to politics, to the goings-on at Vonessen Inc. and the newest buyers to visit Cecilia's gallery. They'd talk about their stresses, their frustrations, their joys, dreams, and desires. And it was in that garden that they discovered that what they both desired more than anything was to hear the pitter-patter of a child's little feet running around the halls of their home.

Their wish came true, and double at that. Only a little more than a year after marrying, the von Essens welcomed not just one, but *two* little bundles of joy into the world when Cecilia gave birth to fraternal twin girls that she and Bruce named Angelina Marie and Blair Rose. Bruce thought it nothing short of a small miracle when he held his daughters in his arms for the first time and looked down into their tiny faces. Angelina looked just like him, with inquisitive chocolate eyes and dark raven hair. And Blair was the spitting image of her mother, but with eyes the color of warm caramel rather than Cecilia's piercing sapphire blues.

Years ago, he could have never pictured this moment; could have never imagined that anything or anyone in his life could be more important to him than running his business. But Cecilia had proven him wrong before, and now these two little girls only reinforced it further. He had a family now. A *family*.

Of course, being a parent wasn't as easy in practice as it was on paper, and fatherhood proved to be a brand new challenge for Bruce. Business matters, money? He could handle those things without blinking an eye. But children? Children were territory that he wasn't familiar with and there were times when Bruce felt like he had gotten in way over his head. Life had been comfortable and easy when it was just him and Cecilia, but when two more girls were added to the mix that was when his true mettle was tested. He and Cecilia shared a lot of sleepless nights in the first few months of parenthood, but Bruce tried his hardest to be the one to get up first when that telltale wailing reached his ears over the baby monitor, solely to give his wife some rest if nothing else.

One night about four months into it was particularly taxing. Angelina was up crying hysterically, already showing herself to be quite the dramatic handful, and Blair was squirming and whimpering in her own crib restlessly, ready to burst into tears and follow her sister's lead at any moment. Bruce struggled to calm the girls down, but nothing was working. Finally, Cecilia came into the room, realizing that the baby monitor wasn't going to stop without a little intervention on her part.

"She won't stop crying!" Bruce gestured at Angelina, frustrated at his inability to pacify her. "What does she want? I've tried everything! Bottles, baby food, toys... she just spits them out or bats them away. I don't know what to do."

It was clear from his expression that he was more upset with himself than his red-faced little girl and Cecilia looked at him sympathetically, compassionate even when she was tired. She rested a gentle hand on his shoulder.

"It's okay. Look," she cooed, reaching into Angelina's crib and handing him the squirming baby. "She doesn't need any of those things, Bruce. She just wants to be held. She just wants to be with her Daddy. See?"

Bruce couldn't believe it, but no sooner than Cecilia had handed him the infant, Angelina started to quiet down, her high-pitched wails regressing to stubborn whimpers. He looked at his wife in amazement as she reached down into Blair's crib next.

"Shh, shh... come here, Blair. It's okay," she said in a soothing murmur. She rocked Blair in her arms and Blair instantly seemed to quiet too, nuzzling into her mother's chest contentedly. Bruce followed Cecilia's lead and mimicked the rocking, and Angelina blinked at him with two big brown mystified eyes before her sad little frown morphed into a happy gurgle.

"See?" Cecilia grinned, sidling up beside him. "You can be just as good a daddy as you are a businessman. I promise."

"How are you so good at this?" he mused in a quiet voice.

Cecilia tucked her hair behind her ear and shrugged in response, always modest when taking a compliment. "Mother's intuition, I guess." Seeing how much calmer Angelina was in his arms, she added, "You're not so bad yourself, you know."

After a few more minutes of quiet rocking, both babies had fallen fast asleep. Although it was never easy when someone else's life was dependent on yours, Bruce saw that night that he and Cecilia made a good team. He grew more confident in his new role every week. Cecilia was right. He *could* be just as good a father as he was a CEO, and he put forth his best effort into giving his wife and two little girls the best lives that they could have; lives that were filled with love, affection, and happy memories.

His good intentions didn't go unrealized, and the first few years of Angelina and Blair's lives were indeed very happy ones... and ones that flew by all too quickly at that. One moment the babies were learning to walk and talk, and the next they weren't babies at all anymore. By the time they were eight years old, the twins had grown to be two beautiful little girls who were quite different from one another despite sharing the same birthday.

Even before they'd started elementary school it had been clear that Blair had taken the most after her mother, and not just because she'd inherited Cecilia's wavy brown hair and soft, delicate features. Blair also had Cecilia's smarts and natural sophistication. She was quiet, serious, and somewhat shy, but her introverted nature didn't make her disagreeable in the least bit. Far from that, she was very caring, well-mannered, loving, and thoughtful, just like her mother. She had a knack for doing sweet, heartfelt things for her family members that brightened their days like making sweet little drawings for Mom, sharing her favorite toys with Angelina, and helping pack work lunches for Dad, making sure to sneak him an extra cookie or two when no one else was looking. She loved to read, write, doodle, and learn, and would often take her picture books, notebooks, and sketchpads to the garden and flip through the pages outside where she could be surrounded by the flowers. But what she loved even more than that - more than reading and writing and learning - was the piano.

As the girls had grown out of their baby clothes and into their toddler years, Cecilia used any free time she had while Bruce was at work and she was at home watching the girls to work on creating new pieces for her gallery. Just like her mother had done for her, she played good music on the radio for Blair and Angelina and let them doodle at her feet while she stood in front of her canvas, turning simple strokes of color into intricate scenes of her trademark red poppies in Tuscany, graceful ballet dancers at the barre, and tiny birds in flight. Blair fell in love with the sound of the piano's tinkling keys that she heard so often in the music her mother listened to, and after a particularly long Chopin marathon, she practically *begged* her parents to let her learn how to play. She began her piano lessons when she was only five years old and would often spend hours at a time sitting at the big black Steinway in her father's study, trying hard to do her best.

Blair had never liked to speak in public, so when writing didn't do the trick, she preferred to let her fingers do the talking. When she played, she would get lost in the music and let it take over. It was impressive how quickly she picked the instrument up. Her teachers even considered her something of a prodigy. But *she* didn't see her playing as that. She simply saw it as doing what she loved. She loved to feel the music flow through her fingertips, and being on-stage at recitals was the only time she felt comfortable in the spotlight. Often, she forgot the audience was even there. Cecilia, especially, loved to listen to her. Sometimes, they would sit in the study alone together, Blair on the piano and Cecilia sitting in front of the fireplace with a book in her hands, the lighting dimmed, and a hot tea or coffee on the table beside her.

Of course, if Blair had a hobby then Angelina insisted that she needed one too. Angelina had also inherited a love for music, but after breaking her first recorder in frustration and only managing a muddled mess on Blair's piano, Bruce and Cecilia realized that she couldn't play an instrument to save her life. So instead of leading her towards picking up the clarinet or flute, they encouraged her to focus on a different kind of instrument: her voice. It probably should've been obvious early on that singing would become Angelina's "thing" anyway, because even as a baby she would gurgle and babble along to the music they played on car rides into the city like she was having the time of her life. By the time she was out of diapers, she was already prancing around the house like a diva, forcing her parents and sister to listen to her sing her favorite pop songs and Disney tunes over and over again, missing lyrics and all. The thing was, she didn't sound half bad despite her age, and her attention-seeking behavior could actually lead to a productive pastime for her with a little guidance. So just like Blair, Angelina began her musical studies at a remarkably young age by taking up voice lessons.

Angelina lacked one thing that her sister had though, and that one thing was discipline. Angelina was unlike Blair in that she wasn't very quiet or shy at all. Instead, she was a rambunctious ball of energy, and part of being a rambunctious ball of energy was the unintended consequence of being a little immature. Maybe a bit *too* immature to actually take her voice lessons seriously... but what *did* an eight year old child take seriously? Singing for Angelina wasn't work - it was fun! And boisterous little Angie always had a penchant for making fun out of any situation. She loved to crack jokes and make people laugh. If there was ever mischief or excitement going on in the house, she more than likely had a big role to play in it, and if there was ever a new friend to be made, she'd be the first to walk up and say hello.

The girls were indeed very different from one another, but one thing that they shared in common was how much Bruce and Cecilia loved them. In no time, their lives had turned into a pleasant, predictable whirlwind of school, recitals, and memorable family milestones. The von Essen family was known around town for not only being one of the richest, but also one of the closest - one whose real wealth wasn't measured solely in money. When it all came down to it, Bruce couldn't have felt more lucky or blessed. Once a successful but lonely man, he wasn't lonesome anymore and his heart had been made whole by the family he loved. He had a wonderful, devoted wife, two caring and talented little girls, and a life's journey to this point that he could be proud of. Say what you will about the von Essens and their money, but this was a family tied together by true love and support - a family that defined the word in every aspect of their existence.

Unfortunately, not everyone in Stirling City had hearts and intentions quite so pure.

CHAPTER THREE
Bad Intentions

THE LATE-AUGUST SUN STREAMED in through the matte-glass windows of Vonessen Inc., brightening the break lounge with hazy rays of speckled light. It was a beautiful day outside, but Victoria Adessi sighed restlessly as she poured herself a cup of coffee in spite of it. The tall, attractive, bottle-blonde woman with a love for lipstick the color of burgundy wine and limit-pushing office wear had been working in the accounting department at Vonessen Inc. for three years now and shouldn't have been feeling so on edge these days, but she just couldn't help herself. Despite being a valuable asset to the company and the admired go-to gal amongst her peers, she still wasn't where she wanted to be.

Victoria wanted more. Not only did she want more, she *needed* more. Her lust for more was insatiable and no matter how well she improved her standing in the world, she'd always craved it and couldn't remember a time when she'd ever been truly satisfied. More material things, more power, and more money - that was what made the world go 'round, wasn't it?

Victoria was convinced that the answer to that question was an overwhelming "yes," and that anyone who claimed otherwise and insisted that crisp green bills couldn't buy you happiness was a liar. In her mind, that was just an excuse that poor people came up with to make themselves feel better about their lot in life. Well, those sorry saps could make whatever assertions they wanted to about the value of money, because Victoria knew the truth: more of it in your pocket *always* made your problems go away, and having unfathomable amounts of it would surely make *her* bitter, gold-digging heart happy. With more money she could buy the best furniture, live in the best house, own the most expensive cars, eat at the most restrictive restaurants, sip the finest champagnes at two in the afternoon solely because why not, and go on the most exotic vacations. In other words, *nobody* could own her. Money was freedom. But alas, here she was despite her good looks, charm, and wit without a rich man to call her own and an *MTV-Cribs* style home to live in. It made her blood boil. She didn't want to be slaving away in an office all day like everyone else. She wanted to live like a queen, and she didn't want to have to work so damn hard to do it.

To not work so hard. To be as lazy as she wanted but have whatever she asked for in spite of it? Now *that* would be some real power. She only knew one person with that kind of clout in these parts, and hell, she was working for him. It was a shame that Bruce von Essen was already married and that she hadn't found him sooner... but then again, that technicality hadn't exactly put a stop to the perverse thoughts that had been setting up residence in her head over the past year. Victoria hadn't been keeping an active tally of just how many times her boss had crossed her mind in ways much less than professional, but if she had to take a guess, a nickel-per-thought would have made her a millionaire by now. And the ironic part was that not a single soul apart from her even had a clue of it, and if anyone who knew her *could've* seen into her head, they would have been shocked at what they'd find.

The thing was, Victoria had never outright *looked* like a greedy sociopath with a lust for dominating others and a knack for manipulation. With her deeply-tanned skin, golden blonde hair, modelesque face, and envy-inducing body, she might have been above average in the looks department, but otherwise she came off as relatively normal. As it turned out, that perceived normalcy was a weapon more powerful than guns or knives or baseball bats, because despite her magnetizing exterior, the real Miss Adessi was as ugly on the inside as a person could come. The real Victoria was cunning, vindictive, and opportunistic, but it was by no means a mistake that she was so good at hiding it. The accountant boasted some killer credentials, and aside from managing money, one of her other great talents was acting.

She'd never been a star on stage or film, but she'd managed to pull the wool over the eyes of her colleagues from the very beginning, putting on a convincing face and masking her true self from the world. Her life had been a life run by games and manipulations and social posturing. That - not knowledge or luck - was what had led her to graduate at the top of her class and earn herself a dual-master's degree in business and accounting. And that was what had helped her solicit the recommendations that she'd needed to rise through the ranks so quickly at Vonessen Inc. Scheming and deception were a means of survival and getting ahead. It was a dog-eat-dog world out there, and to come out on top and not be left wallowing in the dirt you needed three things: control, power, and wealth. Victoria was intent on having those things, and she'd do anything to get what she wanted. No bridge was too far, no mountain too high, and no bystanders immune.

Not even the von Essens.

Fortunately maybe, right now wasn't the time to dwell on it. Right now, the only thing she needed to worry about was the scalding-hot coffee in her hands. She sat down at the break lounge table and took a careful swig, attempting to quell the all-too-familiar storm in her head with limited success.

"Stressed a bit?" a woman's voice asked, calling Victoria from her thoughts. The blonde glanced over her shoulder to see her friend and co-worker Emmalyn O'Dell standing behind her holding a warm, steaming cup of her own. Emmalyn was a nice young woman with .dark-rimmed glasses and auburn-red hair who dressed professionally and worked hard, but for all of her good qualities, Victoria wasn't drawn to her out of a sense of respect. Victoria saw Emmalyn as an underling. Someone not as smart, not as beautiful, and not as capable as her. In fact, she could actually see Em turning out to be a lonely old cat lady one day. Maybe it was the quirky cartoon cat on her mug that did it.

In comparison, Emmalyn had all the respect in the world for Victoria for those same reasons. Victoria was so smart, so beautiful, and so successful! It was no wonder Victoria kept her around. Emmalyn wasn't competition, and she was a great source for the selfish ego boosts that Victoria loved with her misplaced words of admiration or simply her comparable pathetic-ness.

"Morning, Em," she greeted her in a pleasant voice, waving her coffee mug in her direction. "Nothing a little caffeine won't cure." She took another sip and got up to face her, switching her weight to one hip and leaning back against the table. Victoria was wearing a black mock-turtleneck dress and tall ebony heels. A bit tight and short for the office, but when you looked as good as she did, who wouldn't flaunt what they had? "I just have a lot on my mind," she shrugged. "Been working hard, you know?"

"Don't we all? *Especially* you. I don't know how you do it sometimes. But I guess that's a good thing, with that managerial spot opening up. God, I would love to snag that position... but I know I won't. *You* could though." There was that well-placed ego boost, right on cue. Naive Emmalyn never failed.

"We'll see how things fall. But I have to admit, it's been the only thing I can think about since the announcement last week."

"I'm sure it is," Emmalyn mused before adding a little more quietly, "But I know what will take your mind off of it and ease some of that stress. Do I have some gossip for you!"

Victoria shot her a sadistic smile and motioned for her to follow her out of the lounge. She was glad for the distraction. It was one that she and Emmalyn partook in all too often, but

Victoria had always reveled in a little good gossip. There was nothing else quite so gratifying... other than cash and screwing of course. After all, what better way to get away from your own perceived "problems" than to concentrate on those of others?

That better way didn't exist; at least not for Victoria. She and Emmalyn took their mugs with them as they made their way back into the office towards their neighboring desks, pretending to be nonchalant about the stares they received from their male co-workers. Victoria didn't need their wandering eyes to know that she was drop-dead gorgeous. It was a fact she played up on a daily basis with her tight pencil skirts, low-cut blouses, leg-baring sweater dresses, and pointy stilettos. She was narcissistic and liked the attention, but these silly men in department store suits were good enough for a romp or two in bed if it suited her needs or gave her some sort of edge, and that was where it ended. They were nothing but meat to her. As far as long-term went, she was only willing to settle down with someone if his bank account was overflowing like the banks of the Nile, and as much as everyone here was making, it just wasn't good enough. They were all well off, but they weren't the best.

They weren't Bruce.

Emmalyn and Victoria sat down at their desks and the gossip began almost instantaneously.

"Alright," Victoria said as she shuffled through a thick file of papers. "Dish immediately. I need full details."

Emmalyn was happy to oblige her. As she began typing away, the women shared scandalous stories of people in the neighborhood... of one woman's new bankruptcy filing, of another's horrible botched nose job, of one of the wealthy bankers in Stirling City getting caught cheating on his middle-aged trophy wife with a slutty college co-ed... everything and anything that came to mind. For as nice and prim as the Stirling area looked on the outside, it was a breeding ground for gossip-worthy topics. Everyone had their vice; the idea was not to get caught.

The women were right in the middle of discussing how one of the ladies in the Human Resources Department had put on a good twenty-five pounds since her unceremonious divorce when Victoria heard an annoyed - and rather *annoying* - groan come from somewhere behind her.

"Victoria..." a male voice grumbled, as if the groan wasn't enough to grab her attention. She rolled her eyes and huffed crossly. That voice belonged to her least favorite co-worker out of the whole lot, Ben McClafferty, that aggravating potato-head with a giant stick up his ass. Ben was the only person in the office who ever dared to question her perfection, and needless to say she wasn't very fond of him because of it.

"What?" she snapped, irritated that her conversation was being so rudely interrupted by someone she disliked so much.

"Sorry to disrupt your oh-so-important chat, Victoria," he swiveled around in his chair to scowl at the back of her head. "But the dirty laundry you're airing is really starting to stink. It's breaking my concentration on these reports."

Victoria sighed and took a sip of her coffee. "Cut the sarcasm, Ben. Is that all you wanted?"

"I know, God forbid some of us actually want peace and quiet when we work. Anyway, no, that's not all I wanted. The boss is coming. Maybe you'll at least give a shit about that."

Victoria perked up and glanced towards the door. Ben was right. She *did* give a shit. There was the boss in all his glory, standing in the doorway in an expensive black designer suit with his sexy goatee trimmed to *GQ* perfection and his dark hair slicked back, suave and stylish. *Bruce von Essen.* The man only got more attractive every day. Victoria smiled covertly behind her coffee mug. She looked forward to the days when she could share a conversation with her boss and ogle him shamelessly behind his back, even if it didn't help to quiet the voices in her head. She peered over her computer screen and felt herself grow hot at the sight of him. Yes, it was a shame that he was married. But still, the things that she would do to that man...

Actually, there wasn't much that she *wouldn't* do to him. While her desire for "more everything" was causing her plenty of restlessness these days, her desire for this man that had so much of it was only getting worse. The way Victoria saw it, there were only two ways to get the kind of wealth that she so desperately desired: to earn it on her own - which would either be impossible or take her an entire lifetime - or to marry into it and have it handed to her. The second option sounded much more appealing, and considering how high the bar was set, Bruce was the only affluent man around who could satisfy her needs. He was the top dog, the *crème de la crème*. She'd never outright acted upon her lust for him, but she'd never claimed to be a moral woman either. Her obsessive desire for Bruce and his cash was gaining ground over maintaining morality, and while Victoria had been eyeing him up for a while now, she just didn't know what to *do* about it.

Under normal circumstances, she was good at playing these games and manipulating people to screw things up on their own. But Bruce and Cecilia? There was no snag in their rope, no problem she could exploit. All she'd been able to do so far was work her ass off amidst her gossip fests with Emmalyn and hope that he would take notice of her. She'd been putting in plenty of extra hours for this company lately, going above and beyond the call of duty to knock every assignment that she turned in out of the park, and while she might have had underlying personality faults driving it, it couldn't be denied that she was damn good at her job. Bruce began to walk in the direction of her cubicle with that confident CEO stride of his and Victoria had to fight the urge to fan herself. She was practically undressing him with her eyes, envisioning what wonders hid beneath those posh designer suits he wore. From the way he filled them out, she could only imagine.

Emmalyn's voice hissing at Ben from across the gap in their desks was the only snag in her dirty daydream. "Is he coming over here?" she could hear her squeak as she took a nervous sip of her coffee. Emmalyn was the baby amongst the group, just out of business school, and hadn't been in the office for as long as the others. Visits from the boss still made her jumpy.

"Oh yeah, he is definitely heading this way," Ben confirmed, staring at his computer screen and typing away without making eye contact, eager to make a good impression. That manager's position opening up would be a dream come true and Victoria wasn't the only one who wanted it.

But Bruce didn't make it to their particular cluster of desks right away. He visited others first, trying to get a feel for how things were going with end-of-month closing in. If there was one thing that could be said about the CEO's demeanor in the office, it was that he actually seemed to care about keeping everyone satisfied, from the high level executives upstairs all the way down to the ladies answering phones at the front desk. Caring about morale was a philosophy that he'd always believed in, but one that Cecilia had only instilled in him further. Happy employees were productive employees, and productive employees meant a successful business built to last. A win-win for everybody.

When he finally reached Victoria's desk, she was trying hard to look busy on her computer, but the keystrokes were empty and unfocused. She could sense that he was there before he even spoke a word - she could practically *feel* him standing behind her. Her lips pursed tensely in response. He smelled like pricey European cologne, something that made the scent receptors in her nostrils prickle. She knew exactly what it was. *Uomo ricco.* An Italian brand with notes of cinnamon, mint citrus, blood mandarin, and grapefruit, entwining together with Indian patchouli and masculine leather to create an intoxicating mix guaranteed to make a woman weak in the knees. Look, she wasn't perfect, but she damn well knew her perfumes and colognes. Call her a bloodhound for them and she wouldn't take offense.

"Ben, Victoria, Emmalyn," Bruce greeted them, his voice straightforward and all-business. "How are things going over here? Anything I can do for you? Any concerns or issues?"

Ben sure had an issue and thought about asking for a change in desk location so he could get away from these two gossipy little brats, but didn't let on by complaining. Instead, he answered the boss with a professional, "Good morning, sir. Everything's great here. Our clients are happy and things are going smoothly for end-of-month. I'm finishing up my reports right now." He went back to typing feverishly to make a point as the ladies behind him echoed the sentiment. The typical cordialities continued until Bruce turned his attention to Victoria.

"Victoria, I meant to ask you, how is that project I gave you coming along? That last bit of preliminary data you turned in was excellent. I like the pie charts you've been adding. They're very well-organized. Not that I expected any less, mind you."

Victoria restrained the cockiest grin imaginable. "Done," she confirmed, picking up a small presentation binder from her desk and handing it over to him. "Just completed in fact." She leaned back in her chair and watched as Bruce flipped through the binder, perusing her work with an approving nod.

"Excellent," he repeated, impressed with how quickly - and thoroughly - she'd gotten it done. "I'll look through this more closely in my office, but good work. This is just what I needed."

"Anytime," Victoria replied, trying to sound as professional as possible, though her thoughts were less than safe-for-work. '*Hopefully if I continue to impress him with my work, I can impress him in other ways,*' she thought secretly to herself. A mental picture of her molesting him on his office desk came to mind.

Unfortunately for her, a tacky hook-up in the board room didn't look like it was in the stars today. As Bruce bid the group goodbye and walked away to another cluster of cubicles, Victoria's eyes followed him intently. The wheels were turning in her conniving little head. If only he didn't have that damn wife... but then again, people *did* get divorced all the time, didn't they? What was the divorce rate these days, anyway? Fifty-percent?

'Mrs. Victoria von Essen,' she tried the name out in her head, nearly salivating at how good it sounded. *'God, I like the sound of that...'* It had a ring almost like her current name, Adessi, but even better. It had to be fate, there was no other explanation.

Or maybe it was simply delusion, because to mix her name with his and even *consider* the possibility that he'd get divorced was entirely unrealistic. Bruce von Essen was the most faithful man on the planet. Everyone knew it. He made it a *point* to let everyone know it. You could throw a porn star or a supermodel at him and it wouldn't make a damn difference. His love for his precious wife was unwavering and it made Victoria's dreams of winning him over only that much more impractical to pursue. This game would be a challenging one to say the least. Perhaps the most challenging she'd ever signed up for. For once the odds were really *not* in her favor, and it was terribly frustrating for her.

"He's really nice, isn't he?" Emmalyn commented once Bruce was safely out of earshot. "I always get so nervous when I know he's coming down here, but I always feel like an idiot for feeling that way afterwards. I don't know why I freak like that."

"He's a good boss," Ben noted before adding in a bitter aside, "Of course if he knew that you and Vicky over here were always gabbing on about useless drama I'm not sure he'd be so appreciative or give Vic such weighty assignments. I don't even know how they get done with you two never shutting up."

"Ugh, stick a sock in it, Ben. You're such a buzzkill," Emmalyn crinkled her nose at him in annoyance.

Normally at this point, Victoria would chime in with a dismissive eye roll and a *"screw you"* sort of retort of her own to

Ben's obvious jealousy over the fact that he wasn't getting all of the big projects, but right now she just didn't care enough. She had much more important things on her mind besides responding to the death glare she could feel him laser-beaming at her. Whiny, insufferable Ben was just another loser in her eyes, nothing but a walking salami. He had no other purpose in life. Other men, however? Other men could be of much more use to her.

Victoria stole one last glance at the back of Bruce's suit coat before he left the room and felt her insides burn with a dark lust. Damn it, she didn't care how far-fetched it was. She didn't care what she had to do. There was nothing the self-proclaimed seductress wanted more than to snag Mr. von Essen away from that perfect little wife of his and make him, his money, and his life of luxury her own. She swore to herself that she would make it happen one day... even if it was the last thing she'd ever do.

That, in a nutshell, was what made Victoria such a horrible person - her lack of boundaries, lack of morals, and lack of good-will towards her fellow man. It can be difficult for nice, normal people to conceptualize that someone could have such little respect for the lives of others that the notion of altering said lives could be seen as simply a challenging "hurdle" to overcome, but that was Victoria's prerogative. People aren't always what one would call "cookie-cutter cut-and-dry," and in the proverbial potluck of endlessly differing agendas, objectives, and guiding codes of honor, she was undoubtedly sitting somewhere near the bottom of the barrel, teetering the thin line between "shades of gray" and "outright black." She was a woman lost in her own depraved fantasy world; a world that revolved solely around her.

Part of living in that world meant having to get her kicks somehow, and that night Victoria went out to one of the local high-end restaurant bars with Emmalyn and a few other co-workers with just that end in mind. Sometime during the course of dinner and drinks she'd managed to find herself a little late-night "snack" for dessert, and a duo of martinis, some sugared words, and a bit of exposed cleavage later, the man was completely hooked on her. Before the night was over, Victoria brought him home with her - bad snakeskin-patterned jacket and all - for a romp beneath the sheets. At the rate they were going, it didn't even look like they'd make it to the bed. Snakeskin Man was all over her before they even stepped foot through her front door. He latched on to her like an overzealous octopus, his rough hands gripping her body and raking through her hair with an animalistic fervor. It was utterly ridiculous, and Victoria loved it.

She let out an approving gasp as her male comrade groped her ass and gave it a hard squeeze. He backed her against the living room wall, pressed his body hard against hers, and slurred something raunchy and incoherent into her copper skin as he trailed slobbery kisses all over her neck. Victoria's hand made a hasty grab for his crotch, feeling him up over the barrier of his dark jeans while his fingers fumbled with the buttons of her flimsy blouse. They were a tangled mess of limbs and clothes and greedy sex, her sleeve falling down over her shoulder, her lacey red bra peeking through, his tacky snakeskin jacket only half on, his fly already unzipped - but even if Victoria wanted to skip straight to the good parts and have this stranger right here against her living room wall, there was one bothersome thing she had to take care of first. If she was getting lucky tonight - and she was pretty certain that she was - she wanted no interruptions.

Not one single peep.

"Wait," she demanded as she pressed her hand against her soon-to-be one-night-stand's chest. "I need to take care of something. You keep your pants on for one more minute." When the all-too-eager stranger gave her a look of protest, she suggested in a naughty aside, "Don't worry, they'll be off soon enough."

That promise seemed to keep him revved-up enough. Releasing herself from his vice-like grip, Victoria stepped away, sliding past him to open a nearby door and peek inside. From the small sliver that she afforded herself, she could see that her young daughter Nicolette was already fast asleep, tucked up in bed with her dark brown hair fanning messily around her head. Good. She smirked in satisfaction and locked Nicolette's door behind her, giving her impatient guest's shirtfront an aggressive yank and pulling him down the hallway for some fun.

Only Nicolette wasn't really sleeping. As soon as she felt her mother's shadow leave the doorway and heard the lock click in place, the little girl groaned and rolled over in bed, pulling her pillow over her head to muffle the unavoidable noises that would soon be coming from the room next door. She felt a sickening jolt of dread join the sharp pang of hunger in her tummy. She should have been used to this by now. It wasn't rare for Victoria to come home buzzed off of margaritas with strange men that she'd never see again, nor was it rare for Nicolette to go to bed with a rumble in her stomach that the peanut butter and jelly sandwiches she had to make herself for dinner couldn't quite quell.

But being used to it didn't make it better. This was she and her mother's relationship. Barely a relationship at all. And it hurt, like a splinter always there beneath the skin. Victoria only cared about money and getting laid, and Nicolette knew full well that if her mom were given the choice between spending time with her, a brand new Prada bag, or a pair of Gucci heels, one of the inanimate objects would win out. They didn't spend any time together as it was, and any time they *did* was hardly enriching. On the contrary, Nicolette was pretty sure that Victoria hated her. Her mom had never physically laid a hand on her, but Nicolette didn't need to be spanked or slapped to know the truth. She knew that she was a mistake and she knew Victoria didn't want her. She'd been told as much multiple times, and even when she wasn't straight-out told, Victoria's actions spoke louder than words.

Nicolette would've almost rather been hit. The emotional abuse of an uncaring, vindictive mother was just as bad, if not worse, and more than anything she wished that she could just get a little positive attention once in a while. That maybe - just *maybe* - her mom could at least *pretend* to like her. Nice words and attention were things that Victoria never gave her though, not unless it was completely unavoidable or she was putting on her usual act in public. Things were so loveless between them that Nicolette didn't even call her "Mom." Victoria hated the word. In her opinion, it simply oozed with a connotation of being old and fat, neither of which she ever wanted to be. Nicolette clenched her eyes shut and squashed her pillow over her ears. The grunts, moans, and squeaking bedsprings were already starting.

This was *not* going to be a good night.

Clearly, Victoria didn't share this sentiment. It hadn't taken long for her and her boy-toy to strip down to their birthday suits, and no sooner than the clothes had hit the floor, they'd fallen onto the bed in a mangled heap, going at it like a pair of ravenous animals in heat. Victoria was getting exactly what she wanted.

Well... almost.

In reality, this was much more boring for her than all the noise she was making let on. She sometimes had to use her imagination to keep things interesting, and tonight was no exception. Inside her twisted head, she envisioned that this dark-haired stranger bucking on top of her wasn't Snakeskin Man at all. Instead, she pictured her boss in his place. She could see Bruce's perfectly chiseled face, could feel his toned muscles beneath her palms. She could even smell that expensive European cologne that he wore, vividly enough that it made her nose crinkle.

"Mmm, *Bruce...*" she purred as her accomplice gave her what she needed. He was too oblivious to notice that she'd called him another man's name in bed. Then again, it wasn't as if he cared. This wasn't some loving act of passion. He wasn't going to see this woman ever again after tonight and she could call him Charlie, Harry, or William so long as he had a good time. The name "Bruce" meant as little to him as starving children in a third-world country, and Victoria took full advantage of it.

When their raucous rendezvous finally culminated in a noisy, bed-shaking rush, the man groaned in satisfaction and rolled off of her, slumping down against the pillows in exhaustion. It wasn't long before he was snoring. Victoria laid awake while he snorted loudly and turned over in his sleep. If nothing else, her fantasy of him being her boss only strengthened her resolve to snatch away the wealthy businessman. His wife may have been in the way for now... but that could change.

Victoria bit her lip as she stared up at the ceiling and pictured all of Bruce's money. She could imagine bags upon bags of it filling every room in his house. She could see herself swimming in a pool filled with cash, neck deep in gold coins and silver bars. She thought of all the pricey, lavish things that she could buy herself with all of those riches... the purses, the dresses, the cars, the electronics, the classy dinners, the high-end vacations, the knick-knacks, the baubles, the jewelry, the wines... all the fine things that she'd never had before and had always wanted. There was no limit. Oh, what she would give to be a co-possessor of that dough of his... to have *that* kind of power!

The sound of a particularly loud snore broke Victoria from the blissful thought of beautiful green bills, and she grimaced, irritated and disgusted at her life. Swimming in the Federal Reserve wasn't her reality. *This* was. Pining for Bruce's deep pockets and having to resort to bringing home random sausages to satiate her urges. The thought of it was utterly exhausting, and suddenly Victoria realized just how long of a day she'd actually had and just how tired she really was.

So much psychotic obsession could really knock a girl out.

She climbed under her covers with a frustrated sigh, turning away from the stranger and curling her knees up into her chest. Someday things would be different. Someday she'd be with

Bruce, making hot passionate love to him and bathing in riches, romping around in his glorious mansion like the Queen of the World that she'd always been meant to be. Images of him flashed through her mind as she buried herself in her dark cotton sheets.

CHAPTER FOUR
First Meetings

WHILE VICTORIA'S MIND CLOUDED with sinister thoughts, the von Essens carried on with life as usual. Summer was quickly coming to a close, and the departure of long, sunny days by the family pool meant that it was time for the start of another school year at Saint Joan of Arc. Saint Joan was Maple Springs' most prestigious K-thru-8 school. It was rather exclusive for an elementary school and only accepted the best, brightest, and in most cases *richest* in the Stirling City area, but it hadn't taken much to convince the headmaster to let Blair and Angelina in ahead of the waiting list back before kindergarten. If he hadn't been impressed enough by the elaborate decor of the mansion during his grand tour of the place, the potential of the two girls, or their influential last name, Bruce would've been prepared to seal the deal with a hefty monetary donation to the school in a heartbeat. Fortunately, bribery had proven completely unnecessary, though the thought that the school library could have once graced the name "von Essen" still gave him a small chuckle to this day, nonetheless.

The price tag was admittedly hefty and the politics were a bit tedious at Saint Joan, but there was still a lot to like about it. In the girls' case, the fact that music hadn't been pushed out of the curriculum like it seemed to have been at so many other schools in the region was a big part of that. For all of its academic prowess, the school also boasted a superb arts program; one that continued on in its sister high school, Archbishop Wright, which the girls would undoubtedly be attending once they were old enough.

For now though, they were only eight, so they'd just have to focus on getting through elementary school first. On the morning of their first day back to classes, the smell of blueberry pancakes wafted through the house, filling it with the inviting aroma of breakfast. A hearty breakfast was a common staple of mornings in the mansion, but on big days like the first day of school, Cecilia always tried to make her breakfasts extra special.

The smell alone must have acted as a rallying cry, because the pancakes had barely left the pan when the rest of the family came filing into the dining room. Unsurprisingly, it was Angelina who flew through the archway first, dressed in the typical Saint Joan ensemble: a plaid navy pleated skirt, a crisp white button down blouse, knee-high socks, and a navy blazer donning the school emblem. Her short black hair was clipped back in the front with a glittery gold heart clip and matching stud earrings glinted on her ears. She was always trying to find ways to make the school uniform more fun, and she was proud to say that she was one of the first girls in their grade to get her ears pierced.

Her eyes lit up when she saw the whipped cream and blueberry syrup decorating the pancakes her mother was setting at the table, and she let out an excited whoop of "FOOD!" as she scurried towards her normal seat. A much calmer Blair followed behind her, taking care to sit down carefully so as not to ruffle her nice new skirt. The last person to make an entrance was Bruce. The CEO was clad in one of his usual designer suits, today's newspaper already in hand. He practically slept in those suits.

"Good morning, my dear," he greeted his wife with a cheery peck on the cheek as she set down bowls of raspberries and blueberries next. His eyes roved over her pretty navy wrap dress appreciatively. It was very Kate Middleton, like most of her clothes were. Classy and effortless. "You look beautiful today. And check out that breakfast! It must be a special occasion, hmm?"

"The first day of third grade," she reminded him with a charming grin. "I'd say that's pretty special, wouldn't you? So what do you think, girls? Are you excited to go back?"

Blair nodded sweetly but Angelina only seemed to care about the food. "I'm just excited to eat!" she exclaimed. "Mom, this looks *so* good!" She jammed her fork into the raspberry bowl with a hasty stab and Blair winced, almost as if she expected her sister to smash one and get berry juice all over herself - or worse, send it flying in *her* direction. She edged away nervously, fully intent on showing up nice and clean for her first day of classes.

"Ang, you should probably take off your blazer," she suggested with a sheepish grimace. "Remember when you got that strawberry crepe all over it?"

Angelina pouted in defiance. "That was *one* time!"

"Now girls, don't fuss," their mother interrupted, averting a clash of wills with two tall glasses of chocolate milk. "Angelina, you can keep your blazer on, but your sister's right. Try not to get anything on your uniform, okay sweetie?"

"Of course, Mommy," Angelina batted her eyelashes.

Bruce sat down and chuckled at his daughters' antics while he flipped through the pages of the *Stirling City Gazette*, amused that such an innocent response could come out sounding so *not* innocent... but considering who it was coming from, he couldn't exactly say that he was surprised. Every school day started like this without fail: Angelina was always jumpy and excitable in the mornings and soft-spoken little Blair was always the one trying to keep things orderly, calm, and in check. As for him, taking a look at the finance section was his morning routine. Checking out what was going on in the investing world was crucial to operations at Vonessen Inc.; his own personal take on homework.

"What's in the paper, Daddy?" Blair asked him, trying to ignore Angelina's obnoxious cow-like chewing to peek past her at the tiny black and white type.

"Well, Blair Bear... all kinds of things. But here's the article I was looking for. Your mother's made it into the Arts and Culture section. Want to see?" He flipped the section in question towards the girls, giving them a good view of a big color photo of their mother dressed in a pretty pastel pink Alexander McQueen dress, standing proudly in front of a few new paintings hanging against the wall of her Stirling City art gallery. The headline beside the picture read in bold black type, *"Local Artist Celebrates Decade of Gallery Ownership by Unveiling New Pieces for Fall."* The girls gasped. It was only a short human interest feature, but to them even a teeny blurb would have been cause for amazement.

"Wow, Mommy," Angelina said as Cecilia took a seat across from her. "You're in the news. That means you're famous!"

The corners of Cecilia's lips twitched in amusement. She'd always been humble and never cared much for the idea of fame, nor would she ever go so far as to attribute the quality to herself, but she appreciated the notion nonetheless. It was hard to believe that her art gallery had really been open for ten years now... which also meant that she and Bruce had almost been married for just as long. Only a few more months and it would be official.

"Will you read the article to us, Daddy?" Blair asked him.

"Of course," Bruce agreed. He cleared his throat for effect and read the words that followed with all the pizzazz of a professional radio announcer. "Cecilia von Essen may be the wife of a wealthy CEO, but she's far from being anyone's trophy."

Cecilia shot him a look of disbelief. It was hard to believe he hadn't concocted that on his own. "Really? *That's* their opener?"

"I couldn't make this up," Bruce claimed. "See? Right here."

"What's it mean?" Angelina scrunched her eyes.

"It *means* a trophy wife is someone who's only there to look pretty," Blair explained. "That's *not* Mommy." Her eyes widened as she realized the implications of what she'd said, and she corrected herself quickly. "Not that you're not pretty, Mommy. Because you're *very* pretty. But you're also very talented, and trophy wives aren't talented. They're just... well, trophies, I guess."

Cecilia laughed softly. "Thank you, Blair. That's very kind."

"Where do you learn these things?" Bruce chuckled.

"Books," Blair shrugged.

Bruce and Cecilia shared an amused look. Books, indeed.

Angelina wasn't quite as impressed. Blair was such a know-it-all sometimes. "Daddy, keep reading," she demanded with an impatient pout. Not wanting to provoke a temper tantrum by getting sidetracked, Bruce cleared his throat and continued:

Cecilia von Essen may be the wife of a wealthy CEO, but she's far from being anyone's trophy. For the last ten years, Cecilia has seen her own success separate of that of her husband's, investment mogul Bruce von Essen, as the owner of "The Bird and Blossom," a chic, charming, and sophisticated art gallery located in the heart of Stirling City's beautiful Avalon Square neighborhood.

"When I opened The Bird and Blossom a decade ago, I didn't know what to expect," Cecilia admits. "I certainly wasn't anticipating the gallery garnering as much praise and attention as it has. But Stirling City's arts community has been very kind and welcoming, and I appreciate all the support that they've given me."

That support is exactly why Cecilia is expanding her horizons this fall. She loves to paint and is known for clean, elegant pieces of birds and cherry blossoms, as the moniker "The Bird and Blossom" would insinuate. But she has also honed her skills to include complex portraits and detailed renditions of popular world landmarks inspired by her travels. Along with painting in both oils and acrylics, she has also recently tried her hand at watercolors and mixed media. To celebrate ten years of her work, Cecilia is unveiling a brand new selection at her gallery this week. She will also offer a number of price-cut specials and plans to teach a weekly painting class for those wishing to create some art of their own.

"It's a really fun idea [teaching], and I've wanted to do it for a while," she says. "Now that the gallery has been open for ten years, I can't think of a more exciting time to start."

The first class will be held in early October and continue throughout the winter and spring months, with registration available via her website, birdandblossom.com. If you are interested in attending, she asks that you sign up early, as spots are limited.

With one last punctuating clear of his throat, he concluded:

"The end."

"The end?" Angelina repeated. "Aww, that's it?"

"That's it," he affirmed.

"Oh." She kicked her feet back and forth. "Well... at least you're in the paper, Mommy. You really *are* famous."

"I'm not famous, Angelina. Nor do I want to be."

Bruce shrugged. "If you insist. But ten years is still quite an accomplishment. It's important for people to know about."

"Is it?" Cecilia smiled, popping a berry into her mouth.

"*I* thought so anyway," he grinned at her. "But I might be biased. At any rate, it's certainly the prettiest photo in the paper." He reached across the table to give her hand a squeeze and they shared an affectionate glance before Angelina butted in again.

"I hope *I* get to be in the paper someday," she announced bossily. "Everyone will see my picture and they'll all be super jealous. What else is in there, Daddy? Anything about me?"

"Not that I see, Angel," he pretended to search, trailing his finger along the type. "Nothing here... nothing here, either. But I do see a lot of boring news that you wouldn't be very interested in. A lot of stocks bouncing around... and silver is down."

"Silver is down? I thought silver was doing well," Cecilia released his hand to sip her coffee. "Better not tell your brother."

"Gard *is* pretty fond of his precious metals. But it'll jump back up again, I'm sure of it. And hopefully he won't get a chance to call me to go on a neurotic rampage before it does. He's always been a bit overdramatic." Bruce folded his paper in finality and set it aside, taking a big bite of breakfast. "In any case, my appetite will certainly be in the green this morning. I don't know how you juggle so many talents, Cece, but this is delicious."

"Blueberry pancakes are my specialty," she winked.

"Oh? I thought Italian was your specialty."

"Only for dinner. For breakfast it's blueberry pancakes."

"And for dessert?" Bruce gave her a naughty smirk and Cecilia laughed in disbelief, reaching over to push his shoulder away. The look she gave him practically screamed, *Oh my God, Bruce! Not in front of the girls!* But she didn't get to scold him any further than that, because as usual, Angelina always seemed to know just the right time to interrupt a discreet parental flirtation.

"Hey Daddy, can *I* have some silver?" she gave him the big puppy eyes that she always pulled when she wanted something.

"Of course you can," Bruce smiled. "But only if you do well in school this year. Get A's and B's and I'll get you some silver."

"Your father and I will teach both of you girls about investing," Cecilia added. "It'll be fun."

Angelina scrunched up her nose. She didn't think that *investing* sounded very fun at all. But she *did* like the idea of getting what she wanted. "Promise?" she clasped her hands in front of her heart. Next to her, Blair rolled her eyes at her and took a quiet sip of milk, cutting her pancakes neatly with her fork.

"Promise," Bruce swore. Angelina reached across the table to seal it with a satisfied pinky swear and once the family had finished their breakfast - luckily with no messy food spills on her part - it was time for Bruce to head into the city for another busy day at work. Before he left, Angelina and Blair took turns giving him big bear hugs in the foyer. He squeezed them hard enough to elicit a chorus of protesting giggles and consecutive complaints about being crushed, then wished them a fun first day at school and reminded them to do well at their music lessons afterwards and be good for Mommy for the rest of the day.

Angelina put a hand on her hip matter-of-factly.

"Daddy, you know we're *always* good for Mommy."

"Of course you are," Bruce patted her on the head. He shared a knowing glance with Blair, who gave him a secret smile behind Angelina's back and handed him his briefcase. Everyone knew that the reminder about behavior was really meant for her sister. Blair never goofed around, but sometimes Angelina did, and when that goofing around happened at music lessons, it would drive her voice teacher absolutely crazy. Faux-opera voices were her thing, and not the pretty female soprano voice that she was supposed to be learning, but one that was artificially low and bellowing, more like a goofy, warped version of Pavarotti than a beautiful Maria Callas. Luckily, her teacher was a patient woman who would put up with a lot for a decent paycheck.

With paying such generous paychecks in mind, Bruce gave his wife a tender kiss goodbye and Cecilia ushered the girls to the car so they could be on their way as well. Blair couldn't wait to see what she'd be learning in her classes this year. Angelina, on the other hand, was just anxious to see all of her friends again.

The girls might've only been just at the dawn of third grade, but they'd already come to approach their school days very differently. Blair was naturally the more quiet and studious of the two, but although she could be a little serious at times, she was always kind to her fellow students and never shunned anyone. She was known around school for being the smart, somewhat shy girl who was always willing to share her crayons in art class, stayed past the bell to chat up her teachers, and spent her recesses reading chapter books on the wooden bench near the jungle gym. But while many of her classmates liked her and thought that she was nice, she couldn't say that she had a best friend yet. It wasn't that she didn't *want* one. She just didn't *have* one. She was always so busy with piano lessons and studying after school that practice often took precedence over socializing. As it stood, her mom and sister were the closest friends that she had, even if Angelina could admittedly wear her out sometimes with her constant chatter, lack of discipline, and overabounding energy.

Angelina quite favored those aspects of her personality, however - she thought she had a *wonderful* temperament! - so while Blair was the one who kept her focus on her studies during school hours, she was the one who was constantly surrounded by friends and admirers. Fun-loving, popular, brash, and outspoken, most of Angelina's classmates either wanted to know her or be like her. She was sociable, funny, and loved showing off and making people laugh with her silly jokes and spot-on Mariah Carey impressions - the alternate to her grandiose Pavarotti. She was certainly a well-liked little girl, but her love of the spotlight could also be a double-edged sword of sorts. While it had its benefits, it inevitably led some of her more judgmental classmates to perceive her as somewhat of a snob. After all, she was rich, pretty, and talented, and didn't try to downplay it. It wasn't like she *tried* to brag or make anyone feel bad on purpose, but Angelina was always sure of herself... and everyone knew it.

As if her more intense personality traits weren't already polarizing enough, Angelina had also managed to build herself a bit of a "posse," too. She loved talking to everyone and meeting new people, but she, future Bollywood fashionista Gisele Singh, and bubbly redhead Katie Winters were still pretty much the most exclusive little clique in the school. The girls had become quick pals on the first day of kindergarten and their friendship had only grown since. They were practically inseparable now and could almost always be found sitting next to one another in class, eating together at lunch, and walking down the hallways side-by-side, attached at the hip. Outside of school they met for play dates and slumber parties on a near-weekly basis, hung out for hours on end while their moms shared brunch outings and salon excursions, and tied up the family phone lines with their lengthy three-way chitchats. Gisele even took voice lessons with the same teacher as Angelina. They'd hung out all summer long without any sort of hiatus, but Angelina was still just as excited to spot her two best friends in the hallway as she would've been if she hadn't seen them at all. She broke away from Blair's side as soon as she noticed Katie's bright orange pigtails standing out amongst the crowd and ran over to ambush the girls with a pair of giddy hugs.

"Hi Angelina!" Katie greeted her with a perky smile. "Do you like my new backpack?" She slid her bubblegum-pink *Hello Kitty* backpack from her shoulder and shoved it in Angelina's face. The bright colors and bubbly charm fit Katie. She was as girly and cutesy as a girl could come and pink was her favorite color.

"I love it!" Angelina exclaimed with a bright, approving grin. "Check out mine. It's purple! Isn't it awesome?"

"Wow, cool!" Gisele jumped into the fray. "And it's leopard print, too. I *love* leopard print. You girls should see my new pencil case. It's so cute. And my mom bought me gel pens this year."

"Yeah? Well *my* mom was in the newspaper," Angelina bragged. She puffed out her chest proudly and the girls gasped.

"Really?" Katie asked. "What for?"

"She's going to give art lessons or something," Angelina shrugged. "I don't really need them since I'm already good at art. But not everyone can be the next Picasso like me, can they?"

As snotty as it sounded, she was only teasing them. The wink at the end gave it away and the other girls laughed.

"You couldn't paint something if you tried," Gisele snorted.

"Remember that pony she painted last year that looked like a duck?" Katie snickered behind her hand.

Angelina shot them an eye roll. "I've had more practice since then. We'll just see who's talking when art class starts."

"Maybe you should worry more about chorus," Gisele suggested. She jerked her head and motioned down the hallway.

"Ugh..." Angelina grumbled, noticing a pack of snotty girls walking by with their noses stuck up in the air. The brunette in front had hers tilted back so far that Angelina swore if it rained, she might drown. Which wouldn't be so bad. "It's *Jenny Wexler.*"

Jenny Wexler was one of the small handful of girls in school who thought that Angelina was a stuck-up snob. Funny thing about that was that Angelina thought *Jenny* was the stuck-up snob. Jenny was preppy and rude and had a bit of a clique too, just like Angelina did, but hers consisted of Rebecca Aaron and Sarah Rossi. There was usually Mandy Cooper too, but Mandy was more like Jenny's loyal poodle than an *actual* clique member. Angelina and Jenny's cliques never went out of their way to socialize, but when they did there was usually a lot of shade hidden behind sweet niceties. But everyone knew that they didn't particularly like eachother, and the real reason was likely because if there was ever competition to be had regarding who got the best solo parts in chorus, it was usually between Jenny and Angelina.

"Jenny looks even snobbier than last year," Katie frowned.

"I don't really care about her," Angelina dismissed her with a wave. "She won't get any solos this year, anyway. They're mine."

Katie and Gisele shared a look behind her back. Maybe Jenny wouldn't, but Angelina would probably be more of a shoe-in if she didn't goof off in chorus class and voice lessons so much.

"Oh well, who cares?" Katie turned away from Jenny's prissy pack as they disappeared around a corner in the hallway. "Gissy, will you show us the gel pens your mom got you?"

"Yeah," Angelina agreed. "Show us! I want to see them."

"Sure," Gisele nodded. "I can't wait to use them for notes. You girls can borrow some if you want. Katie, do you want pink?"

And just like that, the subject was changed and the back-to-school fervor continued. While the girls giggled and chattered, showing off their new school supplies and raving about all of the fun things they hoped to do this year, two very new faces made their way through the school's double doors. A young brown-haired boy with a blue backpack slung over his shoulder and a slightly younger girl with hair the color of khaki sand stood side-by-side and breathed in deep, sharing a mutual nervous glance. So *this* was the famous Saint Joan of Arc Academy, huh? With its high arched ceilings, spotless polished floors, cream-colored walls, and elaborate decor it was definitely a big change from Maple Springs Elementary. Everything about it looked so... *expensive.*

"Wow..." the girl muttered in a quiet voice. She bit her knuckle and tapped her foot against the marble floor.

"Don't be scared," the boy tried to encourage her, noticing the nervous look of apprehension that had manifested on her small freckled face. "Everyone's going to like you and you'll make lots of new friends here. I'll see you at lunch or something, okay?"

"Okay," she nodded. She wasn't so sure about that making friends part, but at least she wouldn't be eating by herself on day one. She followed the boy to her second grade classroom and bid him goodbye before they parted ways.

"See ya later, sis," he waved at her.

And then he was all alone.

He grasped the strap of his backpack uncertainly as his eyes scoured the unfamiliar hallways. He'd wanted to look tough and calm and totally self-assured in front of his little sister like any other respectable big brother would, but in all honesty, he felt like he was in way over his head here. His family wasn't desperate for money to the point of poverty or anything, but they also weren't as affluent as the families who normally sent their kids to Saint Joan. This place was like an alien world to him, and starting the third grade in a new school was already nerve-wracking enough without all of the spoiled rich kids around to judge him.

Speaking of which...

"Who's that?" Gisele asked, pointing her finger down the hallway in his direction. "Have you girls ever seen him before?"

"Not me," Katie shook her head.

Angelina glanced towards the object of her friends' sudden attention and felt an unexpected somersault rock her stomach. *Holy cow.* What was *that?* The sensation of butterflies was so new and foreign to her that she didn't know what to make of it. Her tummy had never flip-flopped like that before and she could feel her cheeks flushing a hot dark red in response. Screw Jenny and gel pens. She didn't know who this boy was, but *man* was he cute.

"Maybe he's new," she remarked.

"I guess," Gisele assumed with a disinterested shrug. "So, anyway, do you girls want to go to class now? I want to get there before the bell rings and get first dibs on a cubbyhole."

"You girls go ahead," Angelina waved her friends off. Cubbyholes could wait. She was much more interested in figuring out who this mystery boy was. She bid her girlfriends goodbye, bit her bottom lip in determination, mustered up a little courage, and walked decisively towards the new kid. Typical Angie style.

"Hi!" she tapped him on the shoulder to grab his attention.

The boy spun around to face her and her stomach did that weird flip-flop thing again. Up close he was even cuter than from far away. His short brown hair stuck up in the front, his big round eyes were a pretty shade of emerald green, and a light dashing of freckles sprinkled his nose and cheeks. He looked a little out-of-place in his dressy navy blue vest and blazer, as though he'd be a lot more comfortable in a T-shirt and dirt-stained jeans with holes in the knees, but the slight awkwardness made him all the more endearing. Angelina hoped that her face didn't look like a fire hydrant, because her cheeks were positively burning right now.

"Hi," the boy greeted her back.

"You look a little lost," she ventured. "Are you new?"

"Yeah," he admitted. He fiddled with the strap of his backpack. "Do you know how to get to Miss Zhang's class?"

This kid had to get to Miss Zhang's? That meant that he was in the same grade as her! All third graders had either Miss Zhang like she did or Mrs. Pearson like her sister did. Angelina nearly jumped for joy at the realization. "Of course!" she nodded. "That's where I'm going too. Want me to show you where it is?"

The boy shot her a relieved smile. "Sure."

"Okay then," she smiled back. "Follow me."

Angelina took charge and led him past the nurse's office, down the hall, and around the corner from the bathrooms and the water fountain."Ta-da!" she announced with a triumphant swoosh of her hand. "We're here. Since you're new, just ask me if you need any more help finding stuff, okay? I'm a great tour guide."

"Thanks," he agreed. "What's your name?"

"I'm Angelina. What about you?"

"I'm Aiden."

Angelina fought hard against her flushing cheeks. Aiden was such a cute name. She'd never known anyone with that name before. "Well, welcome to Saint Joan of Arc's, Aiden!" she said in cheerful finality. "You're *really* going to like it here, I promise."

Aiden wasn't sure if that was true or not yet, but if it counted for anything, he was starting to feel a little better about his chances. He thanked his friendly tour guide and walked ahead of her into the classroom. As Angelina stood in the doorway staring at the back of his head, a big smile lit her face, a weird feeling tickled her tummy, and hopeful optimism filled her heart.

CHAPTER FIVE
Unbreakable

ANGELINA'S INTENTIONS WERE PURE and innocent; the telltale interest of a child smitten with a sudden first crush. Victoria's intentions, however, were still far from wholesome. Her sordid late-night tryst had offered her a generous distraction at the start of the weekend, but today was already Wednesday, which meant that work had taken precedence over pleasure once again. When she arrived at Vonessen Inc. early that morning, she was still feeling a little groggy and tired from the long night that she'd had before, but she solemnly resolved to work through her crappy feelings, knowing that poor performance wasn't something that would help her cause with Bruce nor her mission to snag the big promotion that everyone else had been talking about. She had to continue knocking assignments out of the park no matter how much it aggravated her; there was simply no other option.

Impress, impress, impress.

Emmalyn took a seat at the desk across from her and set down her purse, stealing a glance at Victoria over her monitor as she waited for her computer to boot up. She didn't need to ask her co-worker how she was feeling. She knew that Victoria was probably tired after seeing her leave last night with a hefty stack of papers and an extra-full briefcase, but the striking blonde sure didn't show it. A pang of good-natured jealousy shot through

Emmalyn as she noted that Victoria always managed to look great, even after rough nights. Her long blonde hair was pulled up into a very sexy librarian-esque bun, her tight gray pencil skirt and frilly white blouse had not a detracting wrinkle to speak of, and not even the slightest hint of a stubborn dark circle tarnished the smooth skin beneath her eyes. Some girls just had all the luck.

"Long night?" Emmalyn remarked over the sound of Victoria's keyboard. Victoria shrugged a shoulder in response.

"You could say that, I guess, depending on your bedtime. I was up until one in the morning finishing for end of month."

Emmalyn's eyes widened behind her glasses. "Wow, one in the morning? You sure don't look like you were up that late. How are you even awake right now? *I'd* feel like I was hit by a truck."

"It's all an illusion, Em," Victoria assured her with a rapt strike of the 'enter' key. "I'm just as tired as you think I am. Strong coffee and the right make-up can do amazing things."

"Hmph. I should've grabbed myself a cup," Emmalyn scolded herself before steering the subject to the usual gossip. The two chatty ladies probably could have done so for hours if it weren't for the interruption of the intercom resonating through the office right as they erupted into a fit of snorts and chortles.

"Victoria Adessi, Bruce von Essen wants to see you in his office. Victoria Adessi to Bruce von Essen's office," a secretary's crisp voice announced over the loudspeaker.

"That damn intercom... haven't they fixed the volume control on that thing yet? I almost had a heart attack!" Victoria exaggerated in a startled voice that she thought only Emmalyn could hear. "I wonder what I'm getting called for?"

"Maybe von Essen is pissed that you two twits won't stop giggling every five seconds and distracting everyone else... specifically *me*," Ben guessed, hunching in his chair irritably.

"Cry me a river," Victoria dismissed him with her usual eye roll as she got up from her seat and pushed in her chair.

Emmalyn groused and shot their co-worker a scathing look. "Ben, why are you always such a drama queen? Don't listen to him, Vicky." She turned to give Victoria a motivational thumbs up and whispered, "Good luck! Tell me how it goes."

"Please. You know I tell you everything."

It may not have been completely true, but Emmalyn didn't need to know that. Victoria headed out the door, up the elevator, and down the hall like a woman on a mission. By the time she got to her boss's office she was practically salivating with anticipation. Bruce was sitting at his long polished desk flipping through a stack of papers, a large white sculpture of the Vonessen Inc. "V" gracing the wall behind him. As she entered the room, he pushed his papers aside and stood up from his cushy leather chair, extending his hand to shake hers, always the professional.

"Good morning, Bruce," Victoria greeted him.

"Good morning, Ms. Adessi. Please, have a seat."

He motioned towards a set of chairs across from him and Victoria settled into the closest one expectantly. 'God, *he's gorgeous*,' she thought as she glanced at his broad shoulders and slicked black hair. His dark eyes looked to be a decadent color somewhere between caramel and chocolate. Bruce was so perfect; so strong and intimidating and impeccably chiseled, looking fully the part of the capable CEO in his custom-tailored Versace suit. Black, of course, with a crisp black shirt beneath a silver-and-black striped tie. And check out those $1,600 David Yurman cufflinks! They were probably more expensive than the suit. She couldn't see his shoes, but she was sure that they were pricey, too. His whole ensemble must have cost him a fortune, and this was only one day's suit. He probably had a whole *closet* of expensive suits, and imagine what he bought for his wife. Just the notion had Victoria mentally drooling at the thought of all the money he possessed. *Mentally* being the key word though, because for being so obsessed with him, she was awfully good at hiding it.

"Well, Victoria," he interrupted her greedy thoughts without a clue. "You must be wondering why I called you here."

"Yes," she played along. "Is anything wrong?"

"No, not at all," he said with an amused chuckle. "Just the opposite, actually. I wanted to talk to you about the work you've been doing lately. I have to admit, I'm impressed."

If Victoria were a lesser human she might've foamed at the mouth at this revelation, but she wasn't a lesser human. She was Victoria Adessi, the master of playing it cool and professional, no stranger to the art of putting on a face.

"Why, thank you," she accepted the compliment with one of her typical charming Victoria smiles. "I appreciate that."

"No… *I* appreciate it," Bruce insisted. He folded his hands in his lap, looking as though he had something important to say. "Victoria, I don't know how much you know about me personally, but I take a lot of pride in this business and what we do. When I see someone who shares my enthusiasm with a work ethic like yours, I feel that kind of dedication shouldn't go unrewarded." He paused to reach into a desk drawer and pulled out something familiar. "This," he continued, holding up the binder she'd turned in to him the week before, "Is a prime example of work done by someone who is invested in what they're doing. You've been working hard for Vonessen Inc. and I can say with confidence that you're one of the best budget analysts we've ever had."

Once again, if Victoria weren't so slick she could've dribbled all over her lap. She crossed one leg over the other and leaned forward, resting her hands on her knee. "Thank you, sir. I've certainly been putting forth my best effort."

"Well, it shows. And your credentials really speak for you. I took another look at your resume today. You graduated summa cum laude with a dual master's in business and accounting. Student president of your university's chapter of Beta Alpha Psi. Member of both the International Business Society and Women in Business club, then passed your CPA test and joined the American Institute of Certified Public Accountants post-graduation. I'm a sucker for academia, and that's all very impressive."

"What can I say? I liked school," Victoria shrugged.

"Well it seems that school liked you, too. You've always been highly recommended by all of your references. I hear nothing but good things about you from past professors and former employers. Your co-workers on the accounting floor respect you and consistently say that when they have questions about their work they feel comfortable going to you."

Could Bruce stroke her already-inflated ego any further? If Victoria were a man this might've actually given her a hard-on. Of course, she knew all these good things about herself already, but it still felt orgasmic to hear them from him. A teeny bit of her act cracked for a moment; a twitch of the lip or an eyebrow, perhaps. Enough to make an oblivious Bruce chuckle ever-so slightly.

"It seems I'm getting carried away," he digressed. "I'll get straight to the point. The reason I've called you here is simply this. If you feel that you're up to it, I think I could trust you to take on more responsibility here. *Much* more. I'm of the opinion that your talents could be put to better use in a higher, more involved position. That being said, I'm sure you know that I've been looking for the right person to fill the Controller's position since it came to my attention that Mr. Davis is ready to retire. Well, I believe that right person is you. So what do you say? Are you interested in becoming a bigger player in this company?"

Victoria didn't bother hiding the big, triumphant smile that spread across her face. It was the promotion that everyone wanted! Vonessen Inc.'s Controller managed all of the financial departments in the company. The accounting department, the budget department, the audit department... this was no wussy one-dollar raise. She'd beat out Ben! And even better than sticking it to that insufferable potato-head, this promotion meant more beautiful, green money and an even closer relationship with the rest of the high-ranking people here than she already had... which also meant more opportunity to interact with Bruce. This was *perfect*. She'd be seducing him on his desk in no time.

"Absolutely. I would be *glad* to take on more responsibility for Vonessen Inc.," she affirmed with an enthusiastic nod.

"Great," Bruce smiled in finality. "Then we'll talk more specifics tomorrow. Glad to have you on board Ms. Adessi."

Victoria stood to shake his hand. "No, thank *you,* Mr. von Essen," she said as his palm made contact with hers. "You have no idea what this means to me. Thank you *very* much."

Victoria's day had just went from average to great, but she wasn't the only lady in town with a brand new pep in her step due to fortunate circumstance. Back at Saint Joan, Angelina had been having a pretty great day herself, and it had all started when she'd muscled up the nerve to approach Aiden in the hallway. During the course of the day, she'd even managed to learn a little more about him from the hushed whispers of her peers. His last name was Andrews, he had a younger sister in the grade below them, and he was going to be playing on the school's peewee football team. It wasn't much, but it was definitely a start, and she was determined to learn even more. She hadn't been able to stop thinking about him, his cute smile, or those big green eyes all day.

Call it sisterly intuition or maybe just common sense, but none of this got past an ever-observant Blair. It wasn't abnormal for Angelina to be in peppy spirits, but there was something funnier than usual about the goofy way she was acting today. Blair decided to bring it up as they waited for their mother to pick them up near the recess yard after school. She sat down next to Angelina on one of the wooden benches by the drop-off zone with a dainty plop. *"You* look pretty happy today," she observed with a suspicious cock of her eyebrow, taking in the ridiculous lovelorn look that hadn't left her sister's face for hours.

"Well, duh! *Of course* I'm happy. It was a good first day," Angelina claimed, acting like that was all there was to her chipper mood. "This is going to be a great year for learning, I just *know* it!"

She must have sounded convincing, because Blair bought it and smiled in approval. "I sure hope so! I've just never seen you this excited about classes before."

Angelina smirked, peeking at Aiden Andrews playing on the jungle gym with some of the other boys nearby. Oh, naïve, clueless Blair - if only she knew! Classes weren't nearly as interesting as cute boys were turning out to be. In fact, just the thought of said cute boy and the new crush-induced butterflies that Angelina was experiencing because of him left her giddy and smiling for the rest of the afternoon. She was smiling when Cecilia picked the girls up, smiling through her voice lesson, and smiling when they arrived back home at the mansion. She was in such a bright mood that she suggested a dinnertime picnic to celebrate.

"We can cook Daddy dinner!" she suggested earnestly. "Please, Mommy, *please* let me and Blair help!"

With the sun shining and the weather outside still warm and pleasant, Cecilia couldn't argue against the idea. Not like she would have wanted to, anyway. She loved whipping up healthy dinners after busy days. Cooking was therapeutic, like painting with food instead of a brush. "Okay girls, you have me convinced. Clean up first and I'll see what we have. By the time you're back I'll have a whole menu planned out for you to help me with."

"YES!" Angelina whooped. She dragged her sister up the staircase, and once they'd traded their rigid school uniforms for casual play clothes, the girls returned to their mother and crowded around the kitchen island with their ingredients. The girls didn't get to help cook every day, but here they were feeling like junior Gordon Ramsays in the von Essen kitchen. Angelina was especially enthusiastic about being tasked with the role of "assistant chef." She couldn't stand still. As her mother worked on slicing fresh peaches for a tasty late-summer tea, she bit her lip in mischievous determination and looked for something to expend her energy on. Ah, the pepper grinder! That would do the trick.

"Look Mommy, I'm Emeril!" she exclaimed as she added a big dash of pepper to the tomato and mozzarella slices that Cecilia had laid out on a plate for Caprese sandwiches. "BAM!"

Cecilia couldn't help but laugh at Angelina's clowning around. Even Blair was peppier than usual, her sister's energy infectious. Angelina was officially on full-throttle now, and she didn't stop with just an enthusiastic Emeril Lagasse impression.

"Mamma Mia, I want to make-a-da green beans!" she chortled in a horrible attempt at an Italian accent.

"We're not even cooking green beans, silly," Blair corrected her like the unintentional know-it-all that she was. "Those are *asparagus*." She tugged at the skirt of Cecilia's dress. "Mom, can I mush the basil for the pesto? *Please?* I *really* want to do that part."

"BAM!" Angelina shouted again for no reason.

Blair giggled. "What is *wrong* with you?"

Angelina stuck her tongue out at her sister and made a rather uncouth noise with it. Blair gasped in horror. *"Eww!"*

"Girls!" Cecilia laughed despite her intention to be stern. "Don't mess around by the stove. I don't want either of you to get burned." She scooped Blair up and sat her on an island stool, handing her a mortar and pestle. "Alright, Blair," she plucked a few sprigs of basil from a jar on the counter. "Get to mashing!"

Blair grinded the herbs, garlic, and pine nuts in her mortar into a perfectly mushy green paste while Cecilia finished prepping the vegetables. All the while, Angelina bobbed around beside them, singing her own butchered version of "Mambo Italiano" as background music complete with missing and made up lyrics. When Bruce finally arrived home some time later, his daughters met him at the front door with a barrage of smiles, hugs, and anxious comments that nearly caused him to drop his briefcase.

"We made dinner!" Angelina announced.

"We made it ourselves!" Blair piped in. "Well, really Mommy made most of it... but we helped."

"We made pasta salad with little bowties and tomato sandwiches with green stuff and peach iced tea with real peaches. And we made green beans, too," Angelina spouted off the menu.

"Asparagus," Blair rolled her eyes and sighed.

"Whatever! They look like green beans to me." Angelina grabbed her daddy's hand and tugged at it in impatience. "Come *on,* enough standing around. Hurry up before it gets cold."

"My, this dinner you made sounds wonderful, girls," Bruce smiled, charmed by his daughters' enthusiasm. "You'd better slow down, though. All this excitement is making me dizzy!" He twirled his head around goofily and acted disoriented, which only made the girls crack up at him all the louder.

Cecilia heard the commotion and came out of the kitchen holding a freshly packed wicker basket. "What are you three doing?" she put her hand to her mouth to stifle a laugh.

"We're driving Daddy crazy," Angelina informed her.

"I can see that. Bruce, stop it. You're going to fall over."

Bruce chuckled, dropping his ridiculous bewildered act and hugging his daughters snugly against his legs. "I assume you can explain all of this fuss to me?" he tilted his chin at his wife.

"The girls are insisting on having a picnic," Cecilia raised her basket in explanation. "The way I understand it, going back to school was so exciting today that one special meal wasn't enough for them. They want to eat outside in the garden."

"Well, I think that's a great idea," Bruce smiled fondly at his little girls. "It's been a beautiful day and the sun is still out. What better way to enjoy it while we still can, hmm? Thank you very much, girls," he gave them both an appreciative squeeze. "This was a nice surprise to come home to." He glanced at Cecilia with affection in his brown eyes. "And thank *you*, Cece. Pancakes and now this? I don't know what I'd do without your cooking."

"Probably starve or survive solely on a microwave diet," she teased him with a sly grin.

"Or maybe I'd lose some weight."

Cecilia gave him a knowing wink and nudged him with her hip before leading the way down the hallway and out the back door. Angelina and Blair followed behind her, pulling Dad along in tow. Once they were outside, Bruce saw that his three favorite ladies had already set up a blanket in the middle of the garden. Everyone took a seat and got comfortable while Cecilia unpacked. As soon as everyone was situated with a plate, fork, first helpings of food, and big glasses of peach tea, Cecilia asked who would like to say grace. In the von Essen household, it was tradition to say grace before every family dinner. Though they didn't always get to eat together thanks to Bruce's busy schedule, Cecilia's art gallery obligations, and the girls' music lessons, they always tried to take a moment to be thankful for the times when they could.

"Ooh, pick me!" Angelina insisted, waving her arm in the air as if she were still in school. "I want to say grace this time."

"Okay, Angelina," Cecilia nodded. "Go ahead."

The family bowed their heads as Angelina began to speak. Her tone was totally serious as she carried out her important duty.

"Thank you for the world so sweet, thank you for the food we eat, thank you for the birds that sing, thank you God for everything," she

recited one of her favorite rhymes, before adding, "And especially thank you for Mommy, Daddy, and Blair. Amen. Now let's eat!"

While the family passed around plates filled with food, they went around in a circle, talking vividly about their days. The girls told their father about their first day of classes, what they'd learned in voice and piano lessons (with an added demonstration from Angelina, of course), and all of the fun they'd had cooking with Mom all afternoon. Cecilia informed her husband of her newest gallery buyers, all the nice feedback she'd been getting from her *Gazette* article, and all the important errands that she'd managed to get done before picking up the girls from school. Finally, Bruce filled his family in on the day he'd had at Vonessen Inc. He assured them that phone conferences were very boring, broke the news about his latest promotion decision, then told them about how his printer had gone off the deep end near the end of the day and sent a stack of papers flying everywhere. His daughters erupted into a fit of giggles at this last part; they could just imagine Daddy running around frantically as papers scattered all over his office like Thanksgiving-parade confetti.

"Victoria Adessi as the new Financial Controller?" Cecilia commented on her husband's promotion pick. "I think that's a good move. She has a very impressive track record, doesn't she?"

Being such an involved member of the Maple Springs community and having a keen interest in her husband's work, Cecilia already knew who Victoria Adessi was. The two women weren't friends or even real acquaintances, but in Cecilia's eyes they weren't exactly enemies either. Like nearly everyone else in town, Cecilia had respect enough for Victoria. Not that she would consider her someone she wanted to hang out with or anything, nor the classiest woman on the planet, but there was no denying that the accountant was good with a ledger. Of course, if Cecilia had known about Victoria's bad intentions she probably would have reevaluated that opinion, but for now ignorance was a sin neither she nor her husband were aware they were committing.

For now, their only conscious offense was gluttony, because the food the ladies had prepared was so good that everyone made sure to come back for second helpings and even thirds.

When they were finished with dinner and sufficiently stuffed, Bruce lounged on the blanket next to his wife and daughters, flipping through his newspaper while Cecilia read the girls a book. Blair had wanted to hear her favorite, *The Velveteen Rabbit,* but they'd settled on *Green Eggs and Ham* when Angelina insisted that they'd just read that boring bunny story and needed to read something less serious instead. Blair was disappointed at first - Angelina *always* got her way. But soon enough, she was enjoying the classic Dr. Seuss tale just as much as her sister was.

The girls listened intently as Cecilia recited the whimsical rhymes, giggling at all of the goofiest parts. They loved when their mother read to them. She always had the best inflection and always made story time fun. As he watched his wife put joyful smiles on their daughters' faces, Bruce couldn't help but smile himself. Work was fine and good, but there was nothing better than spending quality time with the women he loved. These three were the reason he woke up happy and motivated every morning.

It wasn't long before the sun had set and it was time for the girls to go to bed. They were still as wound up as ever come nine o'clock though, and resorted to jumping on Angelina's bed in their pajamas like there was no tomorrow. It had been Angelina's bright idea of course. Mischief was *always* her idea, especially when she'd had a particularly exciting day, and meeting Aiden, getting through a whole voice lesson without being chided for naughtiness, and cooking dinner certainly qualified as exciting.

"Girls, girls!" Cecilia scolded them when she and Bruce came upstairs and realized what all of the ruckus was about. "Calm down. It's time to sleep." She beckoned Blair off the bed. "Come on, Blair. Off to your room. It's bed time."

Angelina pouted and tried to protest for five more minutes, but this time she wasn't going to get her way so easily. Her big plans for being a night owl thwarted, Blair retreated from the room and Cecilia and Bruce took turns tucking the girls in and wishing them goodnight, taking care to go through all of their ordinary nighttime routines in the process. When they put Angelina to bed, they made sure to tuck both her *and* her teddy bear of choice tightly into her comforter. Cecilia closed them both into a cozy little cocoon, just the way Angelina liked.

Then, once Blair was situated rightly in her own bed, Bruce retreated downstairs while Cecilia stuck around to read her *The Velveteen Rabbit* as a bit of a compromise from earlier in the day. Blair listened attentively while she snuggled under her covers and leaned against Mom's shoulder to look at the pictures. She didn't think this book was boring. She loved it, just like she loved the music box she kept on the nightstand beside her. It was the same music box that Bruce had once spotted on the mantle above the fireplace in Cecilia's old apartment; her special music box from France that had been passed down from her grandmother, to her mother, to her, and now finally to Blair. The song that it played was soft and sort of sad but very pretty, and Blair had always adored that music box. While Angelina's stuffed animal burrito was her bedtime tradition, the music box was Blair's. Cecilia made sure to wind it up before leaving the room, and by the time the song was done playing, both of the girls had fallen fast asleep.

With the twins taken care of, Cecilia finally joined her husband in their bedroom and cuddled up against him, admittedly tired but blissfully content. She might not have worked in an office during the daytime anymore, but she still wore many hats. Being a stay-at-home mom, an artist, a cook, a gardener, the official house errand runner, and an active community volunteer was no lazy person's palette of pursuits, but she loved every part of it. Every day was busy with two little girls to attend to, a mansion to keep tidy, and an art gallery to fill, but every day was also a blessing. One that she never took for granted... and neither did Bruce. The happy couple made love far in to the night, so grateful for every day that they spent with one another. This was their life now. Their beautiful, wonderful, loving, predictable life. Nothing could tear their family apart.

The von Essens were unbreakable.

Unbreakable. That word might have described the von Essen family, but there were other things in life - darker things - that could also bear the same descriptor. One of those things was the insatiable lust still festering in Victoria Adessi's tiny pea-sized husk of a heart, because Bruce's new Controller just couldn't get her mind off of him. Each day her obsession grew, like an aggressive cancer that wouldn't let up. Malignant and unchecked.

As she crammed her belongings into a cardboard box at her old desk, getting ready to move her things up to her swanky new office with its breathtaking view of the city, her thoughts drifted to her boss just like they always did. Bruce was already impressed with her, that much was clear. He respected her. Admired her even. And now that she had her promotion, she could finally use it to employ some sort of plan; to turn her dark desires from a wish to a reality. She'd levy her new position to make herself more accessible, gain his interest with her increased presence and a little strategic sex appeal, and then, when the time was right, she'd seduce him just like she'd seduced all of the men who'd come before him. This was only the first step. She stared blankly into her box and imagined what it would be like to call the man, the mansion, and the money her own. Her festering fantasy was only interrupted when she heard Emmalyn's concerned voice calling to her across the gap in their desks.

"Vic, are you okay? You look a little green."

Victoria snapped back to reality and studied her friend, all wavy red hair, long gray cardigan, and aloof naivety written all over her face. Emmalyn was wearing an expression as if she couldn't decide whether to be happy for Victoria or upset that her moving up in the world meant that they'd no longer be desk buddies, and it was actually kind of sad in a way, Victoria thought, that the woman honestly liked her so much.

"Hmm? Oh, yes. Thanks for asking, but I'm perfectly fine," she lied. "I just think that breakfast burrito is starting to take its toll, that's all. I shouldn't have gone spicy so early in the day."

"Aw, hun…" Emmalyn frowned. "You need some Tums?"

"No thanks," Victoria waved her off. "I'm a big girl. I'm sure I can manage a little stomachache."

"Oh," Emmalyn deflated. "Well, feel better then. Do you need any help moving up to your new office?"

Victoria peeked into her box of junk. She didn't have all that much to move. "I'll be alright."

"Well, okay then. But if you change your mind about the Tums, come back and visit me."

"We'll see," Victoria shrugged. Maybe she would, maybe she wouldn't. Em and her Tums were the least of her concerns right now. She grabbed her box and walked through the door with a dark resolve, ready to take on the challenge in front of her.

CHAPTER SIX
Butterflies

FIRST CRUSHES ARE FUNNY THINGS. No one knows when they will come, how they will feel, nor who they will be on. Some first crushes are on peers. Some are on actors or singers, famous people the crusher has never met and more than likely never will. And some first crushes are on older people who are admired and looked up to, like a teacher or a coach. Crushes can be exciting, nerve-wracking, and exhilarating. They're strange, confusing, and completely weird. For some, a real first crush doesn't come until the crusher has moved on to the rigors of that pesky thing called puberty. For Angelina, her first crush hit her in the third grade.

All it had taken was that first meeting in the hallway and she'd found herself utterly, unapologetically smitten with Aiden Andrews. When she woke up in the mornings, she couldn't wait to get to school so she could see him. When she went to bed at night, his cute smile and pretty green eyes were the last things to cross her mind before she fell asleep. All the sappy love songs her favorite singers sang on the radio suddenly seemed to take on a whole new meaning to her. And every time she looked at him in class, she was reminded of the first time they'd met and a lovesick expression would wash over her face and send her spiraling into daydreams. Her little heart would swell inside her chest, filling her with a warm, fluttery sensation. It was an exciting feeling that she didn't know existed and that she didn't understand. It was puppy love... and she was experiencing it for the very first time.

As the school year progressed, the first month and a half of it flying by in a flurry of homework, tests, and extracurricular activities, Angelina took every opportunity to be near her new crush that she could. Their conversations were always short and sweet, but even if they only lasted for a few minutes, simply communicating with Aiden Andrews in any way whatsoever was a bright spot in her day that sent her heart soaring.

"Hey, Aiden!" she would greet him in a perky voice when she managed to catch him in the hallways. She'd smile at him in that lovesick way, and although Aiden was oblivious to what it meant, he couldn't help feeling obligated to say "hi" back. He was starting to fit in at Saint Joan of Arc thanks to his stellar debut season on the school's peewee football team, but he'd still been a little surprised at first to find *her* talking to him once he'd discovered who and how rich she was. Yet despite all of the rumors floating around school (purported mostly by people like Jenny and her clique) that Angelina was sort of a stuck up snob, he'd never really seen that. She'd been the first person to come up to him after all, and she always made it a point to be nice to him.

"Hi, Angelina. What's up?" he'd go with it, shooting her a friendly smile that made her cheeks burn something terrible. Her usual response when she felt that terrible blush coming on was to act cool and nonchalant, like he didn't affect her. But he did.

"Nothing really. Did you do that homework for math?"

"Yeah, why?"

"I was just wondering, because I did mine, but I wasn't sure about some of my answers. Can you show me yours so I can double check what I put?"

Angelina always had some manufactured excuse to talk to him, but Aiden was too clueless to pick up on why. He'd pull out his homework reluctantly. "Well, sure... but I don't really know if what I got is right. I'm not that great at math."

"Oh, it's okay. I don't have to look then." Angelina paused, thinking up an emergency subject change to keep him from walking away. "So do you like Saint Joan of Arc's so far?"

"Yeah, it's great," he shrugged. "I'm glad I got in this year."

"Cool. Me too," she agreed, trying to combat the all-too-familiar butterflies that rendered her stupid and dreamy-eyed.

And typically, that would be the end of that.

That was how many of their conversations went. They were simply small talk, but nice small talk nonetheless. They often revolved around easy, casual things like school and class and football, but the one thing that had never come up was Angelina's crush. In fact, she hadn't told a soul. Instead, she secretly pined for Aiden from afar in that lovelorn way that kids do, doodling silly little deformed hearts with "A.A." written inside of them all over her history notes. It wasn't until mid-October, as she finished doodling her latest bubble-lettered version of Aiden's name on the inside cover of her notebook, that she decided resolutely that a month and a half of keeping her secret to herself was far too difficult. If she didn't tell *somebody* what was going on with her then she just might burst. Besides, weren't crushes supposed to be a lot more fun when you could gush about them with friends?

At this point, she was willing to find out.

"I know something *you* don't know," she taunted Gisele and Katie in a devilish sing-song as soon as the first good opportunity to do so arose. It was lunch period at Saint Joan, and Angelina and her posse were sitting at their usual table against the far wall, away from the prying ears and eyes of the other students where they could do all of their gossiping in private. If there was ever a perfect time to talk about crushes, lunch was it. Angelina decided to be cunning about it for dramatic effect.

"Ooh, tell us!" Gisele demanded, flipping her long black hair behind her shoulder. Katie's eyes lit up eagerly beside her.

Angelina bit her bottom lip. "Can you girls keep a secret?" she whispered, leaning forward in her chair.

"Yes!" the girls exclaimed. They wiggled closer.

"What is it?" Katie asked.

"It's about someone that I *like*," Angelina revealed.

The other girls gasped. "Ooh!"

"I'll tell you who it is if you promise to keep it quiet," she bartered. "No blabbing!"

"We won't tell," Gisele said first.

"Nope, we won't say anything," Katie agreed.

"You have to promise. Pinky swear it!" Angelina demanded. Katie looked at her with conviction in her eyes and stuck out her pinky resolutely, making a totally serious face as if her words meant the difference between life and death.

"Cross my heart, hope to die, stick a needle in my eye," she swore. It was unnecessarily violent, but it got the point across.

"Gissy?"

"Me too," Gisele twisted her finger around Angelina's. "I promise. Now who is it?"

Angelina looked back and forth between them before revealing in a dramatic whisper, "It's Aiden Andrews!"

"Ooh!" her friends squealed again in delight.

"You like *Aiden?*" Katie gasped. She swiveled around to stare in the direction of his lunch table. He was sitting with a few of the other boys under a big green poster that read *'Eat Your Veggies!'* She could see him try to stifle an awkward laugh as one of them poked a hole in their milk carton and spilled milk all over their tray. "Ohmigod, ohmigod! You like the new kid?"

"Shhh!" Angelina hissed at her. She could see Jenny sitting at the table behind Aiden's, probably being as nosy as ever. "Not so loud! And stop looking over at him, you'll give us away."

"He's *really* cute," Gisele approved. "Does he know?"

"No way, and don't tell anybody! Remember, you pinky swore." With the truth revealed and that binding pinky swear in place, the girls carried on in excited whispers about Aiden Andrews and how adorable he was for the next ten minutes flat. *His freckles are so cute! He's really athletic! His smile is so dreamy!* They'd just erupted into a fit of giggles when Angelina stopped suddenly and shushed them with a frantic finger to her lips.

"Wait... sister approaching!" she hissed. Gisele and Katie quieted up and glanced behind their shoulders to see Blair walking towards them, looking prim, proper, and totally overachieving bookworm-chic in her tidy school uniform. There was a satin bow in her hair and she was carrying a tray laden with chocolate milk and a big leafy salad. When she spotted them, her innocent caramel eyes lit up in recognition, but Angelina's lips pursed disappointedly. She and Blair got along fine for the most part, but this was one lunch-time conversation that she was going to have to keep her out of. Knowing Blair and her goody-two-shoes tendencies, there was a pretty good chance that she'd slip and spill the secret to Mom. When Angelina had snuck extra chocolate cake to her room after dinner once when Dad had told her not to, Blair had told Mom. When she'd been keeping a ladybug she'd found in the garden in a jar by her window as a pet, Blair had told Mom. And then there was the time that Angelina had switched the labels for the sugar and salt containers in the kitchen just to play a silly prank and Blair had told Mom that, too. Blair and Mom were super-close and talked about everything, and the last thing that Angelina needed was for her whole family to know that she had a crush. How embarrassing would *that* be?

"Remember girls, not a word about this to anyone," she ordered. "Not even her. I don't want her to know that I like him."

"Why not?" Katie blinked. "Does *she* think he's cute too?"

"No, of course not!" Angelina glowered at her. "That's ridiculous! She'll just tell Mom and Dad. She tattles too much."

Katie pouted glumly, disappointed that their boy talk had to end so soon, but she knew that there was no sense in arguing with Angelina. Any argument with a stubborn diva like her would be an impossible battle to win.

Blair reached their table and put down her tray. "Mind if I join you girls?" she asked in her sugary-sweet voice. "I stayed after Reading class to talk to Mrs. Pearson and now I'm *starving.*"

Gisele and Katie shrugged in indifference. Of course they wouldn't mind. Blair was a little nerdy to think that analyzing short stories one-on-one with the teacher after class was some sick, demented version of fun, but she was still one of them.

"Duh, why couldn't you?" Angelina replied, welcoming her sister to their table as if nothing was amiss. "You missed most of lunch, though. Everyone's pretty much done eating."

"Oh well. Better late than never, right?" Blair shrugged.

The girls nodded and sat through the rest of lunch period without another word about boys, Aiden, or Angelina's crush.

Angelina sat quietly at her desk in History class, her hand under her chin and her mind deep in daydreams. Miss Zhang was busy lecturing the students about the Revolutionary War, but Angelina didn't have the slightest clue as to what she was saying. Normally she'd pay strict attention in class, knowing that she had her sister's annoying straight-A's to live up to, but today she was far too distracted gazing at the back of the head of the boy sitting in front of her to worry about Paul Revere or the Boston Tea Party.

Oh, *Aiden...* Angelina couldn't help but get those fluttering feelings in her tummy every time she looked at him. He was the only person who had ever made her feel remotely shy, and realizing this only made her stomach flutter all the worse. She really wanted to be his friend, not that she'd actually tried outside of their short-and-sweet conversations yet. While she mulled this reality over in her head, Miss Zhang finished her lesson.

"Now class, what I'd like you to do is get with a partner and work together to complete the in-class assignment. And Bobby, don't sigh at me like that. It's just a worksheet for goodness sake." She passed stacks of papers down each row of desks, instructing the students to finish the chain. "When you're done, you can turn your work in to me, then use whatever time is left for silent reading. Just be sure not to disrupt your classmates."

Yeah, yeah, Angelina knew the drill. She usually teamed up with Gisele or Katie on these projects, but before she could, she was totally caught off guard when Aiden turned around in his seat to hand her their row's paper stack and beat her to the punch.

"Want to work with me?" he asked her hopefully.

Angelina blinked at him. "Oh. Um... sure!" she spluttered stupidly. Aiden pulled his chair up to the side of her desk and she nearly squealed out loud with delight. *'Thank you, Miss Zhang, for giving us partner work!'* she thought to herself. *'And thank you Aiden for not working with one of the boys again!'* Across the room, Gisele and Katie stared at her with their mouths agape. It was all Angelina could manage to shoot her girls a bright smile and quick double thumbs-up before ducking her head back down and feeling her cheeks flush that same cherry red that they always did.

"Okay..." Aiden started, peering down at their worksheet and reading the title splashed over the top. "The Revolutionary War. Question one. Who wrote the Declaration of Independence?"

Oh yeah. Angelina had almost forgotten that they actually had a worksheet to do here. She tapped her pencil eraser against the desk, trying to remember what the teacher had been saying while she'd been too busy daydreaming. About *him.*

"Umm... I think that was Thomas Jefferson, wasn't it?"

"Yeah, that's it!" Aiden said brightly. "I was gonna say Ben Franklin, but you're right. It was totally Jefferson."

Angelina breathed a big sigh of relief and smiled at him as he penned the Founding Father's name into the first blank, glad that she'd somehow managed to remember the answer even with the embarrassing distraction. "Easy! What's the next question?"

"How many colonies were there?"

"Thirteen."

"Yep, I knew that one. Who led the American army?"

"George Washington. Let me read the next one." Angelina slid the paper in front of herself so she could see the questions a little easier. "What color were the British army's coats?"

"Red," Aiden interjected. He gave her a mischievous look before adding, "I bet they looked like a bunch of big lobsters."

Angelina giggled and slapped her hand over her mouth before Miss Zhang could get a chance to see it and scold her. "Should we draw a lobster in the blank?" she bit her lip sneakily.

Aiden nodded and Angelina drew a goofy-looking stick-figure lobster with silly pinchy claws next to their answer just for the heck of it. They were already almost halfway done. She was surprised at how quickly they were getting through these questions and couldn't believe that she was having so much fun doing something as mundane as schoolwork. Maybe her hopes to be Aiden's friend weren't totally unreachable after all. She was sure that Gisele and Katie would like him. He was a lot funnier and smarter than he gave himself credit for, and best of all, he didn't ask her annoying questions about her dad's money. Most other kids she talked to brought up how rich her dad was every chance they got. It was almost a relief that he didn't. Uncanny how he could give her that silly unsettling butterfly-filled feeling in her tummy, yet make her feel so comfortable at the same time.

"Alright. One last question," he announced when they finally reached the end of their worksheet. "What country helped the colonists fight the British?"

"Oh, that one's *really* easy. That was France," Angelina said matter-of-factly. She wrote the word neatly in the space that followed, then thought for a moment. "Hey, you know what we should do? We should put down that their leader was Lafayette. Miss Zhang will think we're *really* smart for remembering that."

"Do it," Aiden agreed. "Maybe we'll get bonus points."

Angelina scribbled the difficult name down as best she could without a word bank to help her with spelling it, then Aiden did the honors of walking their assignment up to Miss Zhang's desk. When he plopped back down at his seat, he and Angelina pulled out their history books to pretend that they were reading something for "silent reading," but took the minutes left over at the end of the period to talk a little more freely now that they could concentrate on things other than colonial history. They tried to keep the volume down so they wouldn't get in trouble.

"Okay, Aiden. Do you want to play Twenty Questions?" Angelina proposed, hoping to learn a little more about the boy that she was crushing on. "It's a game. Basically, I have to ask you a bunch of questions, then you have to give me the answers."

"Okay," Aiden shrugged. Why not?

Angelina thought for a moment, then asked him the first good one that came to mind. "If you could have any super power, what would it be?" she quizzed him from behind her book.

"Super speed," he settled on. "Then I could get past everyone in football and no one could stop me. How about you?"

"Flying," Angelina picked. "Or maybe mind-reading."

"I don't think you can have *two* super-powers."

"I can if I can't decide. What's your favorite TV show?"

Aiden answered her question with a question of his own. "Have you ever seen Super Sports Challenge?"

"Yes! I love that show."

He smiled. "Me too. Super Sports Challenge is awesome. I wish I could be on that show and do the Mega Obstacle Course."

Just the mental picture of that made Angelina giggle. Super Sports Challenge was a show on one of the more popular kids' networks where kids their age competed in various sports-related activities like relays, basketball shooting, and soccer free kicks for bragging rights and an ultimate grand prize - usually a trip somewhere really cool. Gold, silver, and bronze metals were even handed out at the end, as if it were the Olympics. In her head, Angelina could totally see Aiden racing through the big Mega Obstacle Course that served as the show's grand finale in orange elbow pads and a big clunky helmet, slamming his buzzer victoriously. Somehow, she didn't think it was so far-fetched.

"Oh, that would be fun! But I think Pyramid Expedition would be even *more* fun to be on," she threw out another of her kiddie game show favorites. "I'd pee myself if one of the Pyramid Mummies came out and grabbed me though. They're scary!"

"For real," Aiden made a face. "They give me the creeps."

"Me too. If I was on that show, I'd be a Purple Pharaoh."

"I'd be a Blue Cobra. Blue Cobras are the best."

Gisele and Katie watched them nosily, squinting their eyes as Angelina and Aiden cracked up over something lame behind their books. The girls couldn't hear what they were saying from where they were sitting all the way across the room, but those two were sure having a giggle fest over there.

"You can *so* tell that she likes him!" Katie hissed at Gisele in an accusatory whisper. "Just look at how red she's getting!"

"I know," Gisele agreed. "But we swore we wouldn't say anything. A pinky swear is a promise, remember?"

"I wasn't *going* to say anything," Katie insisted. "I was just saying you can totally tell. I mean, imagine if Jenny wasn't in Mrs. Pearson's class. It would be terrible!" She watched Angelina slap her hand to her mouth to stifle yet *another* giggle and squinted at her even harder. "I wonder what they're talking about, anyway?"

"I can't hear anything," Gisele grumbled. She kicked one Mary-Jane-clad shoe against the leg of her desk and folded her arms over her chest. "I can't believe they finished already, either. This worksheet is too hard! I wish there was a word bank."

"Me too," Katie pouted. "We're only on number six!"

Luckily, the girls did manage to bunker down and finish in time, but only just barely. When the bell rang to signal that classes were over, they sprinted back to the coat rack, but Angelina lingered behind, actually sad to see the school day end for once. On the bright side, she'd at least managed to learn more about her crush. Aiden liked a lot of the same TV shows that she did, his favorite color was blue, he liked outdoorsy things like camping and fishing, and his family had always lived in Maple Springs, but he and his sister hadn't been able to get into Saint Joan until now. Angelina knew this was probably her best chance to strike up a friendlier relationship with him outside of school, so she mustered up a little courage and ventured, "We should really talk more, Aiden. I had a lot of fun being your partner today."

"Me too," he agreed. "You're really not too bad for a girl."

Angelina felt her cheeks burn and prayed that he couldn't see it. "Then do you want to come over and play at my house this weekend?" she offered. "I *really* want you to visit me."

Aiden shrugged. She was a girl, way out of his social league, and possibly infected with cooties, but maybe this could be fun. "Sure. I'll ask my parents," he promised. And with that, he scooped up his books and shot Angelina one last adorable smile before he left. Her heart fluttered in her chest as she waved goodbye, hopeful beyond hope that his parents would say yes.

CHAPTER SEVEN
Making a Friend

WHEN SATURDAY FINALLY CAME, Angelina was so anxious, nervous, and eager all at once that she could barely sit still. Aiden Andrews calling her after school on Tuesday had been cause for excitement enough, but after a long, boring school week that felt like it had dragged on forever, today was even more exciting, because today he was finally coming over to visit her, just like he'd promised. All morning long she'd been frantic and indecisive as she'd tried to pick out something to wear, and after scouring her closet for something acceptable and making a big mess all over her bedroom floor in the process, she'd finally settled on light blue jeans, a long ruffled lavender tank top over a baby-pink camisole, and her favorite tan-and-pink Gucci sneakers; the ones with the cute floral motifs all over them. Even in third grade, she was already a very fashionable little girl, and once she was certain that she looked cute enough for a play date with Aiden, all that was left to do was wait. She cleaned up her mess and plopped down on her bed impatiently, watching the time on her alarm clock tick by ever-so-slowly. Why was it that time always seemed like it went in slow motion when you really wanted something?

The doorbell couldn't have rang soon enough. When it finally did, she nearly knocked her lamp from her nightstand throwing her stuffed giraffe at it in pure glee. "Ahh! He's here!"

she announced to no one in particular. She flew out of bed, rushed down the stairs, and pulled the front door open to be greeted by Aiden's smiling face. He looked a little apprehensive, like he wasn't really sure that he belonged here, but the apparent nerves only made him all the more endearing. His short brown hair was sticking up in the front like it always did and he was dressed in a striped gray and navy waffle sweater with a tiny embroidered moose on the front. It wasn't the most expensive outfit on the market, but it wasn't the muddy, ripped-up jeans that she'd imagined him wearing outside of school either. Angelina felt her cheeks flush instantly. Oh man - he looked *really* cute today!

"Hi Aiden!" she greeted him chipperly. "Wanna come in?"

"Sure," he said. He waved goodbye to his dad and took one last glance at the leaves changing orange and yellow on the trees outside before peering up at the brown brick mansion in front of him. He'd known before coming that Angelina's family was filthy rich, but he hadn't realized that her house would be so *huge.* He'd never been to a home this big and imposing before. The mansion made *his* house look like a shack in comparison. And if the outside was intimidating, it was nothing compared to inside. His jaw dropped as he entered the foyer. He felt like he'd just stepped into the movie *Scarface,* not like he'd ever stayed up late to sneak watching it when his parents' backs were turned or anything. And not that *Scarface* was really a good comparison, either. Maybe more like Vanity Fair, but Aiden didn't exactly consider himself a home designer, so how would he know?

"Holy cow..." he mused, eyeing up the expensive-looking artwork hanging on the dark-paneled walls. Red and gold Victorian-inspired furniture accented by silky brown brocade-patterned throw pillows was situated next to a tall mahogany coat rack nearby, and intricate brass lighting fixtures were positioned near every archway in the hall. "Your house is *really* fancy."

"If you say so," Angelina shrugged a nonchalant shoulder, though inside she felt like anything but. In actuality, she felt like her heart was going to patter right out of her chest now, but no way was she going to let him see that. The house, however, that was another story. "I can show you around and give you a tour if you want," she offered. "I'm a really good tour guide, remember?"

Aiden scratched his head. "Yeah, okay. A tour would be good. I feel like I might get lost in here without one."

"Oh, it's not *that* big," she insisted. "So, do you want to meet my mom first? You can meet my dad and Blair later, but they're out at a piano lesson right now. Come on, follow me."

It was more of a statement than a question and even if Aiden would have said *no way* and attempted to plant himself right there in the entryway and refuse to budge, she would have pulled him straight into the dining room where her mother was reorganizing the family's collection of vintage wines anyway. She led him into the room, catching Mom's attention with a boisterous announcement of, "Mommy, this is my new friend, Aiden!"

Cecilia swiveled around with a bottle of red merlot in her hand and Aiden gave her a friendly wave, feeling slightly embarrassed and self-conscious as he did it. Angelina's mom was *really* pretty. Her long brown hair was so silky that it looked like it belonged in a shampoo commercial and she was wearing a blue dress with a white lace overlay that was fit for a supermodel or maybe British royalty. His mom didn't wear stuff like this; his mom wore ponytails, jeans, comfy sweaters, and scrubs. And his family wasn't rich like these people. His parents weren't the type that collected expensive wines and put priceless art pieces on the wall. What if Angelina's parents were snooty and didn't like him?

Fortunately for him, there wasn't a snooty bone in Cecilia's body. For all of his trepidation, she didn't seem to mind that he wasn't wearing the latest from the Barney's New York kids' collection nor that his old brown sneakers weren't the newest or the nicest. "Hello, Aiden. It's so nice to meet you," she said in a kind, welcoming candor, setting the bottle down in the wine rack beside her. "While you're here just make yourself at home, okay sweetie? There are plenty of snacks in the pantry and Angelina will show you where everything is if you get hungry. Speaking of which, you are staying for dinner, aren't you?"

She was so nice and had given him such a hospitable welcome that the pang of hidden nervousness that Aiden had felt upon arriving melted away just as quickly as it had come on. He'd expected people as wealthy as the von Essens to treat him like a poor little underling, but if Angelina's dad was anything like her mom, then it would probably be safe to say that they weren't like that. "Yep," he nodded in affirmation. "My dad said I could stay all the way until six-thirty as long as that's alright with you."

"Of course it's alright. I hope you like lasagna."

"I *love* lasagna," he agreed with a relieved smile.

"Great," she smiled right back at him. "It won't be ready for a few hours yet, but I'll let you know when it's done. You two have fun and stay out of trouble until then. And Angelina, why don't you ask your sister to play with you when she comes home with Daddy? I'm sure she would like to join you."

"We will," Angelina promised. She turned back to Aiden and bit her lip anxiously. "So... how about that tour now?"

"Lead the way," he nodded. Feeling a little braver now seeing as things were going well so far, Angelina motioned for him to follow her and showed him all around the mansion. She showed him the fancy dark-wood cabinets in the kitchen, the big, elegant living room with its classy Victorian furniture, and her father's study with its tall shelves full of books that she'd never read, cozy reading area near the fireplace, and the black Steinway piano that Blair played against the far wall. She even peeked in through the slightly cracked door of her parents' bedroom to show him the cool crimson canopy hanging above their bed and Mom's nice mahogany dresser in the corner. When she was done with the bottom floor, she took him outside to the swimming pool, the outdoor bar, and Cecilia's beloved garden. Even in the fall the plot was beautiful, blooming with pretty pink fall asters, blue Russian sage, red sedum, and purple monkshood. Aiden thought it was incredible. He'd never seen a garden so big before.

"Wow!" he exclaimed, taking in all of the vibrant colors. "Does your mom really take care of these flowers all by herself?"

"Yep," Angelina replied with a proud puff of her chest. "She *loves* flowers. This garden is her favorite place in the world and she paints here all the time. Over there. See?"

She motioned towards the wooden easel situated near a patch of yellow goldenrod in the back. A half-painted canvas leaned against it; Cecilia's latest art project. Aiden took a good look around, impressed by all of the pretty colors and the fact that one person could make it all look so beautiful. For some reason, he'd always assumed that all rich people had gardeners and butlers and maids and cooks and a plethora of other doting servants that did all of their work for them, but in this household it was clearly Cecilia who kept the domestic affairs running.

"Wow..." he repeated again. "This place is really cool. We could never have a garden like this at my house. My dog would probably try to eat all of these flowers."

Angelina cocked an eyebrow. "Your dog eats flowers?"

"My dog eats *everything*. I even saw him eat deer poop once. It was gross."

"Eww!"

Aiden grinned. "He's weird sometimes, but he's a good dog. He's a black lab chow mix and he likes to play fetch and go for walks and get scratched behind the ears. His name is Gunner."

"What kind of a name is *Gunner* for a dog?"

"It's just his name. What kind of name is Angelina von Essen for a girl?"

Angelina paused for a moment. He had her there. "A good one, obviously!" she claimed. She folded her arms over her chest and sighed. "You're *so* lucky to have a dog, Aiden. I wish *I* had a puppy or a kitten to play with, but my dad is allergic to pets so we can't have anything. Not even hamsters. It stinks."

Aiden frowned. "That *does* stink. You're missing out. Pets are great. You get to play with them, pet them, cuddle them..."

Angelina made a weird face at the mention of cuddling that he could only assume was from jealousy and he stopped himself there, not wanting to rub salt in her wounds. He was surprised that there was anything that the von Essens couldn't have that his family could, but he was quickly learning that being rich wasn't automatically a catch-all. When Angelina was done showing him around the garden, she took him back inside and up the winding spiral staircase, showing him the big bathroom she shared with her sister, the guest bedroom where visitors spent the night, and the outdoor balcony that looked out over the pool. After showing him almost everything save for Blair's room, Angelina finally got to her last - and favorite - stop of the tour.

"This is *my* room," she announced, propping the door open and giving him a good view inside. Aiden blinked in surprise. Angelina's room didn't look *anything* like the other rooms in the house. It wasn't decorated in dark wood, shades of rich burgundy and plum wine, or expensive-looking fine art. Instead, the walls were a girly violet purple color decorated with a fun vintage damask pattern and a silky lavender comforter was spread over the big queen bed pressed against the far wall. It wasn't hard to tell what Angelina's favorite color was, let alone her favorite toys. Numerous fluffy stuffed animals were scattered all over the room and a eclectic array of Barbie dolls, Beanie Babies, and My Little Ponies spilled out of her toy box. Her shelves were full to bursting with a colorful assortment of young girls' books, her bed was covered in purple patterned accent pillows, her wardrobe overflowed with trendy clothes, and tubes of vibrantly packaged lip balm sticks in fun fruity flavors laid on the desk next to her laptop. A karaoke machine covered in buttons and knobs stood against the wall nearby; a wall that was adorned with whimsical-looking artwork and corkboards covered in magazine pictures of her favorite singers, rainbow-colored Lisa Frank kittens, and her favorite photographs of her posing with family and friends.

"Your room is *really* purple and girly," Aiden observed, picking up a beanie animal from her chaise lounge nearby.

"No kidding... I *am* a girl," Angelina reminded him with a curt hand on her hip. "I still have lots of cool stuff that boys can play with though. What do you want to do first? Do you want to color? I have an art table we can use." She waved her arm at the small white art table in the middle of the room stocked with craft supplies and construction paper to doodle on.

"I guess so," Aiden agreed. At least coloring sounded a bit more appealing than playing with all the girl toys. He put her Beanie Baby back where he found it and plopped down on her floor. She knelt down next to him and handed him some crayons.

"I have all the colors you could want," she boasted. "Plus markers and colored pencils if you like those better."

Aiden was just fine with crayons. He made a grab at one of the brown ones while Angelina chose a green. She pressed it hard against her paper, biting her lip in concentration and trying her damnedest to create a masterpiece that would impress him.

"What are *you* gonna draw?" Aiden asked her.

"I'll show you when it's done. You can't see it before that."

"Okay," he agreed. "Mine will be a surprise too, then. No peeking before I tell you to, okay?"

"Okay."

Satisfied enough with that, Aiden went for a blue next and drew a big curvy squiggle along the bottom of his paper.

"Hey, Angelina... thanks for inviting me over," he said out of the blue. "Before you came up to me on the first day of school I didn't know if I'd make any new friends there. Why did you even want to talk to me in the first place?"

Angelina made a funny face. "What are you talking about? Everybody at school likes you. You have lots of new friends now. Besides, that's a goofy thing to ask. You looked lost and I thought you seemed nice," she said, leaving any mention of crushes and butterflies out of it. She felt her cheeks grow dangerously warm as she remembered that weird feeling she'd gotten in her tummy, but she must have been getting better at hiding it, because Aiden didn't seem to notice. "Why did you *think* I talked to you?"

"I dunno," he shrugged. "Being new in a place like Saint Joan of Arc's is kind of weird."

"I guess being new *anywhere* would be kind of weird."

"Yeah. And everyone there is like, super-rich. My family's not rich like yours. We're just... well... *normal*, I guess."

"So what?"

"So you don't care?"

"Of course not! Why would I care about something like that? That's stupid."

Aiden grinned in approval and tried to sneak a peek at her picture out of the corner of his eye. She gasped and threw her arm over it, covering what little she had drawn so far.

"Hey, stop trying to look! We promised, no peeking."

Aiden made a pouty face. "Please? I just want to see what you're doing with that red," he attempted to sway her.

His blinking puppy eyes weren't going to crack her, even if her stomach felt a little funny. "Well, you can't yet," she stuck her tongue out at him. He went back to his own coloring, and she steered the subject away from herself and back to learning more about him. "What do your parents do anyway?" she asked.

Aiden snagged another crayon from the pile. "My dad fixes cars and my mom's a nurse. She works a lot of weird hours, but she likes to take care of people, so I guess it's okay. And one day my dad's going to help me fix up a really cool car and it's going to be super fast and go a hundred miles an hour."

"A hundred?" Angelina repeated. "Wow, that *is* fast."

"I know. What do *your* parents do?"

"My dad is a boss and my mom stays at home and takes care of me and Blair. Other than that, she paints stuff for her art shop. Most of the paintings in the house are hers, you know."

"Really?" Aiden glanced around the room and pointed at a wide painting hanging above Angelina's bed of two birds sitting together on a black branch against a background of pretty purple blossoms to match her girly purple walls. "How about that one?"

"Yep. She made that one for my birthday last year."

"Wow, she's talented. It must be pretty cool getting to hang out with her all the time. She seems really nice."

"She *is* really nice. And she's a lot of fun, too. She reads me and Blair the best stories and we do all *kinds* of things together."

"I don't think I've ever met your sister," Aiden realized.

Angelina sighed. "That's because Blair's in Mrs. Pearson's class. Plus she's super shy. All she does is read and do homework. She probably wouldn't have *any* friends if it wasn't for me." When she said it, it came off as a little rude, but to Angelina it was only the truth. Sad and unfortunate maybe, but still the truth.

For some reason, it made Aiden feel kind of bad. "Oh," he said. "Well, I have a sister, too. She's younger than me."

"Me and Blair are twins, but she's younger than me too."

"You're twins?"

"Yeah, we were born on the same day."

"I know what a *twin* is..."

"I'm older, though! By three minutes."

Aiden grabbed a green crayon and pressed down hard, drawing straight, sharp, triangular lines to be the teeth for the animal he was creating. He tried to sneak a peek at Angelina's drawing yet again to no avail. "Hey, is your picture finished yet?"

"Hold on, almost," she muttered, sticking her arm in his plane of view. "And... done! How about you?"

"One second." He grit his teeth as if what he was doing was actually taking a lot of effort. And then, "Okay... done!" He flipped his paper over so she couldn't see it. "Alright, you show me yours first," he demanded.

Angelina scooted her paper across the table. She'd drawn a green field of grass with a cross-hatched net in the background. In the foreground, four figures - two in purple shirts and two in red - were kicking a black and white ball between them. "It's not like you haven't looked already, but it's supposed to be people playing soccer. See? My dad told me that in Europe soccer is called football and your kind of football doesn't exist," she declared as though her idea to switch Aiden's sport around on him was the most creative idea ever. "Isn't that weird? What do you think?"

"I think it's *awesome*," Aiden complimented her art skills.

Angelina smiled proudly. "What did you make?"

If Aiden was impressed with her drawing, it was nothing compared to how pleased he was with his. "A big mean alligator of doom!" he announced. He turned his paper around and held it up so she could see the giant angry-looking alligator growling and glaring at them next to a choppy blue riverbank in the corner.

"*Ha!* That's supposed to be an alligator of doom?" she barked. "He doesn't look very mean. He just looks funny!"

"Oh, he might be funny-looking on the outside... but trust me, on the inside he's pure *evil,*" Aiden admired his handiwork proudly. "Animals are my favorite thing to draw. I wish we had art class together. Art and gym are the best, unlike *boring* math."

"Yeah, I like art and gym a lot, too," Angelina agreed. "Especially when we do tennis. But music class is even better."

"Oh yeah... I heard you're good at singing."·

Angelina was surprised that Aiden knew. Then again, it wasn't as if the school chorus was some kind of secret club that nobody knew the members of. Inside, she secretly hoped that in addition to hearing that she was good, that *not only good, but better than Jenny Wexler* was a part of that. "I take lessons for it," she said simply, leaving out the part about her goofing off at said lessons half the time and glancing at her karaoke machine instead. "Hey, I know... I can show you! Do you want to sing karaoke now?"

Again, it wasn't really a question so much as a decision. Aiden abandoned Angelina's drawing table to follow her to the karaoke machine and watched curiously as she flipped through a fat binder of CDs. She popped one into the machine and grabbed a microphone, eager to show off and impress him some more.

"Do you have any good songs?" he asked her.

"*Tons,*" she claimed, putting on something by one of her all-time favorite pop singers, Britney Spears. Pop wasn't what she learned at her music lessons, but it was a lot more fun to sing than all of the fluffy stuff that she did. Angelina held a microphone to her face and belted out the chorus loudly, acting like she was performing at a big concert instead of just her room. Aiden had never sung karaoke before, but she made it look like so much fun that by the time she was finished, he was eager to give it a try.

After searching through Angelina's mostly-girly choices for something that seemed to be the lesser of the evils, he decided on singing "Build Me Up Buttercup" by The Foundations. It was a little cheesy and he wasn't nearly as good at carrying a tune as she was, but his tone-deafness only made him that much cuter. Angelina's efforts not to blush and giggle like an idiot were of no use. He was adorable, even if he sounded horrible and off-key.

Once they'd tired of karaoke, they moved on to making a mess out of the toys in her toy box instead. Aiden was just about to stomp over a Barbie doll's head with one of her ponies when a new sound made its way up the stairs. It was muffled, but still there, soft and tinkling against the walls. Aiden stopped clowning around and listened, trying to figure out what it was.

"Is that a piano?" he squinted his eyes.

Angelina stopped to listen, too. Aiden was right. Blair and Dad must have come home while they'd been preoccupied with her toys, because that was definitely the piano and there was only one person in the house who could actually play it like that.

"Blair's back and she didn't even come up and say hi!" Angelina confirmed with a disappointed frown. "I *told* you she'd have no friends if it wasn't for me. Come on, Aiden. I promised Mom we'd ask her to play with us. Want to go meet her?"

Not bothering to wait for an answer, she grabbed him by the arm and led him back downstairs, stopping at the study doorway and opening it just a crack. Blair was caught in mid-song, looking as though she was deep in concentration. "Err... let's just wait until she's done," Angelina suggested in a quiet whisper.

Aiden followed her lead and hid behind the door, peering into the study and watching Blair's tiny fingers dance across the keys. He'd never claimed to be much of a music critic, but he was amazed at what he was hearing. Blair was playing a song that he'd never heard before, something pretty but sort of sad and bittersweet at the same time. Her hands were small, but she hit each note with the skill and grace of someone who'd been playing much longer than she. Aiden couldn't explain why or how, but he could simply *feel* the emotion of the song as if she put her whole self in to it. Even being as young as he was, he could appreciate that. He'd never heard such beautiful piano playing in his life and was surprised that it was someone his own age that was doing it so well. Angelina had been good at singing, but this was different somehow. He couldn't stop staring at her, completely in awe.

When Blair finished her piece she shut her eyes and sat at the piano in silence, taking it all in. She would have remained completely oblivious to the two people spying on her indefinitely had it not been for the quietness in the room being interrupted by the abrupt sound of clapping coming from the doorway.

"That was awesome!" Aiden cheered for her, stepping out from his hiding place and letting himself inside.

Blair's eyes fluttered open and she gasped in surprise, nearly jumping out of her seat. She stood from the piano bench and blushed sheepishly, tucking a tendril of wavy brown hair behind her ear. How long had Angelina and Aiden been standing there listening to her? She'd really been getting into her song and she hadn't realized that she had an audience. She'd probably been making the most ridiculous faces, too. She *always* made stupid faces when she got lost in the music and wasn't careful about it, and she couldn't help feeling a little self-conscious when she did.

"Sorry! I - I didn't know you were here," she stumbled.

"Well, we were trying to be quiet and sneaky about it," Angelina claimed, shooting a scolding glare at Aiden before introducing him. "Anyway, Aiden, this is Blair." She motioned at her matter-of-factly. "Blair, this is Aiden."

Blair fiddled with the buttons of her cardigan.

"Hi, Aiden," she greeted him with a timid smile. She stepped forward, extending her hand and catching him off guard.

"Hi," he replied, taken aback as he got a good glimpse of her up close. She was wearing a lacey beige shirt under a peachy-pink cardigan covered in tiny little polka dot hearts, a pretty flowered skirt, and brown flats with little ivory bows on the front over matching brown stockings. A very classy, sophisticated look for a third grader. Her eyes were a pretty caramel color, lighter than Angelina's, which were more like chocolate. He wrapped his hand around hers and gave it a polite shake. Maybe a handshake was a strange greeting between two children, but Bruce had always taught his daughters to be courteous and Blair had always been one to use her manners. Aiden's tummy did a weird flip flop, the same goofy flip flop that Angelina's had done when she'd first met him in the hallway at school. He didn't know what was wrong with him, but suddenly his belly was all tied up in knots.

"That was a really pretty song," he complimented her, feeling uncharacteristically bashful himself. "How'd you do that?"

"Oh... thank you," Blair stammered. "I just practice a lot."

Ultra-competitive Angelina might have actually felt jealous of this exchange if she weren't so oblivious and took her uptight cardigan-wearing bookworm of a sister a little more seriously. She butted in bossily, breaking up the introductions.

"Yeah, you practice *too much*. Didn't you just *have* a lesson? Stop playing the piano and come outside with us instead."

The sound of her chiding voice snapped Aiden out of his temporarily-dumbfounded moment and he tried to shake off the embarrassing, goofy tummy feeling that Blair had given him and remember why they were here in the first place.

"Yeah, want to play with us?" he asked her a little more nicely than Angelina had.

Blair tended to be bashful around new company, but playing outside until dinner was done *did* sound like a fun idea. She joined her sister and Aiden in the front yard, and soon the three found themselves playing an impromptu game of cops and robbers which Angelina quickly claimed herself the champion of. As the sneaky sharpshooting robber, she managed to pull off quite a few good sneak attacks on the girls' male counterpart, and Blair was too worried about getting grass stains on her nice new skirt or ripping her stockings to really go for the gold, anyway. Aiden got back at Angelina by sneaking up on her and tickling her until her face turned so red that it looked like she might explode and she reciprocated by pushing him into a pile of freshly-raked leaves. Soon, leaves went flying everywhere, crunching under their feet and scattering all over the yard. When the kids had had enough, they plopped down in the grass and fell into easy chatter, talking about school and classes and whatever else came to mind - including what they wanted to be when they grew up. Blair considered her answer carefully, picking at a piece of grass. The truth was, she'd never actually thought about what she wanted to be when she was older. Grades were really important to her right now, but that kind of decision just seemed so far away.

"I think I'd like to be a music teacher," she decided, even though she wasn't really sure of how true this really was. "Maybe I can teach the piano like Mom teaches art."

"That's a good idea," Aiden shot her a cute smile. "I bet you'd be a great piano teacher. What about you, Angelina?"

Angelina had always been a little outlandish. "Well, *that's* easy. I'm going to be super famous and have my own CD."

Blair let out a soft giggle at her sister's ambitious claim. "If you have a CD then you can go on tour or something."

"Duh!" Angelina agreed like there was no question about it. "I'll be bigger than Britney, just watch. What do *you* want to be, Aiden? Do you want to fix cars like your dad?"

"Nope, I just want to drive them," he said, looking up into the sky with a dreamy look on his face. Being a racecar driver or an astronaut were both pretty high on his career goals list, but there was one thing he wanted even more. "I'm going to be an NFL superstar someday and my team's going to win the Super Bowl. Then I'm going to buy a ton of cars that will all go a hundred miles an hour."

"Awesome! I'll sing the national anthem at your big game," Angelina offered. She glanced at her sister, not wanting her to feel left out. "And Blair can play the piano in the background."

Aiden thought that sounded like a pretty good setup. He started going off on a sports tangent, and the girls listened intently as he talked about all of his favorite players and all the cool, fast cars he would buy with his NFL earnings until it was finally time to eat. By then all of their stomachs were grumbling - in Angelina's case, *loudly*. During dinner, Bruce entertained the kids with funny jokes about how it was nice to have another man in the house for once, then offered everyone yummy cannoli that he'd brought home from the city for dessert. By the time six thirty rolled around, Aiden was one-hundred percent certain that any nerves he'd felt before ringing the doorbell earlier had all been unwarranted. He hadn't known what to expect from a visit to a girl's house, let alone one whose family was so rich, but he'd had a good time. Angelina was really turning out to be good friend material, even if she *was* a girl. He almost felt guilty for getting that weird tummy-feeling over Blair in the study when Angelina was the one he'd come over to hang out with in the first place.

"I had a lot of fun today. We should do this again, okay?" Angelina suggested before he left. She looked up at him with two big brown puppy eyes full of hopeful admiration.

"I had a lot of fun too," he agreed. "Next time you should come over to my house. You need to meet Gunner."

"Okay!" she nodded, totally up for the idea. As Aiden walked down the front walkway towards the car where his dad was waiting for him, Angelina couldn't help frowning despite how elated she felt. What a weird mix of feelings she had inside her. She wished that time could rewind and they could start the day all over again. She'd had so much fun giving him a tour, singing karaoke, playing outside with Blair, drawing pictures...

Oh no, that was right... drawing pictures!

She gasped, remembering the silly doodle he'd left on her drawing table. "Aiden, your alligator!" she called to him. "You forgot it in my room. Do you want me to go and get it for you?"

Aiden looked over his shoulder and gave her a wave.

"Nah, it's okay. You can keep it!"

He got into the car and his dad drove away, honking the horn a few times as they went. Angelina watched until the taillights vanished around a bend in the road, then bounded upstairs to her bedroom, picking up the alligator picture Aiden had left behind. A big smile spread across her face as she laughed out loud at its goofy teeth and stubby chicken legs. It was the most ridiculous looking "Alligator of Doom" she'd ever seen. She tacked it up on the wall right above her karaoke machine where she could always see it, and it stayed there from that day forward: a physical reminder of the first time that Aiden Andrews had come to visit her, and a really fun afternoon with her newest friend.

CHAPTER EIGHT
Wishful Thinking

ANGELINA AND AIDEN QUICKLY became friends after their first play date at the mansion. When she wasn't hanging out with her clique and he wasn't with one of his teammates, it soon became safe to assume that they were more than likely doing something with eachother. As they started playing outside of school more, their activities of choice changed with the seasons. They pulled chunks of orange flesh out of pumpkins at the end of October and admired their funny-faced jack-o-lanterns. They went trick-or-treating with their friends on Halloween and jumped in one last crunchy pile of leaves at the Andrews house before fall was over, squealing as brown, red, orange, and yellow went flying through the air. Once, Aiden even went to one of the art lessons that Cecilia taught in the city with Angelina and Blair. The kids sat in the corner painting scarecrows and harvest scenes on their canvases while Cecilia instructed her students on the use of color, and how certain shades elicited emotions of warmth and comfort, while others drew out feelings of anger, passion, and serenity.

When the first big snow of winter fell in Maple Springs, they built a giant snowman in the schoolyard with Gisele and Katie, went sledding with Aiden's new friend Danny on the biggest hill in town, and baked dozens of delicious cookies in anticipation of Santa. Then, when the buds of early spring finally started to reappear on the trees, they splashed in puddles on rainy afternoons and helped Cecilia tend to her garden. Angelina had always liked helping her mother water the flowers when bending proved too much for her knee, but when Aiden joined in, the task became even more fun. By spring, he had gotten comfortable enough around her to tease and antagonize her just for the fun of it, and for as much as she liked to fight back, she secretly loved it when he heckled her. Usually his evil taunts had to do with some trite comparison between boys and girls, and in the case of gardening, a jab at her weak little muscles tended to suffice.

"Be careful with that watering can!" Cecilia called across the garden one afternoon as Angelina lugged it towards the begonias in determination. Water sloshed from the sides as she went; a horrible waste of sustenance that horrified her sister.

"Angelina, you're spilling!" Blair fretted.

But where Blair saw something to fret about, Aiden saw an opportunity to poke fun. "You're such a weak little girl! You can't even carry a can!" he taunted Angelina with a mischievous sneer. She set her can down and stamped her foot at him in defiance.

"Stop that! I'm just as strong as you are!" she argued hotly. Her comment was met with a flurry of tickling fingers in retaliation and she squealed an earth-shattering squeal, hooting and hollering as she tried to slap his hands away from her ribs.

"Say Uncle!" he shouted when she begged him to stop.

"UNCLE!" Angelina wailed.

"Say 'Aiden is the best!'" he cackled like a sadist.

He knew she wouldn't do it. Angelina was far too stubborn and prideful to ever admit someone else being better than her, *especially* if that someone else was a boy. She flailed and screamed for mercy as Blair watched their play fight with a look of confusion scrunching her face. It was one of the weirdest things she'd ever seen. Tickling? Cackling? *Squealing* like that?

"They're *crazy*," she whispered in a voice that only her mother could hear, handing her the abandoned can. Cecilia stooped over her garden with a knowing smile and shook her head. She knew a little puppy-love when she saw it, and for a nine year old, it was much more harmless and cute than worrisome.

"Crazy indeed," she mused.

Crazy or not, no one could argue that third grade was definitely turning out to be a fun year for the kids. Angelina was getting to hang out with her crush and Aiden wasn't feeling so apprehensive about being the new boy in school anymore. He'd never envisioned becoming friends with someone who wasn't a boy and wasn't his sister, but Angelina was proving to be pretty cool for a girl after all. He liked how over-the-top, goofy, and even *bossy* she could be, and it was easy to see why so many of their classmates liked her so much. Between her and all of the other new friends he was making, he was actually starting to feel like he could fit in after all; something he'd been a lot more nervous about when his parents had informed him of making the switch from public school to private than he'd made common knowledge.

As for Angelina's sister, Blair and Aiden had made a nice sort of acquaintanceship after meeting in the study, but they weren't nearly as good of friends as he and Angelina had become. Perhaps some of that was simply because he'd met Angelina first, but a bigger part of it was probably that Blair really *was* shy just like Angelina had said, and Aiden couldn't help being a little shy around her himself. Weeks passed, but he never fully forgot the goofy, flip-floppy feeling he'd gotten in his tummy when he'd seen her practicing the piano and she'd reached out to touch his hand. Secretly, he kind of found the whole thing unnerving and weird. He didn't know what to make of it so he never mentioned it to anyone else - and *especially* not to Angelina, because for as innocent and involuntary as it had been, he didn't want her to laugh at him or get jealous and not want to be his friend anymore.

Girls were strange like that, and even in third grade he knew to tread lightly around them in hopes of not setting them off.

Coincidentally, this was probably a wise idea, because although Angelina still had a crush on him, she hadn't dared to speak a word of it to his face. She was usually pretty fearless when it came to most things, but something as nerve-wracking as being smitten with puppy love was different. She'd finally found something that scared her: rejection. And in not wanting that fear to be realized, she hid her secret in her heart and kept all damning thoughts of puppy-love and crushes between herself and her two most trusted girlfriends... though *anyone* who paid enough attention could see that she was awfully fond of her new friend.

Blair, perhaps, noticed it the most. Blair had always been an observant little girl even without that fabled "twin sense," and from the very first afternoon that they'd played together at the mansion, she'd been utterly and rightly convinced that Angelina had a crush on Aiden. Conscientiousness and insightfulness were perhaps the biggest benefits of being quiet and introspective, but it wasn't like she would've needed to be a rocket scientist to figure it out. If Angelina's giggling and beet red cheeks during cops and robbers wouldn't have done it on that first afternoon, then the way she'd been prancing around the mansion like she was floating on a big fluffy cloud afterwards definitely would have.

Yet when Blair would bring her suspicions up, her sister always denied them, giving her some lame excuse about how there was nothing wrong with having boys as friends and that just because Aiden was a boy didn't mean that she *liked*-him liked him. Blair didn't buy it for a minute. Angelina was *so* obvious! She would gush and giggle about her new friend every time the girls snuck into each others' rooms past bedtime to talk under the covers while Mom and Dad thought they were asleep, and the mushy smile on her face was a telltale sign of her real affections.

"You like him, don't you?" Blair pried on one such occasion as they hid under her embroidered comforter, faces illuminated by the yellow flashlight they'd found hidden in a storage closet downstairs. "You want him to be your boyfriend, just admit it!"

"No!" Angelina hissed in denial, stuck on her high horse. "That's gross, Blair! I don't even *like* boys right now."

"You don't think *any* of the boys in our class are cute?"

"No! *Eww!*"

"So then, you think Aiden is ugly?"

Angelina's face went white and her expression progressed from shock to irritation in one heated second. "God, shut up, Blair!" she argued, swatting the beam of the flashlight away from her face. She hated when Blair used this weird mental logic trap on her. She was too smart for her own good. "He's *not* ugly."

"So, he's cute then?"

"Ugh, stop it! I don't like him like that!"

It was such a bald-faced lie, and every time Angelina spouted such a bald-faced lie, Blair would shake her head in disbelief at her sister's stubborn refusal to come clean to anyone outside of Gisele and Katie. She didn't get why Angelina had to be such a drama queen anyway. Did she really think that her *twin* couldn't figure out when she *like*-liked someone? Just because they weren't identical didn't mean that Blair was stupid!

But if there was one thing that Blair knew wasn't going to change about her sister, it was that she was horribly stubborn and uncompromising. Blair never exactly managed to convince Angelina to get over her irrational idea that she would tell their parents and admit it, but she'd always known the truth, right from the start. She didn't *need* to hear it. Angelina liked Aiden, plain and simple... and while Blair thought that the new boy was nice and was never anything but courteous to him in return, she kept her distance because of her sister, never wanting to impose.

Meanwhile, Victoria Adessi had been doing nothing *but* attempting to impose for the last few months, yet for all of her efforts she hadn't been making much progress on the "seduce her boss" front. From a strictly "work" standpoint, things were going great. She'd been adjusting well to her new position at Vonessen Inc. and was working in tandem more with Bruce and the other executives high up in the company. Her professional and social statuses were changing for the better - as was the figure showing up in her bank account - but despite the increased cash flow to her pockets and her own swanky office furnished with everything cushy and leather under the sun, the wannabe gold-digger still couldn't help feeling agitated and disgruntled inside.

When Victoria had first snagged her promotion, she'd assumed it would only be a matter of time before she'd be the instigator of a very welcome divorce. But now, her nonsense "good things come to those who wait" approach was starting to sound more and more like just that – *nonsense* —with every month that passed. October, November... it was the start of April now, and her unrequited lust for more material things – and her *boss* — had only grown more insatiable now that she'd gotten a taste.

Victoria could see it so clearly now that she was around him more; just how desirable a life Bruce led. She could hear it as he made plans with colleagues over the phone, reserving tables at the city's most exclusive restaurants and VIP treatment at the most elite wine tastings and charity galas. She could feel it as she sat in on all of the big meetings and witnessed the command he held as CEO. Yet despite the fact that she herself was a constant fixture in his office now, bringing him special reports and updating him on important accounting matters, her "discreet" efforts to impress him didn't seem to be making the sort of headway that she'd hoped for. Bruce was amicable towards her, but he didn't pay her charming personality and form-hugging office wear much mind... and she was reminded of exactly why every time she approached his desk and saw the black-and-white photograph of Cecilia he had displayed there as a constant homage, front and center.

Cecilia was stunning in that photograph, a true classic beauty a la Liz Taylor or Sophia Loren. She was sitting on the beach in a dark lily-printed wrap dress, showing a little leg while she gazed at the camera with a demure, lovelorn smile on her lips. Bruce had been the one holding the camera, insisting on taking a romantic picture before watching the sunset go down. For him, the photo was a reminder of how carefree and happy he could feel around his wife, the beautiful former ballerina who carried on with such poise and positivity in the face of injury and adversity. A picture to look at when the world went too fast and work got daunting. For Victoria, it was a reality check; one that made her greedy fantasies dissolve into naught but wishful thinking.

Her stomach turned with jealousy at the sight of it. And not just jealousy, but a hot, hateful *envy* that sent her blood boiling through her veins, violently enough that it could've made her physically sick. Bruce was so far out of reach. The money, the power, the status, the notoriety, and that castle of a home with all of its *stuff* inside? They already belonged to someone else. Victoria wanted those things so badly that her want had turned to obsession. And in turn, her obsession had become more than just Bruce and his things. It had become Cecilia von Essen herself.

She'd practically become a stalker, the way she snooped around for information on the woman. It was a compulsion, a sickness. She had to know everything - what Cecilia was doing at her art gallery, what accolades she managed to acquire for herself, who she spent her time with and where at. And every time something good appeared to happen for the woman, Victoria felt an intense hatred flare up in the pit of her gut. She just couldn't help herself. The more she saw that picture and the more she was reminded of what was standing in her way, the more she felt her envy grow. If Bruce were any other man, it would have been much easier for her. She'd have no problems getting her grubby little paws on him. But Bruce wasn't a man easily swayed by temptation. Promotion or not, that fact wouldn't change.

But just as Bruce wasn't easy, Victoria wasn't a quitter.

Victoria was becoming more unhinged and unstable every day, but Vonessen Inc.'s new Controller wasn't the only woman with Bruce on the mind, and especially not today on this nice spring day in early April. After much anticipation, it was finally Bruce and Cecilia's tenth wedding anniversary. Though dancing hadn't been easy for Cecilia after her accident, there were certain days that made her want to try... and days like today were it.

She couldn't remember the last time she'd felt so blatantly, unapologetically pampered. In the morning, Bruce had wasted no time in revealing his intentions to spoil her and surprised her with a dozen red roses at the breakfast table - a breakfast table that he had already made, which was endearing despite his horrible lack of cooking skills. And then, before he'd left the house, he'd presented her with an all-inclusive voucher to the spa to enjoy with her girlfriends while he was away at the office. The "ultimate rejuvenating package" that she and her two closest lady friends had been treated to all morning had been just what a busy mom like her had needed and left her feeling more refreshed than ever. The ladies had gotten facials, manicures, pedicures, hot stone massages... the works. And the girls had even gotten in on the festivities after school, presenting their parents with a cute homemade photo album filled with all of their favorite photos of Mom and Dad together. As if all of this hadn't been special enough, then dinner tonight had really been the ultimate treat. Bruce had made reservations at Cecilia's favorite restaurant in the city, and the food had been nothing short of incredible, as always.

The couple sat at their private table quite full and very content as the waiter cleared their plates, just having finished a delicious meal of lobster tail and triple berry torte. The two of them had traveled the world together, been everywhere from Costa Rica to alpine Europe to the California coast, but nowhere were the desserts better than right here in Stirling City. *Le Poisson et la Bête* made the *best* triple berry torte, and Cecilia loved coming to this place. With its soothing mood lighting, crystal vases of roses, relaxing mood music, and burgundy-plum color palette, it was as romantic and classy as a place could get; the perfect way to celebrate a decade of happy memories with the love of her life.

She'd worn one of her favorite dresses to commemorate the occasion: a long midnight blue number with an elegant lace cutout in the back. Something sophisticated and refined with just the right touch of understated glamour. With that dress, the romantic side-swept curls in her hair, and the alluring shade of berry on her pout, she simply emanated the same classic beauty that she did in the photo on her husband's desk; the same that had made him fall for her all those years ago on the banks of the river.

Bruce hadn't been able to take his eyes off of her all night. Even after all this time, he couldn't get over just how captivating she was. He sat across from her in one of his finest suits, sipping contentedly at his leftover Chianti and enjoying the soothing ambiance of the music, the candlelight, and the gently flickering fire burning in the fireplace nearby. Caressing Cecilia's delicate hand, he looked lovingly into her sapphire eyes.

"Have I told you yet that you look beautiful tonight?" he murmured, entwining his fingers between hers.

It didn't matter how many times Cecilia had heard him tell her this. Every time he did, she felt her heart melt inside her chest.

"Bruce, you're too much," she replied with a gentle laugh. "Yes, you have. At least twenty times now. And you look pretty handsome yourself, not that you need me to tell you that. Just as handsome as you did on our wedding day."

"I was a lot younger then. In a bit better shape, too," Bruce teased, resting his hand on his stomach. He smiled affectionately as he remembered their romantic church ceremony with the white roses and the flickering candlelight and her beautiful ivory dress. "It's hard to believe it's been ten years already. *Ten years.*"

"Ten years that I wouldn't trade for anything," Cecilia agreed with a wistful smile. "They've really flown by, haven't they? I could've sworn that Angelina and Blair were just in diapers yesterday, and now Angelina is already planning out play dates with little boys. Soon she'll be sneaking away on *real* dates and giving us a whole world of trouble."

"Our Angelina? Never. Blair won't let her get out of line."

"Want to make a bet? Angelina's going to be a handful, I guarantee it. She already is. Just ask her voice coach."

"I'm sure Margaret can keep her under control."

"Maybe. But we'll see. Somehow I feel like control and our daughter don't really belong in the same sentence." They shared an agreeing chuckle and Cecilia sighed, rubbing her thumb against the wedding band on Bruce's finger. "Can you believe the girls have been taking music lessons for four years now? I feel like tomorrow we'll be sending them off to prom and graduation and college already. I don't know if I'll be able to handle it. Seeing them all grown up like that... having to say goodbye?"

Bruce gave her a bittersweet grin, taking one last sip of the remnants of his wine. "Don't worry, Cece... I think we have plenty of time before we have to worry about that."

"Maybe... but time goes faster than you think. It just goes to show you that life is short. That's why I'm happy I've spent the last ten years of mine with you. They've been the happiest years of my life. The garden, the gallery, our family? God, I feel so lucky. I owe so much to you, Bruce. I just want you to know that." Cecilia shook her head in bemusement at herself, then downed the last droplets of her drink. "It's been quite a journey hasn't it?"

Bruce smiled fondly at the notion. It brought back memories of lunch-time coffee runs and good conversation. Of the first time he'd visited her apartment, seen her Tuscan poppies, and tasted her sweet lips. Of listening to her talk about dancing and music, watching her garden and paint, visiting the city's cultural hot spots, traveling the world together, and learning to live for more than just his work. He could still remember the day she'd told him she was pregnant like it was only yesterday. Could still remember holding Angelina and Blair in his arms for the first time and wondering if he'd ever make a good parent. How far they'd come since then... and how far he still wanted to go.

"It has been," he agreed, putting his glass down on the table. "*Quite* a journey. But it's not over yet. And if anyone owes anyone here, I'm the one who owes you. You've changed me, Cece. For the better. I'm looking forward to the next ten years."

Cecilia leaned forward, her chin in her hand. "Me too. What do you think we'll be doing in a decade?"

"Probably sitting here at this table. Eating lobster and triple berry torte."

Cecilia smiled. She liked the sound of that.

Outside, the sky was dark and the hour was getting late. Bruce stood from his chair and helped his wife out of hers, giving her a gentle peck on the top of her hand before planting one on her lips. He lingered for a moment, appreciating the lovely features she'd inherited from her French and Italian parents.

"You're so beautiful," he admired her for about the millionth time, stroking her cheek tenderly.

"Bruce, stop that..." she smoothed her hair behind her ear.

She'd always been modest and protested when he coddled her, but Bruce knew that she secretly loved it. "Never. I'll never stop. And I have a surprise for you before we go home."

"A surprise? Haven't you pampered me enough already?"

"There's no such thing."

He reached into his breast pocket and pulled out a small gift box, wrapped in shiny pearl-colored wrapping paper.

"*Another* gift?" Cecilia asked in disbelief. "I thought that the spa and this dinner were my anniversary presents. Really, now you *are* trying to spoil me. Why do you insist on doing this?"

Bruce smiled. "Just open it, Cece."

Cecilia peeled the wrapping paper away and peered into the black box inside. "Oh!" she gasped as she held up a rather exquisite - and expensive - piece of jewelry. "Bruce, it's beautiful!"

In her hand she held a gold necklace with a heart and key charm on the chain, embellished with sparkling white diamonds.

"I know you think that jewelry is overkill, but I thought this would be a fitting gift this year," Bruce explained. "Because after ten years, you're still the only woman who could ever hold the key to my heart."

The statement was simple, but so profound that it nearly made Cecilia tear up. She felt herself melting again as she glanced into his eyes. The way that they smoldered, so dark and affectionate, proved his love more than any words. It didn't take lavish gifts of spa time, high-end dinners, or expensive jewelry for her to know her husband's heart was true. And for all of their flash, Bruce's gifts were never about money or showing off. They were about appreciation and admiration. About wanting comfort and fine things for the person he cared about most... and those were the same things that Cecilia wanted for him, too.

"Bruce, you're so cheesy," she shook her head as he took the necklace and slid behind her to help her clasp it around her neck. "But *incredibly* romantic..."

"So is it overkill?" he murmured against her skin. His warm breath sent a pleasant tingle down Cecilia's spine and she glanced down to finger the small charm before turning to face him instead. She lifted a gentle hand to his cheek, feeling the stubble of his dark beard beneath her fingertips. This time, the look in *her* eyes was enough to make Bruce forget how to breathe.

"No, it's not overkill," she said. "I love it. And I love you."

Bruce slipped his hands around her waist and pulled her close. "I love you too, Cece. Happy anniversary."

"Happy anniversary," she agreed. And she showed him just how much she adored him by threading her fingers in his hair and giving him the kind of kiss that money couldn't buy.

Victoria Adessi didn't know where she was, but if she wasn't mistaken, this had to be a jungle paradise. A warm sun shined through the lush green leaves of the tropical foliage surrounding her and she smiled contentedly to herself as the breeze tickled her hair. She couldn't remember the last time she'd felt so relaxed. She laid back on the dewy grass and listened to the soothing sounds of birds calling and the calm murmur of running water nearby. She could lay here forever. Just lay here and forget all of her troubles. No more having to take care of a snotty, annoying brat of a kid that she hadn't asked for in the first place. No more working her life away, playing into this rat race and fighting for social status like some kind of pathetic nobody. No more entertaining mediocre men in her bed. And no more social institution of marriage or aggravating moral codes of conduct to keep her from Bruce.

'Bruce...' she thought to herself, feeling her greedy heart ache. That was all she needed to make this place truly a paradise: Bruce von Essen, in all of his glory, laying here in the grass beside her and feeding her grapes straight from the bunch while their scantily-clad jungle man-slaves fanned them off with peacock feathers. Preferably he'd be naked and they'd be surrounded by money. The plants would be made out of money. Gold bars would dangle from the trees like juicy coconuts ripe for the picking. The thought of this kept Victoria occupied until suddenly she heard footsteps and the rustling of foliage behind her. She stirred from

her comfortable spot on the ground and sat up to face the intruder, angry that they'd broken her peaceful reprieve... but as she realized who had so rudely interrupted her solitude, her irritation quickly diminished.

"Victoria, there you are... I've been looking everywhere for you," none other than Bruce himself murmured. He wasn't dressed in one of his typical suits now; he was wearing a leopard-print loincloth, the defined muscles of his torso glistening with a just-oiled sheen. His dark hair was slicked back, goatee framing a pair of lush lips. The look on his face read equal parts seductive and subtly savage, and Victoria couldn't take her eyes off of him. Desire gripped her like a clenched fist in her gut.

"What a lovely coincidence," she greeted him in a naughty purr. "I've been waiting for you to find me."

"Good," Jungle Bruce smirked. "Come with me. I have something I want to show you."

Coaxing her from her tranquil spot on the ground, he led her through tropical grasses to a beautiful waterfall surrounded by shoots of bamboo, vibrantly colored flowers, and exotic green palm fronds. The water sparkled an exquisite turquoise that took Victoria's breath away.

"Bruce... what is this place?"

"Why, Victoria... don't you know?" he said, brown eyes hot and smoldering. "This is where we're going to make love."

*Victoria felt her pulse quicken as he led her into the water. In an instant, his hands were all over her body and his lips were devouring hers. "I'll give you everything you want," he promised her as he tore her clothes off and rendered her senseless. The sound of the waterfall crashing down behind them made the experience all the more carnal, and Victoria didn't catch for a moment that she was dreaming. No, she wasn't dreaming at all. She was having hot, steamy jungle sex in front of a waterfall with her own personal Tarzan. It all felt so real and tangible. **Too** real and tangible. Their love-making session grew more and more intense. It was the best Victoria had ever had... and surely she'd had plenty in her lifetime. But then the colors started to vanish, Bruce's body went limp and lifeless, and everything began to fade in slow* *motion. She couldn't feel the breeze anymore nor hear the sounds of birds calling or the rhythmic pounding of water... instead her dream world disappeared and was suddenly filled with a dense, stifling fog.*

She was alone in the darkness now, bruised and bleeding, sitting on the floor with her knees curled to her chest. She heard footsteps coming towards her and her heart jumped up into her throat. She hid her face between her legs in terror and felt her body shake. The figure of a man, tall and imposing, stood in front of her, fists clenched. She was too afraid to scream. Then he disappeared, replaced by a harsh woman's voice. "You'll never make anything of yourself!" the terrible voice taunted her, seething with a guttural hatred. "You were born a nobody and you'll die a nobody! Maybe I'll even end it for you myself!"

Another flash, and there was Bruce again, this time in a suit and tie. Still in the darkness, his back was turned to her. He glanced over his shoulder. "I'm leaving now," he said coldly. "Who would want a nobody like you? You'll never be anything to anyone. Especially not to me."

He reached for a doorknob and Victoria cried out in a panic.

"NO!" she tried wildly to ignore the devilish images and go back to her perverse jungle fantasy a little longer. But she couldn't. In a flash, the door slammed, Bruce was gone... and she was left there all alone.

Victoria woke with a start, cold sweat beading on her brow. Her hair was a mangled mess, her tan skin was soaked with perspiration, and her silky black nightgown stuck to her in all the wrong places. *"Damn it!"* she hissed, pushing herself from the couch where she'd fallen asleep with the television still on. On the screen, talking heads were arguing politics, but Victoria couldn't have cared less about their sensationalism. A much bigger concern to her was how she'd managed to doze off here... *again.* This wasn't the first time she'd imagined being with Bruce in her dreams only to wake up sick and sweating and find that he wasn't there. She'd fantasized about having him in his office, on the conference table, in the break lounge, as his maid... if you could name it, she'd probably envisioned it. And every time, that same horrid voice would taunt her in the end and the illusions would fade away into a terrible nightmare. Her hunger for Bruce, his money, and the type of luxurious, *important* life that he was living were taking over her every thought, gnawing away at her insides, driving her to the brink of insanity. Victoria was getting more and more frustrated – and dangerous - with each day that passed.

Aggravated, she flicked off the television and pushed herself from the couch. She walked to her bedroom on wobbly legs, rubbing her shoulders with clammy hands. She shut the door and locked it behind her, not as if Nicolette would care to walk in on her anyway. That wasn't the point. She opened her dresser drawer and pulled out a small black keepsake box. The key was hidden in a box of its own; a discreet trinket box on the dresser meant for loose baubles. She slid the key into the keyhole. Turned it to the right. Her heart pounded in her throat. She opened the lid and rummaged through loose papers. Photographs, newspaper clippings. All about Bruce. She picked one up from the stack. A photo of him that she'd found in the *Gazette*, shaking hands with an investor. Dressed in a black suit, as usual. Strong, confident. Everything she wanted to be. Her lips pursed, mouth went dry.

She wanted him and the life that he lived so badly that it hurt. But her reality had never been compatible with her obsession. Bruce was not going to ravish her in a jungle. He wasn't going to ravish her on the conference table. In fact, Bruce had never given her a sideways glance. Why was he so oblivious to her worth as anything more than an employee or a colleague? Why was he so incapable of giving her a chance? It was April now; she'd been promoted in September. And despite every effort she'd made to garner his attention since, she had nothing at all to show for it. Nothing but this godforsaken box.

And it wasn't as if she hadn't tried. She'd amped up her office wardrobe. Interjected her charismatic charm and wit at managerial staff meetings and managed to make everyone else at the table squirm save for him. She'd even stayed late on days that she'd known he'd be there late too, hoping that with an empty office she'd be able to catch his attention. The woman had tried *everything*. Everything short of being outright blunt about it and grabbing the man by his suit coat and pushing him down onto his desk and ripping off his clothes. If she would have had nothing to lose by doing so, maybe she'd try it just for the hell of it. But Victoria wasn't stupid; that was a sure way to get herself fired. And then what? Forget "the plan." Well, maybe it was time for a new plan. When was a man weakest and most easily manipulated? When they were riding high with all right and perfect in the world?

No. Such was clearly not the case.

Victoria ran her thumb over Bruce's face in the photograph then hastily stashed it back in her box. A photo didn't do him justice. She slid everything else to the side and pulled out a tie instead. Something red, the color of passion and power. It was his. He'd discarded it in the trash bin under his desk, one of the nights that she'd stayed late because he'd stayed late. She'd claimed it was to "run a few numbers." Really, it was more to feel the heat of his presence in the room down the hall. Knowing he was there, untouchable but there, had kept her from running anything but scenarios, over and over in her head. Apparently the tie had begun to fray. Too many motivational speeches at board meetings wearing that one, she supposed. No matter. She'd happily dug it from his trash once he was gone and sprayed it with the cologne he kept in his desk drawer. *Uomo ricco.* Wealthy man. She sniffed the tie, inhaling deeply, and her eyes rolled back into her head.

She wanted him with that cologne on. She wanted him in a red tie. She wanted his attention. She wanted everything. But Bruce von Essen wasn't going to turn over a new leaf and magically start to notice the full extent of what she had to offer him without a little nudge. That damn wife of his was in the way, and so long as Little Miss Goody-Two-Shoes was in the picture, there was literally no hope for her. At that dismal realization, something red-hot and malicious boiled in Victoria's gut. The photograph of Cecilia in Bruce's office came to mind as it always did and her face twisted into an ugly snarl. She wanted to smash that picture frame, to throw it against the ground and stomp all over it in her pointy stilettos. She threw Bruce's tie back into her box resentfully and fished for one last thing. A clipping from the *Gazette*, from back at the end of the summer. On it was a picture of Bruce's wife, dressed in her pastel pink Alexander McQueen dress, standing in front of a collection of equally pastel paintings.

The heading read in bold black type, *"Local Artist Celebrates Decade of Gallery Ownership by Unveiling New Pieces for Fall."*

At that moment, something in Victoria snapped; the last sliver of whatever sanity she might have had left. When there was a pest in the house, there was only one thing to do. And Cecilia, in her warped mind, was just that: a pest, dirtying the perfect endgame fantasy she'd concocted in her head.

Well, not anymore. Wishful thinking would soon be a thing of the past. It was time to make her twisted dreams a reality, no matter what the cost.

CHAPTER NINE
Secrets and Schemes

THAT NIGHT HAD BEEN A TURNING POINT: the night when a closet sociopath's dirty fantasies turned from something strange and creepy but relatively harmless in theory to something unnervingly, seriously dangerous and wrong. With Victoria's insane idea to take matters into her own hands decided, the timeline set in place had been disrupted. The air was heavy with a ticking time bomb; one that might explode at any given moment.

Victoria woke the next morning with her almost too-real dream still stuck in her head and the drastic decision she'd come to overnight burning a toxic hole in her brain. Peering into the bathroom mirror, she wiped the morning crusties from her eyes and studied the modelesque face looking back at her. She didn't look any different despite the make-up wearing off her skin and her golden hair in disarray... but she sure *felt* different. It was a shame her good looks couldn't have won Bruce over on their own. It would've made things much easier. Less complicated.

She pouted bitterly at the morbid thought and slipped out of her satin nightgown, stepping carefully into the shower. As the hot water trickled down her body in haphazard little streams, her mind swirled with dark, depraved thoughts. She knew what she had to do, but *how* should she go about doing it? This wouldn't be easy and she was going to need help. So who could she trust?

Who was indebted to her or infatuated with her enough that she could manipulate them into doing her dirty work?

As Victoria scrubbed the shampoo out of her hair, a light bulb flickered on somewhere and a cruel smile crossed her lips. She knew that *he* would be willing to do anything for her. All she needed to do was snap her fingers and any job she wanted was as good as done. His past crimes were limited to burglaries, substance abuse charges, and the occasional assault or bout of vandalism. Petty stuff, really. He wasn't a professional. But he *was* a drug addict, and such pitiful people would go to any lengths to get their next fix when they were as far gone as him.

Victoria finished getting ready as quickly as she could, eager to make a phone call. As she prepared some oatmeal in the kitchen and mulled over a plan, she could hear the sound of water running in the bathroom. That little annoyance Nicolette was up.

Nicolette sighed deeply and brushed her teeth back and forth, looking in the mirror at her straight brown hair and dark blue eyes, unsure of how she felt about her appearance. When she was around the other kids who attended Maple Springs Elementary with her, she *sort* of felt like she was a decent-looking little girl. But here, at home with Victoria, she always had this depressing feeling like she wasn't good enough. Glancing towards the crack in the bathroom door and making sure her mother wasn't able to see inside, Nicolette reached into the drawer under the sink and pulled out some of Victoria's make-up. Mascara and lipstick... that would do the trick. She popped open a tube of one of her mother's rosiest shades and smeared it all over her lips. Then she brushed the mascara over her lashes, slipped on a thick black headband, ran her fingers through her bangs, and pulled on a pair of blue jeans and a long-sleeved shirt. There... done.

Her morning routine complete, she took a deep breath in preparation and walked out to the kitchen, flabbergasted to see a bowl of oatmeal sitting at her normal place at the table. A surprised grin spread across her face. Sharing breakfast with

Victoria was certainly a rare occurrence; usually she had to make herself something on her own. A cereal bar, some toast, an apple, microwave eggs. Maybe even bacon and toaster waffles if she was feeling really daring and Victoria wasn't around to scream at her for using the stove. But this was a treat. Nice deeds from Victoria were hard to come by and she hadn't had real oatmeal that wasn't the instant kind in ages. Not to mention, this was a perfect opportunity to actually *talk* to her mom for a change. Maybe now that Victoria was enjoying that nice new promotion at work, things would turn over a new leaf for them. She fidgeted with her shirtsleeves and walked towards the table apprehensively. Victoria was indifferent as she sat down beside her.

"Mmm, apple cinnamon. My favorite!" Nicolette hummed as she took a small bite. Victoria forced a fake grin and went back to eating. Nicolette noticed that she looked a little more distracted than usual this morning, like she had something weighing heavily on her mind, but she still wanted to try. She looked at her intently and attempted to break the awkward silence. "Your hair looks really pretty today, Mom," she complimented her, hoping for a smile or maybe even a thank you in return.

She didn't get either. Victoria shot her a look of distaste. She *despised* that "mom" word. It was so old and saggy. What was this little brat trying to pull with an ass-kissing comment like that? Couldn't she just eat her breakfast and keep to herself?

"Don't suck up like that, Nicolette," she scolded her. "I don't know what you're trying to get from me, but whatever it is, you can forget about it. Just eat your food and get ready for school. If you miss your bus, you're stuck here. I don't have time to drive you around like I'm some kind of damn chauffer."

Nicolette frowned, feeling hurt and let down. She looked down into her bowl, poking at her food with her spoon. If they weren't outright fighting, it was this... some kind of rude shutdown. Why did any compliment she ever tried to extend to her mother get interpreted as an attempt at trying to "get something" from her? The only thing Nicolette was ever trying to get was a little love and attention. Well, maybe she'd read too much into her mom's unusual kindness. Perhaps Victoria hadn't made her breakfast out of the goodness of her heart at all. Perhaps she'd really just cooked too much and didn't want it to go to waste. Nicolette wanted to give her the benefit of the doubt, but she couldn't shake that sad, disheartened feeling her mom so often gave her. Maybe any hope of having an amicable relationship really *was* impossible. She felt stupid for trying to be optimistic.

After another moment or two of silence, Victoria looked irritably at her daughter, just then noticing the smear of pink lipstick on her mouth and the dark eye makeup staining her lashes. "Is that my make-up? I hope you're not planning on going to school looking like that," she said curtly. "Don't touch my make-up bag, Nicolette. Those things in there are very expensive."

Nicolette didn't respond; just kept her eyes trained on the cereal in her spoon. Victoria glared at her in annoyance, taking one last bite of oatmeal before picking up her bowl and putting it in the sink. Without a backward glance, she turned her attention to her cell phone screen, dialing someone's number distractedly.

Nicolette frowned, wondering which late-night fling her mom was on the phone with today. Frankly, she didn't care. She'd had enough of Victoria's rudeness for one morning and decided to shake off her letdown mood by watching TV in the living room before leaving for school. One of her favorite cartoons was on, and that was sure to make things better... at least for the half hour that was left before she had to catch the bus.

While Nicolette was engrossed in the colorful pageantry on-screen, Victoria retreated to her bedroom and talked in a hushed voice so her daughter couldn't hear. "Can you meet me tonight? I have a very important favor to ask you. It can't wait."

"A favor?" the gruff voice on the other line asked. "Of course, Vic. What do you need?"

"I can't say," she said forebodingly.

"What? Why not? Bratty little daughter around? Does it involve tits and ass? If so, I'm in."

Victoria rolled her eyes. "I'm charmed, really. I have a paranoia about the government listening in on phone calls, okay? I can't say anything over the line. I have to see you in person. But you can't bring anyone else with you, got it?"

The man chuckled a gritty chuckle. "Shit, all this secrecy! You make it sound like you're plotting a murder or something." When Victoria didn't say anything witty or demeaning in response, he asked, "Wait... *are* you plotting a murder?"

"What did I just tell you?" she snapped at him. "Just remember, you owe me. If I wouldn't have convinced those guys at the casino to forgive your gambling debt a few years back, you'd probably be lying dead in a dumpster somewhere right now, cut up into a million little pieces. Think about that for a minute. A million. Little. Pieces. Nice visual, isn't it?"

"Ugh... you've always been so graphic, Vic. You've made your point. Fine, I'll meet you later and hear you out. I can give you that much. Where and when?"

Victoria hung up a few moments later and a wicked smile crossed her lips. Without wishing Nicolette a good day at school, she walked through the front door and left her behind. It was time for another busy day at work... and if she had things *her* way, there wouldn't be many more of these to deal with in her lifetime.

Inside, Nicolette let herself breathe at last, feeling a huge wave of relief wash over her as soon as she could no longer hear her mother's car idling in the driveway. She was glad that Victoria was gone. That meant that the bus that took her to school would be arriving soon, and she couldn't wait to climb aboard. Homework and classes had never been her favorite things, but school itself wasn't so bad. At least there, people were nice to her and acknowledged that she existed. The *boys* certainly paid attention to her, anyway. After all, Nicolette had inherited her mom's good looks, and even at a young age all the boys knew that she was a certified cutie. Of course, the most that anyone did to her was try to hold her hand, invite her to play at recess, or call her cute amidst giggles over the possibility of cooties, but it was still attention and a desire to be around her nonetheless.

Nicolette liked the attention. It made her feel, even if only for a few hours, that she was actually worth something.

While Nicolette spent her day at school trying to boost her morale, Victoria's day at Vonessen Inc. was busier than ever and by mid-morning she was positive she might crash. After far too many phone calls from aggravating people harassing her for things that they "needed," she took the opportunity to escape from her managerial duties to enjoy a hot, steaming cup of Joe at the coffee machine. Not even a promotion could break the tradition of drinking her daily java in the downstairs lounge when she was stressed. It had become too much of a habit. Sipping on the hot, brown liquid, Victoria thought quietly to herself, hoping beyond all hope that the person she'd called would come through for her. Her future hung in the balance. Her future with Bruce.

Almost as if she'd psychically summoned him with that thought, it was just then that she spotted none other than her boss walking through the break lounge door. It was times like these that she was happy she was a woman who could hide her feelings for the most part and didn't have to worry about pitching a tent in her pants, because *damn* did Bruce look immaculate today. Was that a new suit he was wearing? She suddenly felt a little less overwhelmed about the morning she'd been having. This was why it would all be worth it one day. This was why she was here.

Victoria cleared her throat, approaching him from behind.

"Good morning, Bruce," she said in her typical harmonious tone as he started to make himself a new pot of coffee. "Not a usual thing for you to come down here for your coffee, is it?" She shifted her weight to one leg, placing a hand on her hip. Most of the other men in the office would've probably raised their eyebrows at the stance and admired the way her tight brown pencil skirt and low-cut cream blouse accentuated her slinky curves. But for once, she wasn't so bothered that Bruce was wearing his blinders. She'd fix that. She'd fix all of this. For now, she just had to keep up the act.

"Morning, Victoria," he greeted her. "Maybe not, but the coffee machine upstairs decided to break just now when Jerry tried to make himself a cup. It sprayed all over him and ruined his new suit. It looks like everyone will be heading down here until the interns get back with a replacement."

Victoria shook her head, restraining a sadistic laugh. "Oh my, I can only imagine the look on Jerry's face. Poor guy." Yeah right. She absolutely *hated* Jerry, not like anyone needed to know that. "That sounds like something straight out of a bad sitcom."

Bruce chuckled. "Well, it's all true. I couldn't make it up. And it probably wouldn't have broken if he wouldn't have been wrestling with it the way that he was. Don't worry, I'm sure you'll hear all about it when you come back upstairs, and I'm sure *he'll* be the butt of a few jokes for a good week or so." He gave her a grin and tipped his cup, saying a cordial goodbye. "Have a nice day, Ms. Adessi. Page my office if you need anything."

And just like that, he was gone.

Victoria watched him leave anxiously, folding her arms over her chest. Their relationship was strictly professional for now... but she'd change that, she was sure of it. She just needed to get her man on board, exercise a little more patience, and lay low until the time was right... and then she'd have exactly what she wanted. She could see it all in her sick, twisted head. She finished her coffee downstairs, sipping at the hot liquid gingerly so as not to burn herself. Right as she was prepping to head back upstairs to her office, a much less desirable man walked into the lounge in a hideous grey houndstooth suit. The dirty look and loud sigh of annoyance he heaved upon noticing her wasn't very subtle.

"What's the stink-eye for this time, Ben?" she rolled her eyes at Ben McClafferty dismissively. Ben's jaw tightened. For months now he'd tried to keep his cool and hold his tongue, through all of this fall and the long winter that had followed. But as he took in Victoria standing there at the coffee machine in her huge high heels and inappropriately form-fitting office wear, the frustration he'd kept pent inside for far too long finally won out.

"I just don't get it, Vic," he spat at her resentfully. "You and Emmalyn were always talking up a damn storm while I worked my ass off, and somehow you still managed to snag the big promotion that everybody wanted."

Victoria glowered at him. "What's it to you?"

"Excuse me for saying it," he retorted with a very not-so-subtle hint of sarcasm. "But you didn't deserve it."

"Apparently Mr. von Essen thinks differently."

"I don't give a damn what Mr. von Essen thinks about it."

Victoria snorted in disbelief. "Jealous much?"

"Jealousy has nothing to do with it!" Ben blew up. "I work ten times as hard as you do. I bust my *ass* for this company. What is this, some kind of affirmative action bullshit? You got it because you're a woman or something? I bet if you didn't show so much skin, you'd still be slaving away at your computer in the corner just like the rest of us, not sitting all high and mighty up there in your swanky office counting all the money. Don't think you got in on talent alone… let alone at all. It's bullshit, utter *bullshit.*"

Victoria glared at Ben furiously, her jaw clenching with an unholy rage. Talk about bullshit! The *balls* this man had! There weren't many people who ever questioned her credentials and most of her co-workers and underlings thought that she was the best thing since sliced bread, but *this* little shit had been a thorn in her side since day one. He was the only person in the office who saw through her perfect act and didn't think of her as some kind of deity, and she despised him for it. Purely, utterly loathed him.

"You know what? I don't need your rotten attitude, you annoying little pipsqueak!" she snapped. "I'm above you now, whether you like it or not. Use that tone with me again, and—"

She didn't get to finish that threat.

"Vicky!" Emmalyn exclaimed, rushing between the two. "What's going on in here? Vicky, it's not worth it. Ben, what's wrong with you? You can't talk to her like that. She's your *boss.*"

Of course, Emmalyn the loyal pet, here to save the day. Ben glared at the women with venom in his eyes before turning sharply on his heel and tromping back to his desk. Emmalyn could be as blind as she wanted and believe whatever lies that she wanted, but Victoria having a change in title did *not* make her his boss. "Corporate 'equal opportunity' bullshit," they could hear him muttering under his breath as he left. "Maybe I should start wearing high heels and v-necks. Fucking unbelievable..."

"Vic, are you okay?" Emmalyn put her hand on Victoria's shoulder once he was gone. "He was really being nasty."

Victoria folded her arms across her chest and snarled at the place where Ben had just stood. "It's nothing, Em. I'm fine," she said between clenched teeth. But in reality, the scenarios she was imagining weren't very forgiving. God, did she hate Ben. One day she'd make him sorry that he'd ever shot his mouth off at her.

No one messed with Victoria Adessi.

Later that night, Victoria sat in a secluded corner of a dim, seedy bar in one of the bad neighborhoods of Stirling City, peering across a cramped wooden table at a man whose soul was almost as dark as hers. Wispy, curling tendrils of smoke filled the air with heavy fumes; fumes that mingled pungently with the nauseating reek of beer and urine. This was the part of the city that they didn't put on the postcards or mention in the travel brochures. The part most residents didn't go to or speak of and by default pretended didn't exist. Under normal circumstances, Victoria wouldn't be caught dead mingling in a smelly, low-class shithole like this, but the man she was talking to wasn't exactly a saint. He was gruff, mean, and rotten to the core, yet despite his tiny Grinch-like heart, even *he* was having trouble wrapping his mind around what she'd just laid out on the table in front of him. He'd expected something over-the-top when she'd called him out of the blue, but this was ambitious, even for Victoria.

"Damn, *that* was your big plan?" the gritty man asked, not sure whether to think that she had gigantic balls or was just bat-shit crazy. "I'd do anything for you, baby, you know that. But these people are *legit*. I mean shit... this ain't just some random shmuck on the street you're asking me to-"

"You owe me," she reminded him sternly, glaring at him beneath the rim of a brown fedora. "I told you to remember that."

The man grimaced, dark eyes narrowing. He looked a bit ticked off by the fact, but it was true. If it weren't, she would've been a blast from the past he would've happily kept there. "Damn it, I know that. But these people aren't exactly nothing. And even if I help you, that doesn't mean you're gonna get what you want."

Victoria had to lean in close to hear him over the sounds of pool balls clinking against each other and the noise of someone being nailed in one of the bathroom stalls behind a nearby door. She clutched her leather jacket tighter around her body, her face hidden behind a pair of knockoff sunglasses. "I *will* get what I want," she assured him forebodingly. "There's no question about that. But I need her out of the way to get it. I can't go traditional on this one, I don't have a choice." There was a small pause to let it sink in before she took the liberty of continuing, "The outcome on my end shouldn't matter to you anyway. The important thing as far as this concerns you is that I'll make it worth your while."

"I would hope so. I don't work for free, you know."

"Of course not. I wouldn't expect you to."

"So what, then? You got drugs? Meth, heroin, something? I would do anything for some of that shit right now..."

"I don't have any drugs and you know it," Victoria said sharply. "You know I don't touch that stuff anymore. But with what I can give you, you'll be able to get as much of *that shit* as you want. *Unlimited* shit. So much shit it'll make your head spin. But you and I both know there's something you want more than that. No more debts. No more looking over your shoulder. Well I can do that. I'll make sure that you're set up. As soon as I have the cash locked down I'll pay you handsomely and you'll be able to live comfortably. Even move out of the country if you want to."

"As soon as I have the cash?" the man repeated, pursing his lips. "Where exactly do you plan on getting it?"

"Don't think that I won't have it, because I will. Maybe it won't be able to come all at once, but I can do increments."

"You still didn't say where this money is coming from."

"I work for Vonessen, Inc."

"And?"

"And I'm a *very* good accountant. Trust me. No one will even know that it's gone. Like I said, it might have to be spread out a little bit so it's not caught, but you *will* get it. And I'll pay you ten grand just for agreeing. Think of it as a security deposit."

The man's eyes widened in shock. *"Ten G's* right off the bat? Jesus H. Christ... how can you do that?"

"I just can," Victoria said. She left it at that, but it was clear that this crazy broad wasn't messing around. That amount of money up front as a deposit of good faith was no joke.

And now, she had his attention.

"Alright, Vic," he rested forward on his elbows, brow furrowed and eye contact never wavering. "I'm listening. So, how much we talkin' total here?" She leaned over the table and brought herself close enough to let her nose graze his neck. She whispered an amount against his earlobe that made his toes curl. "Fuck," he breathed. "Fuck me rotten..."

She settled back into her seat and smirked at him smugly. "Oh yeah... fuck you rotten indeed. Think of how nice it'll be to move away. To get away from all your *friends* here in the city and go somewhere nice and sunny where you can shoot yourself up with some of that good shit without a care in the world. No debt, no name, no baggage. This is a business transaction I'm proposing, nothing more, nothing less. We both would benefit from this. You *need* that money. And *I* need a favor. A favor for a favor."

"Fucking hell..." the man dipped his chin down, taking a huge swig of beer and relishing in the tempting mental picture of himself wearing a tropical shirt somewhere off the radar in Latin America, palm trees all around him with a scotch in one hand, a heroin needle in the other, and a line of cocaine on the table. He'd been in serious debt with some bad people for a long time. Considering such, it was a much better vision than the one that entered his head when he imagined not getting out of it. But still...

"This isn't going to be easy," he frowned, clunking his glass back down on the table. "Not to mention the risk..."

"As if a dangerous man like you would be concerned with a little risk?" Victoria put a sultry edge to her voice.

The change in tone made her company squirm with lust. His eyes darkened. "Maybe I'd feel more comfortable being your crony if you upped the ante," he said with a sinister growl.

Victoria chuckled darkly as she slid her hand up the length of his thigh beneath the table. Her palm inched dangerously close to the crotch of his pants.

"Upped the ante?" she repeated with an amused sneer playing on her lips. "There's no need to barter, tough guy. You already know you'll be compensated with more than just the money. For old time's sake, right?"

The man felt a jolt of carnal hunger course through him as she gave him her most suggestive glance. He swallowed hard. She could make a very convincing argument. Most sociopaths could.

"You better not be fucking with me," his lips edged down into a grim frown. "I don't take kindly to people fucking with me. Not even you, Vic. You'd do well to remember that."

Victoria smirked again. *Please.* She wasn't scared of him. As far as she was concerned, *she* was the one holding the cards.

"I'll let you think about it," she said, getting up from the table and reaching into her pocket. She pulled something out and put it in the man's hand before sauntering away. He grimaced at her perfect ass until the front door closed behind her with a solid thud. He opened his palm to see two folded green bills. When he unraveled them, Ben Franklin's face stared up to greet him.

CHAPTER TEN

Art Lessons

CREATING ART HAD ALWAYS BEEN Cecilia's forte, but if she had known that teaching it could be so rewarding, she probably would have started doing it much earlier. It was a Thursday night in Stirling City, and that meant The Bird and Blossom was open much later than usual - now, packed not with prospective buyers looking to purchase something special for their homes and businesses, but students hoping to create some art of their own. The future Van Goghs in-training who occupied the large neutrally-colored room that Cecilia had set aside in her studio for classes were people of all ages, and today there were nine of them.

A duo of teenage girls dressed in urban street fashion stood at two easels, front and center, slathering their brushes with red and black paint. An elderly couple convinced that no age was too old to learn something new together critiqued one another's work in hushed whispers in the back. Cecilia's good friends, Gina and Carmella, stood next to another woman from the country club dressed in a Missoni sweater dress, gushing over Carmella's latest acrylic victory. One quiet young hipster guy who always wore tight jeans, Converse sneakers, and a gray beanie hat stood transfixed in concentration with an art palette balanced against his hip. And one man, who Cecilia knew as a Vonessen Inc. employee named David, worked quietly in the corner, only looking up once in a while to shoot her an appreciative smile when she walked behind him to comment on his work.

David was an interesting one. Everyone here had a reason for attending Cecilia's art lessons - some for fun, others to learn, and some to heal wounds. And for dark-haired David, who was always enthusiastic and eager to learn, painting was something that he claimed helped him work through his stress - fortunately, not stress caused by his job at her husband's firm, but rather personal stress that was more rooted in his strained relationship with his wife.

Cecilia never pried too far into her students' stories unless they chose to tell them, but she was glad when she knew that she was able to help someone find time to relax. She knew how important that was. And she was also glad that Bruce apparently promoted her teaching venture during office hours, because she was sure that a Vonessen Inc. employee more than likely had to have heard it from him. Just the idea of him going on at the table in the board room in that vivid, childlike voice he always got when he was really interested in something sent a current of warmth flowing through her heart.

And heart was something she really hoped she was able to bring to her lessons. They always had a theme. Form, composition, texture, lines, color theory. But for the past few weeks, her students had been working on a lengthier project than usual. Cecilia had tasked them to bring in one of their favorite photos and recreate it - either as it was, or by putting a fun, stylistic twist on it - to create a very personal and meaningful piece of art. Today, many of those students had finished theirs. Seeing the accomplished smiles on their faces made for a much better end to the day than what Cecilia had expected. She'd had to do something rather unpleasant earlier: ground Angelina.

Cecilia didn't have to ground Angelina very often and the groundings never lasted long nor were ever too serious, but even still, Angelina had never taken kindly to them. The words "you're grounded" were usually met with a lot of crying and complaining about how unfair her life was. But what Angelina had done was pretty unfair herself. She'd thought it would be funny to goof off in her chorus rehearsal after school. She'd been showing off a slew of her many musical impressions of singers to some of the other girls before practice commenced, trying to make them laugh. She of course, did her Mariah Carey. She did her Pavarotti, always a favorite. She even did a Britney Spears, followed by a quick Adam Levine and a ridiculous Elvis. But that wasn't what she was in trouble for. She was in trouble for belting out a loud Christina Aguilera right in Jenny Wexler's ear.

"Stop it, Angelina!" Jenny had screamed, stomping her foot and disrupting everyone.

Angelina's argument was that Jenny had deserved it. That she heard her gossiping to another of their classmates about how it was good that Aiden Andrews was good at football, because "when your family is as poor as his, you've got to have something going for you."

That was definitely a mean comment, Cecilia had agreed. But it didn't mean Angelina should disrupt the whole class.

"Be the bigger woman," Cecilia had advised her. "And tonight, no television."

Angelina had argued and whined and cried even though there was nothing on television that she'd wanted to watch anyway, but Cecilia was used to her occasional diva tantrums. Come tomorrow, they'd all be fine.

As for tonight, Cecilia was just glad that she'd managed to live up to the expectations of her students. She smiled in satisfaction at the head of the room as she watched them pack their supplies away and prepare to leave. When she'd been younger, still coping with the aftermath of her knee injury and using art as a way to ease the depression that losing ballet had saddled her with, she'd never thought that her art would be worthy of being shared, let alone that she'd be at the level of "scholar." Thank goodness Bruce had forced her to rethink that. She'd met his insistence to open a gallery with resistance more than ten years ago when he'd suggested she do it, but now The Bird and Blossom was her pride and joy.

The teenage girls in the urban wear were the first to go. "Thanks, Cecilia!" they said in unison, waving at her and giggling all the way out the door with their finished paintings.

"See you next Thursday, girls!" she called after them.

The hipster and the elderly couple left next and Cecilia felt a warm prickle in her heart when she saw the usually quiet hipster hold the door open for the older folks and wish them goodnight. The country club woman in Missoni followed, then Carmella and Gina were next.

"Great lesson, Ceci!" Gina said, leaning in to wrap her friend up into a sisterly hug. "We're so glad you started doing this. Every week gets better and better!"

"Speaking of which, we have a request for next week's lesson, actually," Carmella added. The look on her face was a lot more sneaky than serious and based upon her experience at home with Angelina, Cecilia had a feeling that she was up to no good.

"Uh oh... what's that?" she smirked knowingly.

"Nude models!" Carmella clapped. "Male ones, obviously."

Cecilia laughed her melodic laugh and took a playful swat at her. "Carmella!"

"What? Come on, girl! We just talked referencing, and it'll be an anatomy study! How can we paint a convincing full-body portrait without a proper example? You might have to cover it with Bruce first, but I'm sure we'll get your hubby to agree. For the sake of art! What if my hubby threw in tickets to a gala?"

"There are a few hunky lifeguard boys at the country club I think would make pretty good candidates," Gina agreed.

"No!" Cecilia scolded them. "We're not having naked men in here."

"Please?" Carmella batted her eyes.

"Not a chance. *Goodnight,* ladies. We'll make plans soon."

The ladies could agree to that. The three friends hugged a final goodbye, then Carmella and Gina were on their way.

"Thanks, Cecilia," David said at last, adjusting the buttons on his dark wool peacoat in the empty room before picking up his canvas and approaching her near the door. "Another wonderful lesson. You should have started doing this sooner."

Cecilia smiled, brushing her chestnut hair behind her ear. "Thank you. I'm glad you're finding it interesting." She motioned at the canvas under his arm. "So, can I see the finished product?"

David chuckled and turned it over. "It's not a Rembrandt or anything, but I tried." His painting was of a small, white, fuzzy dog, done in a cartoony style against a yellow background. "Obviously, the background of the real photo wasn't yellow, it was taken in the yard. But I've never been a fan of green and I thought I'd take those stylistic liberties you were talking about."

Cecilia laughed. "Who's the model?"

"Our dog, Mitzy. Rebecca named him that, not me."

"And the photograph?"

He slipped a folded photo out of his coat pocket.

"A stunning likeness. You did a wonderful job."

"Not as wonderful as the job you did," David motioned towards the canvas behind Cecilia's back that she had used as her example prior to the beginning of their project a few weeks ago. "I'm not sure any of us could live up to work like that."

The painting Cecilia had done was one she hadn't showed her family, not yet. It was a portrait of Angelina and Blair at seven years old, posing together in their favorite black formal dresses.

They weren't hugging exactly, but they were leaning in towards eachother, looking at the camera with sweet smiles on their faces, their hands holding each other's arms and their foreheads almost touching. They'd taken the photo that Cecilia had referenced it from after one of their rare dual-recitals. Angelina had sung "Pie Jesu," and Blair had accompanied her on the piano. It was one of her favorite photographs of her daughters together.

"That Blair, she looks just like you," David observed.

"And Angelina looks just like her father," Cecilia agreed.

"Funny how that non-identical twin thing works out, isn't it? Maybe one day Rebecca and I will have them. Kids in general, I mean. Not necessarily twins."

Cecilia smiled. "Well, if you do, I'm sure Mitzy's new portrait would be a great addition to the nursery."

"Or it would give the poor kid nightmares."

Cecilia laughed softly. They barely noticed that the front door had opened until they heard it shut again. A man, dressed in a dark leather jacket and a motorcycle hat with dark stubble on his face and dark circles under his eyes stood in the entryway, shifting his weight as he looked around the room. He looked uncertain and shifty and a little bit strung out. Call it intuition, but there was something off about him. The smile that had been on David's face moments earlier diminished as he cleared his throat.

"I think I left some stuff in the back," he said, walking back to the easel he had been painting at. He watched carefully out of the corners of his eyes as Cecilia greeted the visitor.

"I'm sorry... class is finished for the evening and The Bird and Blossom is actually closed now. Can I help you, sir?"

The man broke his gaze from the painting of her daughters on the easel behind her and shoved his hands into his jean pockets. "Are you Cecilia von Essen?" he asked in a gritty voice.

"Yes," she nodded. "I am."

"Ah, good. I've uh... heard about your classes, Mrs. von Essen. And I was wanting to know what they were all about."

Ah... so, a prospective student. Cecilia offered him a kind, welcoming smile. "Well... we hold them here every Thursday night and we try to learn a variety of different mediums. So far we've done acrylics, oils, and mixed media, and we'll be moving on to watercolors soon. You're welcome to sit in on a class and observe before you decide to join, if you'd like. As a general rule, there are no rules. I provide most of the equipment for classes, but you're certainly welcome to bring your own. If you're interested, you can learn more about pricing if you visit my website."

"That sounds great. I'm definitely interested. Not to say too much, but I'm... ah... a recovering drug addict. And I... well, I don't know, I guess I just kind of want to try something new. You know, try and get a new hobby. Try and get my shit together."

Recovering wasn't exactly the right word, but there was no way she could have known it was a lie. Cecilia skirted past him to a secretary desk near the door. It was covered in art supplies and random knick-knacks. She plucked one of her business cards from the card holder on the ledge, near a brocade-patterned pencil cup.

"Let me take your name down," she offered helpfully. "I should have a slot opening up." She scribbled her name and information on the back of it and slid it into his hand. "I'm so glad to hear you're recovering and would love to help. Thank you for stopping in. We hope to hear from you again. Have a good night."

Shooting her a grim smile before he left, the man let himself out the door and disappeared down the dark city streets. David sidled up beside Cecilia and peered out of the window pane in the door, watching him leave. He was quiet and his jaw was tighter than it had been before. Cecilia's brow creased.

"David? Is something wrong?"

David sighed and blinked his eyes away from the dark street outside and glanced back at Cecilia. He offered her a small smile, but it felt off.

"David..."

"Sorry. He just seemed a little strange. That's all."

Cecilia tilted her chin up. "Ah... maybe a little. But I'd think that would be expected from a recovering drug addict, wouldn't you?" She slipped her arms into her Burberry coat and buttoned the front buttons one at a time before hitching her satchel over her shoulder. "Did you know that art therapy is actually a commonly used therapy in addiction treatment? It allows the person to use his creativity and imagination to make art that expresses himself and the thoughts and feelings that he may not be able to say with words in a healthy and productive way. It's especially helpful for people with underlying psychological issues. It's meant to provide ways for them to understand and cope with their addiction."

"You're very astute, Cecilia," David raised his eyebrows.

"Well, it's only common sense," she shrugged. "I can't say I know much personally about addiction, but as far as coping goes, I know that art has certainly helped me."

David glanced down at her left leg. It was barely visible beneath the skirt of her flowy maroon dress, but he knew that there was a scar on her knee. He'd seen it, before in class.

"A fair point," he said.

"And it helps you, too, does it not?" she added.

He thumbed the wedding band on his left ring finger. It was still there and so was Rebecca, so he supposed he'd consider that a "yes." Cecilia had helped so many people in their class since she'd started it, whether she knew it or not. David knew people in their class who were fighting depression, stuck in creative ruts, or simply looking for a new hobby and wanting to reinvent themselves. There was certainly a real, palpable value to the "therapeutic" powers of what she taught and had to offer. In actuality, she was a work of art herself. Sophisticated, beautiful, graceful, and demure. A talented artist. A loving mother. And from what he could infer, a wonderful wife. Bruce von Essen was lucky. The CEO had managed to procure a lot for himself with his business acumen and his money, but anyone could see what his most valuable possession was. David respected Cecilia and so did everyone else.

How could anyone not respect perfection?

"I suppose I can't argue you there," he admitted.

"Who knows?" Cecilia smiled. "Maybe he'll turn out to be the best in the class."

"Anything is possible," David chuckled, smiling back at her fondly. "Anyway, we'd better get you home. I'm sure that Bruce and the girls are missing you, and frankly, I think your husband's going to kill me if I don't get my reports done tonight. Where are you parked?"

"The garage on Astor."

"Mind if I walk you to your car?"

Cecilia nodded gratefully. "I'd appreciate that. Thank you."

David motioned for her to lead the way and waited as she turned the key in the front door. As the two of them made their way towards the garage on Astor, a pair of dark eyes watched them from around the corner, following the sound of Cecilia's clacking heels against the pavement until they'd been drowned out by the hum of the dark city streets. The man that they belonged to clutched her business card against his chest, then slid it into his wallet in front of a check still waiting to be cashed.

A check for ten thousand dollars, from Victoria Adessi.

There's a well-known idiom that people like to use to describe the quiet, peaceful period that comes right before one of great trouble and difficulty. At first, everything seems fine and dandy. The birds are chirping, the sun is rising, the air is still, and the famous introduction of Rossini's "William Tell Overture" is playing. Then, suddenly, the birds stop singing and retreat to their nests. The air changes, eerie with an ill-omened wind that rustles through the branches. The temperature drops. A line of dark clouds appears on the horizon. One fat raindrop pelts the ground, then another. And then, it's falling in cascades, lightning lashing through the clouds and thunder cracking.

It's the calm before the storm. And as cliché and overused as it might have been, that was exactly the perfect way to describe what the past few months had been in Stirling City. Fall and winter had passed that year with little altercation, but once spring had arrived, the winds of change had begun to pick up and a tempest was brewing courtesy of Victoria Adessi. The smitten accountant had come to one unsettlingly morbid conclusion: outright "seducing" her boss was a long shot, even for her; even with attractiveness, cunning, and charisma on her side. A successful attempt was feeble when he was so frustratingly unavailable to her, and if she were to try it anyway and prove unsuccessful? Well, that would be a deal-breaker.

She would be fired. She would fail. She would never have a chance to make his fortune her own and the dream would be over. Victoria would lose the game, and she couldn't have that.

In her warped vision of the future, the only way that she could see herself having any real luck with the businessman was if his current wife was taken out of the picture. Maybe the woman could have a tragic "accident." Victoria herself would never be implicated because she'd never have made an advance, and there would be no one to implicate anyway because that was typically what an "accident" meant. In the wake of said "accident," Victoria would finally use her new position of power within Vonessen Inc.

to her advantage. With her new status as a fixture in his office solidified, she could be there for Bruce when he needed it most.

And then, like a moth to a flame, he'd be drawn to her.

It was horrible. Repulsive. But that was the despicable plan she'd so nefariously concocted. The reality that she didn't want to come to grips with was that she had *no* reason whatsoever to believe that any of the outcomes she desired could be even remotely justified or plausible. It was a reality her prospective hitman had reminded her of himself, but Victoria wasn't paying him to be reasonable, and as desperate as he was, as strung-out, indebted, and morally compromised, he agreed to get on board with her outlandish schemes in hopes that the cash she promised him in return would pull him out of his miserable stupor.

In the meantime, Victoria did her best to keep her end of the deal while he worked on keeping his. As part of their agreement, she reserved herself to give him time to handle the dirty legwork of creating an "accident" at his own discretion, but hiding her "miscellaneous transactions" in Vonessen Inc.'s accounting books was proving a daunting task for her nonetheless. If it was any comfort, then at least she was good at it and had something else to take her mind off of her rotten schemes when she wasn't writing dirty checks: in particular, this year's Annual Vonessen Inc. Spring Employee Appreciation Banquet.

The Banquet was a pretty big deal for the people who worked in Victoria's office. Every spring, Bruce threw the party as his own special way of showing his appreciation for all of the hard work that his employees did to keep the business afloat. It was a very looked-forward-to event and everyone who attended it always had a great time; maybe none more so than Bruce himself.

Always a gracious host, Bruce loved organizing the get-together. For years, he'd maintained it was the least he could do to treat his employees to the finer things - exotic wines, decadent desserts, cheeses from all over the world, a first-class meal, and live music - and they would dance, drink, and be merry far into the night. Every year he and Cecilia would give out generous vacation vouchers and present awards - usually in the form of big bonuses - to those who stuck out and went the extra mile. For Vonessen Inc. employees, it was practically an early Christmas, and for Bruce it was the perfect opportunity to play Fezziwig.

Emmalyn was particularly excited about the banquet this year. As a new employee, it would be her very first one, and now that she was getting more used to being the baby in the office, she was practically treating it like she was going back to her high school prom.

"I'm so glad I caught you down here! You're up in your office so much that I barely get to see you anymore," she said one morning as Victoria poured herself her traditional cup of coffee.

"Yes, well, this new position has me quite busy," Victoria admitted, looking tired for more reasons than just the job.

"I'm sure the pay is worth it though," Emmalyn tried to lighten the mood. "At least we know Bruce appreciates what you do. He always speaks so highly of you. And speaking of which, the banquet is coming up soon. Are you excited? I can't wait!"

"Oh, the banquet..." Victoria frowned. "I almost forgot."

She sighed heavily and took a seat at the break room table, Emmalyn following suit. For once, it wasn't a lie. She'd been so preoccupied lately that it hadn't even crossed her mind.

"How could you forget? You need to get on that!" Emmalyn exclaimed. "I already have my dress picked out."

Victoria took a long sip of her drink. "The banquet's still a month away. You really have your dress picked out already?"

"Absolutely!" Emmalyn answered in disbelief, shocked that there was anyone else who didn't. "I can't wait for you to see it. It took me forever to find one. What kind of food do you think they'll have at this thing anyway? I bet it's all really fancy..."

"Fancy? Oh yes, it's very fancy," Victoria gave her a forced smile. She humored her friend and let her carry on, but what Emmalyn didn't know was that her priorities had been in much more serious matters than prepping for fancy parties as of late.

She'd been working on getting money to her contact... and if Victoria had things her way, this year's banquet would be the current Mrs. von Essen's last.

CHAPTER ELEVEN

The Unthinkable

THE WARM MAY EVENING OF the much-anticipated Vonessen Inc. Spring Employee Appreciation Banquet had finally arrived. Inside the crowded banquet hall, the mood contrasted with the festering darkness in Victoria's heart as sharply as black and white. Every table was lined with a silken tablecloth and the room was lit by the soft glow of candles and the elaborate crystal chandeliers that hung overhead. Smooth, snazzy jazz music was being performed by a live ensemble at the head of the dance floor and an extravagant catered buffet of the most delicious pre-dinner appetizers was set out for the guests to enjoy. There were cocktail shrimp, creamy dips, numerous types of expensive caviar, crackers with mustards, sausages and cheeses from around the world, and platters of smoked fish. On the dessert table, fluffy mousses, decadent petit fours, fancy cookies, fruity tarts, chocolates, truffles, and spiced gelatins and puddings tempted the attendees to indulge and have something sweet. It was enough to feed a small country, and even before the big boss arrived, the place was already coming alive. Bruce's employees were dressed in their very best formal wear, clinking glasses of the finest, most posh wines that money could buy and looking through bags of favors stuffed with items like personalized engraved silver pens for the office, decadent Swiss chocolates, and French-milled soaps.

Bruce von Essen certainly knew how to throw a party, and this night was promising to be a memorable one for everyone.

Victoria and Emmalyn were among the pampered attendees, chatting at a quiet table near the buffet. Victoria was wearing a slinky crimson dress with her hair pulled back in a sassy up-do while Emmalyn was finally getting to wear the classy strapless black and white number she'd picked out weeks ago. Emmalyn had thought that she'd done a good job in getting herself dolled up for the night, but she sighed as she peered at Victoria sitting across from her. She wished that she could exude the same sexiness that her co-worker did. Even in lace, satin, and a tall pair of pumps she wasn't sure that she could outdo Vic. Really, who could? Victoria could make a paper bag look good.

Emmalyn took a sip of wine, feeling her stomach grumble, and looked around the room at her co-workers. *Everyone* was here, but there was one person in particular who was missing.

Ben McClafferty.

Come to think of it, something fishy had been going on with Ben lately. He'd been snippy and angry and rumors had been flying around about things like "sexism" and "harassment in the workplace." They were all unfounded of course, so when he'd first disappeared from his desk, Emmalyn had thought that maybe he'd finally gotten the seat change that he'd wanted so badly or perhaps moved to a branch office or another department... but now she wasn't so sure. Unhappy about missing out on the big promotion or not, Ben wouldn't have missed this party for the world. Emmalyn recalled the fights he'd always tried to start with Victoria before and couldn't help but wonder.

"No Ben here tonight, I notice," she fished, trying to see if Victoria knew something that she didn't.

Victoria snickered covertly as she downed a bit of her champagne. "As it should be," she commented with a noticeable hint of distaste in her voice.

Ah... so Victoria *did* know something.

"Do you know where he went?" Emmalyn pried, adjusting her glasses interestedly. "Is he at another campus now?"

"Oh, you didn't hear? He's not with the company anymore. Just be happy because the floors of Vonessen Inc. will never be tainted by his dirty footprints ever again."

"You got him *fired?*"

Victoria almost choked on her drink and laughed a sardonic laugh at the naive look of shock and incredulity on Emmalyn's freckled face.

"Goodness, Em! Did I say I got him fired?" she gave her a dismissive wave. "Please, I'm flattered, but I did no such thing. He got *himself* fired with his bad attitude. Vonessen Inc. has a zero-tolerance harassment policy. Other employees took it upon themselves to report his constant outbursts and when I was asked to weigh in as his direct supervisor, I simply agreed that he had a rotten attitude. It may have tipped the iceberg, but I didn't start it and I only spoke the truth. Like I said, he's gone and I'm glad."

She left out the part about how these *other* employees might have only stepped up to bat against Ben thanks to her shedding a few well-placed crocodile tears and giving them a sad sob story whilst dabbing at her eyes with a tissue all a-fluster, and left it where it was. A little manipulation could go a long way.

"Wow... talk about exercising that power of yours," Emmalyn frowned. She took a drink of her own, pausing to think that the company outright firing Ben might have been a little on the excessive side. "Do you think he really deserved it though?" she asked tentatively, wondering if some sort of warning or other disciplinary action might have been more appropriate first.

"Of *course* he did. He was disrespectful. He always has been, especially to the women in the office. And it's completely unrelated, but I can say without question that he's been particularly rude to *me* ever since... well, ever since I let him know that his performance was a little... *unsatisfactory* in certain... *areas."*

Emmalyn stared at her friend, bug-eyed. She didn't need to ask what area that emphasis meant. "Shit, Vic! You and *Ben?"*

"Look, I think it's just as repulsing as you do, but I wasn't going to pretend there was something there when there wasn't," Victoria said in her own defense. "It didn't work out. He wanted it, I didn't, case closed. Besides, it was two years ago, nothing recent. Certainly explains his jealousy since. Anyway, you saw how he was. I've heard plenty of people in the office complain about him. He's a bigoted, sexist, narrow-minded pig and we're all better off without him and his bad temper around." She let out a heavy sigh, glad to get her true feelings off her chest for once.

"Maybe you're right. He *was* kind of rude," Emmalyn admitted, feeling her stomach gurgle loudly as an afterthought. "Oh my God!" she hissed. "Did you hear that?"

"What? Hear what?" Victoria asked, still gloating over Ben getting canned. Like she'd always said, *no one* messed with her.

"My stomach! It sounded like a bomb went off in there," Emmalyn grimaced. She turned around in her seat to eye up the buffet tables, laden with delicious foods that she was just dying to try. Her mouth started to water. "I'm *so* hungry right now. I think I need to grab some grub. Do you want anything to eat, hun?"

"No thanks," Victoria declined. "Dinner is starting soon." She looked at Emmalyn in an almost scolding manner, the same way she looked at Nicolette when her daughter started reaching for second helpings. "You know you'll be getting plenty to eat in a few minutes. Why don't you just wait?"

Emmalyn looked at the buffet tables again.

"No," she replied bluntly. "I'm starving."

As the redhead got up to get a pre-dinner snack to hold her over, Victoria stayed in her seat and pretended to be very interested in her wine glass. Right on cue, Bruce and Cecilia walked in, just as she stole a glance towards the banquet hall's front door. *'Holy shit…'* she mouthed to herself, trying to curb the all-too-familiar desire churning in her gut with little success. Bruce looked amazing in his expensive Bottega Veneta tuxedo: all intimidating, powerful, and undeniably James Bond-esque. She could only imagine what he looked like underneath it.

So much for dirty musings, though. Victoria frowned as he bent down to kiss his wife's hand after a hostess took her coat for her and frowned even harder when Cecilia laughed and fanned herself off at his blatant cheesiness. *'Ugh!'* Victoria thought, shifting her gaze to her boss's wife. Cecilia's hair was pinned half-back in gorgeously romantic chestnut curls and she was wearing an elegant blush-peach evening dress with an open-backed bodice decorated with sparkling beaded embellishments. Admittedly, something very beautiful. Red-hot envy seeped through Victoria's veins like a deadly toxin and she secretly wondered to herself if her accomplice had a plan set in place yet. If he didn't act soon, she was going to have to start getting on his case. Maybe even threaten him. She couldn't keep routing him money and writing herself checks for nothing, after all. She wasn't a damn charity.

She groused at the thought, but wiped the *I just smelled something nasty* look from her face as soon as Emmalyn returned to their table with a plate of something red and jiggly in her hand.

"*Gelatin?*" Victoria crinkled her nose in disbelief. "You whine about how hungry you are and then you come back to this table with gelatin?"

"Well you basically told me not to be fat, so I don't see why you're complaining," Emmalyn shrugged. "Anyway, this isn't just *any* gelatin, Vicky. This is *fancy* gelatin. I've never tasted such immaculate gelatin in my life. I mean, look at it… there's real fig in it! Try some!" She held her fork out to her co-worker and the gelatin wiggled a little as if to say *yes, eat me!*

"Please, Em, I couldn't," Victoria blanched, holding her hand up at the wobbly globule. Emmalyn shrugged again, popping it into her mouth. Victoria would have loved to chastise her further, but she didn't get the chance. The noise in the banquet hall suddenly died down and everyone turned towards the front of the room. The women followed suit and saw Bruce standing up at the head of a long table, clinking a spoon against his glass and looking as though he was about to say something profound.

"Welcome everyone, to the Annual Vonessen Inc. Spring Employee Appreciation Banquet," he greeted the attendees in a purposeful candor. "Thank you all for coming tonight. Tonight is a night of celebration to honor all that we've accomplished this year. Our numbers are better than ever before, we've added new campuses, and we've attracted prime clients. Vonessen Inc. is flourishing, and it's all because of you. Before we begin dinner, I want to extend my very heartfelt thanks to those who have made our celebration possible. Firstly, to our incredible catering company, which has a wonderful dinner menu planned for us... our very talented band... and of course, Celebrations Banquet Hall for providing us once again with this beautiful venue."

Bruce's preliminary "thank you's" and flowery speech went on for quite some time, culminating as he turned to the stunning woman beside him and gave her hand a loving squeeze.

"And lastly, I couldn't end my remarks tonight without thanking my beautiful wife, Cecilia Anne. She is just as passionate about this business as she is about her art, and I can't begin to tell you all how much of an inspiration she is to me every day. Her unwavering strength and support keep me focused on what really matters and our two lovely daughters at home bring me the greatest joy a man could ask for." He lifted her hand to his lips, giving it a tender kiss that elicited a few *aww*'s from the audience.

"And finally, thank all of *you*." He took a hold of the wine glass sitting on the table next to him and raised it in front of him. "Without your hard work and the long hours you dedicate to what you do every day, this company would be nothing. Thank you all for your loyalty, your drive, and for everything that you've done to make Vonessen Inc. an enormous success. I could not be more proud of this company or more honored to have each and every one of you as a part of our family. This is a toast to all of you, and to our continued future success. Cheers!"

Everyone clinked their glasses together and cheered enthusiastically as Bruce finished his feel-good speech. The caterers started to scramble and the band's playing filled the room once more as chatter rose up amongst the excited attendees.

"Nice opening, Bruce," Cecilia smiled at him, a warm mixture of love and pride glinting in her pretty blue eyes.

"My beautiful wife..." he mused affectionately. "You look like an angel tonight. You really *are* an inspiration."

He kissed her delicate hand again and Victoria glowered behind her champagne glass. She couldn't hear them, but she could sure as hell see them, and Bruce and Cecilia were enough to make her sick. *'They may as well enjoy it while it lasts...'* she thought to herself darkly. *'Because soon it'll be **my** turn..."*

"Vicky? Vicky are you paying attention to me?" Emmalyn snapped her fingers in her face, bringing her back to her senses. "What is up with you lately? You seem so distracted."

"Oh, Em... I'm sorry. It's just Nicolette," Victoria lied, masking the true reason for her lack of focus. "She's sick with the flu at home and I'm worried about her. She has a temperature of nearly a hundred degrees. Can you believe it?"

"Oh!" Emmalyn's brow creased in sympathy. "Poor little thing. She must be miserable..."

"Yes, well," Victoria shrugged it off. "It's probably just a one-day bug. I'm sure it's not worth worrying so much over. The babysitter would've called by now if she thought otherwise. I don't want to think about it. Let's just talk about something else."

Emmalyn could agree to that. She dropped the third degree and continued to chat with Victoria about lesser evils until dinner arrived. It all looked absolutely delicious: succulent Wagyu beef steaks, potatoes dashed with rosemary, parmesan asparagus, and steamed mussels. It really *was* fancy and Emmalyn didn't hesitate to dig in. She didn't even care if Victoria raised an eyebrow over it. Fortunately, Victoria was too distracted to care about her gorging herself. She tried to be discreet, but she caught her eyes straying more than once to the long table at the head of the room where Bruce and Cecilia were sitting with the highest-up executives and the advisory board. Cecilia took a bite of her steak and sipped her wine, laughing cheerfully with her husband while a caterer refilled their glasses. The von Essens looked positively jubilant, like they were still trapped in their honeymoon stage. The love looked good on Bruce. Then again, he always looked good. Like he'd stepped straight out of the pages of *GQ*.

Victoria was convinced: he had to be God's gift to women. Wealthy, smart, and accomplished. Built and handsome with that perfectly groomed beard and debonair smile. The smooth dark hair, the rich brown eyes. The strong voice and confident gait. The power to drop a thousand dollars on a whim and have it leave as much effect on his wallet as a common peasant dropping a few measly pennies. Who *wouldn't* be obsessed with him? Was it really her fault that she lusted over him and the lifestyle he lived so badly? Was it really so bad that she wanted a strong man in her life, unlike the men of her past? It was only human nature when it was rubbed in her face like this. Only human nature to want more.

She watched as Bruce fed Cecilia a bite from his fork and sighed restlessly. Why did they still act like two sappy lovesick teenagers around eachother? Was it wrong that she was secretly wishing that the "first lady's" meal had been poisoned? She kept her disappointment at the fact that it hadn't been silent and occupied herself with Emmalyn and the food. At least an oblivious Emmalyn made it easy for her. The woman was so enamored with her meal, the atmosphere of the party, and their conversation that she was practically oblivious to anything else.

"Isn't this the best food you've ever eaten?" Emmalyn carried on like a little kid in a candy store, stuffing her face shamelessly. "I'm so happy that I started working at Vonessen Inc. this year. They *never* had dinners like this at the bank!"

Victoria agreed, playing along. Yes, yes, the best food ever. She took another glance towards the head of the room and downed a long sip of wine. She'd be needing a *lot* more wine. By the time she'd demolished her third glass of cabernet sauvignon, Bruce and Cecilia had finished their food and disappeared from their table to make their rounds amongst the crowd.

The couple walked from table to table, Bruce looking as handsome as ever and Cecilia beautiful and elegant astride his arm. Everyone they spoke to was smiling and laughing, Bruce and Cecilia smiling and laughing with them. Cecilia was a good first lady. She exuded warmth and grace and treated every guest with the same kindness and enthusiasm as she would her own family. She made everyone feel happy, welcome, and at ease, and everyone loved and respected her.

Everyone but Victoria.

Victoria and Emmalyn were still locked in chit-chat by the time the couple got to them. Victoria braced herself for an inevitable encounter with Bruce's wife, knowing that she'd have to let her envy remain unseen if she didn't want to suffer the consequences later. Luckily, she was good at putting on a show, and this was the performance that would win her an Oscar.

"Good evening, ladies!" Bruce's boisterous party-mode voice greeted them. Emmalyn and Victoria swiveled around in their seats to see the von Essens standing behind them.

"Hi, Mr. von Essen. Great party!" Emmalyn stood quickly and gave them an enthusiastic wave.

Victoria took a big, preparatory breath. When she stood, she was face-to-face with Bruce's wife. In truth, this wasn't the first time Victoria had found herself close to Cecilia. They'd chatted at last year's banquet as well, and the women managed to run into eachother from time to time at community events, but Victoria always seemed to forget how pretty Cecilia was during their times apart. Her sapphire blue eyes were far too stunning and her smile was way too charming. Victoria had always been so nice to her to her face, but behind it all, everything about her annoyed her. The very sight of her so close and tangible made Victoria's skin crawl and her brow want to instinctually furrow. Even so, she had never given her true feelings away before, and she wasn't about to start now. She was far too smart for that. She plastered on her best fake smile as Cecilia greeted her.

"Cecilia, it's so nice to see you!" she cooed at her with mock enthusiasm, showing no sense of ill-will whatsoever.

"It's nice to see you too, Victoria," Cecilia smiled. "I've been hearing a lot of good things about you lately. Rumor is that you've been doing some great things for the company."

Next to her, Victoria could see Bruce in heated conversation about the gelatin of all things with Emmalyn.

"There's so much *fig* in it!" she heard Emmalyn exclaim as she motioned dramatically with her hands.

Oh, for crying out loud…

She cringed internally as she realized that she'd actually have to hold a real conversation here. But what better way to cover her tracks later than to be friendly now? She spoke to Cecilia in a chiming, perky voice, continuing on with the pleasantries.

"Well thank you, I certainly try," she boasted. "But enough about me. My, my, do you look positively *gorgeous* tonight! Is that dress a Jean Franc? I *love* his work. It's so classy and elegant."

The fakeness, it burned! She *hated* Jean Franc.

"Oh!" Cecilia put her hand to her chest. "Why, thank you, Victoria. Yes it is. I love him too. His designs are amazing and it makes me like him even more knowing that he's native to Stirling City. It's important to support someone local, you know?"

"Yes, well you look fabulous doing it."

"And you look lovely yourself. Those earrings really look nice on you. They're beautiful. Where did you get them?"

"They're *Tiffany's*," Victoria bragged.

Cecilia grinned. She knew a little passive-aggression. "I should have known. So are you having a good time?"

"Of course. It's a wonderful party."

"Good. I'm glad to see everyone here enjoying it so much. My husband really gets into the planning every year. It's funny how caught up he gets, actually. He always looks forward to it."

"Yes, I'm sure he does." Victoria would have been content to call the obligatory small-talk a wrap there, but her eyes suddenly locked onto the little heart-and-key charm glistening against Cecilia's neck. "My... that's a *gorgeous* necklace," she said, knowing exactly where Cecilia had to have gotten it from.

"Oh, thank you," Cecilia said with a lovelorn glint in her eyes. "Bruce got it for me as an anniversary present." She touched the charm on her necklace lightly with her fingertips and elaborated in a soft voice, as if she were telling a secret to a very old friend. "He said that it symbolizes that I'm the only woman who could ever hold the key to his heart. Isn't he so romantic?"

Victoria's blood burned and for a moment, she felt her jaw tense. She wasn't sure if Cecilia was simply being a typical lovelorn woman or marking her territory, but she had a paranoid feeling that Little Miss Goody-Two-Shoes was going for the latter. Oh, was that so? Well, Victoria wasn't going to bite. "Yes, he's quite a catch, Cecilia," she said, pretending that she hadn't noticed the insinuation behind her sweet words. "You're a lucky woman."

Cecilia grinned in satisfaction and Victoria worked hard to stifle her gag reflex. She wasn't sure how much more of this idle chit-chat she could take, but just at that moment, fate stepped in to save her. Bruce and Emmalyn had stopped raving about the food, and the CEO turned to his wife and Victoria jovially, interrupting their awkward exchange at what was probably just the right time.

"Great party, isn't it, Victoria?" he smiled, oblivious.

Victoria straightened up, putting on her best face and dropping her painful conversation with his wife in lieu of a better option. "Oh, yes," she agreed, trying to sound enthused. "Tons of fun. I love the band. And I was just telling Cecilia this, but I *love* her Jean Franc, too. You two look amazing tonight."

"Why, thank you," Bruce said with a clueless grin. "We try to color-coordinate, you know?" He glanced at his wife with a sappy look on his face and laced his arm around her back. "The credit goes all to her, though. She *is* my better half after all."

"Aww, Bruce," Cecilia made a cutesy face at him. "Stop that, you're embarrassing me. You're too much."

Now *that* was a statement Victoria could certainly agree with. *'Definitely too much,'* she thought. She held her breath and kept the forced grin on her lips to prevent herself from straight-out rolling her eyes at them both. How irritating could one couple be? She'd better get that damn acting award after this.

"Well," Bruce said in finality. "It's nice to see you ladies here having a good time. Both of you enjoy the rest of the party, will you? They're putting out more desserts soon, I hear. The cheesecake is supposed to be particularly good. I believe there will be *eight* different kinds to choose from. New York, chocolate, strawberry, crème brûlée… something for every taste, hmm?"

"It all sounds delicious. I can't wait. Thank you, Bruce," Victoria said. "You enjoy yourselves, too." She exhaled in relief as she watched them walk away. She had managed herself well there, but she couldn't wait until that holier-than-thou wife of his was gone. This was taking too long. What was her idiot of an accomplice doing with his free time anyway? Was he just going to sit around twiddling his thumbs and stalling forever? Did he plan on stiffing her? If that was the case, she'd kill him herself.

"They're very nice, aren't they?" Emmalyn commented.

"Oh, yes," Victoria agreed, though *'nice and annoying'* was what she really thought. But she didn't show it. Right now, she just had to calm down and play it cool like her exchange with the current Mrs. von Essen didn't bother her. Shoulders up, posture tall, brow relaxed, expression un-phased. That was Victoria Adessi at a fancy dinner party. There was no use in getting herself worked up. Was she *really* going to let herself be bothered by something as simple as a few shared words with Bruce's wife? No, she was better than that. Cecilia could make whatever passive aggressive territory-marking comments about necklaces and keys to his heart that she wanted, but she didn't know anything of Victoria's *real* intentions, and that was all that mattered. Victoria kept that reality fresh in her mind as she went back into party mode, intent on enjoying herself as if nothing was amiss.

Soon, the sky outside had grown dark and littered with stars. Inside the banquet hall the revelry of the extravagant party carried on. Couples of friends, co-workers, spouses, and lovers took to the dance floor to show their affections as the band slowed it down a bit. Bruce and Cecilia were amongst them, her cheek on his. Meanwhile, Victoria had split up with Emmalyn to mingle with some of their co-workers, laughing, drinking, and flirting like she didn't have a care in the world. Unsurprisingly, it hadn't taken long for one of them to proposition her. The co-worker, an attractive 40-something dark-skinned man with a handsome face and a broad, muscular build, looked her up and down before asking in a suggestive tone, "Care for a dance, Miss Adessi?"

Victoria smirked at him in approval. At the very least he was easy on the eyes, and paying attention to someone other than

Bruce for five minutes couldn't exactly hurt her. "Well, Guy, I'm flattered," she accepted. "Of *course* I'll dance with you."

Guy grinned and grabbed a hold of her hand, steering her towards an open spot amongst the rest of the couples swaying on the dance floor. Peering over his shoulder, Victoria managed to spot Emmalyn and her auburn hair only a few feet away, dancing with another handsome co-worker with a happy smile lighting her face and a champagne-induced flush in her cheeks. Between the dancing, the music, the company, and the food, it looked like she was having the time of her life at her first von Essen party. It must have been nice to be so innocent and easy to please.

Victoria couldn't be like her. She couldn't settle for her current life. As she swayed back and forth with Guy, she couldn't help glancing out of the corner of her eye to witness Bruce and Cecilia dancing close, seemingly ignorant to everyone else in the world, let alone the room. Bruce stroked his wife's face in a gentle caress, running his thumb along the soft olive skin of her jaw. Anyone could see how much he adored her. You could see it in his eyes, the way he looked at her, the way he held her as if she were the most precious, delicate piece of porcelain on the planet.

Victoria sighed, turning away as longing pierced her calloused heart. Sure, Guy here was hot and steamy... but looks weren't everything. Money was. He wasn't Bruce, nor were any of the other sub-par losers that she brought home with her. Guy was too busy gaping at her abundant cleavage to notice her discontent.

As the slow song ended, Bruce and Cecilia broke apart and Cecilia peered into her husband's familiar brown eyes with love brimming in hers. "I think your party is turning out to be a success," she observed, gazing past him at all the people gathered around them. "Everyone is having a great time."

"It's because you're such a great hostess," Bruce claimed. Cecilia smiled, waving at a few other women over his shoulder as they called her name. "Case in point," he chuckled. "You're very popular with the other ladies here. Why don't you go and mingle with them for a bit? Chat with some people, enjoy yourself."

"I *am* enjoying myself," Cecilia gave him a tender peck on the cheek. For a moment, she looked somewhat distracted as she glanced around the room, but the expression lapsed just as quickly as it came on. "But I really should, shouldn't I? I could use a little fresh air, too. I might step outside for a bit while I'm at it."

Bruce's thumb stroked the smooth skin of her cheek. "You're still not very into these parties are you?" he mused, exposing another secret she kept from the rest of the world; one that only he knew. Cecilia played the role of the accommodating CEO wife well at these company functions, but truth be told she much preferred small get-togethers with her girlfriends or quiet, cozy nights at home with Bruce and their daughters over big, fancy parties like this — a personality trait that she'd seemingly passed on to Blair, and one that Bruce found wholly endearing.

"It's not that I don't enjoy what you do and aren't proud of you. It's just that I don't like big crowds and stuffy rooms."

"I know you don't. You go and talk to your friends then and get your fresh air. Just make sure not to get too carried away and forget about me." Bruce gave her cheek another small caress. God, she was beautiful. Undoubtedly an angel brought down to earth. His eyes peered into Cecilia's stunning Caribbean blues, and suddenly he was feeling like he might be more interested in heading home himself rather than carrying on here much longer. It was too bad it would be considered impolite for the host to leave his own party early. "We'll make up for all of this hubbub with something a little more private later," he promised.

Cecilia let out a small, affectionate laugh. "And you're worried about me forgetting you? How could I forget you when you make promises like that?" She nuzzled her forehead against his. "Don't worry, Bruce. I'll be back before you know it."

"Just in time to give out awards and vacation vouchers?"

"Just in time. You won't even notice that I'm gone."

"On the contrary, I think I will. I love you."

"I love you, too."

Bruce's chest filled with a familiar warmth. It didn't matter how many times she'd uttered those words; they always filled him with such a contentedness. They shared a tender kiss before Cecilia excused herself and disappeared amongst the crowd.

It's a very human quality to look for answers to explain what happens in the world around us. Naturally curious and shaped with an instinctual desire to find meaning, closure, and comprehension, many are guilty of wanting to understand why things happen the way that they do. Why "A" happened instead of "B." Unfortunately, life doesn't always afford us the explanations we seek, nor the finality and understanding we desire. Looking back on it later, Bruce would never understand what had happened only a short time after Cecilia left his side.

Inside the banquet hall, the festivities had been carrying on, loud and unchecked, as bottles of wine and champagne were emptied by the case-full. The host of the party should have been happy, but it was almost time to give out awards and bonus checks and Cecilia still hadn't returned to him. Bruce didn't see her anywhere. Not by the buffet tables, not on the dance floor, not sipping on champagne with the other women by the chocolate fondue bar. He peered out at the noisy crowd, searching for her to no avail. Where *was* she? These awards had always been her favorite part of the night; she was generous and giving like that, a woman with a big heart. She liked to see other people smiling and happy. There was no way she'd forgotten or lost track of time.

Perhaps it seemed so small and inconsequential, but Bruce knew his wife better than anyone else in the world, and he knew something was wrong, even then. What had told him, he'd never be able to explain. But there are times a person can feel a sort of sixth sense about things. Maybe it's leftover animal instinct or shifting auras or simply what happens when your soul is so deeply connected to another's. But as he scanned the room and made his way through the crowd in search of his missing wife, a nagging sense of disquiet materialized in the pit of his gut.

He stepped out of the banquet hall's back door and looked towards the parking area as a burst of cool night wind greeted him. Cecilia had said she might step out to take a breath of fresh air, and if she were to do it anywhere, it would be here where no one would think to bother her while so much else was going on inside. Perhaps she'd retreated to the garden across the lot. Celebrations had always been a good locale for Bruce's parties because of that garden, and many people had told him so. It had tall green hedges, like the garden at the mansion, but even bigger and more expansive, with multiple pathways to traverse that all led to a large stone Baroque fountain in the center. It was a good place for attendees to catch a breather, where they could talk in private and relax on a quiet bench beside the flowers. Maybe Cecilia had gone there. If so, Bruce wouldn't be surprised. He stood in the arch of the door, holding it open and squinting his eyes in an attempt to see. He could barely make anything out in the dark night and could barely hear thanks to another rousing bout of champagne-infused laughter from the revelers inside.

"Cecilia?" he called in concern. "Cecilia, are you out here?"

She didn't answer. That unsettling discomfort swelled forebodingly in the pit of his stomach again and he stepped forward with the intent of searching for her in the garden... but he didn't make it that far, because that was when he saw it: an image that would forever haunt him in his dreams. The most terrible thing he could fathom to see. The reason for his horrible unease.

The first thing that caught his eye was the shimmer of something red and viscous on the ground. And the second was Cecilia's beautiful blush dress. He froze for only a second before a horrific realization dawned on him. A harsh gasp escaped his lips as he grasped the gravity of the scene his eyes had fallen upon.

"Cecilia!" he gasped. There, near a row of cars, was his wife... but not at all how he'd expected to find her. She wasn't getting a breath of fresh air. She was lying motionless on the hard asphalt with blood staining the ground at the back of her head. Her elegant gown was marked with dirt, her hair coming out of the bobby pins that held it in place. Bruce's stomach dropped so violently that it took the breath straight out of his lungs.

The next few minutes were a horrifying blur. Bruce bolted towards his broken wife, and when he reached her he could see with sickening clarity just how dire her injuries were. While the party had carried on inside, someone had hit her with their car. They'd done it with so much force that they'd knocked her to the ground, cracking her skull. And then they'd left the scene in a rush, leaving her there and not caring enough to stop and help.

How had this happened? How long had she been like this, and how could no one have heard the tires screeching where skid marks so clearly showed the slam of brakes and the consecutive peel away from the scene? Bruce grasped Cecilia's hand in desperation, letting her know he was there, but she didn't grasp his back. Her skin was cold and clammy, not the warm, soft skin that he had grown accustomed to. A panicked lump lodged in his throat. His wife was breathing, but her breath was ragged and wrong, and her focus was somewhere he couldn't find, her eyes dilated and vacant. He couldn't tell if she knew he was there - if she could tell that it was him or an apparition. But as he hovered above her, clenching her hand in his, he swore that she could sense him despite the haze in her vision and the confusion that clouded her head. Her slurred, delirious voice was just as desperate as his squeezing hand, her words barely audible, so hard for her to get out as anything but a pained whimper.

But he swore he heard his name. And then, *"I love you."*

She was hard to understand, but he knew what he'd heard. He kissed the hand that he was holding in distress.

"Cecilia do you hear me? I love you. I'm going to help you. You're going to be fine," he encouraged her. "Please hang on. Don't talk or try to move, just squeeze my hand..."

Cecilia still wasn't squeezing. Bruce called for help in anguish, fumbling for the phone in his inside breast pocket.

"Help! Someone help us!" he yelled as he dialed 9-1-1.

He didn't notice just how many people had started to gather outside to see what was going on. He didn't hear their gasps and screams of shock and terror as they came upon the scene. He didn't hear the chorus of calls for help joining his, nor the pattering of feet running down the street in an effort to find any sign of who had hit his wife and where they had disappeared to. He didn't notice those who had clamored around him, trying to aid Cecilia in any way that they could. He didn't hear the emergency phone calls nor the blaring sirens that followed. He didn't hear their determined reassurances of *"She's gonna be okay!"* And he didn't notice Victoria standing at the top of the stairs with Guy's arm around her waist, watching the scene unfold with the same shock and horror on her face as everyone else. All he could do was attempt to comfort his ailing wife as he held her with shaking arms, telling her how much he loved her between his desperate sobs. He tried to be strong, but as the paramedics pushed him aside and loaded her into the back of an ambulance, he broke down in anguish and flustered tears streaked his cheeks. He prayed for something, anything that would save her.

But the light was already leaving Cecilia's ocean blue eyes. The only sparkle left was that of a heart and key pendant, shining softly against her chest.

CHAPTER TWELVE
Innocence Lost

ANGELINA AND BLAIR HAD NEVER BEEN to a hospital before, but they knew right from the moment they stepped through the giant double doors of Mercy that they didn't like them one bit. For one, everything was all one color - a stark, sterile white - and all around them were weird beeping noises and strange machines connected to mazes of tubes. The sights and sounds were overwhelming enough, but the very worst thing about the hospital - even more than the lack of color, the scary diagrams on the walls, and the uncomfortable waiting room chairs - was that the hallways smelled funny. Like death and sickness and disease. The girls had never smelled such things before nor felt that dark, heavy *feeling* hanging stale in the air, but they knew what it was. They knew without understanding. Innately, like an animal instinctively knows a predator without first being bit.

Back and forth, doctors, surgeons, and nurses rushed down the hallways with people on gurneys, their patients stirring in pain and distress. Victims of car accidents, falls, illness, and violence. Behind a closed door at the end of the hall their mother lied on an operating table, surrounded by the most skilled professionals in the Stirling City area. The outlook was grim, but Bruce tried desperately to hold on to hope; to let his wife's inhuman strength pass a little on to him. Blair and Angelina could see him pacing back and forth in front of the door as they sat in the waiting room next to their traumatized babysitter. His stature had deflated to a low they'd never seen before. To them, Daddy had always been strong and invincible, but now his face was white, the lines of his forehead stuck in a permanent crease. He chewed on his fingernails, gnawing them practically to the bone. His nice black suit was stained with the rusty hue of blood. The girls didn't understand what was going on, but they were scared.

"What's happening?" Blair fretted in a tiny voice.

"The doctors are helping your mommy," the babysitter assured her. She patted Blair's brown hair and smoothed it from her face as the little girl clung to her shirt, fearful and trembling. "Don't worry, girls. They're taking good care of her."

Angelina could only whimper in response. She curled up against the armrest and hugged her favorite stuffed giraffe tight as tears trickled down her cheeks. She didn't want to hear reassuring words right now. She just wanted to see her mom. The last time she'd been with her had been only a few short hours ago - just a few short hours, and everything had been okay. She squeezed her eyes shut, remembering the last thing they'd done together.

Of course, it had started with another tantrum.

*"I wish **we** could go to the party!" Angelina pouted stubbornly, crossing her arms over her chest and pulling one of the sourest, brattiest faces she could muster. Beside her, Blair was putting bobby pins in their mother's chestnut hair and brushing it back with a large round brush, biting her lip in concentration as she tried to get every strand just right.*

*Mom had allowed the girls to help her get ready for the banquet by aiding her with her hair and makeup, but while Blair had been content with her impromptu role as a personal stylist, Angelina felt grumpy and fussy about it. Why couldn't **she** go to the banquet, too? She loved parties! All the music and laughing and good food? She wanted to dance and eat yummy cakes, not sit at home with nothing to do!*

Cecilia gave her an apologetic look. It was so typically Angelina to be upset over such a frivolous thing. "Sweetheart, there will be plenty of parties for you to go to in the future. Besides, Maggie is coming over to babysit tonight. You always have fun with Maggie, don't you?"

Angelina scowled harder if that was even possible, and looked at her mother's pretty designer gown with a jealous pout. "Yeah, but I don't care! I want to wear a pretty dress like you and dance and eat and give out awards. Why can't I come? It's just not fair!"

"Done!" Blair interrupted Angelina's temper tantrum with a proud chirp. She set the brush down on the counter, admiring her handiwork and her mother's gorgeous dress, feeling rather accomplished with herself. "You look like a princess from a fairytale, Mommy."

"Thank you, sweetie," Cecilia's reflection in the large antique mirror smiled back at the compliment. "You've done such a nice job. I should ask you to do my hair every day, shouldn't I?"

Blair lifted her chin, beaming with pride. "I'll do your hair whenever you want. I've been practicing a lot."

"I can tell," Cecilia smiled and kissed her forehead. She turned to Angelina as Blair put the rest of the bobby pins and the hairspray away. Blair was humming a content little tune, but Angelina didn't look very keen on being interrupted. She 'hmph!'ed grouchily in aggravation.

Cecilia sighed and reached for her shoulder. "Angie, dear... I know you like to be a part of things, but don't be so upset. You aren't being punished. You just aren't old enough to come to the banquet yet."

"What do I have to be old for?" Angelina muttered, disgruntled.

*"It's just something for grown-ups. Don't worry. You'll be grown up soon enough and it's not always all it's cracked up to be. Enjoy being young and not having responsibilities while you can. One day you'll **wish** you could stay home and have some time to yourself."*

Angelina wasn't sure if Mommy knew what in the world she was talking about, but her words were so kind and comforting that she couldn't help but soften a little. It was hard to be a grouch around Mom for long. Cecilia had always been good at diffusing situations like that.

"Fine," Angelina caved in with a little sigh. She switched her strategy, cutting the bratty pouting and giving Mom hopeful doe eyes instead. "How about next year, though? We can come next year, right?"

"Why do you want to go so bad anyway?" Blair interjected. "It's just a boring dinner party."

"Because I want to try fish eggs!" Angelina revealed.

Blair made a disgusted face. "Really? Eww! Why would you want to eat caviar? It sounds so gross..."

"It **is** gross," Cecilia winked. The girls giggled as their mother wrapped her arms around them and pulled them close. "Maybe you girls will be able to come next year, but we'll worry about that when the time comes. This year you're going to play with Maggie for the night, okay?"

Angelina seemed to be satisfied enough with that.

Mommy **hadn't** said no.

The girls helped Cecilia with a few last-minute touches - jewelry and the right coat - and then it was time to tell their parents goodbye. Before they left, Cecilia thanked them for helping her get ready, telling them that they'd done a good job. Then she gave them both big hugs, as did their father. Angelina made sure to interject a hopeful: "Bye Mommy, bye Daddy! Have fun! But not too much fun! And please bring back some food!," and Bruce chuckled.

"Oh, we will, dear," he assured her. "We'll bring home plenty of leftovers, I promise. We'll be feasting like kings for weeks."

"Bring back fish eggs!" Angelina insisted.

Blair shook her head and did a little face-palm just as Cecilia laughed and bent down, gathering the girls against her sides for one last loving squeeze. She gave them two big kisses, right on their foreheads.

"We'll see. Be good Angelina. Be good Blair," she bid them farewell. "Be nice to your babysitter. Mommy loves you."

And then she'd left. It had all seemed so simple and ordinary at the time. The girls couldn't have possibly imagined that their night would end with them sitting here in this dreary hospital instead of greeting their mom and dad at the door.

But the unthinkable had happened. Mom had been hurt, and from the way everyone was acting, it had to be bad. It felt like they spent hours in that waiting room worrying, going back and forth from hopeful, desperate optimism to desolate, defeated devastation. Everything was touch and go. Good news, then bad, then good again. But that meant that there was still hope, didn't it? Cecilia was typically a docile person, but anyone knew how much she loved her family. She loved her children and her husband with an unwavering passion that only a mother and wife could know. When it came to them, she'd do anything. She was fighting. Even unconscious, with major injuries, she was fighting.

But sometimes there are battles that even the strongest fighters can't win. When the head surgeon stepped out of the operating room some time later and placed his hand on Bruce's shoulder, Dad's gutted, heartbroken sobs confirmed the worst.

Mom was gone.

Childhood is innocent. Children by their nature are blameless, honest, and free of prejudice and contempt. They're able to see the good in humanity with such untainted clarity, eager to believe that those who inhabit the world they live in are like them; inherently kind and genuine and good. The naivety of children allows them to view life in a way that adults can't hope to see it once jaded. But in a flash, that innocence, that carefree state can be lost... tarnished by some horrible event that forever scars the child. That scarring moment had come for Angelina and Blair; the moment that would forever change the course of their childhoods, and by default the rest of their lives.

The dim yellow glow of candles lit the inside of Saint Thomas Church, flickering gently against the gray stone walls and reflecting off of the stained glass windows. The atmosphere inside was heavy and startlingly quiet, save for the lone sounds of a weeping violin and somber cello playing in tribute to the memory of Cecilia Anne DeAngelis-von Essen. At the head of the church, her casket lay surrounded by countless flower arrangements from family, friends, and admirers, and the pews were filled beyond capacity, the muffled sound of crying coming from each and every one of them... but for all of the heartbreak in the room, no one felt the depth of her loss so much as Bruce and his two little girls.

Angelina and Blair sat next to their father in matching black dresses, desolate tears streaming down their faces as they grieved for a life cruelly cut short for no good reason at all. Their innocent naivety was gone, their hearts broken, and their view of the world behind rose-colored glasses forever distorted. What had happened to their mother felt so sudden and cheap and confusing and unfair. But when was death ever fair? All it had taken was one moment and one act of unthinkable cruelty... and now everything they'd once known to be their reality was lost.

As the priest spoke at the head of the congregation, speaking of the dedicated mother, loving and faithful wife, cherished daughter, loyal friend, and talented artist who the mourners in attendance had lost, the girls listened to his words, but they didn't really *hear* them. They didn't feel comfort. They didn't feel hope or like their mother had "found true peace" or was "in a better place." They only felt sadness. Just a few short days ago, their biggest concerns were keeping up with their homework, getting through the third grade, and hiding secret crushes. Now this. They couldn't fathom why it had happened. Why someone would do such a terrible thing to their mom, a woman who'd never done anything wrong or spiteful to anyone else in her life. It wasn't fair and didn't make sense. And the worst part was that they hadn't even gotten to say a real goodbye. Their heads swam with unanswered questions and a horrible sense of helplessness.

And Bruce couldn't help them, because he felt the same things. The girls' father knew that they were hurting, but he didn't know what he could do for them... and frankly, it was difficult for him to do anything at all. The terrible moment when he'd first laid eyes on his broken and bloodied Cecilia would haunt him for the rest of his life. The vision visited him in his nightmares and hounded his sleep. Since the banquet, he'd heard so many people tell him that they were sorry. That they understood his pain. But they didn't. Nobody knew the agony he was living with. So many people, throughout history, had spoken so ignorantly of love. But how many of them had actually gotten to experience it to the depth that he had? How many knew what it was like to feel a heart hemorrhage like his? Cecilia wasn't just a woman that he'd loved. She was the love of his life. And the pain that he'd felt upon seeing her forced to suffer like she had agonized him relentlessly.

He'd held her in his arms as she'd slipped away, and the fact that all she could think to do in her last conscious moments was to tell him that she loved him - and God help anyone who told him he'd imagined it - left him with a horrible feeling that he wouldn't wish upon his worst enemy. He was faced with a grim reality now: the reality that each day of his life from this point on, he would be dying a slow, painful death. Not a single day would go by that he didn't hurt.

He - and his family - would never be the same again.

When it came time for the von Essens to approach the casket and say their last goodbyes, Bruce led his daughters to the head of the church, resting his hands on the smalls of their backs. Everyone was watching them, but Blair couldn't see anything but the box in front of her. She broke down and her little body shook with sobs, knowing that her mother was inside, never to come out again. She silently wished that Mommy would lift herself up and climb out of it, alive and well, but she was smart enough to know that it was impossible. She'd never again play her piano for her, or be tucked in to sleep while Mom hummed her music box melody, or hear her read stories like *The Velveteen Rabbit* in the garden.

Beside her, Angelina stared at the casket numbly, tears staining her cheeks and her chapped lips quivering. Mom had always told her that she had a pretty voice and that she should take chorus class and her voice lessons more seriously. Now, she was wishing that she would have listened more and goofed off less. That she would have made Mom just as proud of her singing as she was of Blair's piano. How many times had she gotten in trouble for doing one of her goofy Pavarotti's or a loud, obnoxious Christina Aguilera in Jenny Wexler's ear during chorus class just to make the other girls laugh? How many times had Mom driven her home from a voice lesson at Margaret's with her hand on the wheel and gaze steady ahead, not saying anything, but clearly saddened by the way Angelina squandered being able to do something that she loved, when she herself had had ballet taken from her? Angelina *did* appreciate singing lessons. She told Mom that she did, all the time. But right now, although it may not have been the truth, she felt like she'd done nothing but disappoint her.

"I love you, Mommy," she whimpered in a tiny voice, her small fingers shaking as she ran them over the casket. "Every time I sing, I'll do it for you. I'll be a good girl and take it seriously just like you wanted me to. I'll make you proud of me, I promise."

She sat down next to Blair and their father, sobbing as she hugged them tight. As the service ended and the pallbearers escorted the casket from the church, Father John offered his condolences to Bruce and his kin. The priest felt a great sympathy towards the von Essens. He'd long been a friend of the family, especially Cecilia who was always volunteering her time at church fundraisers and Lenten fish fries. It was he who had comforted her when she'd sought guidance after breaking her knee, when the loss of her dream to be a professional ballerina had begun to overwhelm her. And it was she who had suggested that Father

John marry her and Bruce ten years ago, which he had done proudly in this very same church. He knew the pain that Bruce and his daughters had to be feeling right now was tremendous, but he tried to offer them hope in their dark time; a reminder that God was with them, even when it felt like He wasn't.

"She was a beautiful spirit," Father John said as he wrapped his arms around the businessman's back. "And you gave her a good life. She was very happy with you and there's no doubt she's looking down on you and your family right now. This isn't the end. You'll meet her again one day." He sighed, giving Brue one last pat on the shoulder. "Stay strong, Bruce. Stay strong."

Bruce appreciated the thought, but he didn't make any promises. He wasn't sure that this was one he could keep.

Cecilia was buried in the Saint Thomas Church Cemetery, and when the emotional ceremony was finally over, family and friends retreated to the von Essen mansion to lay a memorial marker dedicated to her memory in a private part of the garden that she had loved so much. The garden had been her pride and joy, the place where she'd done all of her painting, and it only seemed fitting that her name forever lay etched in stone amongst the flowers. Among the visitors to come to the house and pay their last respects was little Aiden. Aiden had arrived with his dad as soon as the funeral had ended, intent on comforting his friends to the best of his abilities, but he'd never experienced something like this before and everything about it was hard. It was hard seeing his friends like this. Hard being around all of this sadness. Hard knowing what to do - or if he could do anything at all. And hard understanding what had happened in the first place.

Aiden had only met Mrs. von Essen a few short months ago, but now she was gone, and the suddenness and cruelty of it left a terrible, unsettled, sick feeling in the pit of his stomach. For all of the money and riches and nice things that Angelina's family had, and despite how much better off they were than everyone else, the von Essens were still nice people. Bad things weren't supposed to happen to nice people. It didn't make any sense.

The entire situation boggled his mind. But maybe what confused him the most about it was that *he* had been the first person who Angelina had called when she'd found out the bad news. He didn't know why she would call him over all of her other friends – even Gisele and Katie - but he could still remember the way her whimpering, tear-filled voice had sounded on the other line and it had absolutely broken his heart.

"Aiden, please, I need to talk to somebody," she'd said, her voice a strained whisper distorted by sniffles and sobs. *"I don't know what to do. My mom is dead."* They'd talked for over an hour that night, and although he hadn't really known how to react or what to say or how to process this new, sad concept, he knew that he needed to be there for his friend. Then, and now.

So that was what he did. He held a weeping Angelina close in front of Cecilia's memorial marker, his arms wrapped around her back as she buried her face into his chest. He didn't know what he could say that would make her feel any better and talking didn't feel right anyway, so he simply kept quiet, hugging her tight as her tears stained his suit coat. As her body shook against him and she bawled into his shoulder, he couldn't help but get teary-eyed and start to cry himself. Angelina was one of the best friends that he had made at Saint Joan of Arc so far, and he felt terrible that she was going through this. He wanted nothing more than to make her feel better again, but he didn't know how. So for now, this would have to be enough.

And it was more than enough. At least to Angelina.

She held Aiden close, taking comfort in the feeling of his arms around her. His cheek was on her forehead, his hand gently rubbing her back. Normally she would have blushed at such an intimate, caring gesture, but she wasn't thinking about her crush on him today. Silly, stupid things like crushes were the last thing on her mind. Reality had put a dart through her daydreams and what she really needed right now wasn't a crush at all. It was a friend. And Aiden *was* her friend. She knew it. Because nobody who wasn't your friend held you like this, or talked to you on the phone for an hour when you were blubbering and crying and not making any sense, or tried to make you feel safe and like everything was going to be okay again, even if it wasn't.

They stayed like that for a long time, and would have even longer if it weren't for Gisele and Katie approaching Angelina to envelop her in teary hugs of their own. Aiden stepped away and wiped the tears from his eyes with his coat sleeve as Angelina's girlfriends attempted to comfort her. Once he felt composed enough, he scanned the backyard for Blair. A part of him felt a little timid about comforting her since he wasn't nearly as close to her as he was to Angelina, but he knew that he needed to do it. It hurt him to know that she was hurting the way that she was... especially considering how much he secretly admired her.

He spotted her near one of the hedges. She'd tried to sneak off from everyone else, but she hadn't gotten far. She was crying so hard, but barely making a sound, and seeing her cherubic face stained with tears and her eyes red and bloodshot like that nearly killed him inside. He didn't feel butterflies. He just felt sad. He approached her cautiously before reaching out to wrap his arms around her, and for once she didn't protest or push him away.

"Aiden..." she said his name in a soft whimper. It came out muffled and pained against his shoulder. He felt sad and sick to his stomach when she said it like that, like someone had tied his tummy into a big knot and given it a hard yank.

"I'm really sorry about your mom," he murmured against the wavy brown hair of her ponytail. He noticed for the first time, because he'd never been so close to her before, that her hair smelled like flowers. "If you need anything, just let me know, okay? I don't like you and Angelina being sad like this."

He could feel her head nod in response and she squeezed him gratefully. "Thank you," she said, her voice still shaky but the rest of her slightly calmer, at least for the moment. "You're so nice. Angelina's really lucky to have a friend like you."

"I'm *your* friend, too," he reminded her.

Blair went quiet. She nuzzled her face deeper into his shoulder. "Aiden?"

"Yeah?"

"Please help my sister, okay? She really needs you."

Aiden was surprised by Blair's sudden - and rather grown-up - request. He didn't know how to respond to her other than to simply say, "I will. I promise."

It felt significant to make such a promise to her.

He wouldn't break it.

The crowd in the garden gradually thinned, and at long last, day faded into night. Once all of the well-wishers who had followed the family home to the mansion had finally taken their leave, Bruce and his daughters lingered outside, tired and worn out from their taxing ordeal. Bruce held his little girls' hands, one on each side, as they stood in front of Cecilia's memorial marker.

"I miss her," Blair whimpered against his pant leg.

"So do I," Angelina clutched his hand a bit tighter.

Bruce brought his girls close to him, wrapping his arms around their backs. He could feel tears forming in his eyes and squeezed his lids shut in an attempt to quell them, but it was no use. Hearing their voices break like that and knowing that he couldn't do anything about it destroyed him. Made him feel like less of a man and destroyed him, too. He wasn't used to this. To feeling powerless. But he'd never felt more out of control than he did tonight. Never felt more gutted and rudderless.

Cecilia was *gone*. Even after the funeral, the burial, and the garden memorial, a part of him still didn't want to believe it.

"We all miss her," he frowned. "But we have to be strong, girls. We'll be strong for Mommy."

The words sounded contrived and he knew it, but he also knew that he had to try. To help Blair and Angelina right now and say something that would comfort them, even if he had no comfort reserved for himself. His daughters peered at him with reddened eyes as he continued in a pained murmur, "Remember, girls... she'll always be with us. She might not be here where we can see her anymore, but she'll always be in our hearts. We'll never forget her. And the bad person who did this will go to jail."

"Do you promise?" Angelina sniffled. "Will they really go to jail? Forever?"

"Forever," Bruce repeated, hatred and sadness darkening his voice. "I swear it to you."

He glanced at his girls' quivering lips and a new wave of sorrow overtook him. He and Cecilia had created these two beautiful little girls... they both looked so much like her.

"I love you, girls," he said to them, kissing them gently on their foreheads, just like their mother had done on the last night she'd been with them. "I love you both very much and Mommy loves you, too. She always will. Never forget that."

He took a hold of their hands again, and together, the von Essens walked in to the mansion and left the cold stone marker behind them. Life as the family knew it would never be the same.

With Cecilia gone, they all had a dark and difficult road ahead of them.

CHAPTER THIRTEEN
In the Midst of Tragedy

AFTER CECILIA WAS BURIED, a strange and unnatural silence filled the von Essen home. For a house once so vibrant and alive, the mansion felt startlingly quiet and empty without her. Bruce and his daughters had no choice but to attempt to carry on, but coping with their harsh new reality was a task much easier said than done. The entire situation was a nightmare, and perhaps what hurt the most about it was the heartbreaking lack of answers that surrounded the whole ordeal. This wasn't like a drawn-out sickness, which despite its sadness, allowed a person's loved ones to prepare for the inevitable. It had been cruel and sudden and left them with a terrible sense of emptiness and bewilderment. The identity of Cecilia's killer and the motivations behind the crime were a mystery that police were trying hard to make sense of; one that splattered the headlines of local print, radio, and television news. In the aftermath of the banquet, the truth wasn't clear, but Bruce needed answers like he needed air to breathe.

"Someone *has* to know something," he insisted, holding his crossed palms against his lips to keep his simultaneous urges to both cry and yell in frustration in check. "Someone doesn't just run another person down and then disappear from the face of the earth."

The investigator sitting across from him at a small table in the Stirling City police station gave the distraught businessman a sympathetic look. Bruce had been meeting with officers and detectives nearly every day since the funeral, trying desperately to find whoever had killed his wife so that they could be brought to justice. But unfortunately, the police weren't delivering.

"I'm very sorry, Mr. von Essen," the detective cleared his throat with a disappointed frown. "We're doing as much as we can. There's no security cam footage to help us, no witnesses coming forward, and no description of the vehicle, so without any of those things we don't have much in the way of solid information to go off of. It's hard to pinpoint exactly what we're looking for here and we're still trying to determine if this crime was intentional or an unfortunate case of wrong place, wrong time committed by someone too afraid to turn themselves in and face the consequences... but whatever the truth is, I assure you your wife's case is high on our list of priorities. We'll get the answers, Bruce. It's just going to be difficult without a bit of legwork."

Bruce's eyebrows creased angrily. How could this man say these things? What was so damn difficult about this? He refrained from making eye contact with the detective, his gaze going straight through a mug half-filled with old, stale coffee. He didn't want to hear excuses. In his head, all he could see was an image of his bruised and broken wife failing in his arms, trying to tell him that she loved him. Those were her last words. *I love you.* It spoke a lot about someone when their dying words were an expression of love, and it damn well broke Bruce's heart. A woman like that - a woman with such a big heart and selfless, loving nature, even when afraid and dying and in horrible pain - deserved better than some half-assed bullshit from an inept PD. She deserved justice.

She deserved vengeance.

"What does intent matter? Whoever did this left my wife there to die. It was *no* accident. They ran my beautiful Cecilia down and didn't even think to stop and help her. She was *murdered,* detective. I want the bastard who did this to suffer. They need to pay for what they did to her... for what they did to my family. We can't even live in our own house now without security on the grounds. My little girls can't sleep. They're traumatized. They cry for their mother every night. How am I supposed to tell them that I don't have the answers? How can I look them in their eyes and tell them that justice isn't being served? How are we supposed to heal?"

"I assure you, Mr. von Essen," the detective repeated. "We are doing absolutely everything in our power to find the person who did this. We've questioned every attendee at that party, down to the caterers. Do you have any enemies, Bruce? Anyone who would wish to cripple Vonessen Inc. by crippling its CEO?"

"I certainly have competitors, but no one would be that heartless. That's absurd."

"What about your wife? Was there anyone she was fighting with, anyone that was giving her trouble?"

"No. Not that I was aware of. Cecilia was loved by everyone. She *couldn't* fight with anyone. She was a sweet, honest, loving person..."

Bruce's voice trailed off as his lips began to tremble. This investigation tired him. It sucked the life out of him, pained him, made him feel helpless and broken. He was a powerful man, always in charge. But this destroyed him. Every day he relived that terrible night in his mind and it tore apart his very soul.

"We'll keep looking, sir," the detective assured him, leaning forward on his elbows pointedly. "I promise you. If we find out anything new whatsoever, you'll be the first to know."

"Thank you," Bruce pushed himself from his seat, trying to have faith lest he go insane otherwise. "I appreciate your efforts."

As he turned to leave, he could no longer hold back the tears that began to fall from his eyes. Why was he here? Even if the police managed to solve this crime, none of it would matter.

Nothing they could tell him would bring Cecilia back.

Unfortunately for Bruce and his family, things only got more disheartening as time went by. The police were coming up empty handed and running out of leads; not as if they'd managed to find any solid ones to begin with. There were only a few people who had been let go by Bruce's company within the past year, and even the most recent and angry, Ben McClafferty, ended up being a dead end... although it didn't seem that way in the beginning.

Ben McClafferty, the scorned employee passed up for the big promotion he'd been more qualified for than the person who'd gotten it. Let go by Human Resources for alleged sexism in the workplace, repeated harassment, and generally "disturbing the peace" after multiple complaints filed by anonymous female sources. An employee who *hadn't* been present at the party itself, but knew exactly where and when it would be happening.

A motive was there, and Ben *could* have been a prime suspect considering how furious he'd been when he'd been fired. Investigators even thought that they had something when they discovered that his car had been taken to a body shop with a fresh dent on the hood and a broken headlight. But after weeks of being accused in the media of being an evil murderer, Ben was able to prove with the help of his lawyer and a separate investigation that the damage done hadn't been caused by him hitting a person at all; he had, in fact, hit a deer just like he'd claimed from the beginning. Bad timing perhaps, but the fact of the matter was he damn well hadn't committed any crimes. The police finally admitted that it was simply an unfortunate coincidence, but only after Ben's good name had been dragged through the mud.

The whole debacle had been an absolute hell for him. He'd dealt with nonstop interrogations and constant backlash. Death threats, even. He snapped at the investigators as they gave him their consensus, saying that he would sue them for defamation of character and adding that they were off their damn rockers if they thought that he was some sort of deranged lunatic that would resort to killing an innocent person because of a lost job. Suspicion would always be attached to his name solely on principle, but his alibi placed him nowhere near the scene of the crime.

It was back to square one. Cecilia's killer was simply a mystery. That parking lot had been dark and empty and the revelries inside had been loud and jovial. The police were short on ideas and dismayed at the lack of witnesses, and their words of reassurance started to sound emptier and emptier as one month passed, then two months, then three. With the cops giving up hope, the von Essens were also starting to lose hope. Bruce had tried everything. He'd even made a televised plea to the public on the steps of the Stirling City Courthouse, begging for help, but it hadn't yielded the results that he wanted. The huge sum of money that he was offering as a reward had only brought investigators phony information from liars trying to get their hands on the cash. The aura of hopelessness and hurt surrounding the investigation became stifling, and with every disappointment, Bruce lost a little bit of himself and his fervor with it.

Meanwhile, Victoria had done well to keep her hands clean in this mess and continued living out her life as though everything was normal. She - along with everyone else who had been there - had been questioned relentlessly on the night of the banquet, but not once had the police suspected her of being anything more than another shocked party attendee. Maybe that was because aside from having no clear motive considering her recent promotion, she really *had* been shocked at the time. All night, the envious woman had been thinking of how nice it would be to have Cecilia out of her way, but when everyone else had run to the door, she'd been just as horrified as the rest of them.

'*Oh my God...*' she'd thought to herself as she leaned against the doorway, frozen in shock while her co-workers looked on. '*What the hell did he do? It wasn't supposed to happen this way...*'

Victoria hadn't known of any of her cohort's immediate plans, nor that he'd followed the von Essens to the party, but as soon as she'd laid eyes on the scene played out in front of her, she'd known without a doubt that this hit-and-run had to have been her hitman's doing. And even though he'd technically come through for her and kept his end of their bargain by doing it, she was *not* very happy with his dramatic performance. She'd been very clear when she'd told him what she'd expected of him:

"*Make it look like a tragic accident,*" she'd said. "*Make it clean, so that no one will be implicated and no one suspects ill-intent or foul play. In time it will go away. No one will ask questions and they won't even be looking for a killer... and that will be the end of it.*"

Well, so much for that. What had happened did *not* look like an accident and it *wasn't* going away. She was now in an uncomfortable position that she'd been hoping she wouldn't find herself in. She was going to have to be careful for a while. *Very* careful. She was lucky that she was such an incredible actress, that her hitman hadn't been caught despite committing his crime in a crowded place, and that Cecilia hadn't lived long enough to give a description of his vehicle nor the man himself to the police, because the night of the banquet could have easily ended much differently if any of those bullet-points weren't true.

Of course, such perfect luck couldn't last forever. There was finally a glimmer of hope when one anonymous woman did come forward, saying that she'd been fooling around in the bushes with a co-worker she'd been having an affair with near the back entrance of the banquet hall when she'd heard a loud screech and a bang, then seen a black sedan peeling down the road away from the direction of the parking lot only moments before Bruce had come upon his injured wife. At the time, the woman hadn't realized that it was a person who'd been hit - she'd thought that maybe someone had just sideswiped a car. But now that she knew the truth, she felt horrible that she'd hid. She wished that she could tell the detectives more, but she hadn't gotten a good look at the license plate nor much else, and wasn't sure of the make or the model. It could have been a Town Car, maybe a Marauder or a Crown Victoria... she wasn't sure. She didn't know anything about cars. All she'd known was that it was black, it was long, it was a sedan, and one of the back lights had been burned out. It was the only lead the authorities had, but it was more than they'd started out with, and that had to count for something at this point.

Needless to say, if Victoria had been unhappy about her hitman's unorthodox methods before this revelation, then she was positively furious once it came out. He'd been seen by at least one person running from the scene of the crime, and if the police found him and he ratted... well, she wouldn't let that happen. Vonessen Inc.'s star employee vowed to herself that she'd go to great lengths to ensure that the authorities never connected her to the murder in spite of her cohort nearly botching it if she had to.

Great lengths, indeed.

But not so fast. There was no sense in getting ahead of herself. While the von Essen family tried their best to cope in the aftermath of their unexpected tragedy by leaning on friendships new and old, Victoria's time outside of work was spent keeping her name clean and free from suspicion while she waited for enough time to pass before setting her plans into motion. She knew that in order to maintain her innocence it would be necessary to keep her double-life a secret and pull the wool over the eyes of even her closest friends - so that was exactly what she did. She carried on with normalcy. She didn't entertain any inkling of a guilty conscience. She even went out a few times with Guy, the co-worker she'd danced with at the banquet, and pretended to be genuinely interested in him and make sure that everyone knew just how "wonderful" she thought he was. And when she and Emmalyn finally talked about what had happened that fateful night over frozen lattes outside of one of Maple Springs' coziest coffee shops after a successful low-key shopping trip, Victoria acted like Cecilia's untimely death actually upset her.

Emmalyn sipped her drink quietly, an uncomfortable frown on her face and a menthol cigarette burning in hand. Taking a short puff on the smoldering cancer stick, she fretted, "I still can't believe what happened at the party... of all the terrible things... Cecilia von Essen getting run over by a car!" She shook her head in disbelief, clearly shaken and upset over the whole thing despite a little credit card therapy to take her mind off of reality. "I just don't understand. It was such a great party up until that happened. Who would *do* a rotten thing like that?"

Victoria furrowed her brow, feigning concern. "I don't know, but to do something so cruel, they'd have to be a monster," she agreed darkly. "That was just appalling. Absolutely barbaric."

"Definitely," Emmalyn agreed. "That had to be one sick, disgusting human being to do something so horrible... to run someone down like that. What could their reasoning possibly be? And God, even if it was an *accident*, what kind of pig could plow someone over and then just *leave* them there and not even try to find help? A drunk? Someone on drugs? It's *so* messed up. I would never do something like that. I didn't know Bruce's wife very well, but she was just so *nice*. They were such a fairytale couple and their daughters are so young... it must be terrible for them. I heard that she wasn't even all the way dead when he found her, either. People are saying that she died in his arms. Isn't that sad? I cried for nights when I heard that. I feel so awful... I'm traumatized. God, I can't eat, I can't sleep..." Emmalyn stopped and took a long drag on her cigarette, glancing at her friend. A glazed look was in Victoria's eyes. "Vicky? Are you alright?"

Victoria drummed her fingertips against the tabletop and frowned. "I just feel terrible for Bruce," she said. "He's such a generous boss... you couldn't ask for someone more appreciative of his employees. You wouldn't expect it from someone with the power and influence that he has, but he's a good man. He didn't deserve for someone to do something like that to his family."

"No... no, he really didn't. Nobody does. It's horrible."

"No kidding. If it was an employee that did this... well, frankly, they'd have to be *insane.*"

Emmalyn sighed, unaware of the irony. She blew out one last punctuating cloud of smoke before plunging her cigarette down into the ashtray between them, extinguishing it with a rapt clear of her throat. "Well... I think the police have ruled that out. I hear they're looking into the possibility of an overzealous art gallery admirer now. Like maybe she had a jealous stalker or something that was coming to those classes she was doing. Can you believe that? I don't know if that's more likely or that someone had it out for Bruce, but the whole thing is really unnerving. People always joke that they could get hit by a car crossing the street. I guess you never really know how many days you have left." She paused and shook her head. "Did you know that the advisory board is questioning Bruce's ability to run the company now? He hasn't been himself, it's true. But who would expect him to be? It's just so disrespectful..."

Victoria frowned. It was true. Bruce had been so distraught that the Vonessen Inc. Advisory Board had been considering giving him some "time off" until he was feeling a little better. Bullshit, in her opinion. And not a good look when her entire plan had been to snag the *acting* CEO of Vonessen Inc.; not a man who had *once* been the respected CEO of Vonessen Inc. but had been downgraded to being pushed and bossed around within his own company by a bunch of ungrateful pigs in a board room.

"Don't remind me," she said, sliding her coffee away in disgust. "You'd think the board would show a little more sympathy. The man just lost his damn wife for crying out loud."

"I'm sure they'll back off. Anyway, I think I've had enough talk about this for one day," Emmalyn declared with finality. "It's way too morbid and depressing. I can't take it. Want to meet up again later tonight and head to one of the bars downtown for a little change in atmosphere? After work this week and everything that's been happening, I really need to have a stiff drink and forget about it for a while. And forget about the bill I just rang up."

Victoria almost agreed. After all, picking up a little booze and a possible late-night fling sounded mighty fine right about now... at least, much better than talking about this anymore. But if she wanted to be a part of Bruce's world, she had to leave this kind of lifestyle behind. She was young, but she couldn't act like a teenager who'd just landed a fake ID. No CEO was going to get with someone who spent their free time getting tipsy and picking up one-night stands at bars, no matter how swanky the locale. It was time to get serious and focus on pursuing the man that she *really* wanted. She just had to wait a bit until the dust settled.

"I would, Em, but I can't tonight," Victoria declined.

"Going out with Guy?"

"Just have a lot of work to do. Maybe some other time."

"Suit yourself," Emmalyn shrugged. She pushed in her chair and grabbed her shopping bags, none the wiser to the evil sitting across from her. Naive Emmalyn was just another casualty.

Just another notch to add to Victoria's belt of deception.

With everything that was going on, the prospect of returning to work was hard for Bruce to stomach. He finally returned to the office after a few weeks away, but even then, he didn't feel like he was completely up to it. When he sat at his desk, there was an empty feeling that completely encompassed his insides. When he went home there would be no more Cecilia there waiting for him. Just a house filled with memories of her.

Despite his attempts to be strong, he was having a difficult time coming to terms with what had happened and what he had seen. He felt a horrible guilt always there in the back of his head, like it was all his fault. Why had he suggested she go out and "mingle?" Why had he left her alone? Maybe if he'd been with her, he could've prevented this. But hypotheticals were hypotheticals. What he really wished, more than anything, was that he was simply having a nightmare that he'd soon wake up from, and that everything would go back to normal again. That he would open his eyes and Cecilia would wrap her arms around him and kiss him and hold him, and tell him that it had all been a dream and everything was alright. But nothing would be ever be "normal" or "alright" for him again, and that was the reality he had to face.

It was a reality the girls had to cope with too. Angelina and Blair were devastated by the loss of their mother, and for Angelina, the sadness, frustration, and anger that came with that manifested in anxiety. Usually happy-go-lucky and full of rambunctious energy, Angelina now found herself falling all too often into dramatic spur of the moment temper tantrums and crying sessions. And when she got too worked up, that was when the hyperventilating fits started. Panic attacks, the doctor said. Brought on by severe acute stress. That was how Angelina knew she was really upset - when her lungs would constrict on her and her sudden fear of suffocating to death sent her heart racing in a dizzying double-time. For a little girl who loved to sing, the sensation of not being able to breathe properly was a terribly scary one. Her new inhaler never left her side.

Blair, on the other hand, didn't have the panic attacks that Angelina did - she just had the depression. Stifling depression. A depression that was dark and deep and all-consuming. As a child, it was hard to grasp exactly what she was feeling, but all she knew was that bubbles weren't quite so fun to blow anymore, butterflies weren't as pretty, and silly games like cops and robbers didn't hold the same novelty value as they once had. She went through the same sort of sadness that her sister did, but Blair's expressions of it weren't quite as public and dramatic. She'd always been more reserved to begin with, but now she resorted to bottling up most of her pain inside, choosing to cry when no one else was watching. When she wasn't in school she spent most of her time alone in her room or sitting by herself at the piano in the study, attempting to push her pain out through her fingertips.

Behind her locked bedroom door, Blair would open her music box and trace her thumb over the Latin inscription engraved inside as she listened to the bittersweet melody tinkling out. *"Faber est quisque fortunae suae"* - every man is the architect of his own fortune. How could that be true, she wondered? How could every man be the architect of his own fortune, when fate decided that fortune for him, regardless of his consent or desires?

Blair's tears would flow as she thought of this and thought of Mom and the last time that she'd seen her. If she would have known that night that it would've been the last time she'd ever get to feel her mother's warm hug or hear her soft, velvety voice, she would have treasured it more and held on to that hug a little longer. It was all so overwhelming for her. Death was so final, so absolute. And although it was a new concept for the von Essen girls, they were learning the cruel realities of it all too quickly.

And yet another new reality for the girls to get used to was the presence of a nanny in their lives. Before, Mom would always stay home to watch them while Dad was away. She would cook lunch with them, take them on errands with her and make them feel important and accomplished, like they were her own personal assistants, and let them doodle in the garden while she painted new pieces for her gallery. But now she was gone, and Bruce couldn't do it all on his own with a business to run and his own grief to attend to. He hired a nanny to help make sure that the girls got to their music lessons and had food to eat, and that nanny did her very best to help them get through their day to day.

Her name was Elena Montoya, and she was a pretty woman in her early thirties who'd recently become a proud naturalized citizen. She didn't have any children of her own, but had grown up as the second eldest in a family of eight, so had plenty of experience caring for her younger siblings. Elena had warm almond-shaped eyes that always seemed to make a room brighter, and a kind, soft-spoken voice with a melodic Spanish accent that soothed the girls when they were feeling sad and lonely. Angelina and Blair had hesitated to open up to Elena when they'd first met her, because it was odd having a stranger in the house who wasn't their mother. But when they learned that Elena had lost her mother too, it made them see her in another light. Like she was someone who they could talk to and connect with.

"What was your mom like?" Blair asked her one rainy afternoon as they baked cut-out cookies together in the kitchen. They couldn't go outside when the weather was dark and dreary like this, so they'd stayed inside to partake in an activity that would make the day a little brighter. The dough was out on the countertop, a rolling pin was in Angelina's hands, tubes of colorful sprinkles and icing were within easy reach, and traditional Mexican mariachi music was playing on the radio.

Elena's eyes softened as she remembered her mother. She had been young, too, when *Mamá* had died. Not as young as the girls, but still far too young to have to bury a parent.

"She was very beautiful, just like your mommy," she said. "She had pretty black hair that she always wore in a braid, and she loved to cook and make beautiful things for us."

"What kind of things did she make?" Angelina pried.

"All kinds of things. Scarves, dolls, blankets. But jewelry was her favorite. Beaded jewelry, like bracelets and earrings."

"That's really cool. Our mom made paintings."

"I've seen them. They're very nice paintings."

"Yeah. I miss watching her paint. Do you miss your mom?"

"I miss my *mamá* every day, *querida*."

Angelina paused, her rolling pin suspended over the dough, her hands powdery with flour and lips pursed in uncertainty. "Elena... what's a *querida?*"

"It means *sweetheart* in Spanish."

"Do you speak Spanish?"

"*Sí*, Angelina. I speak it very well."

"Will you teach me?"

"I'd love to teach you."

"Will you teach me, too?" Blair asked. She pressed a flower-shaped cookie cutter against the rolled-out dough in front of her and added it to the other cookies waiting on their pan.

Elena patted her hair gently. "Absolutely."

The girls went quiet and got back to work. It was Blair who spoke up again. Her voice was soft and had a slight wobble to it when she did. "Elena? What do you do when you miss her?"

What a weighted question. Simple, but weighted.

Elena cast Blair an empathetic frown. She took the cookie cutter from her hand, took the rolling pin from Angelina's, and set the objects on the counter. Then she took the girls' palms in hers, looking at them with a sad sort of warmth in her eyes.

"I remember all the good times that we had together. We have a special holiday in Mexico called *Día de Muertos*, and every year when it comes, I travel home to meet my brothers and sisters and we talk about all of our favorite jokes that *mamá* told us and all of the good cookies we learned how to bake because of her. I honor her by being kind and patient and treating everyone who I meet in the way that she would have wanted me to treat them. And I tell stories about her and look at pictures and try to be happy when I do, because I know that I was very blessed and lucky to know someone with so much love in her heart and to have such a wonderful *mamá*." She paused, her tone more serious and almond-eyes creasing. "But sometimes, I can't be happy and I can't smile. And that's okay, too. It's okay to feel sad, because feeling sad means you care, and caring means that you loved her. Love is something you should never be ashamed about. So most importantly, when I miss *mamá,* I let myself cry when I need to."

That day, and that conversation, were turning points for the girls. The point when Angelina and Blair began to see Elena not as a replacement for Mom - because there could never be a replacement for Mom - but as the big sister they'd never had. Grief can be a lonely experience for children *and* adults, but it helped to have someone like Elena there who understood. She encouraged the girls to tell stories about their mother. To simply talk about her and remember. And she always listened. It didn't fix the holes in their hearts, but it made them a little smaller.

Needless to say, the girls quickly came to like her. They liked when Elena took them to the park, colored with them, taught them Spanish during trips to the store, and did crafts in the study with them like her *mamá* had done with her. Having Elena around made the task of getting through what little of the school year they had left that much easier.

Concentrating on school at Saint Joan of Arc was still hard though, even with the help of their nice new nanny and the outpouring of support that they received from their classmates. It was difficult to focus on concepts like numbers and grammar when the only thing that seemed to matter was not having Mom around. Nevertheless, their fellow students banded together to try their best to help them feel better. Even "snobs" like Jenny Wexler and her cronies cast their catty differences aside. Soon, homemade cards, bouquets of flowers, and kind words of sympathy flowed towards Blair and Angelina like a steady river. The compassion was nice, but no one helped them more than their closest friends.

Gisele and Katie had understandably been a little jealous when Angelina had first started getting close to Aiden earlier in the school year. After all, she'd been *their* best friend first. For the first time, they'd had to share her with another person - a boy, at that! - and Gisele specifically had had her moments when she'd felt rather put-off and hurt about it, even if she'd always acted like she didn't. Now, the girls no longer cared. Aiden became a part of their group, an important piece of the puzzle, someone who Gisele and Katie knew Angelina needed on her side if she was ever going to heal. The three of them did their best to offer Angelina and her sister their shoulders to cry on, and to brighten their days with nice notes, shared lunches, plans for fun play dates, and any other positive mood-boosters they could think of.

Gisele's usual go-to for cheering the girls up was offering to give them makeovers or do their hair or convince her mom to take them on shopping trips to look for trendy new clothes and cute jewelry. For Katie, the offer was typically even more cutesy, because she was a pretty cutesy girl herself. She would bring them kawaii little trinkets that her father sent her from his business trips to Japan and share colorful Japanese sodas with them. A few times, she even helped her mom make the girls adorable bento boxes for lunch. And Aiden would simply be there to tell a good joke or to talk - sometimes, all that Angelina really needed.

The unwavering support of their friends was something that got her in particular through even her saddest, most anxious days. She was thankful to have such good people in her corner.

It reminded her that there were still nice things in the world, even if it was a much darker place now.

CHAPTER FOURTEEN
Gaining Trust

ASHLEIGH ANDREWS DIDN'T WANT to admit it, but she was seriously struggling. The second grader's good marks had been the reason that she and her big brother had been accepted into Saint Joan in the first place, but almost an entire school year had passed her by, and she just wasn't sure that she fit in. Aiden had had a much easier time making friends and assimilating than she had. He was much more outgoing than she was, more charismatic than she was, and more adept to change. Not to mention that since he was such a great peewee football prodigy, she was often overlooked. If Ashleigh ever *was* noticed by anyone, it was usually as "Aiden's little sister," and although she'd always looked up to him and tried not to hold any contempt for him over the fact, it was still kind of a bummer. Pretend as she might, facts were still facts. And the fact of the matter was that if anyone was going to run with the "popular," "rich" crowd at this new school and make a lot of new friends, it was much more likely to be Aiden than her.

He'd already proven that by making friends with Angelina von Essen, hadn't he? Ashleigh didn't typically play with them when Angelina came over to visit, but it wasn't necessarily like she *wanted* to. Angelina had always been a little standoffish and intimidating. She gave off this bitchy sort of vibe like she thought that she was *better* than her. Well, no matter. Ashleigh didn't need to be involved in their fun to be reminded of just how different from Angelina and the other Saint Joan girls she really was.

Ashleigh had sandy hair and light skin dotted with freckles. She was a bit of a tomboy, and the other girls were all so girly and superficial. They gossiped, snuck make-up on in the girls' bathroom between classes even though it wasn't allowed, and talked in hushed giggles about how cute all the boys were. Ashleigh couldn't have cared less about cute boys or make-up. The girliest thing she ever did was Irish dancing, but she didn't even consider that "girly." She did wear a skirt for it though, and it was about the only time when she had to and it didn't bother her.

She much preferred being outside in her sneakers and jeans. Hiking and kayaking with Dad on the lake and riding her bike. Reading books and learning about how everything worked and playing soccer. She was quiet and liked to think things through before she said them. Ashleigh was the kind of girl who would never grow up to be one to go out and get her nails done, nor drop a hundred dollars on a stupid purse, nor prance around in pointy high heels. She felt uncomfortable putting more on her face than chapstick. And while the other girls in school constantly played around with trendy hairstyles, she was content to put hers up in a messy ponytail and call it a day. She liked to pretend it didn't bother her, but she'd had so much trouble finding other people to connect with in school that by the end of May she was convinced that she was destined to be a social reject forever.

As Ashleigh clutched her hall pass in her hand and trudged down the empty hallway, she couldn't help feeling lonely and deflated. If only she could make a *few* friends here... one or two, even. Maybe then she wouldn't feel like such an outcast.

She tried not to think about it; just focused on her destination. And there it was - the girls' bathroom. She sighed as she pressed her hand against the door, but just as she was about to push it open, she stopped short. Pressing her ear against the wood, she could clearly hear the muffled sound of crying coming from the other side. She froze, unsure of what to do. She already felt awkward enough. Should she just leave? She didn't want to interrupt anything, but in the end her throbbing bladder won out and she stepped inside, hoping to sneak in unnoticed.

It was then that Ashleigh saw her: Blair von Essen, standing in front of one of the sinks, sobbing into her hands. Blair had never been to the Andrews house before and Ashleigh didn't know her - not that she'd ever tried to. Ashleigh had always seen the von Essens as unapproachable, way out of her social circle, and strictly Aiden's territory. But the sight of Blair so upset - a girl who was always so prim and proper and put together and perfect - made her feel horribly uncomfortable inside. She'd never seen anyone cry like that. *Real* crying, guttural crying, the kind that people did when they thought nobody was looking. There was something that Ashleigh thought would be very wrong - and totally rude - about walking in and then walking right back out without so much as asking if Blair was alright, so she took a deep breath and hoped against rejection as she approached her.

"Blair?" she asked softly. Blair didn't seem to notice her. Ashleigh took another breath, then put a tentative hand on Blair's shoulder and tried again. "Um, Blair? Are you okay?"

Blair gasped in surprise, her shoulder going rigid and jerking away. She choked back her sobs and spun around to look her comforter in the face. In that moment, Ashleigh saw more sadness in her eyes than she could have ever imagined, and any intimidation she might have felt before vanished in an instant.

"Are you alright?" she asked with a sympathetic frown, already knowing the answer.

"I'm sorry! You scared me," Blair whimpered, flustered that she'd been caught in such a state. She tried to push her hair from her face with shaky fingers, but it was no use. She was a mess. She couldn't even seem to make decent eye contact without being embarrassed at herself. "I - I didn't hear you come in."

"I'm sorry," Ashleigh apologized. "I didn't mean to frighten you." She paused awkwardly before venturing, "Um... I feel really bad about what happened to your mom. Do you need somebody to talk to? You can talk to me if you want."

Blair didn't say anything back at first. Just frowned at her, her little pixie nose crinkling. Ashleigh tried to fill the silence in the only way she could think of.

"My grandma died last year," she said, trying to make Blair feel like she wasn't alone. "She was sick with cancer. I know it's not the same thing, but I guess what I'm trying to say is I know what it's like to lose somebody you love. So you can trust me."

Blair inhaled a small, sharp breath and her bottom lip quivered. She looked at Ashleigh for a long moment. Pensive.

And then, she seemingly came to a conclusion.

"I just don't understand," she said in barely a whisper. "I don't know why Mom can't be here anymore. I miss her so much."

Ashleigh had never spoken a word to Blair before and she didn't know if Blair even knew who she was, but she did what her gut instinct told her to do. She didn't speak again, she didn't even nod her head in agreement. She simply reached out and hugged her... and that was what Blair needed more than anything.

The next day in school, Blair was the one who approached Ashleigh. It happened in the hallway, before classes. The hair Blair typically wore long and wavy was styled straight and clipped back with a lacey bow, her caramel eyes were no longer reddened by tears but thankful and expectant, and she was holding something small and square in her hands. Ashleigh couldn't tell what it was until she held it out to her. It was a gift box.

"You got me a present?" Ashleigh's brows pulled together in confusion. Sure, they'd had a bit of a moment yesterday, but

Ashleigh hadn't thought that something as simple as giving Blair a hug and being there for her for a few short minutes should have warranted anything special in return. Perhaps she hadn't realized just how much her random act of kindness meant, or how much Blair had needed it. Blair nodded shyly in response and Ashleigh took the box from her, sliding the lid off to peek inside. A carefully-folded red origami crane and a stack of saran-wrapped cut-out cookies stared back up at her. *'THANK YOU'* was written on one of the crane's wings in black permanent marker.

"My nanny helped me bake the cookies," Blair explained, clasping her hands and tracing her shoe along a line in the floor. "And some of the other girls told me that they see you doing origami at recess sometimes, so I brought some paper with me today. Do you want to sit with me at lunch later and make some?"

Ashleigh smiled brightly, feeling her heart flutter. "Sure... that would be great! I can teach you how to make a boat. Or maybe a flower. They're not very hard. If you want to, I mean."

"I would love to," Blair's lips curved up into a small smile of her own.

"Great! I'll do a couple practice ones before lunch then," Ashleigh concluded. "Just to make sure I teach them right." She took one of Blair's cookies, one that was shaped like a flower, and popped it into her mouth. "Thanks for the cookies, too, by the way. I *love* cut-out cookies! These are really good."

"You're welcome," Blair smiled sweetly. Then she waved goodbye and turned on her heel, looking forward to having lunch with a potential new friend. And there was a *funny thing about making this new friend,* she thought as she walked to class with her books clutched hopefully against her chest. *For once she hadn't needed Angelina's help.* And Ashleigh hadn't needed Aiden's.

Maybe they weren't destined to be social rejects after all.

204 | *Stephanie Rose Vigano*

Angelina didn't know if she could do this. It wasn't the song she had to sing that was giving her such anxiety; she wasn't the least bit worried about forgetting the lyrics to "Think of Me." *The Phantom of the Opera* was one of her favorite musicals, and she knew all the lyrics by heart. It was just that this was the very first recital she'd ever sang at without her mom in the audience.

Elena was there. Dad was there, too. Gisele's parents were there, since Gisele had a song to sing herself. And even Aiden and the Andrews were in attendance. But there was no Mom. It didn't feel right having no Mom. Even with the prospect of Blair playing the piano to accompany her - a surprisingly rare occurrence, considering how very entrenched in music the both of them were - she still had a horrible feeling like she might throw up.

Even worse, have an anxiety attack in front of everyone.

But there was no turning back now. She felt her pulse quicken as she walked onto the stage in her new gold-brocade dress where Blair was already seated at the piano. Her stomach hurt. She had so many memories of these recitals. Of mom helping her get ready beforehand, like she and Blair had helped her get ready for the banquet on the night that she'd died. Doing her hair, tidying her dress. Helping her remember that there was nothing to be afraid of. Mom had always told her that what the audience thought of her didn't matter; that all that mattered was her and the music and how much she loved it. So many of Angelina's memories of past recitals were fond ones. But there were also memories that hurt now. Some, because they weren't possible to duplicate ever again - Mom scooping her up into a huge hug after she'd nailed a particularly difficult piece, the big smile on her face as she'd watched from her seat in the crowd. But there were also ones that hurt now not because they were bittersweet, but because there was no way for Angelina to make them up to her anymore.

Like once, after she'd been bad at a voice lesson with Margaret, purposely overdoing run after run as if the prim song she was learning was some kind of vocal gymnastics-ridden pop hit, Mom had driven her home in silence, her jaw set and rigid. Her disappointment had hurt Angelina more than her anger. Mom never got upset, and Angelina hated making her upset because of that. *"Angelina, I'm very disappointed in you,"* she'd said, her voice even and quiet. Granted, Mom had also told Angelina that she was proud of her many, many more times than that. But for some reason, now that Mom was gone, it was the times that she was disappointed in her that bothered Angelina the most.

Angelina was scared to sing. There was no Mom here, and for the first time she felt truly alone on stage. But at the same time, a strong resolve washed over her despite her jitters, and as she looked down at the crowd, she found a strength in herself that she didn't know she had. She didn't want to disappoint her mother anymore. She wanted to show her that she'd worked hard. She wanted her singing to be as beautiful as Blair's piano playing and Cecilia's pretty paintings. She took a deep breath, clasping her hand around the microphone in front of her. She peered into the audience, and suddenly she made eye contact with Aiden, sitting next to his family. Her heart constricted in her chest as he shot her a silent thumbs-up. Blair began to play the introduction and she tried to will away her nerves, her fear, and her uncertainty.

And then, she started to sing... and the entire room went silent. Her voice was beautiful. Captivating and ethereal. And so was Blair's playing. But in the audience, Bruce's eyes welled with tears and his chest tightened with an awful discomfort. A startling realization came to him as his daughters' music filled the concert hall. He couldn't watch them. He couldn't listen. With Cecilia gone, the music he had once loved so much only hurt now.

Flashes of memory flooded his mind. Cecilia sitting with the girls in the study, reading a book to Angelina while Blair played the piano. Singing along with them to Christmas tunes. Sitting on the bench next to Blair, playing the left hand of Heart and Soul. A peel of laughter as Angelina instructed them, "play it faster!" His wife tearing up at Angelina's first recital.

As Angelina finished her song, she fought hard to hold back tears of her own. She didn't want to cry; she was tired of it, it made her eyes hurt. But someone must have realized how hard she was fighting it, because as she stared out at the audience with her chest heaving in defiant composure, she felt a hand clasp hers.

"I love you, sis," Blair whispered, sidling next to her.

Angelina closed her eyes. "I love you, too."

She felt Blair give her hand a squeeze and she squeezed it back, happy that she had her sister. She and Blair might have approached many things differently, but they were in this together, no matter what. And together, they left the spotlight and retreated backstage, accompanied by the sound of applause.

It wasn't until more than half a year after Cecilia had been buried that Victoria finally attempted to chisel her way into their father's broken heart. Until that point, she'd been careful not to make any moves on him too quickly or come across too strong. Though she hadn't been the one to personally run Cecilia over herself and had been seen inside the party schmoozing with Guy by many other attendees at the time, she still hadn't wanted to arouse any suspicion. Now however, more than enough time had passed, and when she noticed that Bruce had been staying at the office later and later, she decided to finally take advantage of it.

Bruce was sitting in his office, the lights dim, hunched over his desk. He was staring blankly at a stack of papers in front of him, holding his forehead in one hand and a pen in the other. He was in another one of his melancholy moods. The police had searched for every black sedan in Stirling City, but there was still nothing in the way of answers relating to his wife's case. That hopeless feeling had settled in again, the nightmare never ending.

Glancing at his watch, Bruce could see that it was late, but he knew that the nanny was taking care of the girls and didn't feel much need to rush home. Really, he didn't have a desire to do much of *anything* anymore. He was tired. There was no telling how long it would've taken him to be pulled from his miserable stupor had it not been for a light knock on his office door.

"Come in," he instructed in an unenthused grumble.

He was greeted by a familiar face framed by golden blonde hair. Victoria Adessi. There was a look of concern on her face and the top button of her dark blouse was strategically unbuttoned. Her signal was subtle. Practically unnoticeable. But still there.

"Bruce?" she greeted him pensively.

"Hello, Victoria," he nodded back, noticing that she was holding a paper bag in her hands but not caring much about what was in it. "A little late for you to still be in the office, isn't it?"

"I could ask you the same thing," she pointed out. She made her way into the room on tall ebony heels. "I've been busy, but it's nothing I can't handle. I've noticed you've been cooped up in your office more than usual, so I brought you a little something to make it more bearable." She placed the paper bag that she was holding on his desk. He could smell bread and meat inside.

"What's this?" he asked, taking a peek.

"It's dinner. A Pastrami-Reuben from the deli down the street. I heard you liked them. And you have to be hungry."

Bruce grimaced, surprised. "You brought me a sandwich?"

"And potato salad. With a pickle."

"What for?"

"You've been staying at the office late, Bruce. People have been saying you're not taking your lunches. It's really not good for you to skip out on meals. You should be eating something."

Bruce paused, looking into the bag at the sandwich and potato salad inside. It was a nice gesture, albeit he was a tad confused. "I wasn't aware that you were so concerned about me."

"*All* of us are concerned. And we're all here for you. You know that," she reminded him. She didn't have to say it, but she knew that Bruce would only have to think of the petition that she and some of the other employees had turned in a few months ago to convince the advisory board that Bruce was a great boss and more than fit to remain in the office to believe it. He'd been thankful for that; the loyalty of those working for him had been touching and the board had instantly backed off and apologized profusely for doubting him. Victoria didn't want to leave it at that, though. She paused before elaborating, "Bruce... working for you has changed my life. My daughter Nicolette and I are on our feet and doing well for the first time. I can't begin to express my appreciation for all that you and your company have done for me, and I'm sure that I'm not the only one who feels that way. So, I know that this food isn't much... but I wanted to do something for you personally. I don't like seeing you upset like this."

"There's not much I can do about that. Those are very kind words, though. Thank you," Bruce responded, caving in and pulling out the sandwich to take a bite. He *was* hungry. And he *did* like Pastrami-Reubens. "Hmm... this is very good."

Victoria offered him a small smile, but despite his thanks, she could still see that Bruce's spirits were dampened and he was unfocused and distracted. She followed his gaze to the photo frame in front of him with Cecilia's picture still inside. The picture of her on the beach in her lily-printed wrap dress. That picture had always filled Victoria with such a sick, hateful envy, but she knew that she would have to play nice to get what she wanted.

"She was very beautiful," she remarked, causing Bruce to pause mid-chew. Sadness washed over his face and creased his lids, but she continued. "I'm so sorry for what your family is going through. If there's anything that I can do to help..."

She leaned over the desk as she said it, just enough to give him a slight view of tanned cleavage. Bruce blinked, pretending not to notice. It was probably an accident. He highly doubted that

Victoria meant to "help" him in the way her leaning would insinuate. Ms. Adessi was far too nice and professional for that.

"I appreciate the thought, but no one can perform miracles," he dissuaded her. "Unless you can reverse time or raise the dead, there's nothing you can do."

Victoria frowned. She wished that Bruce would stop being so damn depressive and get over his dead wife already.

She wasn't going to give up that easily, though.

"Bruce... I know that you're my boss, and it may not be my place," she ventured. "If so, forgive me. But if you ever need someone to talk to... I can't say that I know what you're going through. But I *can* say that I'm a good listener. If you ever need anything, you know that my office is only a few doors away. Please don't hesitate to knock. And any time you feel like skipping lunch, I'll run to the deli and get you your sandwich."

He almost seemed to smile a little as he glanced back at her in appreciation. "Thank you, Victoria. That's very nice for you to offer," he gave in. "Maybe a turkey on rye next time."

"Of course. Have a good night Mr. von Essen."

"The same to you," he replied.

Victoria excused herself from Bruce's office and made her way towards the elevator, smirking in satisfaction as the automated doors shut behind her. That had started out rocky... but it had ended quite well. She knew that she'd have to work for it, but she was convinced that if she continued to be kind to Bruce and show him that she was caring and concerned, she could see this through. And all the while, Bruce, the police, and everyone else around them would remain oblivious to her evil ways.

CHAPTER FIFTEEN

Lean On Me

THE WORLD DIDN'T STOP; it never does. Months passed, sometimes crawling, and sometimes going by so quickly that they left Bruce wondering where they had went. Two years after his family's tragedy, the head of the household finally seemed to be pulling himself together in the public eye, but inside, he would never truly be the same person that he once was again. Once a certain innocence in life is gone, you can't go back to before, and Bruce could feel that truth in each stabbing ache of his heart, in each night when sleep forgot him. No amount of time could deaden the pain, and his sadness ate away at him, numbing all other emotions. Not even his daughters could console him now. When Bruce saw Angelina and Blair, he could only see Cecilia and the life that once was. He didn't mean to distance himself from them, but he did... and it had quite an ill effect on the girls.

When you're a child and don't know any better, it can be easy to mistake a parent's distance for apathy. But grief can be a powerful emotion that can take a person over if they're not careful. When the body is in physical pain, the brain can shut the sensation down to prevent it from overwhelming the person. When a person is in emotional pain, that same thing can happen to the heart. To prevent pain, the heart must grow numb and cold, and that was exactly what was happening to Bruce. Despite his early good intentions, the sting of losing Cecilia and his attempts to move on with his life and appear strong in the face of so many unanswered questions left him disconnected and closed-off from the rest of the world. Work had become his only refuge, a distraction that occupied the majority of his concentration. Drowning himself in as much of it as humanly possible and keeping the world at arm's length was a coping mechanism. For the girls, it just felt like one disappointment after another.

Two years after their mother's death, there was much that had changed about their relationships with their father. Dad would often come home late. Sometimes he wouldn't come home at all. He didn't attend recitals often anymore, and when he actually *did* manage to fit them into his oh-so-busy schedule, he didn't pay as much attention to them as he'd used to, tapping away on his Blackberry or looking generally distracted instead, as though watching his girls on stage pained him somehow. The girls started noticing that Elena would be home with them later and later, and that Dad's physical presence in their lives had been replaced by his attempts to satiate them with items bought rather than time given. The promises he had once made went left unfulfilled, forgotten somewhere along the line. While Blair took it all in and stayed silent, Angelina got frustrated and lashed out

Angelina had never been timid before, but these days she challenged Bruce with that ballsy attitude of hers a little more often than he would've liked. It was almost as if her panic attacks had been replaced with something else - namely, the desire to never allow herself to be seen as weak or compromising. For a girl her age, her methods could be infuriating. Sometimes she would actually *try* to pick fights with him; to *make* him pay attention to her with her challenges, to get some sort of emotion out of him even if it was only anger. As Angelina threw her temper tantrums and Bruce lost his own temper and yelled back at her in a fruitless attempt to reign her in, poor Blair - always the one stuck in the middle, gunning for peace and order - would cover her ears with her hands, begging them to stop. Sometimes it worked, sometimes it didn't, but either way Angelina would be sent to her room and stomp up the stairs bitterly. She would snatch her phone off the hook and call Gisele, Katie, or Aiden to vent some more, unaware of the guilt and sadness these encounters made her father feel beneath his angry facade. It was a vicious cycle for both father and daughters; something that none of them wanted, but none of them seemed to know how to fix without Mom around, either.

Angelina and Blair missed the closeness they'd once had with their father. They missed their mother, too. Everything was confusing and difficult anymore... but at least they had their music. For the girls, it was fitting that Saint Cecilia, their mother's namesake, was the patron saint of music and musicians, because through all of their hardships, they still kept up with their lessons. Blair could still be found sitting in front of the piano tinkling away at the keys more often than not, and Angelina fended off her much more infrequent, manageable panic attacks by concentrating on her singing. Mom's death had truly been a turning point when it came to her outlook on her voice lessons. She didn't goof around at them anymore - now, she was dead serious. With Mom gone and Dad more distant, her determination to do well manifested in more walk and less talk, and was spurred on by her convictions to make her mother proud. As for Blair, perfecting the piano was a comforting routine that gave her back a sense that she had some bastion of control in her life. If she could control that instrument, then at least one thing was in her own hands.

So that was how the girls coped. Music. Music was something universal and beautiful. Something that lit up the world even when it was dark. It was something that had become more than just hobbies for the both of them; its healing power had kept them together in the most difficult time of their lives.

Yet for as much as music helped them, perhaps their friends helped even more. Angelina had remained good friends with her best gal pals Gisele and Katie over the last two years, but it was she and Aiden who had grown especially close. After the funeral, he had been adamant about keeping his promise to be there for her, and now he and Angelina were practically inseparable. They'd gone from being decent friends before Cecilia had died to the very best of friends after, and in Angelina's mind, he'd probably helped her more than anyone. Time and time again he'd been there for her. Consistently. It had started out as gestures as simple as picking up the phone when she needed someone to talk to at night. In time, it had grown to be more than that.

There was one specific time that stuck out the most to her. She and Dad had gotten into a pretty bad argument. She'd practiced particularly hard for one of her recitals and she'd really wanted him to come - he'd *promised* that he'd come. But when the big day actually arrived, he didn't show up. She'd looked out at the crowd expectantly, hoping to see him smiling back up at her, but there in the front row next to her nanny was the seat that was supposed to be his... and it was empty. Empty like it always was. She'd almost choked on stage, almost totally blew it because she was so damn upset that he'd lied to her *again*. By the time she'd gotten to the end of her song, she was shaking with embarrassment over how close she'd come to butchering her "Ave Maria." She hated that she was getting worked up. She never wanted to be seen as weak, never again. She was humiliated, face red, eyes stinging. And when Dad had arrived back home that night - late as usual - that was when the argument had ensued.

"You *never* have time for me anymore!" she hollered at him with angry tears welling in her eyes.

"I'm sorry, Angelina," he waffled. "I didn't mean to miss your recital, but I got tied up with something very important at work and I couldn't leave. I'll make the next one, I promise."

Angelina had long given up on his promises. "Yeah right! You're a liar!" She stomped her foot and balled her palms into fists at her side. "I hate you! I'm running away and you can't stop me!"

This wasn't the first time she'd made such a dramatic threat, but this time she wasn't bluffing. She was so upset that she stormed right out of the house, running out the front door and pattering down the street as she ignored him yelling behind her to stop. She didn't bother grabbing her bike. Just ran and ran with no real destination in mind as the evening sky quickly lost its light and the sun faded purple on the horizon. She didn't care. All she knew right now was that she needed to be with somebody else - *anybody* else. The only question was who? Katie's family was out of town for the weekend, so that wouldn't do. And without her bike, there was no way she'd make it to the other side of town where Gisele lived. The only person close enough was Aiden. She turned down his street, huffing and puffing and crying, wondering if forgetting her inhaler was a mistake she'd regret.

By the time she got to his house it was dark. The yard was dark, the windows were dark, and there was no Gunner in sight. The little pup was probably fast asleep in his dog bed, or she was sure he'd be barking up a storm right now. But no matter – she'd rather not be announced. Angelina knew which window was Aiden's like she knew the back of her hand. She found a small rock on the ground, pulled her arm back, and threw.

Clunk!

Aiden sat up in bed as he heard the soft thunk against his window. What was that? He heard it again, and when he climbed out from his blue striped comforter and peeked outside, he saw Angelina sitting by the bushes against the backyard fence, looking small and lost and peering up at his window. He couldn't see her well, but he thought that there were tears staining her cheeks.

"Psst! Aiden!" she hissed, clutching her knees to her chest.

"What are you doing here?" he hissed back. He glanced to the side, as if he were trying to be careful not to wake his sister in the next room. "It's late already. Tomorrow's a school night!"

"I know," Angelina's bottom lip quivered. "But I didn't know where else to go. I just need somebody to talk to."

Aiden frowned. To come all the way over here this late, Angelina *must* have needed someone... and he wasn't going to leave her there, not when she sounded so desperate and upset.

"Hold on, I'll be right down," he promised. He slid out of bed, slipped on his tennis shoes, and crept down the stairs. He peeked towards the sliding glass door in the living room that led to the backyard. Gunner's dog bed was in-between him and salvation. He grit his jaw and tip-toed past his sleeping pup as quietly as he could. One of the floorboards creaked, but Gunner didn't notice. He snorted in his sleep and rolled over, letting his tail flop over the side. Aiden exhaled in relief. *Phew.* Out the door.

Angelina was still beneath the bushes when he found her. There *were* tears running down her cheeks. Her short black hair was still tied back in a French braid from her recital, but it wasn't as neat as it had been before. Wisps of it stuck out from the sides and her side-swept bangs were damp with perspiration. The satin black ribbon she'd tied it with was no longer in a bow; just two long strings hanging down, disheveled. She wrapped her arms around her legs, pulling her knees closer to her chest. She didn't care that Aiden was wearing plaid blue pajama pants and a ratty old shirt. He was a sight for sore eyes - and considering how upset and flustered she was feeling, her eyes were definitely sore.

"Are you okay?" he whispered, plopping down on the grass beside her, letting the bushes form a protective canopy over their heads that hid them from the house's darkened windows.

"He's an *asshole*," Angelina responded. Her voice was bitter and trembling. Aiden couldn't tell if it was more mad or sad, but either way, he didn't like to see her like this or hear her use swears. If she was swearing, there was usually a good reason, though, so he didn't tell her not to. "He promised me he would come to my recital, but he didn't," she said. "He never does."

Aiden could have tried to make it better, but he knew that nothing he said could do that. It wasn't worth it to say *it's alright* or make an excuse for Angelina's father or tell her he was sorry.

So he didn't. Just let her vent.

"He doesn't even care about me," she continued. "All he does is yell at me and tell me to go to my room. As if going to my room is a punishment! I'd rather be *there* than be around *him."*

Aiden frowned. "That's messed up. *I* would have come to see you sing."

Angelina sighed. "Thanks, Aiden. I'm sorry to bug you right now. I'm just really mad. I miss the way things used to be."

Aiden put his hand over hers and Angelina felt the apples of her cheeks burn. She'd gotten better at hiding the involuntary reaction around him, but then again, he didn't always put his hand on hers. He did, however, have a secret weapon that he liked to employ often. Humor. And now was no exception.

"You know what I think we should do?" he suggested.

"What?"

"We should race."

Angelina stopped fuming, stopped crying, stopped everything, and stared at him like he had three heads. *"What?"*

"When I'm really mad about something, I run it off."

"'*A,*' that's because you're fast. And '*B,*' I just ran all the way here and it didn't help, so why would that be different now?"

"Just trust me."

Aiden stood from the ground and offered Angelina his hand, yanking her up as she took it. She shifted her weight to one hip and crossed her arms over her chest skeptically. "This isn't going to work, Aiden. It won't make my dad not a giant asshole."

"No. He'll still be an asshole. But it *will* be fun."

Angelina's head turned this way and that. "But it's dark out here. Where would we even race to?"

"To the street light at the end of the road and back."

She shot him an uncertain look, but he was already stretching. He stretched one quad, then the other. Put his hands to the ground and touched his toes. Tugged a little on the laces of his shoes. Then stood up, jumped up and down, and acted like he was psyching himself out. By the time he'd started lifting his legs like a marching soldier with an expression of over-determination on his face, hamming it up with the sole purpose of making her laugh, a small giggle escaped Angelina's lips in spite of herself.

"What are you *doing?*"

"You have to warm up first. Come on, do it."

"This is dumber than dumb, Aiden..."

"What, are you afraid of losing?"

Angelina rolled her eyes at him and mimicked his stretching. When he seemed satisfied enough that she wasn't likely to pull something, he took her by the hand and led her around the house to the driveway. He glanced up at the windows of his house. Everyone was still asleep. The road ahead was dark and empty. The sound of chirping crickets filled the night sky. Down the sidewalk, the street light he had chosen as their checkpoint was illuminated like the lustrous orb of a second moon. Moths and flitting nighttime bugs congregated in its halo.

"Ready?" Aiden nudged Angelina with his shoulder.

She nodded and got into position, one leg in front of the other, her back hunched forward and arms at her sides. "Ready."

"Okay then. Three, two... POW!" he made a noise like the crack of a gunshot and they were off. Angelina pumped her arms and let her legs fly. The breath caught in her lungs, her heart pounded in her throat. Aiden was ahead of her - of course he was ahead of her. He was fast, like some weird human-gazelle hybrid.

His pajama pants whipped in the wind, two plaid blue curtains billowing around his legs. His arms thrust back and forth.

She wasn't going to let him beat her. No damn way. She tried harder. Panted for breath. Felt the breeze whisk across her face, felt her messy braid loosen even further, and felt...

Not sad. Not happy, either. But relieved. *Alive.*

Thank goodness for those little things called endorphins.

She reached the street light right after he did. Ran into it and caught herself with her hands before whipping around to make her way back towards the house, back towards the bushes. She pushed herself faster, harder. She could see Aiden's surprise as she started to catch up to him. He slid through the backyard gate. She came in right after him. They laughed all the way to the bushes, feeling the excitement of competition, the release of adrenaline. Right when it looked like Aiden would be victorious, Angelina pushed in front of him with one hard burst of energy and raised her arms in the air, pumping her fists in victory.

"I did it!" she exclaimed. Then, jerking her gaze towards the house and back to him, a little quieter, *"I did it!* I beat you!"

Aiden didn't care to be a sore loser. He beamed at her, then plopped back down on the ground, scooting under the bushes once more. She slid down beside him and rested on her stomach, kicking her legs in the air and smiling at him triumphantly.

"Did you see that, Aiden? I kicked your butt!"

"You got lucky," he claimed. "So did it work?"

She stopped, paused, considered it, smiled again. "Yes."

"I *told* you running always worked," he smirked.

"I guess you're not as dumb as you look then."

"And I guess you're not as wussy as you look."

Angelina giggled softly and slapped at his shoulder.

"You're a jerk."

"But I'm your favorite jerk."

"In your dreams."

They both went quiet. Angelina rolled onto her back and looked at the stars dotting the velvety night sky above them. It was funny. Go into the city, and you wouldn't see all of these stars. But here in the suburbs, there were so many of them. Angelina noticed that one of them was blinking at her. Not a star, an airplane. She watched it until it disappeared out of view.

"Do you see that up there?" Aiden asked, pointing up at the cosmos. "That thing that looks like a soup spoon?"

Angelina followed his finger to the heavens. "Yeah?"

"That's the Big Dipper."

"It's so cool..."

"And if you look over there -"

"The Little Dipper, I guess?"

"Uh huh. And the North Star. That bright one."

Angelina stared at the star, shining like a faraway beacon.

"My uncle who lives in Colorado told me that if you're ever lost, just look for the North Star and you can find your way home again," Aiden explained. "I know how to find Orion, too. It's a constellation of a guy with a bow and arrow. You can find him by looking for the three stars that make up his belt. Once you know where they are, it's really easy. I see him all the time now."

Angelina was sure that a guy with a bow and arrow would be a pretty cool thing to find in the night sky, but she was much more fixated on the North Star. What was that, that Aiden had said? If you were ever lost, you should look for it and you would find your way again? She wasn't sure if she needed a star for that.

When she felt lost, she just looked for him.

She stayed there with him for a long time, staring up at the stars. She didn't know how he'd managed to do it, but she'd gone from being furious and fuming and sad and hurt to laughing and smiling and feeling calm and content, like everything was right in the world again. It was almost as if her problems went away when he was near. Or at least, were made a little less daunting.

When she finally returned home, she felt so much better that she didn't even care that she'd been grounded for storming off and scaring Dad like she had. Any length of grounding would be worth it if it meant spending time with her North Star.

And *that* was exactly why Angelina liked Aiden so much. Why she needed him so much. He had become more to her than a butterfly-inducing pair of green eyes and a cute freckled face. He had an uncanny ability for making her feel like everything was going to be okay again, like nothing was so bad that she couldn't get through it and survive so long as he was there. Aiden was fun to be around, always had good jokes to tell, and always knew how to make her laugh even when she didn't feel like it. She loved spending time with him, whether they were racing to a lamp post, playing in the park, drawing pictures of stupid animals at her art table, seeing who could stay underwater the longest in the von Essen pool, sharing a huge banana split at their favorite ice cream shop, or sitting around playing video games. It didn't matter *what* they were doing, so long as they were together. His friendship made her happy in times when she wouldn't have been otherwise.

In a word, they just *clicked*.

Blair, too, had found someone who she clicked with in Aiden's little sister, Ashleigh. The girls had become instant friends after Ashleigh had comforted her in the girls' bathroom, and soon they had started sharing their lunches together every day. Sometimes they would make origami together, just like on that first day - animals and birds and pinwheels and flowers. Sometimes they would talk about all of the interesting things that they were learning in class; about solar systems and proper grammar and historical events that made their voices heighten with enthusiasm. They would share their views on world cultures and scientific theories and discuss their favorite books and short stories, analyzing them with more fervor than most other kids in their grades ever did. And through the course of their conversations, they discovered that they had a lot in common, even if Ashleigh was more of an athletic type and Blair gave off that prim and proper tea-party vibe with her frilly bohemian dresses, lacy bows, dainty ballet flats, and flowered skirts.

They both had a thirst for learning, a hunger for discovery, and an enthusiasm for literature and art and many niche-type things that their peers considered "bookwormish" or "nerdy." Eventually, they started to have sleepovers nearly every weekend and stayed up late to talk on the phone. They drank loose-leaf tea together in thermoses during recess, flipping through new books and coming up with creative projects to do. After school, they would meet up to do their homework or make crafts with Elena, creating pretty things like glistening sun-catchers, Japanese flying carp streamers for the garden, baked clay magnets to hang on their refrigerators, and mixed media paintings to put in their rooms. They loved to come up with characters and stories, and would fill notebooks upon notebooks with writing together, collaborating to create different worlds full of fleshed-out personalities. Sometimes Blair would go to Ashleigh's Irish dancing shows to watch her tap her feet to the festive music or cheer her on at her soccer games, and Ashleigh would attend all of Blair's piano recitals in turn. Even though she couldn't play an instrument herself to save her life, she had a good time watching Blair grow as a pianist and loved listening to her play.

Despite all of this, Ashleigh had been surprised to find herself getting close to Blair at first, because before she'd gotten to know her better, she'd never expected that someone like Blair would want to be friends with someone like her. But Blair had quickly shown her that not everyone who had a wealthy CEO for a dad was a stuck-up, snotty, spoiled snob who would instantly judge her because her family wasn't as well off as theirs. Ashleigh had found a kind, benevolent companion in Blair who cared about what she had to say and didn't make her feel invisible. And Blair had found a good listener to confide in who was honest and genuine and *real* - something she really respected and valued. What you saw was what you got with Ashleigh Andrews, and Blair loved that about her. Blair didn't mind the girls that Angelina hung out with most of the time, but Ashleigh was much more down-to-earth and less high-maintenance than they were. It was ironic in a way, because Ashleigh had always viewed her disposition as a hindrance to making friends, when it had proven quite the opposite. In time, the girls were two peas in a pod, just as close as Angelina and Aiden. There wasn't anyone else in the world who Blair would've rather called her best friend - and that was exactly what the girls had become. For Blair, who'd never had a best friend before, and Ashleigh, who didn't think she'd be likely to make *any* friends in her new school let alone a *best* one, this was a pretty big deal. One that neither of them took for granted.

It was one particular weekend, while Angelina and Aiden were occupied elsewhere, that Ashleigh and Blair solidified their new "best friends" status. They'd spent the entirety of a sunny Saturday afternoon making "dream jars" in Blair's room - pretty decorated mason jars to slip tiny pieces of paper marked with "dreams" into; dreams that hadn't happened yet and dreams that had already come to fruition. The jars were meant to remind them of happy hopes and happy memories and happy wishes to look at on days that weren't so happy. Ashleigh had read somewhere that a dream written down was more likely to come true, and whether that was true in itself or not, she wasn't so sure. But either way, the craft idea had made for an awfully fun afternoon.

Blair had covered her mason jar in light pink lace, lined the lid with tiny pearls, and hot-glued a delicate pink cloth flower adorned with silver beads near the top as an accent. Much different than Ashleigh's jar, which was covered in green and yellow tissue paper cut into an ambitious quatrefoil pattern. The girls' jars seemed to match their personalities perfectly, echoing their creators in flawless, if subconscious fashion. Classy and demure and romantic for Blair. Fun but logical for Ashleigh.

They cut small pieces of stationary paper once their jars were complete, writing their dreams down one by one and dropping them inside, never to be removed until they were realized or no longer resonated. Big things, small things, long term, short term. Things that were serious and things that weren't. *Score ten goals in soccer next season* and *survive middle school* were probably two of the most wanted goals for Ashleigh. As for Blair, *become a published author* and *teach someone else how to play the piano* were at the top of her list, right up there with *go to college, read 40 books in a year,* and *maintain straight A's through middle school.*

"What's that one say?" Ashleigh asked, peeking at her friend's latest scribbling. It read in Blair's perfect cursive:

Go To Paris.

"Hey!" she brightened. "Mine says that, too!"

She showed Blair the slip that she had just finished.

"Visit Paris," Blair read, a small grin of recognition forming on her lips. "Maybe we can go together some day."

Ashleigh smiled back. "That would be awesome! I bet we would see so many cool things there."

"Like Notre Dame."

"And the Eiffel Tower."

"And the Louvre!"

"And the Arc de Triomphe?"

"Yes! And we'd go to all the cafes," Blair agreed.

224 | Stephanie Rose Vigano

Ashleigh paused, chewing on the inside of her lip. "You'd really want to go with me?" It wasn't like Blair wanting to go to France in general was a surprise. Just that aspect. After all, Blair was part-French on her mom's side and her room was pretty Parisian as it was. Decorated with all things feminine and vintage and classy and European-inspired. Shabby chic frames with romantic prints of Paris inside. The Eiffel Tower paperweight on her desk. The striped light blue wallpaper. The vanity along the far wall with fancy cabriole legs. Her four-poster canopy bed with its flowy curtains. Of *course* Blair would want to go to France.

And *of course* she would want to take a friend with her.

"Ash, I have to give you something," she said, seemingly out of nowhere. Ashleigh sat up and set down her jar and the silver gel pen she'd been writing her dreams with, squinting in curiosity as Blair walked to her bedside table and opened the music box she'd had on it since before she could remember. The music box from her mom, the one from France where she wanted to go. For a few seconds, the bittersweet melody played as Blair reached inside and pulled something out that Ashleigh couldn't see. Then, she shut the lid with a soft clunk and it stopped.

When she turned around, she was holding two small gold necklaces in her hand. She reached out and handed one to Ashleigh. When Ashleigh peeked into her palm she saw a simple gold four-leaf clover charm hanging from the chain. She noticed that Blair's was a miniature Eiffel Tower. She flipped her charm around. There was an engraving on the back. *Best Friends.*

She couldn't say anything at first. Just stared at it.

"Friendship necklaces," Blair explained the obvious.

"Wow, Blair... they're really pretty," Ashleigh fumbled.

"Elena helped me pick them," Blair tucked her hair behind her ear, a bashful nervous tic that she'd unknowingly inherited from her mom. "You don't have to wear it all the time if you don't want to, but I thought they were nice and I wanted you to have one. I've never really had anyone to give one to before."

Ashleigh felt her heart swell. And to think, she'd once considered herself a loser. "I'll wear it every day," she promised.

Blair smiled and reached out to give her a grateful hug. She might have been the one giving a physical gift, but Ashleigh had given her something even more valuable. One that meant the difference between staying grounded and giving in to the hurt. Blair knew that she and Ashleigh would continue filling their dream jars together for a long time. Maybe someday they really *would* go to Paris together. Either way, just the idea gave Blair a glimmer of optimism that she sorely needed.

She and Ashleigh spent many afternoons together like that, enjoying one another's company. Dreaming of the future, chatting about the present, and trying to forget the past. The girls kept themselves busy, and if nothing else, it helped Blair take her mind off of sad things and keep it on things that were happier.

Indeed, friendship had played a big role in helping the von Essen girls two years after their mother's death. But friendships weren't the only dynamics that had played their part. The hidden crushes amongst the group hadn't exactly disappeared over the months, but they hadn't been brought to the forefront, either. Aiden's tummy would still tie itself in knots when Blair was around, but he tried to ignore it. He was always amicable and friendly towards her, but he was still a little shy, and she was usually too occupied with Ashleigh to pay him much mind anyway. She was already way out of his league as it was, but perhaps the biggest factor that kept him quiet was Angelina. For as cool as Angelina could be, she was a little touch-and-go emotion-wise after losing her mom, and considering how close he was to her now, he didn't want to upset her by paying too much attention to her sister. Instead, he kept his mouth shut and bit the bullet, admiring Blair from afar in that quiet, secretive way that kids do and concentrating his energy on other pursuits. He felt like he could talk to Angelina about anything and everything, but that had always been the one thing that was a little too embarrassing and awkward; the place where he drew the line.

Little did he know, Angelina had bitten the bullet and kept secrets from him, too. She wasn't afraid of much, but rejection and failure were two things that were very scary to her... and equally scary was the idea of messing up the close friendship that they had. When she'd first met Aiden, he was her crush, but over the past two years what she'd really needed wasn't a crush to doodle her name next to inside her notebooks - it was a friend. Aiden had become the brother she'd never had, and that was exactly why she'd never said anything to him about liking him as anything more than that. She couldn't help but always have that little pang of puppy-love hidden in her heart, but that puppy-love was secondary now. She zipped her lips, guarded her heart, and effectively reserved herself to the friend zone. It was for the best. They were just kids anyway, even if they'd grown up a little since they'd first started getting to know each other... and even if that growing up had been expedited by the trauma they'd endured.

As for other "hidden crushes" - or rather "hidden unbridled lusts" if you wanted to get technical about it - Victoria was still in the picture two years post-tragedy, and maybe now more so than ever before. While work had become Bruce's biggest distraction, she was determined to become his second biggest. In time, her efforts to sway him had finally begun to pay off, and though it was a slow, careful process, she was winning over his vulnerable, fragile heart one day at a time, just as she'd sworn she would. The low-cut tops, skinny pencil skirts, super-high heels and form-fitting dresses that she wore to work and flaunted on a daily basis didn't hurt her cause now that Bruce was a lonely widower, yet as forward and direct as she would've preferred to be, she wasn't stupid. She wasn't interested in being a one-time "fling" that Bruce would simply have his way with for a short time and then toss away like an old sock when he was finished.

She knew what her main role would be by default, and it was a role that she not only didn't mind, but *wanted...* but even more so than that, she wanted to seduce him into a longer-term commitment. Instead of focusing purely on the physical laws of attraction, she took a more conservative, sneaky, "appeal-to-his-emotions" type of approach. It was dishonest and snakelike and disgustingly sick and depraved for her to offer him any sort of emotional comfort after what she had done to his family, but she tried it all the same... and it seemed to be working.

Ever since she'd defended him against the advisory board with her petition and "broken the ice" with her simple but effective surprise sandwich run, she and Bruce had begun to associate more and more. She'd worked her way into his life and gained his trust, providing him with an easy outlet. She'd showered him with supportive words, made it a point to never be too far out of reach when he needed it, brought him lunches, did him favors as though she were his personal assistant, and made sure to throw in the occasional manipulative come-hither glance whenever it felt appropriate. It was slow work, but Bruce had come to expect her interest and concern... and even began to open up to her because of it. First it was business. Then, it got personal.

Victoria, despite her hidden agenda, was a very good actress when it came to showing sympathy for him - and ironically enough, sometimes she wasn't even acting. Once she got to know him better and became more personally involved with him, it actually *did* bother her to see Bruce hurting sometimes. Sometimes, she even forgot that she was the one who had caused it all. But although she diminished her role in the situation when she felt it was convenient like the sociopathic bitch that she was, she never forgot her true goals and motivations.

Money. Money and power and status. Those were her incentives. The culmination of the twisted games she'd played in life thus far. The final step on her personal ladder.

And she was almost there.

The chance to actually act upon those true goals and motivations didn't come right away, though. Not until autumn had arrived in Stirling City and Victoria had finally managed to persuade Bruce into accompanying her to one of the local coffee shops for a drink and a bit of good company. Going out for coffee was something that Bruce had always associated with Cecilia, but he'd been trying to convince himself that he couldn't avoid the drink and be sad at the thought of java forever. So when Victoria had asked him to join her for a cup during lunch break to go over some important accounting business, he'd accepted.

Bruce sat across from her in the dimly-lit cranberry-walled locale, lost in thought as he sipped gingerly at a hot cup of Sumatra blend and listened to the soothing murmur of the obligatory hipster music that was playing on the sound system. He'd known Victoria as an office fixture for quite a while now, but only in recent months had some odd feelings arisen in him and he'd started to see her as more than just a conveniently-placed employee and colleague. He couldn't put his finger on the exact moment when things had taken this turn, but he did know that he'd been grateful for the concern she'd shown him since he'd lost his wife in such a terrible and tragic way. Apparently, that appreciation was having an effect on him. More of an effect than he'd expected. He glanced at her cautiously before speaking up, taking in the steely gray of her eyes and the matching gray leopard-print scarf wrapped around her slender neck. Her golden hair was pulled back in an alligator clip, away from her face.

Admittedly, she looked particularly attractive today.

"Victoria... I know we're supposed to be talking about the budget," he said. "But if I can be candid for a moment, I really have to thank you."

His claim had come out of the blue. Victoria's gaze perked up from her coffee and she blinked in what appeared to be quizzical surprise. "For what?" she asked in an innocent voice.

"For being so..." he fished for the right word. "*Supportive* over the past two years. They haven't been easy, with all of the dead ends in the investigation. But even something as mundane as coffee can really brighten a man's day when nothing else is going right. It's meant a lot to me that you've put forth the effort," he confessed, showing a vulnerability that he all too often hid behind his no-nonsense business suits and stern exterior.

Victoria relinquished the urge to smile in triumph at this admission and kept her expression one of true care and concern. She reached across the table and placed her manicured hand over his. When he didn't pull away from her, she knew that she was finally getting somewhere.

"I care, Bruce," she said simply. "It's hurt me to see you hurting so badly. The night Cecilia died was horrible and sudden for all of us. She was a wonderful woman and I can't even imagine what you've had to go through since then..."

She stopped herself, noticing the lines in his forehead crease as a grimace formed on Bruce's face. His expression turned uncomfortable and pained at the mention of that terrible night. Even after all this time, he felt somehow at fault about it... though what had happened had technically been *Victoria's* doing. But Victoria didn't allow the pang of guilt that any normal person would feel to enter her mind. She couldn't. Even if she *did* feel bad at times that it had taken such extreme measures to make any headway with him, the ends justified the means. If she wouldn't have put her terrible but necessary plan into motion, she wouldn't be sitting across from Bruce now. This "relationship" that she'd so patiently and methodically cultivated over the past year and a half was her big chance at having him, his money, an easier life, and an early retirement. She wouldn't apologize for that. But she *would* apologize for bringing up something dreary and reminding him of events that she herself had orchestrated to unceremoniously disband his marriage when it wasn't necessary.

"I'm sorry, Bruce. I wasn't trying to upset you, I just-"

"It's okay," he shook his head. "I know you're not trying to upset me. What happened to my wife is just a reality that I'm going to have to learn to accept." He paused, looking down into his cup. His eyes darkened as his fingers unintentionally squeezed the cardboard sleeve. "But mark my words... I *will* find whoever hurt her one day and I'll make them pay. I've promised myself and my children that. I've promised *her* that. But in the meantime, I'm just trying to take comfort in knowing that she lived a happy life and was loved by many people. It's all I can do."

Victoria studied his face, silent for a moment. She didn't doubt his intentions, but he wasn't going to find that person. Not if she could help it. "You'll have your justice one day," she lied through her teeth, keeping up the charade and ignoring his nameless threat. "You'll find whoever did it. I'm sure of it."

"I'm glad you think so," he sighed. "Most people don't."

The statement felt profound; profound enough to nip that conversation in the bud. The two sat in silence for a few moments, sipping their coffees quietly. Finally, Bruce looked at Victoria again, hesitant but hopeful. Maybe for the first time in a while.

"You know, I have to tell you..." he admitted. "I'm glad that I can say these things to you. I never would have expected to become close to an employee. I don't like to mix business with pleasure. It's not professional. This isn't something that's normal for me. I don't like to make it a habit. But I enjoy your company. It's been one of the few things that's gotten me through this mess."

Victoria reveled at his words. "I'm glad to have helped."

"You have," he confirmed.

A coy smirk played on Victoria's lips. Now was her chance. "Then would you like to join me and Nicolette for dinner sometime?" she offered. "I'm sure she'd love to meet the girls."

CHAPTER SIXTEEN
A Plan Unfolds

ANGELINA COULDN'T REMEMBER the last time she had felt so infuriated. Dad had done a lot of things to make her mad over the past two years, but this time he'd really managed to outdo himself. She'd much rather be hanging out with Elena or one of her friends than going on a stupid spur-of-the-moment dinner date with some *woman* tonight, but *no*. Here she was, about to get in the car and do just that, and she was *not* very happy about it.

"Ugh... do we *have* to go?" she whined as she made her way down the front walk to where her father's Mercedes-Benz was already parked on the road waiting for them. She pouted in contempt and kicked at the ground, folding her arms over her chest like a diva. Blair frowned quietly in agreement behind her, just as apprehensive, if maybe not as dramatic. The girls had dolled themselves up enough to play their obligatory parts tonight – Angelina in a nice (although in her opinion rather nerdy and itchy) tumbleweed cardigan over one of her favorite leopard-print tops, and Blair in a vintage baby blue flowered dress decorated with pretty cream lace – but neither of them had any desire to meet this random lady Dad had told them about. Unfortunately, they didn't have much choice in the matter. Bruce had made their minds up for them and there was no getting out of it this time. Angelina couldn't run away or throw a tantrum now.

"Yes, Angelina, you have to go," he insisted, shooing her into the car. "I'd really like you girls to meet this friend of mine. She asked us to come over for dinner tonight and it's only courteous to accept her kind offer. I think the two of you may even end up liking her. She's very nice and she has a daughter your age, too. Wouldn't you like to make a new friend?"

"I already *have* friends," Angelina groused as she yanked her seatbelt across her waist, uttering the words with such ballsy disregard that her sister's eyes widened in shock. "I don't *need* any new ones. This is stupid!"

"Excuse me?" Bruce scolded her in a tone that let her know that she'd overstepped her bounds and the chance of winning this particular argument was null. "I am your father. Do *not* speak to me in that tone, young lady. You're going to go to this dinner and you're going to behave yourself."

"But I don't want to-"

"Behave yourself," Bruce repeated sternly.

Angelina could see that she wasn't going to get her way.

"Fine," she groaned in defeat.

"Fine and what else?" he prompted her.

She rolled her eyes. "I'm sorry, Daddy."

"Good, that's better. Blair Bear, buckle your seatbelt."

Blair obediently followed suit, clicking down on her restraint and leaning her head against the car window with a sigh. Bruce turned the keys in the ignition and sighed himself. He didn't show it on the outside, but inside he could empathize with the girls' unease. He was feeling a bit more unsettled than he let on, too. He'd found himself in a situation that he'd never thought he'd be in: having dinner at the home of an attractive employee, his wife dead, his girls putting up a fuss. But despite it, he tried to be hopeful and optimistic. Life had been so dark for the last two years. He was exhausted. He needed a distraction to take his mind off of things, and a friendly dinner outing had potential to do that.

He just needed his girls to get on board and make things a little easier for him. Just for a few hours, that was all that he asked. He'd see if he got his wishes - and just how bad Angelina wanted to be grounded this particular week - soon enough. It didn't take long for them to arrive at a modest cream-colored ranch house with yellow rose-bushes lining the walkway out front. Bruce parked the car and beckoned his begrudging daughters out of it.

"Now, her name is Victoria," he told them as they walked up the front steps of her porch. He glanced at Angelina and Blair, taking in the disgruntled looks on their faces. "Just be nice to her, will you? Remember your manners."

Angelina and Blair grumbled in acceptance and Bruce rang the doorbell, hoping that his daughters would cheer up and stop being difficult once they were inside. The bell had barely rung when a tall, tanned, golden-haired woman with a big, toothy grin on her face propped the door open and greeted them. She was wearing a tight turquoise wrap dress that would have looked cute had it not been for the fact that her cleavage was nearly spilling out of its dramatic plunge. She certainly didn't leave much to the imagination. Any more of a "V" in the front of that dress and there could have easily been a major wardrobe malfunction going on.

"I'm so glad you could make it, Bruce! This must be Angelina and Blair. It's *so* nice to finally meet you girls!" Victoria coddled them in her most enthusiastic sing-song, going for the interested, innocent, and overly-nice persona. She waved them inside with a hearty flourish. "Come in, come in! I just finished cooking. You're going to *love* what we're having for dinner."

Angelina and Blair raised their eyebrows at eachother as Victoria led them through the front door. It didn't matter if this woman was acting friendly; they'd already had their pre-

234 | Stephanie Rose Vigano

conceived notions about her before they'd even stepped foot in the car, and the sooner this visit was over with, the better.

At least it appeared that they wouldn't have to suffer through an awkward dinner alone. Once they were inside, they could see a young girl who looked to be about their age sitting down on the living room couch watching cartoons. She looked just like Victoria, except her hair was dark brown instead of a dandelion bottle-blonde, and her choice in clothing - a simple brown waffle shirt and swishy light blue skirt over a pair of cute beige boat shoes - was much less flashy and offensive. She glanced at her mother's visitors and waved at them cautiously.

"Don't just sit there and wave, come over here and greet our guests," Victoria reprimanded her. God, what a slow little brat her daughter was! The girl held her tongue and pushed herself up from the couch, flicking off the television set.

"I presume this is Nicolette," Bruce smiled at her, reaching out to give her hand a shake. "It's nice to finally meet you."

"This is Bruce von Essen," Victoria interjected somewhat bossily. "And his daughters, Angelina and Blair. They're in the same grade as you."

"Nice to meet you," Nicolette said in a compulsory mumble, looking back and forth between the twins and their father and giving the latter of the three an uncertain half-smile in return. This situation might have been odd for the von Essen twins, but it was equally weird for Nicolette. Bruce seemed alright so far, but she couldn't help feeling apprehensive. After all, it wasn't like she normally *met* her mother's visitors, at least not formally. They'd never been friendly, nor were they ever over for dinner, and when they weren't straight-out ignoring her, the most interaction she'd ever had with the men who had come over in the past was being stared at like a piece of meat or made fun of like she was some sort of comic relief. This was a little... different to say the least. Hopefully it would be a good kind of different.

When the awkward introductions were through, Nicolette, Angelina, Blair, and Bruce took a seat at the dinner table while Victoria laid down steaming hot plates of salmon, couscous, and cucumber salad. On the kitchen island, a chip and dip platter was laid out with pretzels and other snacks for the girls, and a big bowl nearby held what wasn't already passed out of her homemade gazpacho. "Get it while it's hot!" she announced annoyingly as she put down her potholders and picked up a fork. As she sat down in her chair she leaned forward, exposing far more skin than Blair or Angelina had ever wanted to see.

Angelina shot a grossed-out look at Blair, whose innocent caramel eyes were nearly popping out of her head.

"Eww, boobs!" she hissed in an antagonizing whisper despite Bruce's instructions to mind their manners. Blair giggled at her quietly, the others completely oblivious to their exchange.

Soon enough, the food had made its rounds and the sound of clinking silverware filled the room. Blair took small bites of her cucumber salad, pretending to like what was on her plate, but the meal Victoria had prepared wasn't anything like her mother's cooking, nor the nanny's for that matter. She was sure Victoria had honestly tried, but the salmon was a bit overdone and the couscous wasn't done enough. She tried to be respectful and discreet, but it was hard to refrain from giggling when Angelina was making faces behind Dad's back. Angelina thought that she was being cute and sneaky, but unlike her earlier quip, her dinnertime antics didn't go unnoticed by her hostess in the least.

'Spoiled little shits,' Victoria thought in annoyance as Angelina squashed a mushy smiley face into her salmon with her fork. *'Damn it, why does Bruce have to have such snotty little children?'*

This wasn't what she said out loud, of course.

"You know, it really is nice to have you all over. I usually don't have such a full table in here," she commented as if she were stupid and oblivious, ignoring Angelina's prima donna attitude and Blair's unfortunate susceptibility to follow her lead.

"Well, thank you for inviting us, Victoria. It was a very kind gesture," Bruce smiled at her cordially.

Angelina stuck her tongue out at Blair and pointed towards her mouth, making a gagging noise. This time Bruce definitely noticed. He shot her a stern look and cleared his throat, and Blair barely managed to clamp her hand over her mouth to stifle another giggle. Across the table, Nicolette pretended to be very interested in her gazpacho, but her attempt to hide a silent smile of approval was unsuccessful. She didn't know what the twins thought of her yet, but she was starting to like these girls already. Especially Angelina. Nicolette thought that Angelina was funny, but Victoria was *not* amused by these irritating little brats in the slightest. She resumed her façade of innocence and interest nonetheless, sipping from her champagne glass thoughtfully.

"So, I hear that the two of you are very musically gifted girls," she complimented them sweetly. "Your father has said so many nice things about you. Blair, you play the piano?"

Blair nearly choked on a piece of fish. "Oh, yes, ma'am," she caught herself quickly. "I'm classically trained. I like it a lot."

"How nice. Piano is such a pretty instrument. I wish I could play," Victoria bullshitted. "And Angelina, you're a singer? I hear you're very good. I'd love to hear you sing sometime."

Angelina wanted to say something cold and sarcastic back like '*I bet you would*' or '*get in line,*' but caught the look of '*please, be nice and give her a chance or you're going to be grounded again*' on her father's face and thought better of it. She caved with a forced fake smile and a simple, unenthused, "Yeah, thanks," instead.

"I'm looking forward to it," Victoria grinned back.

Angelina dug a hole in her couscous.

"Angelina and Blair are both very talented," Bruce interjected before his more rebellious daughter could be tempted to start acting up again. "They certainly have a knack for the arts." He turned his attention to Nicolette diplomatically, not wanting her to be left out of the exchange. "Nicolette dear, you must have a hobby you enjoy," he ventured. "What do you like to do?"

"Me?" Nicolette asked, surprised. She couldn't say that any of her mother's visitors had ever taken an interest in her pastimes before. She wasn't sure how to respond at first. The von Essen sisters sounded like they were pretty serious when it came to their hobbies, but she didn't have any talents like that. Her biggest talent was probably her ability to feed herself when her mom didn't make her anything for dinner, but she wasn't about to say that while Victoria was sitting there staring at her as though how mean she planned on being to her later hinged upon her answer.

The truth was, Nicolette's hobbies were just normal kid stuff like doodling, watching cartoon re-runs, and playing with what few toys and video games she had. "Umm... I don't really know," she shrugged, thinking of something random. "I like... umm... watercolors, I guess? Painting's pretty fun."

The thought of painting and the memories such a hobby evoked made the corners of Bruce's lips twitch, but he wasn't here to dwell on the past. He smiled at Victoria's daughter, trying to make her comfortable. "Well, that's wonderful. Maybe you could share some of your artwork sometime. I'm sure it's very nice."

Nicolette couldn't believe her ears. Had Victoria actually brought home a decent guy for once? She didn't want to get her hopes up, because she knew better than anyone that her mother was no saint and none of her flings ever lasted, but she decided to take the compliment for what it was worth.

"Thanks. Maybe I will," she grinned back, happy for something other than a put down for once. She went back to munching on her salmon and Victoria interrupted with more of her fake pleasantries, turning the attention away from her daughter and on to other things; none of which interested the girls very much.

Throughout the remainder of the meal, Angelina and Blair did their best to behave themselves and ignore Victoria's dense remarks, nearly malfunctioning push-up bra, and blatant flirtations with their father just to make him happy, but despite their efforts to be cordial, they weren't very happy and they couldn't help but notice the way he stared at her googly-eyed like a lovesick puppy the entire time. What was he doing? It was *gross!* And who was this woman, anyway? Why were they even here?

The girls avoided too much Victoria overload by concentrating on small-talking with Nicolette, but they still couldn't wait to get done with this food, out of this house, and back home. This whole dinner thing was awkward and weird.

But apparently, for Bruce, very satisfying.

"That was scrumptious!" he said enthusiastically, placing his fork on the table when they were finished. "I didn't know you were such a good cook, Victoria. Thank you very much."

Victoria smiled in triumph at all of the full tummies sitting around her table. "Well, we all have hidden talents. I know it may surprise you to learn that crunching numbers isn't all that I'm good at, but I'm more than a one-trick pony, Bruce."

"I certainly can't argue with that."

Angelina coughed in disgust and Victoria snickered.

"I'm glad you enjoyed dinner," she said before glancing towards Nicolette. "Clean up the dishes for us, will you, Nic?"

She said it nicely in front of Bruce and his girls, but Nicolette knew that it wasn't really a question, nor a suggestion. It was a demand. While she stood over the sink with a soapy sponge in hand and did what she was told, Angelina and Blair got up from the table and glanced at their father hopefully. He'd told them they were just visiting for dinner, hadn't he? Well, dinner was over now, and that meant it should be time to leave... but it didn't look like they'd have any such luck. Victoria and Dad were locked in some stupid conversation about their "hidden talents" or something ridiculous like that - *"I have a sailboat I keep docked at Saint George and I play a mean round of golf,"* Bruce was saying, while Victoria countered, *"I love to sketch fashion and can tell you exactly what any cologne or perfume is comprised of"* - and it appeared that they would be staying that way for quite some time.

Nicolette approached the sisters, wiping her hands on her skirt. "Your dad is really nice," she commented out of their parents' earshot. "You girls are lucky to have such a cool dad."

Angelina snorted. Sure, Nicolette thought he was nice. Dad was *plenty* nice when he was trying to look good in front of other people. But if missing recitals and yelling at her and acting distant and never being home was nice, then she was kind of afraid to know what not nice was. "Thanks, I guess," she shrugged indifferently, not fully believing it. "Your mom is... umm..."

She meant to give Nicolette a compliment back just for posterity's sake, but as she glanced at Victoria in her slutty blue wrap dress giggling at something lame her father had said, she was having trouble finding something about her that she liked.

"She's weird, I know," Nicolette finished for her, preventing her from having to strain herself too much. "It's okay, you don't have to pretend to like her. *I* don't even like her. You were really funny at dinner by the way. It was hard not to laugh."

Angelina beamed at the well-placed compliment, but Blair couldn't help being surprised. "You don't like your mom?" she asked, unable to fathom how something like that could even be possible, especially when she missed her own mother so much.

"Victoria's kind of hard to live with," Nicolette scrunched her nose. "That slave driver *always* makes me wash the dishes."

"You call her by her first name?" Blair blinked in disbelief.

Nicolette made a face. "She's weird about the 'M' word."

"Wow..." Angelina raised her eyebrows. She'd never heard of such a bizarre thing. "She really *is* weird."

Nicolette peeked over her shoulder. "She *has* been better lately. I guess your dad has something to do with that. It's kind of weird though... I don't think she's ever actually invited anyone over here for dinner before. Or spent so much time cooking it."

The von Essen girls went quiet. Victoria already had an uphill battle to fight with them and they didn't need to know the truth about her or the horrible things that she'd done to feel that way. The thing was, anyone who wasn't their mom had their disapproval when it came to closeness with their dad by default. Maybe it wasn't fair, maybe it wasn't right, but that was just the way it was. The only reason Elena had ever been different was because it had always been clear that she was only the nanny. But this situation wasn't so clear. Dad had never said that this woman was his "girlfriend" or anything, but it sure was starting to seem that way with the dumb eyeballs they were giving each other.

"Well, anyway... do you girls want to go play video games or something?" Nicolette offered. "I have a Nintendo in my room and it looks like they'll be talking about boring stuff for a while."

"Sure," Angelina shrugged. There wasn't anything better to do, so playing games had to be better than staying out here.

The girls followed Nicolette to her room, away from their chatting parents and Victoria's bad plunge dress. The whole Adessi house was decorated in neutral shades of white, beige, brown, and black, with the only real pops of color coming from strategically-placed décor items like vases, throw pillows, and the giant *Vogue* print that Victoria had hung up on the dining room wall, but Nicolette's room was noticeably plainer than the others they'd seen so far. The walls were a bland off-white, the rug was knobby and gray, and the only color came from Nicolette's green and blue butterfly quilt, the tween magazines on her bedside table, the few hand-drawn pictures she'd taped on the wall, and the half-finished dolphin painting on her flimsy wooden easel. Apparently she hadn't just been reaching for something when she'd said she liked watercolors. As she booted up her Nintendo, something pink in the corner of the room caught Blair's attention.

"Hey... did you paint this?" she asked, pointing at the finished canvas hanging slightly-off-center on the wall.

"Oh... yeah," Nicolette answered self-consciously.

"That's Paris!" Blair smiled. "I *really* want to go to Paris."

Nicolette squirmed in response. "It's not that good."

Angelina glanced at the painting. It was a likeness of the Eiffel Tower, done in bright strokes of hot pink, yellow, and lime green. It was no Monet, but it was still cute, and there was something nice about seeing someone putting homemade art on the wall again. It had been so long since Mom had done the same.

"Are you kidding? That's *really* good," she said. "I like it."

Nicolette smiled graciously. She knew that Blair and Angelina had to be feeling awkward, even without the mischievous comic relief at the dinner table to tell her that. But for two girls who didn't want to be here and felt just as confused as her, she couldn't say that she minded the compliments. She didn't get to hear such nice things often, especially not in this house.

"Thanks," she grinned, holding out a Nintendo controller. "Come on, let's play *Mario Kart*. I'm gonna be Princess Peach."

The ice broken, the girls plopped down on Nicolette's butterfly comforter and played the racing game together to pass the time and make it more bearable. While they tried to navigate one treacherous course after another, Bruce and Victoria stayed in the dining room, talking mostly about the goings-on at the office and current events in the news. Perhaps it didn't seem like much, but getting out and simply talking over dinner wasn't a luxury

Bruce afforded himself very often anymore. It was nice to take a breather. So nice, in fact, that he completely lost track of time.

Day had inevitably turned to night. The girls eventually grew tired of playing video games and flipping through Nicolette's tween magazines and ventured back to the living room to turn on the television instead. Bruce and Victoria barely noticed their re-arrival until the sound of their snores broke through the conversation. The girls were dozing off midway through another late-night preteen sitcom rerun. Angelina had already made a bed out of the couch, Blair was slumped back blinking as she tried fruitlessly to stay awake, and Nicolette kept nodding off, then jerking her head back up in an attempt not to pass out. Bruce hadn't realized just how late it was until he took a good look at the girls. He turned to Victoria apologetically as Nicolette finally gave up and trudged to her room, too tired to fight it any longer.

"My, it must be getting late," he noted, checking his watch and relinquishing his seat. "Time really does fly when you're having fun, doesn't it? We'd better get going. I'm sorry, Victoria, I'd love to stay, but my girls look like they need to get to bed."

Victoria was disappointed that her evening with Bruce was coming to an end so soon. This was the most substantial one-on-one time she'd snagged with him yet.

"Oh, it's alright," she played along, smiling and flipping her long blonde hair over her shoulder. "Your girls *do* look a little tired. Thank you for coming over, though. I *really* enjoyed your company." She shot him a suggestive glance as an afterthought, sticking her chest out as she added, "It's nice to get together for something other than business for a change, isn't it?"

Bruce was taken a bit by surprise at Victoria's apparent attempt at advancement. This time, unlike all of the other times she'd nonchalantly leaned forward at desks and tables around him before, it couldn't have been an accident. He averted his eyes from the abundant cleavage he realized he'd been staring at dumbly for the last few seconds and spluttered, "Yes, and thank you for having us. It was very pleasant. Again sometime, hmm?"

As he walked towards Angelina and Blair, Victoria pouted childishly behind his back. She wasn't finished yet, damn it!

"Girls, it's time to go," he told them, patting them on their backs to get them up and moving. "Say thank you for dinner."

Angelina and Blair didn't want to thank this skanky stranger for dinner, but they were brought up better than that despite Angelina's troublesome mealtime mischief and smiled their sweetest obligatory smiles in response, complying with their father's wishes. *"Thank you, Victoria,"* they sing-songed at her.

"Good, girls. I'm going to use the restroom and then I'll meet you two at the car," he said. He turned to Victoria and asked her where her bathroom was while Blair and Angelina walked out the door. The girls breathed a mutual sigh of relief as they finally made their way to the car - and salvation. They'd admittedly had fun playing video games and hanging out with Nicolette, but they were still more than happy to get out of Victoria's house.

Angelina yawned like a drama queen as she trudged down the walkway with her hands in her pockets. "Jeez, do you think that could have lasted any longer? I'm *so* beat," she complained.

"Me too," Blair agreed. "I can't wait to get to bed."

"Seriously."

Angelina reached forward to open the door to the backseat, but stopped just short, turning to face her sister with a heavy sigh instead. "You know... Nicolette's pretty cool," she admitted despite her earlier claim that she already had friends and didn't need any new ones. "But I *really* don't like Victoria."

Blair wrinkled her nose. "Oh. She's... okay," she shrugged, trying to be nice just for principle's sake. "She *did* invite us over and cook us dinner. At least she's *sort* of nice..."

"Nice? Yeah right. She's *too* nice, and you know what that means? It means she didn't even *want* us there. Not to mention her boobs are gross," Angelina reminded her sister stubbornly. Blair frowned at her for being so blunt, but Angelina wasn't one to mince words. She screwed up her face at the mental picture of all of that tan, mushy flesh. "I hope if we ever see Nicolette again, we don't have to come over for dinner. I *hate* dinner dates, I hate being roped into things that I don't want, and I *hate* icky fish."

For all of Blair's attempted niceties she seemed to agree with that sentiment. "I don't want Dad to have a girlfriend," she said with a worried frown, putting into words what the girls' real problem was with his new companion. The sisters shared a look.

"Me neither," Angelina agreed.

They stood there in the dark for a few long moments, staring back at the front door as an uncomfortable, awkward silence that was void of all but chirping crickets settled in, letting what they'd just said to each other sink in. Dad was spending time with a woman and it wasn't Mom. It just wasn't *right*.

"I miss Mom," Blair wrapped up with a sigh.

"Me too," Angelina nodded. She followed her sister into the car where they waited uneasily for their father to join them.

Meanwhile, Victoria had been waiting for Bruce to join her back in the house as well – and quite impatiently at that. She folded her arms over her chest and tapped her heeled foot in irritation. Luckily, it didn't take him long to gather his thoughts and return to her. After all, the real reason he'd stayed behind was to say goodbye to his hostess in private, not to actually use the facilities. Victoria straightened up and turned to face him with a pleasant smile as she heard him re-enter the room.

"Thanks again for having us, Victoria," he adjusted his shirtsleeves and reached for his leather coat. "The food was wonderful and it was very nice of you to invite my girls over to meet your daughter. I'm sorry that they were a bit misbehaved.

They're just stubborn, that's all. They've had a hard time coping since losing their mother. I hope you weren't offended."

"No offense taken," Victoria claimed with a dismissive wave. "I completely understand. I didn't expect them to be very enthusiastic. They just need time... that is, of course, if you wouldn't mind spending more time with me yourself."

She blinked her eyelashes at him irresistibly, her insides burning with an insatiable lust. Who really cared about those stupid little brats of his or their stupid little opinions? The only thing *she* cared about was staying in his good graces so she could get into other things - namely, his pocketbook and his pants.

Bruce's palm closed around his keys as he peered back at the come-hither expression on her face. In an agonizing moment, he could feel his heart being pulled in two different directions. He hadn't come here looking for anything other than her company, but Victoria was certainly attractive. *Immensely* attractive, actually. Any man would be entranced to see her golden hair pulled half-back from her face like that, her eyes rimmed with kohl, and that bold turquoise wrap dress hugging her body as snugly as it was in all the right places. And although he was technically her boss, Bruce was still just like any other man. He thought for one fleeting moment that perhaps he might like to do something about it... to thank her for the dinner and the conversation and for dressing up so nicely for him in more appropriate fashion. But he pushed the impulsive thought out of his mind in discomfort. He offered her a cordial grin and an honest "of course," instead, wishing her goodnight and turning for the door. He was about to turn the knob when he was stopped by the sharp sound of her voice.

"Wait!" she called to him.

He turned.

"Bruce... wait," she repeated, a bit calmer this time. She sauntered up to him, all swaying hips and hooded eyes, and prevented him from leaving with a purposeful hand on his chest.

Her manicured fingernails grazed the buttons on his shirt. "Don't go yet. I want to say goodnight more properly..." she said.

This was it; the opportunity she'd been waiting for. For a second, Bruce was stunned stupid by the closeness of her body, the desire that laced her catlike features, and the stony flecks of gray that flickered in her eyes... but just as she leaned in to kiss him goodnight, he caught himself and resisted her. Victoria could feel him edge away from her uncertainly, but she didn't let his confusion discourage her. Many a time before she'd worked her seduction skills with other men to get what she wanted, and she'd just have to do the same with Mr. von Essen. She'd already come this far, and from the looks of things, he'd been cracking.

So, what would it take to make that crack splinter?

"Bruce... I know that you're unhappy. And I know that you're lonely," she purred in her sultriest murmur. "But you don't have to go on like this. You should let me help you..."

Her words were the deadliest poison. Manipulative and effective. She leaned in once more, twisting her fingers in the fabric of his shirt, and this time he didn't pull away. He kissed her hesitantly at first, then harder as he felt a wave of *something* wash over him. He didn't know what it was - maybe relief. He didn't "love" Victoria, so it wasn't that. Nor was it fireworks or butterflies or a choir of angels singing in the heavens. But after feeling so dead and so empty for so long, he finally felt like something was happening again. Like he could actually feel something other than the dull ache in his chest that time hadn't been able to mend.

He pulled her closer and deepened the kiss, and in that moment, Victoria knew that she had him. At last, after months of plotting and scheming and obsessing, it would only be a matter of time before the von Essen fortune was firmly in her grasp.

CHAPTER SEVENTEEN
Pulling the Strings

FROM THE DAY OF THAT first kiss - that first taste of physical contact - the relationship between Bruce and Victoria escalated quickly. There was no question for the girls anymore as to whether this woman was Dad's new "girlfriend" or not, and while Bruce knew that he'd never care for another woman in the same way that he had for Cecilia, the hard truth was that his wife was gone now, and had been for more than two years. He had to start to move on with his life again, or at least appear to do so. And Victoria could help him with that, just like she'd promised.

Bruce hadn't paid her pencil skirts, high heels, and tight blouses much mind before, but a lonely, broken man in need of a distraction and some semblance of normalcy to fill the void noticed such things a little more than a man who was happily married to the love of his life. The ball was in Victoria's court now, and the cruel-hearted seductress was more than happy about the forward momentum in her at-one-time completely unrealistic schemes. Bruce's piqued interest instilled in her an extreme amount of self-gratification and arrogance unrivaled by any she'd ever had before. Things could not have gone more perfectly.

Looking back, her big "plan" had never been much of a plan. Honestly, after that whole banquet debacle, *anything* could have happened. But all of a sudden, she was the puppeteer pulling the strings... and Bruce was her helpless marionette.

He was smitten with her. Totally besotted. But Blair and Angelina weren't so easily won over by sugared words and batted eyelashes. The girls didn't always agree on everything, but one thing they *could* agree on without a sliver of a doubt was that Dad having a girlfriend - *any* girlfriend - was just plain wrong, and they didn't like it. Bruce's daughters knew nothing of Victoria's wicked schemes and never suspected her of anything truly "evil," but Victoria was still an outsider nonetheless. She wasn't Mom and would never *be* Mom, and therefore didn't belong in this picture. This intruder could've farted rainbows and unicorns and they still would've felt the same. Everything about her being a part of Dad's life irked them. They dealt with her solely because they didn't have a choice, but secretly wished that Victoria would go away, leave them alone, and stop trying to take Mom's place.

But Victoria didn't go away. Dad's new girlfriend stuck around like a tick, and you know what they say about ticks. A tick cannot be lured off or gently wiped off; it has to be burned off.

Alas, here were Angelina and Blair without any matches.

It would have taken a hefty fire to change the course their father was traveling down, however. Desperate hearts called for reckless amends, and the momentum wasn't faltering. Victoria and Bruce began going on dates. Secret ones to dinners, plays, and the occasional musical performance. He took her to museums, to art galleries, and to the orchestra. She attended fashion shows and charity galas at his side. Most of these outings were disguised as business outings, but no matter what you called them, they were a taste of the life that Victoria had always wanted so badly, a taste of the life Cecilia had with Bruce before... and she reveled in it.

She and Bruce kept their new relationship status on the down-low since she was still a manager at his company in light of avoiding claims of favoritism and special treatment, but Bruce's perturbed little girls didn't adhere to the same restraint. They knew better than to spout the news to everyone and their mother, but kept it within the circle of their closest friends, confiding in Aiden, Ashleigh, Gisele, and Katie when Dad wasn't around and listening. These days, that was often... because if Dad hadn't been around much before, he *certainly* wasn't now.

"Her boobs are always out!" Angelina hooted brazenly on the phone one afternoon after school as she three-wayed her posse in the sanctuary of her room. "And they're HUGE!"

"Gross!" Katie giggled. "That's nasty!"

"You're telling me!" Angelina carried on. "They're like two big floppy water balloons filled with mashed potatoes. You're just lucky that you two don't have to see them all the time like I do."

"Eww!" Katie squealed at the mental visual.

"Eww is right! Icky Vicky is *so* annoying and stupid. She always tries to act so nice and sweet and *perfect* all the time, but I know better. It's not real nice, it's *fake* nice. I can't *stand* it!"

"Well, if you want to get rid of her, then maybe you could prank her," Gisele suggested helpfully. "Next time she comes over, put a tack on her seat. That'll get her to back off."

"Yeah! First make her sit on it. Then poke her in the boob with it and see if it pops," Katie added immaturely.

"I should!" Angelina agreed with a devilish cackle. The thought sent a surge of sick, sadistic glee through her. She rubbed her hands together. "Ooh, can you imagine how mad she would be? Her dumb face would get so red! That would be *so* funny!"

The girls cracked up in evil hysterics as they pictured this scenario in their heads, but for as much as Angelina would've loved to try it and follow through with the cruel and demented means of eliminating Victoria that they came up with, she never did. Forget being grounded; her father would *kill* her if she stabbed a guest with a thumbtack. And Blair, despite her mutual dislike for Dad being in a new relationship, would probably kill her too just for doing something so mean. Elena wouldn't kill her, but she *would* scold her for it and take away her dessert privileges for a while... and that was deterrent enough, because Elena made a mean chocolate chip cookie. Angelina would just have to think of less violent ways to show her distaste for Victoria. Annoying her or defying her maybe. That would do it. It didn't make Dad happy when Angelina caused him such difficulty, but Angelina didn't care. She acted up all the same, and inevitably saw the rift between herself and her father grow even wider because of it.

Meanwhile, Victoria's own daughter wasn't sure *what* to make of her mother's new romance with the wealthy businessman. Nicolette didn't know what it was like to have a dad in her life, nor *any* male presence for that matter. But for what it was worth, she liked what little of Bruce she got to see and thought that he was a nice enough man to have around. On one hand she was hopeful. Yet on the other she was honestly confused, because she'd expected this to be another one of her mother's flings. After all, Victoria had always been promiscuous before and was completely incapable of real love. There was no sense in denying that. Yet regardless of Nicolette's trepidation, things were changing. There was no denying *that* either. Victoria didn't bring home random strange men anymore and she was snapping at Nicolette a lot less, too. That was undoubtedly a step in the right direction, and as far as Nicolette was concerned, she could handle the weirdness and confusion of having a man around if it meant that her life was improving. The longer her mother stayed with Bruce and kept this up, the better... and as it looked, Bruce wasn't going anywhere any time soon.

He'd found his distraction.

The first time Victoria had slept with him had been nothing short of a fantasy-come-true for her. Sure, the location might not have been the conference table at the office nor some weird jungle love den like in her twisted fantasies, but finally managing to lure him into bed had been an accomplishment that she'd been quite proud of all the same. She would never forget the satisfaction she had felt in knowing that the wait, the patience, and the drastic measures had truly been *worth* it.

Bruce had been everything she'd dreamed of and more.

He had been standing in the living room at the Adessi house that night, waiting for Victoria to finish getting ready to go out. He'd arrived to pick her up for a date - or another "business-related outing," rather - and Victoria had insisted that she needed just a few more minutes in her room before they could set off.

"Are you almost done in there?" Bruce called to her impatiently, checking the silver Rolex latched around his wrist. "We have reservations, Vicky. You didn't forget that, right?"

"I'm almost ready!" Victoria called back to him. "Can you come in here a minute? I really need your help with something."

Bruce shook his head impatiently. He couldn't fathom why it always took women so long to get ready. He almost felt like scolding her for it. But when he opened the door to her bedroom, all thoughts of discipline fled his mind. His jaw dropped at what he saw. He'd assumed that the help Victoria needed would be with a stubborn zipper at most... but apparently he'd been wrong.

Very wrong.

The room was dark. A candle flickered on the nightstand. There she was, lounging seductively on her bed wearing nothing but frilly black lingerie and a pair of strappy high heels. Her makeup was smoky and seductive. Her hair was wild and loose. Her skin was toned and tanned. Her breasts were barely contained in her dark lace push-up bra. And thigh-high stockings attached to a satin garter belt at the inviting curve of her hips. On a frame like hers, the look was nothing short of pornographic.

"Victoria-" he murmured, startled by her brazenness. "I was *not* expecting this..."

"Of course you weren't. But it looks like you're happy to see me," she noted, pushing herself from the bed and raising a suggestive eyebrow as she eyed up the crotch of his pants. Bruce's face turned a very uncharacteristic shade of crimson as he realized just how right she was. As she walked towards him, swaying her hips enticingly, beads of sweat formed on Bruce's brow. He couldn't tear his eyes away from her svelte body. She was a perfect canvas of curves and skin, and like all the men before him, he was falling swiftly into her trap. It didn't matter that he was a successful CEO. Behind the money and status, he was still only a man. He wanted her, he knew it… and that dangerous look in her feline eyes made him forget to care if it was right or wrong.

She wrapped her arms around his strong, broad shoulders, lacing her fingernails in his hair and brushing her body against his shamelessly. It was easy to see how excited he was. A primal flare pulsed through her veins.

"What do you say we screw the reservations and get you out of these fancy clothes?" she purred in her sultriest voice, breath hot against the shell of his ear. When she was looking at him like that, all sex-kitten and lust, it was hard to tell her no.

So he didn't.

Bruce's lips crashed against hers. His tongue pushed into her mouth. His palms groped for any part of her body they could find. She peeled off his suit coat in a heated rush and made a hasty grab for his tie. Soon they'd forgotten all about their dinner reservations. It wasn't a meal Bruce was hungry for anymore, and there was more than one way to work off excess baggage.

It was like another person had taken over his very being. He wasn't nice or romantic or gentle with her. He was rough and feral, and Victoria swooned at his assertiveness. Usually she was the one who had to play the dominant aggressor with men, but her boss was proving to be just as hot and steamy as she'd fantasized him to be. He took her in bed, against the wall, on the dresser. Right-side up, upside down. The act was much less about love than it was about releasing pent-up pain and frustration, but that was just fine and dandy with Victoria. She didn't care much about love anyway, and pain had always been a good motivator.

As Bruce forgot himself and left the once gentle and familial man he was behind, Victoria could practically taste the impending victory on the horizon. She was finally getting what she wanted. She let herself enjoy the prize, determined that when she was done with him, he wouldn't know left from right.

The first time inevitably did not end up being the last. Rather, sex soon became a staple of Bruce and Victoria's budding relationship. Perhaps it was lewd, but partaking in the sordid act with the blonde bombshell served as a means of coping and escape for Bruce; yet another distraction from the rest of the world and all of his troubles. It was a time when he could revert back to primal instincts and focus solely on pleasure, not on all the sorrow and pain and unanswered questions in his life. Bruce craved more the more he got, and Victoria was always willing to slip under the sheets with him at any given moment to satisfy that craving. Or anywhere else, for that matter. She got her wish to have him on his desk. She got her wish to have him in the conference room. And somehow, she'd managed to convince Bruce that it was all his idea. It was subtle and cold, but she was gaining control.

Bit by bit, the puppeteer's strings grew tauter.

These escapades could only stay fun and games for so long, however. Bruce was a man with a sex drive, yes. But he was also a man with a reputation, an image to uphold, and a place of power to reinforce at the very company he'd created. For the past two years it had felt like a pity party in the office for him - *"oh, poor broken Bruce!"* But Bruce didn't want a pity party. As the relationship between he and Victoria progressed, he realized that he had a very important decision to make. He couldn't keep this a secret forever, and he wanted to appear in control of the life that had been broken. He didn't want the advisory board to ever question his capabilities again. And besides, he wasn't a fling-with-employees man. He was a support-a-family-and-look-presentable-to-society man. He had two choices: put an end to his trysts with Victoria, or consider a more concrete arrangement.

But before he could make that decision, he needed pay a visit to someone very important first.

Bruce stood in front of Cecilia's grave in the Saint Thomas Church Cemetery, holding a small bundle of red flowers from the von Essen garden against his chest. A gardener had been taking care of Cecilia's old plot over the past few years, but as soon as Bruce had noticed the Tuscan poppies blooming, he'd picked a few to bring back to her. It had been a while since he'd been able to muster the courage to visit this place, and as he peered down at the outline of Cecilia's name etched in the stone, his heart was heavy and soul conflicted. His mind was swirling with thoughts of his past with her, of his current relationship with Victoria, and of his desire to take things with his new girlfriend to the next level. Standing before his dead wife's grave, he couldn't help but feel guilty, like he was being unfaithful somehow, even though she had passed away a long time ago. It was an uncomfortable feeling that he wished would go away and leave him alone... but would it ever? He'd always been a big believer in "till death do us part." He just hadn't been expecting that part to come so soon.

Bruce felt... stuck. But even more than that, he felt lonely and depressed. Victoria's attention had undeniably helped him cope in the time that had passed, and his feelings for her had grown to be more than just professional. She didn't take Cecilia's place - no one would *ever* be able to take Cecilia's place. And he'd never imagined in a million years that he would ever be with another woman, because sweet Cecilia was all that he'd needed. But there was still something there. It had to be more than just a coping mechanism. More than just physical desire or a distraction or wanting to look good within society by having a wife and appearing grounded and sane. He had to believe that. Victoria was a friend to him now, a confidante. Someone he appreciated.

And then there was little Nicolette. Bruce had fallen for the darling girl as soon as he'd met her. She was a little awkward sometimes, as though having a man around baffled her somehow, but she was still endearing despite her quirks. Maybe it was because she painted or because she had blue eyes, like Cecilia had.

Who could say? Victoria hadn't shared much with him about her romantic past, but all that Bruce needed to know about Nicolette was that her father was no longer in the picture. According to Victoria, he'd left as soon as he'd discovered that she was pregnant. He was certain that Nicolette didn't even know who the man was nor cared to know, because she never spoke of him nor talked about wanting to meet him. Well, she deserved to have someone in her life who would take care of her. And she seemed to get along well with his daughters, especially Angelina. Bruce had never planned on having more children after the twins, but he was sure that he'd like for her to be a part of his family.

His family.

Bruce's stomach twisted as he thought of how Blair and Angelina would react to something as big as what he was considering. Surely their stubbornness and undying devotion to their mother would cause them to be upset about the prospect of him remarrying; he had no doubts of that. They'd already expressed so enough and he'd found Angelina challenging him more times than not about more than just this. But he didn't want to remarry to disrespect Cecilia's memory. He just didn't want to be alone for the rest of his life. He wanted to be happy again, to feel cared for again by another human being. He wanted a way to fill the void that wasn't available to him through work. They could understand the need to heal and rebuild, couldn't they?

Bruce ran a hand over Cecilia's headstone, thinking of his beautiful wife and remembering how her Caribbean-blue eyes had lit up when he'd proposed to her at the river. He'd never forget that look on her face, the hug she'd wrapped him in, nor the tears of joy that had run down her soft flushed cheeks. It had been an afternoon straight out of a fairytale... but he'd learned that fairytales were for children. Naive and unrealistic. The world didn't stop when bad things happened. It kept going, and he had to do the same. Even when he didn't want to. Even when it hurt.

That was it then. The answer to his question.

He sighed as he placed his flowers down on the ground and pulled his hand away from the stone marker in front of him. He knew that it was time to move on from all of this sadness and try to heal his wounded heart. He couldn't go on like this.

"I hope you will not think ill of me," he whispered to the empty air, tracing his fingers over Cecilia's name. "I love you, Cecilia. I always will. Nothing will ever change that."

And then he turned away from the cold stone grave, leaving the beautiful bundle of Tuscan poppies - and his old life - behind him.

CHAPTER EIGHTEEN

Very Big Changes

VICTORIA LAID ACROSS FROM BRUCE on the deck of his thirty-five foot cruising sailboat, The Sapphire Goddess, wearing nothing but a black and gold-sequined La Perla bikini and a flowy black unbuttoned cover-up, looking very much like a goddess herself. The water on Lake Saint George was wide and calm and even bluer than the sky, and the sun beating down on it left shimmering patterns in its wake. Bruce spent most of his time in Stirling, but sometimes he liked to drive to this lake and sail his boat. In the same way that Cecilia had loved to paint and garden, he found the task of sailing strangely and wholly therapeutic. To smell the water and see the trees and look out at the Adirondacks beyond and feel that telltale ache in his back and shoulders the next day left him with a gratifying feeling unlike much else. He'd never been very interested in giant luxury yachts, though he had plenty of money for them and had been on them for parties and business meetings. But huge yachts didn't feel quite as intimate and personal, and when you had a woman like Victoria on your boat, you'd want to get as intimate and personal as possible.

Victoria situated herself on her side, propping herself up on her elbow and resting her head in her hand as she smirked at the shirtless captain beside her and took a long sip of *Chateau Lafite* from the tall wine glass positioned on the deck in front of

258 | *Stephanie Rose Vigano*

her. They'd nearly reached the end of the bottle, but it was a special occasion to be invited on her first weekend getaway with her boss - and they'd celebrated not just with this wine and a delicious seafood lunch on the water, but with some rather spine-tingling sex only a few moments prior. Victoria couldn't get over what a good lover Bruce was. At one point, she'd had a worrisome concern that maybe she'd been overblowing her expectations of him. But twice already on the floor of this boat, he'd proven her fantasies as right as ever, and prior to this, many times before. She'd certainly been treated to the finer things since pursuing her affair with him, and after an afternoon like this, she was certain that she could get used to these "business outings."

She could get very used to them indeed.

"That was incredible, Bruce," she grinned a naughty grin, reaching forward to trail a French-manicured fingernail down the center of his exposed chest as she appreciated the way that working the sails - and her body, more recently - had left his muscles taut and slick with sweat. "I mean, what you just did right now wasn't bad, but the prosciutto-wrapped shrimp was to-die for. And this wine?" She put her fingers to her lips, making a puckery kissing noise like an old, seasoned chef. *"Che bello."*

"Hmm... yes, well you'll have to humor me," Bruce twirled a strand of her golden blonde hair around his finger in amusement. "I have a thing for red wines, particularly vintage."

"Something we have in common, then," she claimed egotistically, as if she'd really been in the market to drink vintage red wines that cost the price of a rather well-off person's salary before. She smiled a smug smile, taking a glance at the label on the bottle before turning her gaze from Bruce's physique to the lake. This was really a beautiful place. The mountains, the pine trees, the water... she wasn't much of an outdoors girl, but it was heaven. And the best part about it was that nobody knew where she was. Victoria kind of liked the thrill of sneaking around like this, but Bruce's motivation for finding some isolation away from the city was a bit more complex than usual this time. He had something very personal planned for this trip and wanted privacy to handle it. Having sex with Victoria was one thing - that didn't take much effort, with a drive and a body like hers and the escape that they provided him. But this would be a big step after all that he'd been through, and he'd wanted to know he was ready for it.

"Victoria... there's been something I've been meaning to talk to you about," he admitted, peering into her kohl-rimmed eyes with a thoughtful look in his. He was reminded, not for the first time since the start of their affair, that her eyes weren't the pretty sapphire blue that Cecilia's had been - the sapphire blue that he'd named this very boat after - but rather a steely gray. Still nice... just different. Mysterious, in a way. "You've been a big help to me over the past few months," he continued. "More than you know. I'll never be able to thank you enough for that."

"Oh, there's no need to thank me," Victoria insisted, her words ironic in that they were probably the most honest ones she'd ever spoken. An oblivious Bruce seemed to think otherwise.

"No, I do need to," he insisted. He sat up, taking her wine glass from her fingertips and holding her hand in his. "Victoria, listen... almost three years ago, I thought my life had ended. But I've come to believe in second chances and new beginnings."

Victoria cut the bashful act and listened to him intently.

"My life has been very painful for a long time now, but I can't live like this anymore. I'd like to have a second chance at being happy. I don't want to live the rest of my life in sadness, especially when I see how happy I can be when I'm with you. Like we are here, on this boat. What I'm asking for is for you to give me that second chance. For a new beginning... for you and I to start a life together... and for us to be something more."

He reached into a small compartment that he kept loose items in and pulled out the black box he'd been hiding from her the whole afternoon and placed it on the deck in front of her.

Victoria gasped as her hands flew to her mouth. She almost wanted to scream or cry or maybe do a combination of the two. Typically, uncontrolled screaming and crying were things she never did, emotions she never let take control of her, but the exhilaration that had suddenly swelled inside of her chest was almost too much to bear. That box could only mean one thing, and for all of her scheming and manipulating, she hadn't expected Bruce to ask what she presumed he was asking so soon. She'd thought she'd still need to work for it longer; after all, she'd waited long enough to get this far. This was only their first time venturing outside of Stirling and the realization that her schemes were finally coming a head made her beam uncontrollably, like a shark in a feeding frenzy, gorging on its bloodlust.

There weren't any sharks in the water at Lake Saint George, but there sure as hell was one on this boat. Of course, that wasn't what Bruce saw. Bruce didn't see a deadly predator. He saw a woman in love with a happy smile on her face.

And in seeing that, something warm welled in his heart.

"Open it," he said in amusement. "Please."

Victoria grabbed the box and did as she was asked. She gasped again at the sight of the sparkling diamond ring inside. It was huge. Gigantic. An exquisite round-cut diamond solitaire surrounded by an intricate pavé diamond halo, set in an 18-karat white gold band lined with diamonds. It was the most beautiful piece of jewelry she'd ever seen, let alone worn. She couldn't imagine in her wildest dreams how much this ring had cost, but was sure it had to be pocket change to a man like Bruce. She thought of all the other expensive things she could help herself to once she was Mrs. von Essen and bubbled over with glee.

"Oh, Bruce!" she put her hand to her chest. "It's incredible!"

He chuckled and slid the ring on her finger. As she admired the radiant, gleaming diamond there contrasting with the bronzed tan of her skin, happy tears began to cloud her vision.

"Victoria... I think this goes without saying. But I suppose what I'm asking is... will you marry me?" he asked her officially.

Victoria's answer was a no-brainer. She leaned across the deck and pulled him towards her, meeting his lips with a hungry kiss. In no time her bikini top was unlaced and the bottoms were cast aside on the floor again. Hell yes, she'd marry him.

And soon, she'd have everything she'd ever dreamed of.

Two other ladies would not be so excited about the big engagement. Bruce knew that informing his girls of his impending wedding plans would be a bit of a shock for them, but it was a shock that he could no longer avoid. Marriage was something that would affect Angelina and Blair just as much - if not even more - as him, but while the presence of a new stepmother and stepsister in the house would undoubtedly be a big change for them to adjust to, he was certain they'd be able to do it and be happy about it in time if only they'd give it a chance. On the evening after he returned from his trip to Saint George with Victoria, he called the girls to the study for a family meeting and prepared to break the news. Angelina and Blair sat on the couch in front of the fireplace, looking at him apprehensively as the flickering flames behind him cast an orange glow across the tanned skin of his face.

"Girls," he addressed them firmly. "I have something very important to tell you." His daughters shared a quiet glance, wondering what in the world Dad had to spring on them this time. He continued with a deep breath, electing to be direct. "There are going to be some very big changes in this house."

"What kind of changes?" Blair fidgeted uneasily.

There was no use in stalling. "I proposed to Victoria last night, and she said yes," he confessed. "We're getting married."

The air felt like it had been sucked right out of the room. Dad hadn't hesitated, hadn't even pre-empted. It was clear from his straightforwardness on the matter that he was dead set on this and wouldn't take any arguments, and the color instantly drained from his daughters' faces. Blair gasped and turned away, unable to speak or even look at him and Angelina's expression turned to one of pure shock and mortification. The girls had hoped against this. They'd hoped that the presumably physically-driven relationship wouldn't last and that they'd never have to see Dad's new girlfriend again after a few more months of this charade. But this level of intrusion into their lives was completely different than the ending they'd envisioned. Angelina was sure that her mother was rolling over in her grave right now and the thought nearly sent her into one of her horrible hyperventilating fits. The only thing preventing her from falling into another anxiety attack and forgetting how to breathe was the pure shock of it all.

"Daddy, why would you *do* that?" she asked in utter disgust, a lump forming in her throat. Blair, who was desperately trying to hold back the tears that threatened to come rushing from her eyes finally lost the battle and bolted out of the study bawling.

"Blair!" Bruce called to her. "Blair, come back."

Angelina shot him a dirty look of contempt and ran after her sister, pounding up the spiral staircase as quickly as she could. Bruce frowned. He'd expected a poor reaction, but not something this dramatic. He trudged after the twins with a heavy sigh.

When he found them, they were in Blair's room, sitting cross-legged on her comforter. Blair was crying and Angelina looked like she'd just drank a glass of sour milk. She patted her sister's back, muttering to her under her breath. Bruce hated to see his girls so broken up over this. This was supposed to be a happy moment; a new and positive beginning for all of them. He walked towards them and pulled Blair's desk chair over to the bed. They hadn't really "talked" in a long time now and it almost felt awkward to give it a try, but he didn't know what else to do.

"Girls… what's on your minds?" he asked them, preparing for a long chat. "Why are you so upset about this?"

To his surprise, it was Blair who spoke up first.

"Victoria's going to replace Mom," she answered gloomily. "You're going to be with her and you're going to forget all about Mom and not love her anymore…"

Sadness washed over Bruce's face. "Oh, Blair Bear…" he said quietly, using the affectionate nickname he'd once called her more often. "Is that what all of this resistance has been about? It doesn't work that way. No one could ever replace your mother. I could never forget about how much I love her, and I would never want to. I'll always love her with all my heart."

"Then if you love her, why do you want to marry *Victoria* so badly?" Angelina argued back hotly. "I don't *want* you to get married! I want *Mom,* and Victoria's *not* Mom."

Blair nodded her head in feeble agreement.

"I miss her too," Bruce frowned. "And you're right… Victoria's *not* Mom. But I think that Mom would want us to try to move on and be happy again, don't you?"

Angelina crossed her arms over her chest defiantly. "No. I don't want to move on. This is stupid. I hate it."

Bruce sighed. They weren't getting anywhere. "Look, girls… I understand that this is a big change. But I'm *tired,*" he admitted, the dark circles under his eyes that much more noticeable once he'd said it. "I want Mom back just as much as you two do, but the thing is, we can't always get what we want."

"Well, why not? We have money! Why can't you just… buy a scientist or something that can bring her back?" Angelina pouted unrealistically in frustration. "That man in the movie we watched with Miss Montoya last week could bring people back…"

Bruce sighed. He was going to have to keep tabs on what kinds of movies Elena was watching with the girls, apparently.

"Because, Angelina," he said simply. "That was a movie, not real life. You can't do that in real life. You're very stubborn and I know you mean well, but you're going to have to start understanding the difference between what's reality and what's pretend or you're going to end up hurting yourself one day."

Blair sniffled and let out a tiny whimper. What her father had just said felt so harsh. Next to her, Angelina kept her arms crossed, but her stature was noticeably deflating. She was indeed a stubborn little girl, yet even *she* realized when she had to give in.

"Angelina?" Bruce said in that stern boss-of-the-family voice of his. "Can't you try?"

After a few tense moments, his daughter finally loosened her arms in defeat and they dropped to her sides. The hard eye contact she was making faltered. "I guess," she caved sullenly.

Once the girls were ready to talk, Bruce sat with them for a long time, having a heart-to-heart. Or at least what counted as a heart-to-heart for them now: basically him saying that he was sympathetic, but this was just the way things were going to be. Still, for a few fleeting moments, there were glimpses of the old Dad again. A gentleness in his voice, his hand on their shoulders, a few well-placed *Blair Bears* when it felt appropriate. After a while, Blair and Angelina started to feel a little better, but no matter what words were said or how Dad tried to reassure them and rationalize it, they still weren't thrilled about the idea of him marrying again. By the end of their conversation it was clear that they had no choice but to accept it, though... and for what it was worth, they *did* want to see Dad happy and smiling again. It was something that he hadn't been in a really long time, and if it was Victoria that would bring that smile to his face, then they would try to give her a chance. Even if it didn't make them happy and even if they didn't like it.

If for no other reason, then they'd do it for him.

Because even if Dad had forgotten it, even if he broke his promises, that was just what you did for the people you cared about. You tried to make them smile... even when it hurt.

Whether they liked what was happening or not, the girls still had their friends to confide in. It helped to be able to vent to people they could trust, and in Angelina's case, those people were predictably Aiden, Gisele, and Katie. Gisele and Katie were particularly good at mocking Victoria and making light of the situation behind her back. Maybe it was the latent mean girls hiding in them, but humor always seemed to be the best medicine.

"Look at me! Who am I?" Gisele chortled, grabbing two hand towels from the bathroom she shared with her little sister Priyanka and shoving them down her shirt amid another after-school makeover. Angelina and Katie giggled as she put her hands on her hips and stuck out her chest, strutting around the room like a narcissistic diva. "You're going to *love* what we're having for dinner. Delicious raw fish! Aren't I so hot?"

"Yes, that's perfect!" Katie clapped. "Mashed potato boobs!"

"You look just like her! Wait, you're forgetting something," Angelina insisted. She reached for the bathroom counter and found one of Gisele's mother's tubes of lipstick. Gisele leaned forward and puckered up dramatically as Angelina smeared it all over her lips. It was a dark burgundy wine color, the same color that Victoria always wore on her pillowy pout. It practically screamed *I'm a drama queen!* and the girls cracked up in hysterics.

"I hear you're a very good singer," Gisele mocked her and stuck her chest out even further. One of the towels in her shirt started to slip out and she made a hasty grab for it, stuffing it back where it belonged and clearing her throat. For some reason she was talking in a British accent, which Victoria didn't have, but made the whole thing even funnier. She put on a pompous facade.

"I hear you're a *very* good singer, Angelina. I would just *love* to hear you sing sometime. Won't you please sing a song for me?"

Angelina laughed and did one of her goofy Pavarotti's in response. *"Big stupid bimbo - I'm a big stupid bimbo!"* she bellowed to the tune of the only song she knew from *Pagliacci* - or as she liked to call it, the sad clown opera. The girls cracked up all over again, giggling and hooting and hollering until Gisele's little sister Priyanka found them and stole Gisele's towels, threatening to tell higher powers that they were making a huge mess and leading the girls on a wild chase that had them tearing all over the house. This had become a common scene for the girls, one replayed over and over again with no less amusement no matter how many iterations they repeated and rehashed. Angelina had learned that being defiant and turning everything into a joke and a farce took a whole lot of power away from the bad, and her girls were always up for joining in on her fun. Gisele's mother often wondered why so many towels were thrown into the dirty laundry, but never figured it out. Mocking Victoria became the girls' little coping mechanism. Tried and true... and *way* too fun for words.

Laughing and making things into a farce wasn't really Blair's style for coping, though. She was far too analytical for such foolish games. She always needed to talk things out, to know the reasons why things happened, to understand and grasp. She liked to organize everything and put it into its own little box. That was why Ashleigh was good for her, because Ashleigh was the same way, analytic and logical, even if not to the extreme that Blair was.

Blair had gone straight to Ashleigh after being hit with the news of her father's engagement, and Ashleigh listened like she always did, in the same way that she had listened when she'd first met Blair in the girls' restroom at Saint Joan. Blair was thankful for it. When she was in front of her father, she had to resist complaining about the big changes that were ahead for the family out of respect for his wishes and not wanting to hurt his feelings or be difficult, but around Ashleigh she didn't have to fake it.

"I can't believe my dad is getting married," Blair lamented as she and Ashleigh sat across from each other on a patch of grass in the park making friendship bracelets. It was a sunny weekend afternoon and the girls were on a play-date with Ashleigh and Aiden, supervised by Elena and Mrs. Andrews. The two women were busy chatting and thumbing through the pages of a cooking magazine on a nearby bench, trying to come up with something to make the kids for dinner later, and not far away Aiden and Angelina were playing on the playground and chasing each other up the jungle gym. Blair glanced over at her sister enviously. How could Angelina giggle and laugh at a time like this when everything was about to be turned upside down? "I never thought something like this would happen," she continued in disbelief. "He spends more time with Victoria than with us."

"I'm sorry," Ashleigh frowned. "That really sucks. But at least she makes him happy, right?"

Blair frowned and braided a few strands of string. "I guess so. I try to be nice and I try to like her, but she's just not Mom."

"Maybe Victoria won't be so bad once you get to know her better," Ashleigh shrugged, trying to be positive about it and look on the bright side. "You should give her a chance. It has to be better than seeing your dad sad all the time."

That was true. But still, anyone with Dad other than Mom would never sit well. Distracted from her bracelet-making, Blair glanced at a patch of nearby flowers, her gaze falling onto a bee buzzing between the orange and purple buds. Life was so simple for that stupid bee. All it had to do was pollinate, make honey, and try not to get swatted or crushed. It didn't even feel anything. Not sadness, not fear, not loneliness. It worked on a hive mind and did its appointed task and that was it. If only life for people could be that cut and dry, and emotions didn't exist.

"I don't want Dad to be sad... but it's still weird," she shook her head uncomfortably. "I don't think I'll ever get used to having Victoria or a new stepsister in the house."

"Maybe it'll be nice to have new people around," Ashleigh shrugged again. "Maybe having a new stepsister will be a *good* thing and Nicolette will turn out to be pretty cool."

"Maybe," Blair sighed.

Ashleigh sighed back. She knew that she probably sounded overly-hopeful, but what else was she supposed to say?

"I'm sorry, Blair. I'm trying," she frowned.

"I know," Blair apologized. "It's just a lot to deal with. I don't know if I'm really *ready* for this. But I guess it's not like we have much choice. It's going to happen anyway."

"Exactly. You can't change it so you might as well try to make the best of it, right? Sometimes that's all you can do."

A loud ear-splitting scream from the area by the sliding board caused the girls to turn their heads, interrupting their talk. Aiden had finally caught up to Angelina. He was tickling her like he always did, and she was doubled over with laughter, barely able to breathe. "STOP!" she pleaded as she swatted at him feebly. Aiden cackled sadistically at her, knowing full well how much she hated to be tickled, but doing it anyway for solely that reason.

"Say Uncle, you heathen!" he taunted her in an evil voice.

Blair couldn't help but smile and shake her head despite her worries. She looked back at Ashleigh gratefully and noticed the gold four leaf clover charm dangling from her neck. "You're right," she conceded. "I guess sometimes that's all we can do. Take what you can and try to be good. I'm just glad that I have you."

"Me too," Ashleigh smiled in satisfaction. She held up her finished bracelet, showing off the braided strands of varying shades of blue string. "I'm done. Do you like my bracelet?"

"It's really pretty," Blair nodded.

She held out her arm and Ashleigh secured it around her wrist with a tight little double-knot. Things were definitely going to be different for Blair and her sister soon, but not everything was so bad. They still had good friends like Ashleigh and Aiden to talk to, and that had to count for something.

Feathers went flying all over Angelina's room, littering her purple rug with tufts of gray and white fluff. Her loud, piercing squeals and Aiden's consecutive whoops of cantankerous laughter filled the air. She tried to shield herself, but it was no use. A fluffy down pillow came crashing down over her head.

"Stop it, Aiden!" she screeched, her face beet red and tears streaming from her eyes as she tried desperately to catch her breath. It wasn't working. She clutched at her stomach, crumpling over. Laughing hurt so bad right now, but she couldn't stop doing it. In a desperate bid to slow him down, she swung her arm around, hitting him the ribs with a pillow of her own.

"You hit like a sissy!" he chortled at her.

"You're a jerk!" she wailed back. He pummeled her into submission until she finally admitted, "I give up!" and slid down to the floor laughing and crying. He laid down next to her victoriously, forgoing using his pillow as a deadly weapon anymore and using it as an elbow rest instead. He propped his head up in his hand and rested his cheek in his palm. He was laughing, too. Angelina was so funny when she got red and flustered. She always made this horrible loud gasping sound deep in her throat that was hilarious. The apples of her cheeks were hot and scalded and she looked like a beet. A red little beet.

"I think I won that one," he claimed smugly. Angelina rolled onto her back and stared up at the ceiling, panting.

"You cheated!" she disagreed, trying to calm her racing heart. "You jumped me before I even had a chance. It wasn't a fair fight. If I would have been ready, I would have won."

"If you would have been ready, you *still* would have went down crying like a girl. Just like you did at the park."

Angelina jabbed him in the stomach with her closed fist and he laughed at her again. "I hate you, Aiden."

"No you don't. You love me."

She smiled at him, then went quiet and looked away.

He was right.

"Aiden..." she said, her tone suddenly serious. "Everything is going to be so different now. Everything is changing."

Aiden went quiet, too. Everything *was* changing. Angelina's dad was getting married again, to a woman Aiden didn't really know, but who he'd met a few times in passing. Victoria had never interacted with him much; not like Angelina's mom had. Angelina's mom had always offered him snacks when he'd come over, told him to feel at home, and let him join in when the girls helped her in the garden. At most, if Victoria was ever over when he was, she would put on a weird super-nice act and feed him a fake overly-sweet smile, but after that, she dismissed him and pretended that he didn't exist, just like she dismissed Angelina and Blair. Angelina was going to have her as a stepmother now. She was going to have a stepsister. It was crazy.

But one thing wasn't going to change.

"I'll still be here," he said. "This will still be the same."

There was such an honest, simple sincerity in his statement that it made Angelina's bottom lip tremble. Just for a second, then she got a hold of herself and straightened up. She wouldn't cry anymore, not around him. She wouldn't be weak. But her heart softened all the same, warmed her chest, made her feel that puppy love all over again. Aiden was always there for her. Always.

She rolled from her back to her side and bit her lip, reaching her hand forward. Aiden was surprised when she took her palm in his. She looked him dead in the eyes. Those emerald green eyes that had given her butterflies on the first day of third grade and would probably never stop giving her butterflies.

"You're my best friend," she said. "You know that, right?"

He blinked at her. She had a totally serious, vulnerable expression on her face. One that said a lot more than her words.

"You're my best friend, too," he said.

"Then we're in this together?" she asked. "No matter what happens, we're always going to be best friends?"

"No matter what," Aiden promised. "BFF's for life."

Angelina smiled again. She leaned forward, and when she pressed her lips to his freckled cheek, he didn't pull away.

"BFF's for life," she agreed.

And suddenly, all the big changes that her family was about to go through didn't seem so scary anymore.

CHAPTER NINETEEN
Blinded

VICTORIA'S HEART SOARED. AFTER ONLY a short engagement to her wealthy fiancé, today was finally the big day: the day that she would inherit Bruce von Essen's fortune and snag him as her husband. She smiled in wicked satisfaction as she admired the beautiful woman in the tight white mermaid dress reflected in the long mirror in front of her. It was almost too good to be true. This was what she had worked for - this was what she had *killed* for. What would naysayers like Ben McClafferty have to say now?

Nothing, that was what.

It wasn't like Victoria cared what any of her former co-workers had to say, anyway. She never really had. The news that she and Bruce had become an item had been quite scandalous in the office at first, but like any other scandal in Stirling City, the gossip had subsided once people had gotten bored enough with it. As word of an impending wedding broke, she inevitably left her job at Vonessen Inc., but instead of being upset about giving up the big promotion that had once filled her with such smug satisfaction, retiring before the age of thirty-five and only having to show up at the office to consult the new Controller on an as-needed basis was something that filled her with nothing short of pure glee. Luckily, this was a wedding, so no one would question her for being so jubilant. They wouldn't see the years of scheming and manipulating coming to a head. They wouldn't see a murderer who'd dreamed of never having to work again finally getting her wish. Even her Maid of Honor was none the wiser. Emmalyn smiled affectionately as she entered the room in an elegant rose taffeta dress to check on the soon-to-be-bride.

"Do you need anything, babe?" she cooed behind her.

Victoria made one last narcissistic kissy face in front of the mirror before swiveling around with a hand on her hip. "Not a thing. All I need is for this damn wedding to start!" she declared.

Emmalyn laughed and beamed at her tenderly, remembering their wild bar-hopping excursions of the past. Victoria had always been a bit of a man-eater back then and had gotten plenty of attention from the opposite sex because of it, not that she'd ever considered it malicious. But damn, did Victoria look happier now. "You know, it's nice seeing you like this, Vicky. I never thought I'd live to see the day that you got married."

Victoria smirked at her friend and motioned towards her ivory frock. "Well, I guess you thought wrong, didn't you?"

"I guess I did," Emmalyn admitted. "But damn, girl... marriage looks good on you. You make one smoking hot bride!"

"Do you like the dress?" Victoria bragged, twirling around and making the bottom of the skirt swish a little.

"I do! It's beautiful."

"It was custom made in Italy. Sent straight from Milan."

"Well, it's *gorgeous*. I love the diamond accents and the shape. And let me just make myself feel a little better by saying that your Maid of Honor is looking pretty damn hot herself!"

Victoria laughed a haughty laugh. "Of course you are, Em. The boys are going to be drooling all over you. I hope you brought your pepper spray. You might need it to fend off all of the lost little puppies that try to follow you home after the reception."

"Oh my, I hope not!" Emmalyn joked, a look of mock concern on her face. She and Victoria giggled obnoxiously before wrapping each other up into a sisterly hug. "Congratulations, Vicky," Emmalyn praised her genuinely, her voice softer now, more sincere, no more giggles or bullshit. "You and Bruce will have a good life together. I'm glad to see someone finally tame you and glad to see Mr. von Essen happy again. You're good for each other. I love you, girl. I'm *so* proud to be your bridesmaid."

"Oh you! Look at you getting all sappy. Stop that or you're going to make me cry," Victoria teased. She gave Emmalyn another appreciative squeeze, and for once, she actually meant it. If only Em knew how hard she'd *really* had to work for today to be possible... but no matter how good of a friend or a reliable ego-boost the naive redhead had proven to be since the day they'd first met on the accounting floor at Vonessen Inc., Victoria would never tell. She'd take her secrets to her grave, keeping the rest of the world blinded to the monster that she truly was.

And maybe even blinding herself in the process.

Outside, the sky was clear and the sun was warm. It was the perfect day for an opulent outdoor ceremony; not a single cloud was in sight. Rows of white wooden chairs lined a long ivory carpet running down the center, leading to a beautiful altar decorated with candles and giant arrangements of elegant white roses at the front, and a large stone arch adorned with flowers stood as the site where vows would be exchanged. Bruce and his affianced had chosen the exterior of an historical gothic church as their venue, and the weathered gray stone and high arches surrounded by tall leafy trees, marble and bronze statues, wrought-iron gates, and elegant garden beds made for an almost dream-like backdrop. In the courtyard where the reception would be held, caterers were already working on preparing the exquisite dinner that would be served afterwards under a canopy of thousands of twinkling white lights, and hostesses were busily placing elegant floral centerpieces and gift bags with his-and-hers Rolexes at every table. The entire event was extravagant and pricey, just like Victoria's custom-imported dress from Milan.

But Blair and Angelina weren't quite so impressed about all of the hubbub as many of the others in attendance. They were dressed in their formal best - Blair in a pretty peach-colored dress with ruffles on the bodice and a matching sash tied around her waist, and Angelina in an short flutter-sleeved lavender chiffon dress - but for them, this wasn't a celebration; it was merely a formality. They sat next to Nicolette and their nanny in the front row as they waited impatiently for the ceremony to begin, shooting glances at their friends, who were sitting with their families, and trying to ignore the excited chatter that had arisen amongst the other guests congregated around them. Nicolette played with the skirt of her ruffled pink dress anxiously and kicked her feet back and forth, clunking them against the leg of her chair. It was odd to see her acting so giddy with nervous energy, but while her impatience was more of an excited one, the von Essen girls' impatience had been borne more out of dread and uncertainty over what was to come. Despite their heart-to-hearts with Dad and their friends leading up to this point, they'd never fully accepted the life-changing event that was about to happen. Change was scary, even when it was supposed to be good change.

"This is awesome! These flowers look so nice! Isn't it pretty out here?" Nicolette went on and on, her mouth moving a mile a minute as she fidgeted relentlessly. Ugh, she wasn't helping. This was the most Blair and Angelina had ever heard her speak, but right about now they wished that she would just shut it already.

Angelina turned around in her seat and glanced at Aiden sitting a few rows back. He was dressed in a tux, which she found rather endearing despite how horribly awkward it looked, and he was fussing with the sleeves of it as if he'd never been more uncomfortable in an outfit in his life. Ashleigh was beside him, looking even more awkward than he did in her new emerald frock, which considering the girl's distaste for wearing anything other than jeans or corduroys, didn't really surprise Angelina. She managed to catch Aiden's eye and jerked her head in her soon-to-be-stepsister's direction. Nicolette looked like she might explode.

"She's driving me crazy!" she mouthed at him.

"What?" Aiden mouthed back.

Angelina repeated it again, and when he still squinted at her with a look of confusion on his face and put his hands up in defeat, she rolled her eyes and jerked her head at Nicolette again, throwing her finger to her head and swiveling it around in a sign for "crazy" before turning back to face front in her seat.

"You know what else I was thinking?" Nicolette continued on obliviously, a positively jubilant look on her face. "I was thinking that since my mom and your dad are getting married, that means that we're going to be *sisters* now! Isn't that cool?"

Angelina and Blair shot her annoyed looks, but Nicolette was too wound up to realize that they weren't into talking right now. She gasped as a sudden realization hit her.

"Holy crap, I've never had sisters before! Oh wow, we're going to have so much fun together! I'm so excited!"

Blair whimpered in protest and squirmed in her seat.

"Nic, shut up already!" Angelina finally cracked. "I can't take it anymore! You're talking my ear off!"

"I can't help it!" Nicolette smiled, rubbing her palms together in anticipation. These girls just didn't get it. Having a stepdad and stepsisters in the house meant no longer having to live alone with Victoria. And maybe - just maybe! - being happily married would inspire her mother to treat her a little better, too. It was worth hoping for at least, and that was cause enough for plenty of cheer on Nicolette's part. She was practically bouncing around in her seat. This was like Christmas, but better, because this time it felt like she was actually getting presents for once.

Her giddiness was almost too much to take. Angelina was tempted to smack her right over her head if she didn't shut up and stop wriggling around already, but fortunately for Nicolette she was saved by the sound of a wedding march beginning to play. The guests instantly quieted down and looked on anxiously for the arrival of the bride, craning their necks to see behind them.

When Victoria started to make her way down the aisle with a huge bouquet of white roses in hand, astonished gasps and shocked whispers could be heard all around. What an extravagant wedding dress! What a beautiful up-do! Bruce's soon-to-be-bride looked absolutely gorgeous. She had the body of a goddess, the face of a model, and a flawless, bronzed tan. Her entire look screamed Old Hollywood Glamour, but nothing was more radiant than the beaming grin on her face. Victoria was glowing.

"Oh, she looks beautiful!"

"My, what a figure!"

"What an incredible dress!" came the astounded whispers from the chairs lining the aisle. The von Essen sisters didn't share the rest of the guests' awe, even if Victoria *did* look good. Angelina felt an uncomfortable twinge in her stomach, and judging by the way that Blair was nibbling at her fingernails, she could only assume her sister felt the same. Beneath the arch, the girls could see their father looking like he might tear up. After all he had been through and all that his family had been through, this was an incredibly emotional moment for him, and the girls knew it - which was exactly why they hadn't antagonized him all day. Beside them, Nicolette looked on excitedly, nearly squealing as Victoria reached the altar. Her mom looked so pretty... and *happy!*

As the ceremony got underway, that happiness only multiplied. Bruce and Victoria stood beneath the arch of beautiful white flowers as they exchanged their vows, hand in hand.

"Bruce von Essen, do you take Victoria Adessi to be your lawfully wedded wife?" the priest asked officially at last.

Angelina whispered in Blair's ear:

"I think he means *awfully* wedded wife."

Blair *hmph*'ed in agreement, but she'd taken what Ashleigh had said to heart. She didn't have to be excited about Dad marrying again, but she'd at least give this a chance. Her father looked so happy next to Victoria. She missed Mom and she wanted this to be Mom and it would never be right that it wasn't... but her dad being unhappy and miserable and alone wasn't right, either. She reached across the gap between she and Angelina's seats and took a hold of her sister's hand. Angelina stopped joking around and being obnoxious and squeezed hers back as the girls shared a silent, serious look - a look that said no matter what, they had each other's backs and they were going to survive. But it only lasted for a second, because it was then that they heard the two words that they'd been dreading more than any others.

"I do," their father said with conviction.

"Then by the power vested in me, I now pronounce you man and wife," the priest declared. "You may kiss the bride!"

Bruce and Victoria shared a passionate kiss as cheers and applause resounded amongst the wedding guests. With that kiss, Victoria Adessi - the devilish gold-digger, the murderess in disguise - sealed her fate. She was officially Bruce's second wife, the girls' stepmother, and the co-possessor of the massive von Essen fortune - from this day forward, for better and for worse, in sickness and in health, until death did them part. The new Mrs. von Essen could practically taste the posh lifestyle that she'd always dreamed of as her husband's lips met hers; she could feel it envelop her in a crisp green paper-blanket. Happy tears began to fall down her cheeks, but no one could possibly know the full extent of why. The puppeteer's plans were finally fulfilled.

Victoria stood victorious, once and for all.

CHAPTER TWENTY
A New Reality

AFTER MONTHS OF MANIPULATION AND scheming, Victoria had finally gotten what she wanted. In the weeks that followed the sealing of their deceptive union, Bruce's new trophy wife settled quickly and cozily into his mansion, his bed, and his pocketbook. The new Mrs. von Essen had expensive taste, but Bruce didn't seem to mind that she used him for his money; rather, the recently remarried businessman was simply content to no longer be a lonely widower and determined to make his new wife happy.

Angelina and Blair, however, never exactly "fell in love" with their new stepmother like he did. Over the next few years they honestly tried to put forth an effort to accept their new situation, but there was no getting around the fact that life wasn't the same without Mom around. Mom had been compassionate, caring, nurturing, and involved, and "Vicky" seemed more than content to strut around the mansion in her costly designer dresses like she was Queen of the World, enjoying that early retirement. She wasn't Mom, she'd never be Mom, and there was no use in pretending that someone else could fill the void left by Mom in their hearts. The girls eventually learned to put up with the fact that a new woman was a part of their lives, but they never fully accepted her as "family" nor believed that their father had married purely for love. Nothing about her screamed "doting stepmother," so they didn't see her as that. She was just "Victoria"... a typical, superficial Maple Springs woman who somehow knew voodoo, mind-controlled Dad into thinking she was the best thing since sliced bread, and basically took up space in the house. Blair was always kind and courteous to Victoria, and tried to be politically correct about it to let it be what it was, but Angelina didn't see much point in undue niceties. She made her aversion quite clear no sooner than Victoria had moved herself into the mansion.

Bruce's raven-haired daughter had always been the more outspoken and rebellious of the twins, so perhaps it should have stood as no surprise that she'd be difficult. Even just having finished the sixth grade, she'd known that "ground rules" needed to be set and confronted Victoria in the dining room one afternoon while her new stepmother was looking through the family's vintage wine collection with a greedy glint in her eyes; the same vintage wine collection that Cecilia had been rearranging on the first day that Aiden had visited the mansion years ago. Victoria had just been eyeing up a bottle of a particularly fancy red reserve when she stopped and turned to glance behind her shoulder, feeling someone's eyes boring a hole in her back. It was Angelina, leaning against the archway with her arms folded across her chest, glaring at her through side-swept bangs with a judgmental pair of chocolate eyes. Such a look of smug indignation she had never seen on a child's face. And yes, that was exactly what Angelina was, whether she wanted to believe it or not. Just a child. Victoria put on her usual nice act and shot her a charming smile.

"Hello, Angelina. Can I do something for you?"

"Yeah. You can, actually," Angelina scowled, pushing against the arch with her shoulder and taking a step forward. Her arms stayed laced where they were. She wasn't buying the crap. "If you're going to live in my house, there need to be rules," she said firmly. "Like just-between-you-and-me kinda rules."

Victoria's lip twitched. *Her* house? Sorry to bust this little girl's bubble, but Victoria having married her father meant that she had a lot more ownership of this house than Angelina did. This brat was going to be a problem. Victoria could already see the challenge she was going to pose in her teenage years written all over that sour little face. She didn't know whether to admire her gusto or simply despise her for it.

"Whatever are you talking about?" she asked sweetly.

Angelina's response was short and curt.

"You don't have to act nice to me. You're not my mom."

"I'm not *acting* nice to you, Angelina," Victoria shook her head. "I *want* to be nice to you. We're family now."

Angelina grimaced at the claim.

"We're *not* family."

Victoria wasn't sure how to respond to that. She set the bottle she was holding down on the table and crossed her arms over her chest, mirroring the middle-schooler and sizing her up.

"Okay then," she played ball. "If it will make you happy, then we can have it your way. What are your rules, Angelina?"

"Rule one, you're not my mom, so don't pretend that you are," Angelina said.

"Done," Victoria agreed.

"Rule two, don't try to be my friend or tell me what to do."

Victoria's eyes narrowed. *"Done. Is there anything else?"*

"Yeah. I know that you only married my dad because he's rich, so act how you want around everyone else, but don't try to convince *me* you didn't, because I'm not stupid. That's rule three."

"That's not true," Victoria shrugged nonchalantly. "I love your father and your father loves me. But if it pleases you to believe it, then you can think whatever you want."

"Whatever," Angelina snorted.

Victoria wanted to slap those rolling eyes right out of her head, but she kept her voice nice and even. "Will that be all?"

"No," Angelina glared at her.

She glared back. "Then you certainly have a lot of rules."

"Well this is the last one. Just so you know, I'm going to find out who killed my mom. I don't care if everyone else gives up, I won't. And I'll do whatever I have to do to find them. So rule number four, don't get in my way and I'll stay out of yours. Fair?"

"Perfectly," Victoria agreed darkly.

Having said what she felt she needed to say and satisfied enough with Victoria's responses, Angelina turned on her heel and left the blonde standing there bewildered and irritated. It was clear that Angelina's rules for their relationship moving forward didn't involve any attempt at forging new "bonds," and that seemed to be the end of that. The same rules were never set out loud with Blair, but although Angelina's twin never went out of her way to shun her new stepmother, she also didn't go out of her way to be Victoria's friend, so they still seemed to apply. Victoria could have been bothered by the girls' natural inclination to keep her at arm's length if she'd cared enough, but in truth she rather *preferred* their new arrangement this way. The alternative was far too cuddly and cozy, and she'd never been one to get cuddly and cozy with kids - not even with her own daughter for that matter. Marriage or no marriage, that wasn't going to change.

It was a reality that was a huge let-down for Nicolette. Although Victoria refrained from being outright mean or degrading towards her in front of the other members of the family, she still treated her daughter with distaste and disdain when their backs were turned, and when she wasn't straight-out being mean and nasty, she was ignoring and cold-shouldering her like she didn't exist. So much for Nicolette's wedding-day hopes. While it was a huge disappointment to see her relationship with her mother fail to improve, there was nothing she could do about it and eventually she gave up on trying. Motherhood had never been something Victoria had been crazy about in the past anyway. As far as she was concerned, that was what the nanny was for.

As for her new stepdaughters, Victoria's only true interest in them was in using their academic and extracurricular successes to make herself look good in front of all of the other well-to-do housewives in town. While Bruce busied himself at work and Elena watched the kids, Victoria chose to do what she wanted when she wanted as opposed to petty tasks like child-rearing and homemaking. More often than not that meant alternating between shopping at expensive stores and lounging around at the Maple Springs Country Club. When she was doing the latter of the two she had plenty of opportunity for self-marketing and never hesitated to take it. Any time she had a poolside chat with one of the other moms about Angelina's singing or Blair's piano it was solely a bragging point and it wasn't as if she actually gave a damn about anything they got out of it for themselves. The other women would "ooh" and "ahh" all the while, and Victoria was never suspect of being anything other than perfectly normal, because every other woman at the club did the exact same thing.

Ultimately, she fit in well with Maple Springs' upper-class socialite demographic, but no matter how well she played the part, she was still very different from the rest of them. For all of their similarities, none of her new gal pals had quite the same lethal track record nor uncanny talent for personal manipulation that she did. No one could con and charm quite like her, and Victoria von Essen practically defined charisma. Her new marital status had shot her straight to the top of the social ladder. The women at the country club loved and envied her and the people in town admired her bold fashion sense and posh lifestyle. Victoria became such a local style icon that she even took up modeling for her own fashion blog, *"Affascinante,"* which quickly gained followers and acclaim. Clearly, the rest of the world was oblivious to the real her, but while the "real her" might not have been a very good role model or motherly figure, she made up for whatever nurturing qualities she was lacking for in the bedroom.

Bruce had been changed by his new wife. He didn't realize it, but his girls had certainly noticed just how much less attention he paid to matters of family now and how much more into money, his work, and his sex life he was. It was even worse than before. Dad still encouraged the twins to continue on with their music lessons and other interests on the outside, but inside he wasn't nearly as invested as he could have or should have been. In the public eye he smiled at all the right times, said all the right things, and bought the girls things that he thought would please them to make up for his lack of presence in their lives, but there was still something off about him... a disconnect and a distancing.

Even though he was a married man again, his relationship with his daughters hadn't gotten any better. Much to the contrary, Angelina and Blair sometimes felt like he didn't care about them at all anymore, and it hurt. It hurt because they missed him, because they loved him. But so much for heart-to-hearts. Dad was like a robot; programmed, almost. They missed their old Dad. The one who would sit in the living room playing Go Fish with them and teach them about investing in silver and stocks. The one who would have picnics outside in the garden and tuck them in at night. They missed the Dad that wasn't constantly coming home with bags from expensive lingerie stores or going straight to his study to bring his work home with him. And they missed the Dad that would rather spend time with them than at the office or in his bedroom or on pricey weekend getaways with Victoria.

The girls certainly missed all of those things, but what they missed most of all wasn't just their old Dad; it was their parents being together and how close they'd all been as a family back then. Life had been so perfect when Cecilia and Bruce were so happy and young and shamelessly in-love. Their life had been predictably cliché and cheesy and wonderful, like they were living out some kind of real-life happy ending from a *Disney* movie. At the time, the girls had taken it completely for granted... but now that they didn't have it, it was the only thing they wanted.

And the one thing they knew they could never have.

Reality was that they'd never be as close as they'd once been again. That part of their lives wasn't coming back. It was unfortunate, but true. And as if to add insult to injury, it didn't seem like they'd be getting retribution for their mother's death, either. The answers just weren't there. No who, no why... nothing. Cecilia's murder remained shrouded in mystery as the months dragged on with no real progress. The police hadn't been able to show the von Essen family anything but their own ineffectiveness and it was something that made Angelina particularly angry and bitter. As a rebellious preteen, she couldn't stand authority figures that she saw as having no real authority, and as far as she was concerned, the SCPD fit right into that category. Apparently they could give out frivolous traffic citations and sit on the side of the road holding a radar gun just fine judging by the amount of driving tickets given out in Stirling on an annual basis, but when it came to actually solving a serious crime that had ultimately taken a person's life? They were useless, and as unfair as this was, nothing anyone told Angelina could convince her of otherwise.

"Don't worry, Blair. I'm not giving up on Mom," she told her sister every time they felt sad and empty and were missing her. Her determination would add a serious edge to her voice and put passionate darts of fire in her eyes. "I'm going to find a way to get answers from somebody. I don't care what I have to do or how long it takes. One day we're going to know who did this, and I'm going to make sure they get exactly what they deserve."

It was a strong conviction. A promise she took seriously, even if she had no clue how she was going to fulfill it. But if there was one thing that could be said about Angelina von Essen, it was that she was very resourceful and didn't take kindly to hearing no.

Unfortunately, her voice of hope and determination was one among many other disheartened others. For as much fire and fervor as she had, the authorities weren't so optimistic about solving the crime. In fact, it felt like they were giving up hope of *ever* finding answers. They had no evidence to speak of aside from a half-assed description of the vehicle, no motives, and no suspects. Ben McClafferty was the closest thing they'd ever had to a legitimate lead, and with him ending up a bust just like so many other dead ends, they were lost... and what was even worse than being lost was that in their frustration it looked like they were becoming content to throw their hands up and brush off what had happened as a tragic accident or simply "random impersonal violence" committed by a killer who would never be caught. Even with Victoria - the one who had set this whole plan into motion - dangling right beneath their noses, they still couldn't sniff out the rotten truth. And it wasn't as if they'd never had the chance.

Being Bruce's new bride, Victoria had gone through extensive questioning prior to the wedding solely on principle; questioning that was maybe even more rigorous than it had been on the night of the banquet when every attendee there had been grilled and kept locked in that dining room until the wee hours of the morning like prisoners. Bruce had been furious that the police would do such a thing, even if it was simply a formality and no real suspicion was being directed at her. Yet Victoria had agreed to cooperate, and when she'd talked to the cops she hadn't raised any red flags. Years after the banquet, they still couldn't see past the lies, the crocodile tears, and her supposedly sorrowful demeanor about the loss of the "wonderful," "beautiful," and "talented" former Mrs. von Essen, and when it was all said and done, it was ironically clear that Victoria really *could* have tried out for acting roles with the way she was able to pull the wool over everyone's eyes. She could've taken home a damn Oscar.

In actuality, she was the one and only person who had any idea of who had really killed Cecilia, and she'd made sure a long time ago that he would never speak a word of it to the authorities, nor to anyone else for that matter. She'd made *damn* sure.

It wasn't what she'd wanted, but he hadn't given her much choice. Back then, in the early days when Cecilia's murder was still a fresh memory in everyone's minds and the police hadn't yet given up and were still pushing hard, the pressure had been starting to get to Victoria's accomplice. The television pleas for answers from Bruce, the constant news coverage, the obtained description of his car, and the reward posters hanging up on every telephone pole on every street corner in every Stirling City block had been chiseling away at him. He wasn't sure how he'd gotten himself involved in this mess in the first place, but Victoria had been so *convincing* and with her having routed him plenty of money, he worried that it was only a matter of time before someone linked the missing money to the murder and then linked the murder to him. It was all this bitch's fault. *She* was the one who had brought herself back into his life and put him up to this, and maybe if he came clean to the cops - came up with some sort of plea deal and gave her up, revealing her as the architect - he would be spared a life of imprisonment... or worse.

When Victoria hadn't heard from him for a few weeks she got concerned. She got even more concerned when she learned that he hadn't used the money she'd gotten him to skip town. When she was finally able to get a hold of him, she enticed him to meet her with the promise that she was ready to reward him with that *other* form of payment she'd promised him; the one that had nothing to do with money. Against his better judgment, he agreed to meet her in a private place, a secluded spot in the woods that few people really knew about or would bother getting to. It was a place he'd gone to before to do his drugs, away from the prying eyes of cops and tattle-tales. But when he'd met her there, she wasn't exactly dressed for the occasion and the look on her face was anything but seductive. She confronted him immediately, and as she grilled him for his absence, he finally cracked under the pressure. Victoria could clearly see that he'd been weighing his options and keeping her in the dark, and that infuriated her.

"They're going to fuck me," he fretted as he paced back and forth on a matted patch of grass and weeds with a cigarette burning in his hand. "Fuck, I have enough problems without this."

"Well, you're the one who botched it," Victoria reminded him. "You were supposed to make it look like an accident. What did you expect, running someone down in public like that?"

The man shot her an angry snarl. "Fuck you!"

"Excuse me?" Victoria growled back at him, disgusted.

"You heard me," he exclaimed, throwing his arms in the air. "*Fuck. You!* You don't know *shit*, Victoria. You don't know *shit!* And this is all *your* fault. Why should I rot in prison for this fucking mess while you sip on Dom Pérignon? I'm done with this, bitch! If anyone gets it in the ass here, it ain't gonna be me."

Victoria knew it then: she couldn't trust him and she couldn't have him around as a liability anymore. He was too out-there, too dangerous, too unstable, and too impeded by the presence of at least some inkling of a guilty conscience... or maybe just a fear for his own disgusting skin. If he opened his mouth and turned her in, her life was over. Everything she wanted would never happen. Well, she couldn't have that. She *needed* the chance to snag Bruce, and she wasn't going to let this strung-out sack of shit stand in her way. Luckily, he was a lowlife, a drug addict, and a piece of scum. No one would miss him or even notice that he was gone. If anyone did notice by chance, the guys who he constantly owed gambled-away drug money to would be blamed, not her. No one even knew that they associated anyway; she'd done well to hide her dabblings with undesirable individuals.

She'd hidden it back when she'd met him and she hid it now. Who could possibly know that they'd met in college, when she was only a freshman? When she would party on the weekends and get high to forget the fucked up life she'd left behind at home?

Who would know all the times she'd been in his bed, not because she'd cared, but because it was an easy fix? As easy a fix as the pills and potions he'd shared with her, the pills and potions that she'd pushed aside when circumstance and ambition had called for her to do so, but he'd been so addicted to that pushing them aside had never been on his table, let alone attempted?

He'd been a short-term fling. Much to his dismay, at the time. He'd been obsessed with her. Who that she'd lied with *hadn't* become obsessed with her? But she'd moved on to bigger and better things. To bigger goals, to bigger ambitions, to manipulations and ministrations *worth* making. She only sought her fix with people who could better her position in the world. In college, she'd used sex to get ahead - either the act itself or the threat of exposing the act. And she had forgotten this man until she'd run into him again while working a part-time night job at a casino, not far from her college campus. She was a senior then. The girl who would walk around in skimpy little nothings, trying to get patrons to buy booze, which would in turn keep them gambling longer. And then, when she was through with that, she would balance the books. When she met him again at that casino, he'd been thousands in debt, having gambled away most of his money to purchase his same tired pills and potions - the ones that her leaving him in the dust had only gotten him *more* addicted to, not that he would've ever admitted that to her out loud.

There were people who'd wanted to hurt him for not repaying his debts. People from the city who weren't exactly the friendliest of sorts. The ones nobody talked about when they mentioned Stirling, the ones that didn't fit into the prim and proper picturesque postcard world of Stirling that its society had created. When Victoria had caught them holding him at gunpoint in the back parking lot, she'd felt a glimmer of compassion and helped him. Or maybe it was just a glimmer of coming to the realization that if she did so, he would owe her... and big time.

She'd convinced the thugs with her honeyed, sugared words - and some strategic posturing of the manipulative hourglass figure that had garnered her so much attention from the opposite sex, to leave him be. Promised to pay off a portion of his debts in return for them backing off - at least for a little while.

They'd agreed. Because they'd liked her body and her fire, nothing more. That had been the first time she'd skimmed money from someone else's books and not gotten caught. It had given her a sick sense of satisfaction, coming to the realization that *yes*, she was a very good accountant, even before her degree was in her hands. She'd paid the men. And *this* man now owed her his life.

And inevitably, because he'd owed her, and because his lust for her had never fully gone away, nor his gambling problem, nor his enemies, nor his need for sharp needles and white powder, he'd remembered it... and now he was waffling at the finish line.

Apparently, things had changed. Shit had gotten too real for him. There would be no turning back now. Their argument in the woods culminated with Victoria pointing a gun in his face.

"Do you think this is a game?" she snapped at him, her expression contorted in anger and hatred. Her eyes blazed, her hand shook, not with fear, but rage and desperation. She looked like a woman possessed. "Do you really think I'd let you rat?"

He shirked back at her sudden movement, then lunged towards her. He grabbed her wrist and she shrieked.

"You wouldn't *dare*, you bitch!"

He was wrong. There was a struggle as he tried to wrestle her for the gun. His calloused hands left bruise marks on her wrist, marks she'd have to cover for the next few weeks with long sleeves and chunky bracelets. His knee left an angry purple welt on her thigh. He yanked at a fistful of her hair and she screamed. But it was no use. The adrenaline had kicked in and Victoria was more nimble than she looked. Her finger tightened on the trigger.

CRACK!

She could still remember the sharp sound ringing in her ears, could still remember the look on his face in the milliseconds before she shot him... in that moment when he realized he wasn't fast enough. She remembered the way that his eyes had widened with fear, with disappointment, with shame, and with heartbreak, pleading silently in that moment without words for her not to kill him. Asking her *'were we not something more, once? Don't we have history?'* But she didn't flinch. She shot him square in the chest, taking him out with two well-placed .45 millimeter rounds. She could remember the tinny, sickening smell of blood and the heavy thud that his body had made as he'd fallen dead to the ground.

"*Damn* it!" she snapped, her hands flying into her hair. "You did this to yourself, you bastard!" She looked with disgust at the blood splattered across the front of her jacket and the crumpled figure of her accomplice lying dead at her feet, regretting that she'd ever been so short-sighted as to hire a hitman who didn't even have a set to stand on. But what was done was done. Still... what the hell was she supposed to do with a corpse?

She turned her head this way and that, taking in her surroundings before dragging his body away and hiding it where she was certain that no one would ever find it.

And so far, no one ever had.

Now, both her hitman's murder and Cecilia's hit-and-run were a part of Victoria's past. The cold-hearted woman didn't think of them anymore and her involvement in the dark pair of incidents remained undiscovered. As the years went by, the police put Cecilia's case on the backburner, the von Essen girls traversed the awkward mazes of middle school and puberty while hanging on to hope that one day justice would be served, and Victoria settled comfortably into her new role as Bruce's second wife. She used all of her newfound power to get things that she could have only dreamed of having before: overpriced jewelry, purses, and shoes, gorgeous dresses, spur-of-the-moment sex-filled vacations to exotic locations, VIP treatment at fancy social gatherings and dinner parties, and everything decadent under the sun. Bruce had not a clue of the dark scandal that had gone on behind his back for years now, nor did he realize just how much he'd changed from the loving, fostering father that he'd once been to the disconnected, all-business, stereotypical CEO that he was now.

Things were different and there was no denying it, but life went on as it always does. The story belonged to his daughters now. Angelina, Blair, and Nicolette's stories were the next chapters in the von Essen legacy.

TO BE CONTINUED

AFTERWORD

"DECEIVED" IS THE STORY OF the von Essen family, a wealthy but troubled family living in the affluent suburbs of the fictional metro of Stirling City. It is part tragedy, part drama, part romance, and part coming-of-age, focusing on the members of this family, their struggles in the face of unthinkable tragedy, the way that tragedy shapes their lives, their ongoing search for answers and closure, and the people they come in contact with along the way.

Keep an eye out for the other novels in the *Deceived* series:

DECEIVED

STEPSISTERS

To connect with the author, please visit:

www.writerstephanierose.wordpress.com.

ABOUT THE AUTHOR

STEPHANIE ROSE VIGANO was born in Pittsburgh, Pennsylvania. She currently lives near Philadelphia with her husband, but is a wanderer at heart and has a special fondness for Montana and the mountains. She loves undertaking new creative projects, and when she isn't writing, enjoys traveling, cooking, wandering through bookstores, target shooting, tinkling the piano keys, engrossing herself in video games, drinking copious amounts of coffee, and practicing yoga. *Deceived* is her first published work.

44686108R00183

Made in the USA
Middletown, DE
13 June 2017